As good as Jam

money back!

Jack Kerley's *The Broken Souls* has everything you want from a thriller – twisted villains, killer action and brilliant characters.

We're so sure about this, that if you don't enjoy it as much as international bestseller James Patterson, we'll give you your money back. All you have to do is send us back the book, along with a copy of the sales receipt and a letter outlining your reasons for returning it to:

Kerley Moneyback Offer
Fiction Marketing
HarperCollins Publishers
77-85 Fulham Palace Road
London
W6 8JB

We'll refund the price you paid for the book, plus 65p to cover your postage costs.

It's that simple. And there's only one way to find out if we're right – so read on.

THE BROKEN SOULS

Jack Kerley worked in advertising and teaching before becoming a full-time novelist. He lives in Newport, Kentucky, but also spends a good deal of time in Southern Alabama, the setting for his Carson Ryder novels. He is married with two children.

Visit www.AuthorTracker.co.uk for exclusive updates on Jack Kerley.

www.jackkerley.com

Also by Jack Kerley

The Hundredth Man
The Death Collectors

JACK KERLEY

The Broken Souls

HARPER

This novel is entirely a work of fiction. The names, characters and incidents portrayed in it are the work of the author's imagination. Any resemblance to actual persons, living or dead, events or localities is entirely coincidental.

Harper
An imprint of HarperCollins*Publishers*
77–85 Fulham Palace Road,
Hammersmith, London W6 8JB

www.harpercollins.co.uk

This paperback edition 2011
1

First published in Great Britain by
HarperCollins*Publishers* 2006

A catalogue record for this book is
available from the British Library

ISBN 978 0 00 789664 6

Set in Meridien by
Palimpsest Book Production Ltd,
Grangemouth, Stirlingshire

Printed and bound in Great Britain by
Clays Ltd, St Ives plc

For my children,
Amanda and John.
They make life shine.

ACKNOWLEDGEMENTS

To them that talk, them that listen, and all of them stuck in between . . .

The Six a.m. Thursday Morning socio-politico-religio discussion group and kaffee-gargle: Steve Burke, Andy Hartzell, Roger Peterman, and Rick Rafferty. Camaraderie combined with the mesh and clash of ideas; what a way to wake up.

My good friend and neighbor in Fairhope, Alabama: Gerard Lawson, who keeps me abreast of Mobile-area happenings when I'm home in Kentucky. Just up the highway are Bill and Toni Riales; thanks for the great food and conversation, guys. Can't forget Captain Bobby Abruscato, fishing guide and storyteller deluxe.

Sandy Carroll and Mike Whitehead, who fill my kitchen with words and music.

My children, with whom I can discuss anything from philosophy to the lyrics of Green Day.

On the publishing side, my "dynamic duo" at HarperCollins, UK: Julia Wisdom and Anne O'Brien. Our chats are generally by e-mail, and keep my writing in time and tune.

All the folks at the Aaron Priest Literary Agency, especially Aaron, who's not shy about saying, "This isn't working, Jack. Try something else."

My wife, Elaine, who told me to get my hindquarters out of advertising and write novels.

AUTHOR'S NOTE

I exercised broad license in bending settings and institutions to the whims of the story. All should be regarded as fiction save for the natural beauty of Mobile and its environs. Any similarities between characters in this work and real characters, living or otherwise, is purely coincidental.

PROLOGUE

Eastern Mobile County,
Alabama, early 2000s

"Are you sure he ran this way? I don't see anything."

"Keep your damn voice down. Don't touch the blood. And just use light when you need it."

Lucas heard voices in the distance and his eyes snapped open. The world was spinning slowly, like he was caught in a syrupy vortex. Lucas threw his arms out to his sides to hold on and felt his fingers touch grass. It was night, but he saw the dark shadows of nearby trees. Comets were spinning between their trunks, blinking on and off: comet, no comet. It smelled fresh here in cometland, like dew and wet leaves. A very peculiar effect, he thought. Also peculiar: a single star straight up in the sky, flashing, like the comets and the star were conversing.

"I see a car! Hidden behind the trees, branches over it. He's around here."

"We'll have to get rid of the car. Fast. Call for a trailer."

Lucas closed his eyes and took a deep breath of cool air. The solitary star blinked. Another comet flashed across the sky. No, not comets, his clearing mind registered, it was flashlights pressing through fog. He was in a field beside a woods, damp weeds bristling against the sides of his face. Why was he in farmland? Had he gotten drunk? Why were there flashlights? Looking for something.

Looking for him.

What had he done?

The footsteps resumed, with the sound of bodies pushing aside branches, stepping on twigs. Flashlight beams swept through the weeds and trees. Lucas's world turned white as a beam crossed him. He made himself lay absolutely still. The light passed by.

But in the moment of illumination he had seen something odd: his hand was red. He stared at his dark fingers, perversely entranced.

Then he realized it wasn't just his hand: his blue institutional pajamas were soaked with blood.

The voices started again. Louder and closer.

"I saw something at the base of the microwave tower. It should be to your left; can you see the tower light blinking above the trees?"

"Be careful. He's . . . resourceful."

A montage of pictures formed in Lucas's head, recent memories playing like a jittery movie. He started to remember and his gut went cold. He should have figured they'd be coming. He knew too much.

"Shouldn't the doctor be here? Why didn't you bring him?"

"Shut up. I'll circle to the far side of the tower. Keep the walkie-talkie low, light off. I'll tell you when to move in."

It was black and quiet for several minutes. Lucas wiped the blood from his hands to his pants, flexed fingers, arms, legs. He could move now, escape. He drew himself into an unsteady crouch as the comets started flashing again. His world turned white. Black. He stumbled to his feet, his knees like gimbals, seeming to wobble every direction. *Run!* his mind screamed.

"I see him, he's up."

"I'm coming in from my side. Get the stunner out."

Lucas took a deep breath, calculated the angles his pursuers had chosen, figured his way past them. He gathered his energy into his core.

Just as he ran, the world turned white.

"Damn, he just ran into a tower support. He's down and rolling around."

"Go!"

He heard running feet. Felt bodies fall over him, wrestle him over, his face pressing deep into the wet grass. He felt metal wrap his wrists, pain. He smelled sweat. Aftershave. And a piercing reek of fear, not his own.

"Zap him!"

"He's not fighting."

"I told you to –"

There was a shivering blue explosion and the comets returned, each bringing a hundred stars to the party. They whooshed and tumbled and danced. It was beautiful.

In the distance, the voices started up again.

"There's something all over him. Jesus, Crandell, it's blood."

"Get him up and moving. We've got to get out of here."

And then a mouth at his ear, hot and wet.

A happy mouth, it seemed, like it had just consumed a delicious meal.

"What did you do, Lucas?" the happy mouth whispered. "What terrible thing have you done this time?"

CHAPTER 1

Present time

A stalled weather front bred thunderstorm cells from New Orleans to Pensacola. Rain dropped in sheets and lightning shredded the sky. Then, as if on a switch, the deluge halted and the air turned sweet and balmy. Ten minutes later, earth and sky were at war again. Mobile, Alabama, was dead center in the conflict.

"What do you think, Carson?" My detective partner, Harry Nautilus, peered through the windshield wipers. "Time to start loading up animals two by two?"

"How about this time we leave the mosquitoes behind?"

It was nine thirty p.m., the streets almost

dead, sane people safe at home. Harry and I were parked near the downtown library. We were working four to midnight, something we did a couple times a week, most bad guys being nocturnal as owls. Not that we'd see much of them tonight; of the five hours we'd been in the car, two were spent against the curb, blinded by rain.

The radio came to life, the signal mangled by nearby lightning.

"DB . . . Eldredge and . . . truck driver heading to hosp . . . ains."

"Did I hear DB?" Harry said. DB was Dead Body. He grabbed the microphone.

"Nautilus here, Dispatch. You're breaking up. Repeat."

"DB . . . corner of Industrial and Eldredge. Called in by a truck driver. Driver en route to hospital with chest pains."

We were eight blocks away.

"Nautilus and Ryder confirm message received," Harry said. "We're on our way."

Harry jammed the Crown Vic into gear, roared toward the scene. I figured we left a wake like a speedboat. The radio crackled again. Not Dispatch, but another detective team in the vicinity.

"This is Logan and Shuttles. We're closer, just five blocks. We'll take it."

Harry growled and keyed the mike again. "Nautilus and Ryder have the call."

"Why's Logan out at this hour?" I said. "I've never seen his lazy ass work past five thirty."

The radio crackled with Pace Logan's voice. "Dispatch, this is Logan. Mark this one ours, we're almost there."

I felt the car accelerate. Harry growled, "Negative on that, Dispatch. Carson and me are making the run."

"Goddamn it, Nautilus, it's ours," Pace Logan barked over the radio, no longer using Dispatch as an intermediary.

Harry threw the microphone to the floor. "It's whoever gets there first," he muttered, flicking on the lights and screamer and taking a right so fast it about threw me in his lap.

Pace Logan was a disgruntled, hotheaded old-timer waiting to grab his retirement pay, buy a trailer in Florida or Branson, and make life miserable for a succession of lonely women picked up in bowling alley bars. Logan's twenty-seven-year-old partner, Tyree Shuttles, was a new-made detective with the misfortune of being chained to a dinosaur.

Harry cut another corner hard, skidding toward a line of parked cars barely visible through the rain. I held my breath and braced for an impact that somehow never arrived. We blew through a deserted intersection and I saw a flashing red light paralleling us one block over: Logan and Shuttles. We were three blocks from the scene.

"Jeez, Harry. It's a drag race."

"I'm not picking up after Logan again," he said. "No goddamn way."

Six or seven weeks back, Logan's mishandled evidence in a homicide case almost bought the defense a dismissal. Harry and I got called in at the eleventh hour, eleven forty-five, maybe. It took weeks of twelve-hour-a-day work to retrace Logan's investigative steps, supplanting tainted evidence with new finds. Harry'd finally nailed it using information Logan had overlooked in his own records.

I'd spent the bulk of my time handling our standard overweight caseload, meaning Harry had mopped up pretty much on his own. Both of us had worked doubles most days, and Harry'd ended up postponing a vacation with family in Memphis. He was still royally steamed about Logan's screw-up.

I rolled the window down an inch. Between the beats of our screamer, I heard Logan and Shuttles's siren. It would be close.

"Next block, Harry. Turn right."

A radio car at each end of the block had secured an intersection at the edge of a warehouse district. On one corner was a restaurant equipment wholesaler, cattycorner was an industrial laundry.

We raced down the street from one direction, Logan and Shuttles from the other. A semi sat dead in the street, a red Mazda a dozen feet from the big truck's grille. Harry skidded to a stop and dove into the rain, no time to pull on his rain gear. I slid into a plastic slicker and followed.

Harry splashed toward the Mazda as Logan jumped from his vehicle, almost on the Mazda's bumper. Logan stepped in front of Harry, finger jabbing, voice angry. The uniformed officers closed in, drawn by the smell of confrontation. I hurried over, rain pouring into my eyes.

"I've got the scene, Nautilus," Logan said. "Get back in your vehicle and haul ass."

"Not gonna happen, Logan," Harry said. "It's ours."

"I got seniority, Nautilus."

"Then join AARP," Harry said. "I'm not saving your worthless ass anymore."

Logan froze. His eyes tightened. "It was a Forensics screw-up, not mine."

"You almost blew the case, Logan," Harry said. "Have the balls to own up to it."

Logan's hands squeezed into fists. "For a simple fuck, Nautilus, you're a sanctimonious son of a bitch."

"And for a cop, Logan, you're a helluva defense lawyer."

Logan made a guttural sound and launched a punch toward Harry's gut. Harry blocked it, grabbed Logan's wrist, twisted, dropped to a knee. Logan went down. Harry rammed Logan's arm behind his back. He writhed on the wet pavement, cursing and threatening.

"Knife!" someone yelled, a nightmare word. Everyone froze, heads turning, hands dropping to holsters.

"Easy, guys," Tyree Shuttles said, a few feet behind the Mazda. He pointed into shadows by the curb. "I found a big-ass knife. Over here in the gutter."

Harry released Logan's wrist. Logan squirmed up, gasping and wheezing, a heavy smoker. He leaned against the Mazda to catch his breath.

Something grabbed his eye, and for a moment he seemed transfixed by an image near the sidewalk. I turned to look, but all I saw was water rushing down the gutter, dumping into a storm sewer.

Harry and I jogged to Shuttles, kneeling beside a metal object in the gutter. Logan wheezed up, looked at the weapon, then at Shuttles. Harry backed away and sighed, having the civility to invent an ad hoc protocol.

"Shuttles found evidence, Logan. You guys get the case."

Logan leaned against the driver's side of the Mazda, looked inside. He stared a moment, pulled a flashlight from his pocket, checked again, shook his head. Logan laughed without a trace of humor.

"You want this one, Nautilus? It's yours."

Logan turned away, walked back to his car, climbed in the passenger's side. Shuttles shot a glance at his vehicle, Logan sulking within. The young detective looked embarrassed.

"I'm sorry about what went down with Pace," Shuttles said. "He's been in a shitty mood the last couple weeks."

Harry brushed rain from his face, stepped closer to Shuttles, lowering his voice so the uniforms couldn't hear. "I know you won't request a new-partner assignment, Tyree. I respect that. But transfer to another district. Get a new partner that way. Logan's not doing your career any good."

"Pace is retiring in two months, Harry. He'll be gone soon."

"You sure?"

Shuttles nodded.

Harry bounced a gentle punch off the young detective's shoulder, said, "Hang in there."

The slender black officer walked back toward his car. He paused, turned to Harry and mouthed *Thanks*. Shuttles climbed in, flicked off the flashers behind the grille, pulled away. I didn't envy him the rest of his shift with Logan pissing and moaning and inventing ways he got screwed.

Harry told the uniforms the show was over and to get back to diverting traffic, if any happened to show up. I put on latex gloves, opened the door of the Mazda. The victim's bowels had released and the car was thick with the smell of blood and excrement. She was tumbled across the transmission hump, her head on the passenger seat, braided and beaded hair flung like a rag doll's. Her nose appeared broken. Her lower lip was torn. There were wounds across her torso, her blouse glossy with blood. Her throat had been slit.

I took a deep breath and continued my visual inventory. One of her hands looked odd. It was hanging down on the passenger side, in shadow. I went to the passenger side and opened the door, my fears confirmed. Three fingers broken, the digits bent backward. It was unsettling, like a hand assembled incorrectly.

I made myself concentrate on the pillaging of the vehicle – sound system removed, wires dangling. The glove box was open, contents scattered. Maps half-open on the floor, registration, manual, tire-pressure gauge. Sun visors pulled forward. Sometimes folks clipped a few spare bucks there, for toll roads and the like. Blood was everywhere, like the interior had been hosed down with an artery.

I knew why Logan had passed on the case. This one had an immediate bad feel, a one-glance Creep Factor. I studied the woman again, a cold wave spreading through my gut. The smell overwhelmed me and I withdrew.

"She was beaten and cut," I told Harry. "It's bad."

Harry had gone to the car for his rain gear,

not that it would do much good. He leaned in and scanned the scene for several minutes, his mind taking pictures. Now and then a detail pulled a grunt or a sigh. He studied the floor at the woman's feet, put his hand in, touched the floor, looked at his fingertips. Then, aiming the flashlight close to the floor, he repeated the motion.

"What is it, bro?" I asked.

Harry didn't hear me. He turned his face to the sky, as if looking for the answer to something.

CHAPTER 2

Lucas crouched in shadow beside the fast-food restaurant's stinking dumpster, wadding cold French fries in his fist and jamming them into his mouth. Untouched fries were safest, he figured. The cast-off sandwiches all had bite marks.

Lucas pushed sodden, foot-long black hair from his eyes, brushed French-fry salt from his thick beard. He leaned out into the light. There was a bank beside the restaurant, a small branch office with an ATM in the drive-through. Getting money was critical to Lucas's plan. Money breeds money, hadn't he heard that a thousand times? Like a mantra: Money breeds money.

In the half-hour he'd been waiting, over a

dozen cars had slipped to the ATM, drivers making transactions, zooming away. Two of the drivers had pulled to the side, close to the rear of the restaurant. Lucas had watched as the drivers turned on their interior light and fiddled with banking paperwork.

The door at the back of the restaurant slammed open. Lucas froze in the shadows and stench.

"You there, you," a voice yelled, angry. Lucas felt his muscles tighten, his hands ball into hard fists.

"Me?" said someone inside the place.

"You – Darryl, is it?"

"Daniel," a voice grunted.

"I got soft-drink canisters out here. Get 'em inside."

"I still got to finish mopping the –"

"Now."

The door banged shut. Lucas slithered beneath the wheeled trash bin. His heart sank when he saw he'd forgotten his purse. Made of cheap white vinyl, it lay past the dumpster, almost in the cone of light from the restaurant. The door reopened and feet appeared. Canisters were hefted in the door.

The door shut. Lucas squirmed from beneath

the dumpster, pavement grease now added to his shirt and pants, pulled from a donations pile outside a Goodwill store. He'd left his institutional clothing with the other cast-offs.

Lucas clutched the purse to his chest and turned his eyes back to the ATM. Women afforded the best opportunities. But he'd take whatever fate provided and work with it.

He waited twenty minutes, only one vehicle stopping at the ATM in that time, a pickup truck with dual tracks and a stars'n'bars decal on the window. A good ol' boy, Lucas thought. The type to keep a pipe under the seat. Or a gun.

Not worth the risk.

Minutes later a compact car entered the bank lot: a woman, driving slow. Lucas gathered the purse in his hand and threw it into the shadowy corner of the bank lot, twenty feet away. It landed as the car's headlights washed over the pavement. The lights hit the purse, passed by, angled toward the ATM.

Slowed.

Stopped a dozen feet short of the ATM. Lucas held his breath.

Take the bait.

The car began backing up. Lucas raised to a

crouch. Tensed his muscles. The car parked beside the purse. He heard the door locks snap off.

Lucas was up and running.

CHAPTER 3

The next morning I arose to a sky the color of unfired clay. Harry and I had worked until three in the morning, ascertaining what we could from the victim's name and vehicle papers. Thunder rumbled in the distance, another storm cell rolling through. The phone rang as I was pouring coffee. It was Danielle Danbury – my girlfriend.

"Carson, can you stop by before work?" Her voice was somber.

"What's wrong, Dani?"

"Please hurry."

"On my way."

Though Dani's profession as a TV journalist made us natural adversaries, we'd been thrown into an uneasy alliance last year, tracking collectors of serial-killer memorabilia. The bizarre episode had taken Dani and me – I simply couldn't use her on-air moniker, DeeDee – to Paris to interview an elderly art professor. While in the City of Light we'd become lovers, a condition that remained.

The erratic and overlong hours of our jobs made getting together more chance than certainty, and not counting sleeping, we grabbed maybe fifteen hours a week together. At least that had been the norm until a couple months back when Harry jumped into Logan's mess and I'd played catch-up eighteen hours a day.

I raced down the steps of my stilt-standing beachfront home and jumped in my old pickup, making Dani's house in twenty minutes. She was in reporter garb: good jeans, white silk blouse, burgundy linen jacket, strand of pearls at her neck, tiny matching earrings. Her blonde hair was lacquered, a concession to the cameras. She clutched a copy of Woodward and Bernstein's book on Watergate, *All the President's Men*, to her breast. Her eyes were red and swollen.

I stepped inside, my heart racing. "What's wrong, Dani? Are you all right?"

"I'm fine, Carson. It's a friend . . . she was killed last night. Murdered. I just read it in the paper."

There was only one murder last night.

"Taneesha Franklin," I said, reaching to hold Dani. "I was there. I'm sorry. Was she a good friend?"

Dani wiped her eyes, leaned back to look into my face.

"More like mentor and mentee, I guess. But she was a wonderful person."

"She was a reporter?"

"For a tiny radio station, WTSJ. She was a newbie, spent her days covering city meetings, ribbon-cuttings, yapping politicians . . . the usual starter crapola. I'd had lunch with her a few times, Teesh asking questions about journalism, me answering. She was bright and dedicated and excited about her little reporting job. What happened, Carson? The paper had maybe four column inches. I can read between the lines. It sounded . . . brutal."

"It was bad. Probably a robbery that went haywire."

Dani and I hear so many lies in our jobs that we don't lie to one another, not even the little white ones. Dani was still holding

All the President's Men. I tapped its cover, tried a smile.

"You're about thirty years behind on your reading, babe."

"It was a gift from Teesh. I told her my copy of the book was about to turn to dust, and she bought me a new one. She dropped it off a few weeks back. Read the dedication, Carson."

Dani opened the book to the inside cover. I saw script in a neat and flowing hand.

> *To DeeDee . . . Who told me how things are supposed to work, and when they don't, how to maul the bastards messing in the machinery. Love, Teesh.*

"Isn't that great?" Dani asked.

"Maybe a tad strident."

"It's how the good ones start out," Dani said, a tear tracing her cheek.

I met Harry at the department and we went to the hospital. Last night we hadn't been allowed to interview the trucker who'd discovered the crime scene – he'd suffered a heart attack – but he was now stable.

Arlin Dell was a strapping guy with about five bedside devices either measuring or dripping something. The doc gave us five minutes. I pulled up a chair, Harry leaned against the wall. Dell was pale, his voice light. He seemed a bit fuzzy, like on a mild narcotic.

"I'd just left the yard with a full load of electronic gizmos headed for Memphis. I cut down that side street, rain pouring, me wondering if it's gonna be like this all the way to Tennessee, when I see this red car in the middle of the street. No lights. I jam on my brakes, about jackknife the rig."

"You see anyone near the Mazda?"

Dell made a whistling noise, like laughing or choking. "An ape jumped out of the car, ran straight at my headlights, then cut to the side and jumped into the shadows."

"Ape?" Harry said.

Dell said, "I climbed from the rig and looked in the car. When I saw what was inside, my heart grabbed in me like a fist. I made it back to the cab, called 911."

"Tell me you didn't really see an ape."

"It was a hairy guy." Dell patted his cheeks. "Furry face, long hair. Like an ape. Or the thing in those *Star Wars* movies."

"A Wookiee?" I asked.

Dell shrugged. "Ape. Wookiee. Or maybe one of those guys from ZZ Top."

"I hate a bearded perp," Harry said as we left the hospital and aimed the Crown Vic for WTSJ, the victim's employer. "The bastard shaves and he's got a brand-new face."

I'd been replaying Dell's recollections in my head, picturing myself high above the ground in a cab-over Mack. "You know what really got me, bro? The perp ran straight for the rig, then juked at the last second, disappearing. He ran a dozen feet directly into the truck's headlights."

Harry tapped his thumbs on the wheel. "Headlights, engine rumble, windows like eyes . . . the truck should have scared the hell out of a guy just committed a capital crime. Standard response is haul ass the opposite direction."

"Maybe he thought he could attack the truck," I said. "Roaring on crack or PCP. Or maybe insane."

"He'd already pitched his knife. It was on the other side of the vehicle. If he was going to war with the semi, he was going at it barehanded."

"Ballsy son of a bitch," I said. "Or a full whack-out."

"Never a good thing," Harry noted. "Either choice."

WTSJ was in a squat concrete-block building near Pritchard, a town abutting Mobile to the north. The receptionist's eyes were shadowed with grief, but she forced a smile.

"Lincoln's the station manager. He's on the air two more minutes."

She put us in a small anteroom. Lincoln Haley was in the adjoining studio, visible through a thick window. Haley was mid-forties, square-jawed, a neat beard. His forehead was high and protruding, like it was filled with songs. Racks of CDs were at his back. He wore a black headset and spoke into a microphone the size of a beer can. He saw us looking, flashed *two minutes* with his fingers, leaned over the microphone. Speakers filled the anteroom with his voice.

" . . . coming up on the hour, time for Newsbreak. After the hour it's the Queen Bee, Miss Pearlie Winston, bringing you the best in funk'n'blues in the whole United States . . . Now I'm gonna take you to the top with Marlon Saunders . . ."

Music kicked in. Haley stood, set the headset on the table, rubbed his face. A man worn past the tread. The studio door admitted a large and brightly dressed woman. She gave Haley's hand a squeeze. He appeared in the anteroom seconds later, khakis, sandals, sweater, hands in his pockets.

"I'll do anything if it helps find the animal who hurt Teesh."

Through the glass I saw the woman put on the headphones, pull the microphone close. She took a deep breath, a big fake smile rising to her face.

"This is Pearlie Winston, queen of the funky scene . . ."

Haley reached to a switch, killed the speakers.

"Pearlie's heart is broken, but she sounds like she's about to break into song. It's tough. Taneesha was like my daughter, everybody's daughter. She was . . . w-was . . ."

"Tell me about Ms Franklin's job," Harry said. "At your own pace."

Haley nodded, composed himself.

"We're a small station, Detective. When Pearlie's not on the air, she's selling advertising time. When I'm not broadcasting or managing things, I'm the electrician. Teesh was our reporter, but sometimes wrote ads."

"You're probably not ripe for a takeover by Clarity Broadcasting," I said. Clarity owned Channel 14, Dani's employer.

Haley's eyes darkened. "Everything Clarity touches turns to garbage; profitable garbage, but soulless."

"Ms Franklin worked here how long?" Harry said.

"Started as an intern two years back. That girl had boundless enthusiasm."

"Did she want to be a DJ or whatever, on the air?"

"She did the midnight show for several months. But talking between tunes was too tame for Teesh. Her dream was to be a reporter. Teesh had the aggression, the drive. She just needed more polish. I moved her into our tiny news department. You would have thought I'd given her a job on CNN."

Harry said, "Was she working a story last night?"

"Not an assignment. But Teesh was always looking to break that big story, find something no one was supposed to know, putting the light on it. I told her we didn't have money for investigations. But she thought of it as training, kept at it on her own time."

"Self-propelled," I said.

"Know who she wanted to be like? That investigator on Channel 14, uh, I can't recall names . . . blonde, big eyes, kind of in-your-face, but sexy with it . . ."

"Uh, Danbury?" I said.

Haley snapped his fingers. "DeeDee Danbury. Teesh spoke with Ms Danbury a few times, asked questions. Teesh called her a kick-ass lady with a mind all her own."

"I've heard that about Ms Danbury," I said.

CHAPTER 4

We left the station and headed for Forensics. We walked into the main lab and found deputy director Wayne Hembree sprawled across the white floor, tie flapped over his shoulder, glasses askew on his black, clock-round face, one bony arm beneath the small of his back, the other flung above his head.

"I've been shot," he moaned.

"Who did it?" I asked. Detectives get paid to ask insightful questions like that.

Hembree nodded to the far side of the room where an older guy in a neon-bright aloha shirt held a dummy gun and grinned like he'd just discovered orgasm pills.

"Not Thaddeus over there," Hembree said. "From his angle the momentum would have flung me the opposite direction. My arm wouldn't have been beneath my back, but across my belly."

I grabbed Hembree's hand, pulled him up. He brushed down his lab coat, made notes on a clipboard, then told the shooter they'd act it out from another angle in a few minutes. The Thaddeus guy flicked a salute, faked a couple shots at Harry and me, retreated from the room. Hembree scanned a report and gave us the preliminaries.

"Reads like a robbery gone bad. The car stops at the intersection, the perp runs from the shadows, busts the driver's-side window, takes over."

"Why the torture?" I asked.

"Motivation's not my bailiwick," Hembree said. "Maybe she said something that set him off."

"Must have been a hell of a something," I said.

Harry had been listening quietly. He stepped up.

"I got something feels off, myself. How long had she been dead when your people got there, Bree?"

"Under a half-hour, I'd bet. Your trucker saw the perp jump out when he arrived. Why?"

"The driver's-side window, the busted one, was windward," Harry said. "Close, anyway."

Hembree frowned. "I'm not getting you."

"I stuck my finger down on the floor. There was over two inches of rain there. I mean, it was raining like hell last night, but four inches an hour?"

Hembree frowned. "Rain fell in moving pockets, the storm-cell effect. If a string of cells went over that location, three or more inches an hour is possible. But a location a mile away might get an inch or less."

"Makes sense," Harry said. "One less thing to think about."

I heard my ring tone, grabbed the phone from my pocket. The call was from the front desk at headquarters.

"This is Jim Haskins, Carson. You and Harry are leads on that robbery-murder last night, right?"

"Ours. What's up?"

"Got a woman here at the desk who brought in her elderly mother. Mama's wrought up, mumbling about a purse, an ATM and a long-hair in her car. Thought you'd want to know."

Harry and I arrived twelve minutes later, the

wonder of a siren and flashing lights. The daughter was Gina Lovett, forty or thereabouts, plump and bespectacled. Her mother was Tessie Atkins, late sixties, nervous. She kept her arms tight to herself, as if cold.

"What happened, Miz Atkins?" Harry asked as we sat.

She tugged at her sleeve. "I had been visiting a friend at the hospital and passed the bank on my way home. I needed to pay bills. Maybe it wasn't smart at that hour . . ."

"What hour, ma'am?" I asked.

"Almost midnight. It was late, but there was a restaurant next door, a fast-food place. It made me feel safer. I pulled in and saw something white to the side of the lot. At first I thought it was a cat or some poor animal run down by a car. But then I saw it was a purse. I thought someone's purse fell out by accident. It happened with my wallet once in the lot at Bruno's. Some nice Samaritan took it inside the store. I thought . . ."

"You'd repay the favor," Harry said.

"I pulled next to it and got out to pick it up. The next thing I knew a hand was across my mouth and I was back in the car. It was a man with all kinds of hair, bad smelling. He got down in the passenger side, on the floor, and said if I didn't perform to expectations, he had a gun."

"Perform to expectations?" I said.

She nodded, arms crossed, shaking fingers clasping her shoulders. "He made me take six hundred dollars from my account and three hundred from my two credit cards. It's my limit. I was too shook up to drive. He drove south of Bienville Square a few blocks and jumped out. I just sat there and cried until my hands stopped shaking. I don't know how I got home."

"Why didn't you call the police?"

"He took my driver's license. He said if I told the police, he was going to come to my house."

Mrs Atkins looked away. The daughter spoke up.

"I stopped by Mama's this morning to pick up some sewing. She wouldn't look at me and I knew something was wrong. She finally told me."

We spoke to Mrs Atkins for a few more minutes, honed in on details, what few had registered beyond her fear. She consented to have her car checked by Forensics. Though sure the perp had made his threats just to keep her quiet, we made a quick call to the uniform commander in her district, requested his troops keep a tight watch on Mrs Atkins's house the next few days.

"Bait," Harry said, setting his can of soda on the hood of the cruiser, leaning back against its fender. "He used a purse as bait."

"It's brilliant," I said. "Who can resist a purse? The good want to help, the bad see money and credit cards."

We were parked on the causeway connecting the eastern shore of Mobile Bay with the city. Twilight was an orange lantern hung below the horizon of an indigo sky. Fresh stars shimmered in the east. A hundred feet distant, three elderly black men fished from lawn chairs, frequently consulting the brown bags beside them.

"After pushing her back into the car, he didn't touch Mrs Atkins," I said. "Didn't lay a hand on her."

"He threatened her with death," Harry reminded me.

"He said he had a gun. Two hours earlier he'd just butchered a woman with a five-inch knife. Why didn't he threaten to stab her, slice her? Why didn't he ransack the car? And what's with that 'perform to expectations' line? It sounds like a damn stockbroker."

Harry looked south at the dark horizon, the mouth of Mobile Bay thirty miles distant.

"He probably tried the purse bit with Taneesha but she heard him running up. She closed the door, locked it. Maybe that's what pissed him off."

"Something sure did. How many wounds did Ms Franklin have?"

"Over thirty. But he broke her fingers first. I don't get it. Why he'd kill one woman, two hours later give another a break?"

I forced myself to revisit the Franklin crime scene: the Wookiee breaking the young woman's fingers, getting off on her pain, then going wild with the knife – poke, slash, jab. Then, interrupted by the sudden appearance of the semi, the perp bails out, runs wildly into the truck's headlights, veers away into the night.

"Did Forensics find any blood in Mrs Atkins's vehicle?"

Harry said, "No blood, no hair, no trace of any evidence."

"At least we got a knife."

Harry finished his can of soda, crumpled the can like paper, bouncing it in his hand.

"With nada on the prints. An uncharted whacko."

"Is this going to turn weird, brother?" I asked.

"Going to?" he said.

We heard a ship's horn and turned to watch a freighter slipping from the mouth of the Mobile River. The ship's bridge was at the stern and lighted. The only other light was at the bow. Somewhere between the two points were hundreds of feet of invisible ship. A minute later, its wake reached us, hissing against the shoreline with a sound like rain.

CHAPTER 5

Lucas stood in the piss-stinking service station restroom, door locked, and foamed restroom soap over his torso, patting dry with rough paper towels. Once more he counted his money, tight clean bills, over a thousand dollars' worth. Seed money. The next step was to turn it into working capital. A quick way of doing that was to find and supply a product for which there was great demand.

He could get product. What he needed was a distributorship.

Lucas studied the face in the grimy mirror: nothing but black eyes and round hole of mouth deep in a sea of black hair. Scary, hideous even, like he'd escaped from hell. But then, how else was he supposed to look?

Lucas scowled into the mirror, bared his teeth like a rabid dog, growled. Snapped his teeth at his image.

What's that face mean, Lucas?

Dr Rudolnick's voice suddenly in Lucas's head.

"It's how pissed off I am, Doctor."

"You look angry enough to kill, Lucas. Are you really that angry?"

"I guess not, Doctor. Not today, at least."

"Good, Lucas. Let's do some deep breathing and visualizations, all right?"

Lucas laughed and tucked the shirt into his pants. He opened the restroom door. Lights in the distance, bars, clubs. Lowlife joints with lowlife people, the kind of folks attuned to nontraditional distribution networks. Something in the automotive segment of the market.

The nearest bar, a hundred feet distant, had a window blinking LUCKY'S in green neon script. Maybe it was an omen.

Lucas stepped out into the night, music playing loud in his head, snapping his fingers to an old funk piece by Bootsy Collins, "Psychoticbumpschool". He angled toward Lucky's.

CHAPTER 6

"Give me a couple minutes with Ms Franklin, Clair?" I said. "Please?"

Dr Clair Peltier, chief pathologist for the Mobile office of the Alabama Forensics Bureau, stared at me with breathtaking blue eyes. Between us, on a stainless steel table, rested the draped body of Taneesha Franklin. Her face bore the misshaping of the blows she'd been dealt; her bare arms outside the drape displayed puckered knife wounds. Her head lolled to the side, the gaping slash beneath her chin like a wide and hungry second mouth.

"Ryder . . ."

"Three minutes?"

She sighed. "I'll run down the hall and get a coffee. It's a two-minute run."

"Thanks, Clair."

She waved my appreciation away and left the room, her green surgical gown flowing as she moved. Not many women could make a formless cotton wrapping look good, but Clair pulled it off.

Perhaps it was peculiar only to me, but as an investigator – or maybe just as a human being – I always sought a few moments with the deceased before the Y-cut opened the body, transformed it. I wanted time alone with my employer. Not the city, nor the blind concept of justice. But the person I was truly working for, removed from life by the hand of another, early, wrongfully. Sometimes I stood with the Good, and often I stood with the Bad. Most of the human beings I stood with fell, like the bulk of us, into a vast middle distance, feet in the clay, head in the firmament, the heart suspended between.

From what Harry and I had discerned, Taneesha Franklin had lived her brief life with honor, focus, and a need to be of service to others. She had only recently discovered journalism and through it hoped to better the world.

Good for you, Teesh, I thought.

Clair stepped back through the door. Without

a word, she walked to the body, picked up a scalpel, and went to work. I stood across the table, sometimes watching, sometimes closing my eyes.

I generally attended the postmortems, while Harry spent more time with the Prosecutor's Office. We joked that I preferred dead bodies to live lawyers. The truth was that I felt comfortable in the morgue. It was cool and quiet and orderly.

"Where was she found, Carson?" Clair asked, staring into the bisected throat, muscles splayed outward.

"Semi-industrial area by the docks. Warehouses, light industry."

"Not crowded, then? No one very near?"

"It's normally sort of a hooker hangout. But the rain kept them in that night. Why?"

"Her vocal cords were injured. Lacerated."

"From manual strangulation? The knife wound?"

Clair pursed her roseate lips. "Screaming, probably. I wondered why no one heard her."

The procedure took a bit over two hours. Clair snapped off her latex gloves and dropped them into the biohazard receptacle beside the table. She removed her cloth mask and I saw a lipstick kiss printed in the fabric. Clair uncovered her head, shaking out neat, brief hair, as black and glossy as anthracite. She pressed her fists against her hips and stretched her spine backward.

"I'm getting too old for this, Ryder."

"You're forty-four. And in better shape than most people ten years younger."

"Don't try charm, Ryder," she said. "Unless it's absolutely necessary."

I was perhaps her only colleague this side of God who used Clair's first name. Not knowing of her insistence on formality, I'd used it when we were introduced. Those with us had grimaced in anticipation of a scorching correction, but for some reason, she'd let it stand, addressing me solely by my last name as a countermeasure.

When I'd first met Clair, I'd considered her five years older than her actual age, the result of a stern visage and a husband in his sixties. I would later come to realize the latter bore certain responsibility for the former, Clair's visage softening appreciably after hubby was sent a-packing.

Two years ago, a murder investigation had cut directly through the center of Clair's personal life. The revelations of the investigation had wounded her, and I'd been present at a moment of her vulnerability, a time she'd needed to talk.

We'd stood beneath an arbor of roses in her garden and Clair had revealed pieces of her past – less to me than to herself – suddenly grasping meaning from the shadows of long-gone events.

They were startling revelations, and though I disavowed the notion, she had believed me the vehicle for the transformative moment.

"When will the preliminary be ready?" I asked, pulling my jacket from a hanger on the wall.

"In the a.m. And don't expect it before ten thirty."

Though our relationship was professional, there had been times – as in her garden – when the world shifted and for fleeting moments we seemed able to look into one another with a strange form of clarity. A believer in reincarnation might have suspected we'd touched in a former life, spinning some thread that even time and distance left unsevered.

"I'll be here tomorrow at ten thirty-one, Clair."

She walked away, talking over her shoulder. "How about sending Harry? Be nice to see someone with some sense for a change."

Though at times the thread seemed tenuous.

* * *

I was climbing into the Crown Victoria when my cellphone rang, Harry on the other end. "Hembree wants to see us at the lab. How about you whip by and grab me. I'll be out front."

We blew into Forensics fifteen minutes later. Hembree leaned against a lab table outside his office. He was so skinny, the lab coat hung in white folds like a wizard's robe.

He said, "You got great eyes, Harry."

Harry winked. "Thanks, Bree. You got a nice ass. Wanna grab a drink after work?"

Hembree frowned. "I meant catching the water depth on the floorboards. I called the regional office of the National Weather Service, talked to the head meteorologist. They archive Dopplers. He reran the night's readings, checking time, location, and storm cell activity."

"Upshot?" Harry asked.

"The area where the vic's vehicle sat took pretty light rain, overall. Lightest in the city, at least in the hour before it was spotted. About an inch fell in that hour."

"Why so much in the car, Bree? It was a lake."

"Maybe a leak along the roof guttering caught rain, channeled it inside. I'll check it out."

"Anything else turn up?"

Hembree said, "The knife Shuttles pulled off the street? Made years ago by the Braxton Knife Company in Denver. The handle's bone. The blade's carbon steel, not stainless, why it looks corroded. It's a damn nice knife."

"How about prints? Anything new?"

"Pulled a thumb, forefinger and middle finger, some palm. Ran every possible database. Nada. Nothing. Zip."

"You got a Wookiee database?" Harry said.

"What?"

We waved it off and walked out the door.

CHAPTER 7

Harry and I spent the rest of the day wandering the industrial neighborhood where Taneesha Franklin had died. Normally, the area was a cruising ground for hookers, but rain was keeping them inside. We corralled as many denizens as possible, asking about the bearded longhair. The killing had frightened most of the girls, guys, and question marks that hawked wares from the corners. They tried to be helpful, but we ended the day with a zero, heading home at six.

Home, to me, was thirty miles south, to Dauphin Island. It's an expensive community, but when my mother passed away, I inherited enough to buy it outright. It was actually my second home on the island, the first turned to kindling by Hurricane Katrina. I never complain about paying insurance premiums anymore.

I pulled onto my short street and saw a white Audi in my drive, Danielle Danbury's car, the bumper festooned with birdwatching and wildlife stickers. I parked beneath my house, climbed the stairs and stepped inside.

Dani yelled, "I'm heading out to the deck. Join me." The deck doors slid closed with a thump. I stood in the living room hearing only the soft hiss of the air conditioner. Normally Dani would have met me at the door.

What was up?

I paused to yank off my tie, toss it over a chair, follow it with my jacket. The shoulder holster and weapon went to my bedside table.

I heard the deck door slide open. "Where you at, Carson?"

"Changing."

"Get it in gear, Pogobo."

Pogobo – and its diminutive, *Pogie* – came from *po*-lice *go*-lden *bo*-y, coined by Dani after Harry and I were made Officers of the Year by the Mayor. Most of the time we were homicide detectives, but once in a great while we were the Psychopathological and Sociopathological Investigative Team. PSIT, or *Piss-it*, as everyone called it, started as a public relations gimmick a few years back, never intended to be activated. But somehow it was, somehow it worked, and somehow it bought us Officers of the Year commendations. The honor turned out to be, as Harry had promised, worth less than mud.

I slipped into cutoffs, T-shirt, and running shoes a half-mile short of disintegrating. At the kitchen sink I slapped cool water over my face and glanced out the window. Dani paced beside the deck table; on it something hidden beneath my kitchen towel. I dried my face on an oven mitt and went to the deck.

The waning day remained beautiful and springlike, enhanced by a salt tang breezing up from the strand. Gulls followed a school of bait-fish in the small breakers, keening and diving. Several pleasure boats bounced across the Gulf, including a big white Bertram I'd seen a lot lately. High above, a single-engine plane banked at the far edge of the sky, so small it looked like a lost kite.

Dani stood beside the towel-shrouded tabletop in white shorts and red tank top. Sunlight shimmered from her ash-blonde hair, her big gray eyes made blue by the bright sky. I raised my eyebrows at the table.

"A magic show? You're going to make a rabbit appear?"

She snapped off the towel. Centering the table was a bottle of pricey champagne iced down in a plastic salad bowl, flanked by my two champagne flutes, $1.49 apiece at Big Lots.

Dani thumbed the cork from the bottle and froth raced out behind it. She filled the glasses, handed one to me.

"We're drinking to my elevation from reporter to . . ." she lifted her glass in toast, "a full-fledged anchor."

I stared like she was speaking in tongues. "What?"

"They're making me an anchor, Carson. I start this week."

"This is out of the blue."

I saw the edge of a frown. "Not really. I've felt it coming for a few weeks, caught hints. Heard a few feelers."

"Why didn't you tell me?"

"It's June, Carson. When was the last time we had a real conversation? Early April?"

"I was working." I heard myself get defensive.

"I tried to tell you a couple weeks back. But one time you shushed me and went on writing in your notepad, and the other time I looked over and you were asleep."

"Why not a third attempt?"

She didn't appear to hear the question.

"I'll start by subbing for anchors when they're out. Do weekends. Get viewers used to me."

"They're already used to you."

"People only know me as a woman holding a microphone. It's important the audience comes to know me as an approachable presence. Someone they want to spend time with. Someone they trust. It's like a relationship with the viewer, something you give them."

It sounded like the kind of hoo-hah she'd always laughed at in the past. I was wondering what I'd missed or who she'd been talking to about viewer relationships and approachable whatevers.

"What's this lead to?" I said.

"Regular hours, at least for this biz."

"All we have now are weekends, and only sometimes at that. Didn't you just say that's when you'll be –"

"A trial period, that's all. Break-in period. Things will change."

"Seeing less of each other is better for each other?"

"I can't help it, Carson. This is my chance to try a high-profile position. Plus the money is almost double." She changed subjects. "You already rented your tuxedo for Saturday, right?"

I slapped my forehead. Channel 14 was having their annual to-do on Saturday night, a formal event. I guess I'd figured if I didn't have a tux, I didn't have to attend; sartorial solipsism, perhaps.

"Get it tomorrow, Carson. This is the big wing-ding of the year and all the honchos from Clarity will be there. I've got to make an anchor-level impression."

We sat on the deck and I listened as Dani told me things I probably should have heard weeks back. Her job change seemed rational and good for us in the long run; more time, regular hours. But somewhere, behind the hiss of the waves and gentle blues drifting from the deck speakers, I heard a faint but insistent note of discord, like my mind and heart were playing opposing notes.

CHAPTER 8

I arrived at the department at eight the next morning. It was quiet, a couple of dicks on the phones, digging. Most of the gray cubicles were empty. Pace Logan was sitting at his desk and staring into the air. I didn't see Shuttles and figured he was out doing something Logan didn't understand, detective work maybe. After grabbing a cup of coffee from the urn and tossing a buck in the kitty for a pair of powdered doughnuts, I headed to the cubicled, double-desk combo forming Harry's and my office.

I walked into our space, saw Harry on his hands and knees on the floor, looking under his desk.

"That's right. Crawl, you miserable worm," I snarled.

He looked up and rolled his eyes. "There's a couple photos missing from the murder book. I figured they dropped down here."

The murder books – binders holding the investigational records of cases – had sections with plastic sleeves to hold crime-scene and relevant photos, trouble being the sleeves didn't hold very well.

"What's in the pix?" I asked.

Harry stood, brushed the knees of his lemon yellow pants, and cast a baleful eye at the wastebasket beside the desk. It wouldn't be the first time something disappeared over the side, dumped by the janitorial crew.

"I dunno. I got the file numbers. I'll call over and get some reprints."

I looked at the pile on his desk. Harry had been checking records and information removed from Taneesha Franklin's office, adding potentially useful pieces to the book.

"Finding anything interesting, bro?" I asked.

"Funny you should ask. I was going over Ms Franklin's long-distance records. Here's a couple calls caught my eye."

He tapped the paper with a thick digit. I looked at the name.

"The state pen at Holman?" I said. "What's that about?"

"Eight calls in two days. Seven are under a minute. The final one lasts for eleven minutes."

I nodded. "Like she finally got through to someone."

Harry jammed the phone under his ear, tapped in the numbers. "I'll call the warden, see when we can come up and hang out. You want a king or two doubles in your cell?"

The warden was a pro, not a bureaucrat, and said we'd be welcome any time. We pointed the Crown Vic north. Two hours later, we were checking into prison.

Warden Malone was a big, fiftyish guy with rolled-up white sleeves and a tie adorning his desk instead of his neck. His hair was gray and buzz-cut. Loop a whistle around his neck and he'd have been Hollywood's idea of a high school football coach. We sat in his spartan office overlooking the main yard.

"I had the visitor logs checked," Malone said, patting a sheaf of copies. "T. Franklin was here on Wednesday before last, nine a.m. She designated herself as Media, representing WTSJ. Ms Franklin spent twenty-one minutes with Leland

Harwood. It appears to have been her sole visit to the prison."

"What's Leland Harwood's story?" Harry asked.

Malone leaned back in his chair and laced his fingers behind his head. "Low-level enforcer type, legbreaker. A couple thefts in his package, assaults. He bought his ticket here last spring, when he shot a guy dead in an alley behind a bar. A fight."

"The guy he killed was in Mobile?" Harry asked.

"Harwood and some other moke got into a tussle at a Mobile bar. Went outside. Bar patrons heard a shot, found the other guy dead. Come court day, everyone in the bar swore the other guy started the fight. The prosecution had no choice but to let Harwood plea to Manslaughter two, light time."

"Maybe that's how it went down," Harry said.

"My boy's an attorney in Daphne," Malone said. "Prosecutor, naturally. He knows a lot of folks at the Mobile Prosecutor's Office, including the lady who handled Harwood's case. She says the patrons weren't so in tune with Harwood's story on the night of the action. Only when they hit the stand did they sing his innocence. Note for note, too. Like they'd had some choral training, you know what I mean."

"Paid performances," I said.

"Sure sounded like it," Malone said, tossing the file back on his desk and looking between Harry and me. "Harwood's a white guy. Thirty-one years old. Probably establish a better bond with Detective Ryder. I'd suggest the visitors' room, not the interrogation facility. He'll clam in an interrogation room. But Leland's a talkative sort in a visitors'-room environment. Probably yap your ear off."

"Outside of chatty," I asked, "what's Harwood like?"

"An eel," Malone said. "Or maybe a chameleon."

"Whatever he needs to be," Harry said. It was a common trait in the con community.

CHAPTER 9

"I have a new girlfriend here in the joint, Detective Ryder. She likes for me to use Listerine. You use Listerine, Detective? My little girlie thinks the Listerine keeps me kissing-sweet. Fresh, you know?"

I looked through an inch of smeared Plexiglas at the face of Leland Harwood, babbling into the phone. It was a short-distance call: three feet to the visitor's phone in my hand. Harwood had a scrinched face set into a head outsize for his body, like his mama birthed the head a couple years before the rest of him dropped out, the head getting a head start on growing.

"There's only one problem, Detective Ryder . . ."

I shifted my gaze to Harwood's hands.

Scarred and ugly, tats scrawled across them, the classic LOVE on one set of knuckles, HATE on the other. Couldn't these guys ever think of something different: DAMN/DUMB or LOST/LIFE or FLAT/LINE?

"The Listerine kinda burns when I rub it on my asshole."

Harwood started laughing, a start-stop keening like the shower scene from *Psycho.* He laughed with his mouth wide, showing a squirming tongue and the black ruination of his molars. He tapped the glass with his phone, stuck it back to his lips.

"Hey Dick-tective, stop daydreaming. I'm telling you about my love life. You should be takin' notes or something."

"All I want to know is what you talked about with Taneesha Franklin."

"Who?" The outsized head grinned like a jack o'lantern.

"A reporter. From WTSJ in Mobile. She signed in for a visit a week back. The sheet shows you spent twenty minutes talking to her."

Harwood pretended to pout. "Why isn't the little sweetie coming to see me anymore? You're cute, Ryder. But she was cuter. A touch plump, but I like cushion when I'm pushin'." He did the *Psycho* laugh again.

"She's dead, Leland."

He froze. The smart-ass attitude fell from the milky eyes, replaced with a glimmer of fear. "How'd she die?" No more comedian in his voice.

"Robbery, looks like. She took a bad beating, Leland. Torture, even."

Harwood leaned toward the glass. "Torture how?"

"She had three broken fingers, Leland. That sounds like something an enforcer type might do to get information. Wasn't that your line of work?"

"I had a lotta lines of work. Man's got to make a liv—" His lip curled. I thought it was a sneer, but it turned into a pained face. He punched his sternum, belched. I swear I could smell it through the glass.

"I'm clean, Ryder. I been behaving. Taking classes. Working in the library. Being a good boy. First time I get up before the parole board, I'm out."

"For about two weeks. I know your type, Leland. You got no other talent than crime."

He grinned, a man holding four aces with a backup ace in his shoe.

"I'm set up this time. No more day laborer. I'm made in the shade from here on out." Harwood caught himself. Winced.

"What is it?" I said.

He belched again, thumped his belly with his fist. "Indigestion. A year of eating the crap they serve in this joint."

"You reserved your table here when you killed a man, Leland. Bon appetit."

"Fuck you." He winced again. "Jeez, I need a fucking tub of Bromo."

Another prisoner entered the convict side of the visitors' room, a man with piercing gray eyes and dark hair falling in unwashed ringlets. His forehead was deeply scarred between both temples, as if an ax blade had been drawn through the flesh like a plow. He was rock-muscled, and I took him for one of those guys with nothing to do but pump iron all day. I've never understood why prisons give violent criminals the equipment to turn themselves into weapons. They should give them canasta lessons.

The guy walked over and sat two chairs down from Harwood, dividers between sections allowing a modicum of privacy. Harwood shot the guy a glance, frowned, looked quickly away.

The door to the visitors' side opened. I glanced over and saw a wide-shouldered Caucasian with curly yellow-blond hair, eyes deep-set above high cheekbones. He was dressed in a suit: silk, brown. A gold watch flashed from his wrist. He seemed guided by unseen currents in the room, pausing, turning, evaluating. Then pulling out the chair one booth over, a half-dozen feet away. His eyes looked through me, then turned to the man across the Plexiglas. He picked up the phone, started a whispered conversation. A lawyer, I figured.

I turned back to Harwood. He was spitting on the floor, wiping away saliva with the back of his hand.

"I'm done talking, Ryder. I'm sorry about the little sweetie. She was nice. Sincere, you know. But naïve."

"Naïve?"

"It's a mean old world, Detective. Little sweetie-tush was too busy playing reporter to understand there are people out there who can . . ." Harwood paused, swallowed heavily, made a wet noise.

"You all right, Leland?" I asked. "You're looking strange."

"'Flu coming on, maybe. I don't feel good."

"What didn't Taneesha understand, Harwood?"

Harwood wiped sweat from his forehead with the back of his hand. "I'm feeling rotten all of a sudden."

"Tell me about Taneesha. Then you can head to the infirmary."

Harwood suddenly stopped speaking and looked into his lap. His eyes widened.

"Jesus."

"What is it, Leland?"

"I pissed myself, and didn't even feel it. What the hell's happening?"

He dropped the phone to the counter and stood unsteadily. His blue institutional pants were dark to the knees with urine. His face was white, his hair sweat-matted to his forehead. He convulsed from somewhere in his midsection, dropping to his knees, toppling the chair.

"Guard," I yelled to the uniformed man in the corner of the visitors' area. "Sick man here."

Harwood clung to the counter with his tattooed fingers, weaving. I watched him shudder to restrain vomit, saw his cheeks fill, his mouth open. A flood of yellow foam poured over his tongue. His eyes rolled into white and he slid to the floor.

Doors on the containment side burst open and two uniformed men rushed to Harwood. He convulsed on the floor, heels and head slamming the gray concrete. His bowels opened.

I suddenly found myself alone on the visitors' side, the man beside me having retreated from the horrific spectacle. The monstrous convict visitee was still across the glass, watching as the two guards rolled Harwood onto a stretcher. I saw the convict lean over for a closer look, his eyes a mix of fear and concern.

Then, for the span of a heartbeat, I saw him smile.

We pulled away from the prison. Harwood had been taken to the infirmary. When we'd gone a couple miles, I climbed in the back seat, lay down with my hands behind my head. Harry and I had traveled this way often, him driving, me reclining in back. When I was a child and my father's psychotic angers would infest his brain, I slipped from the house and hid in the back seat of our station wagon. A back seat felt secure to this day. It wasn't the officially sanctioned method of travel, thus we limited it to backroads and anonymous highways.

"Harwood exploded like a volcano?" Harry asked the rearview mirror. "Think it has anything to do with our case?"

I thought a moment. "He was a smug smart-ass, a gamester," I said to the back of Harry's square head. "Probably didn't make a lot of friends. Could have been payback."

"Or just some bad prune-o," Harry said, referring to an alcoholic concoction brewed up in prisons everywhere. "What'd he say about Taneesha?"

"He was being a funny boy, but when I mentioned her murder it was like throwing ice water in his face. He seriousced up a bit, said she was naïve and didn't know how the world worked. And that he was going to be set up when he got out. He wasn't going to be a day laborer anymore."

"Set up? Like being taken care of financially?"

I said, "That's what I took it to mean."

"So Harwood thought Taneesha didn't know how the world worked?"

"We've met a hundred guys like Harwood, Harry, how do all of them think the world works?"

Harry thought a moment. Looked in the rear view.

"You got enough money, you do what you want. When you want. To whoever you want."

"That about sums it up," I said.

CHAPTER 10

To Lucas it looked like any deserted warehouse near the State Docks: brown brick, busted windows with boards behind them, shattered glass on the sidewalk. There was a single door in front, rippled steel painted green, the kind of closure that retracted upward. A loading dock was to the side of the building, strewn with crumbling pallets. He could smell the river in the distance.

Lucas took a seat on a short wall a quarter block away, dropped shoplifted sunglasses over his eyes, and watched as twilight settled in. Friday night would be a good night, Lucas figured. If, that is, the name his five hundred dollars bought wasn't bogus. If he'd been lied to by the guy, he'd go back to that bar and cut the obese bastard's lying throat – what was his name? Leroy Dinkins? – slice Leroy's fat throat open like a –

"Clouds, Lucas. Concentrate on the clouds."

Lucas heard the words in his head and closed his eyes. He replaced the violent thoughts with pictures of clouds. White and puffy and gentle. Clouds from earth to sky.

"Float on the clouds, Lucas," he heard Dr Rudolnick intone in a hypnotist's voice, deep and soothing. *"Float like a boat on a calm pond. Breathe away the anger as you float. Out goes a breath, out goes anger . . . Let it flow out like water."*

Lucas listened to Dr Rudolnick for two minutes, breathing deeply and floating on the clouds. When his eyes opened, he felt calm and refreshed.

He resumed watching the warehouse. The street was one-way. Semis drove by with containerized cargo racked on trailers. It was almost twilight before the first car arrived, a Corvette as white as snow. The second, a half-hour later, was a black Benz. Forty-five minutes passed before the third car rolled into view, a silvery T-bird, a classic. The green door swallowed them whole and quickly.

I bought the right name, Lucas thought, slapping his knee in delight. *I invested well.* He stood and ambled to the warehouse. Stars were beginning to poke through a darkening sky. He walked past the door to the corner of the building, leaned against it and waited.

Twenty minutes later he heard a vehicle enter from a block down, headlights shining across the deserted street. The car stopped and Lucas figured the driver was phoning inside the warehouse. Seconds later, he heard a whining electric motor and the sound of the door ratcheting open.

He stepped around the corner and saw the taillights of a gold Lexus disappearing inside the warehouse, the door dropping like a portcullis. Lucas sprinted to the door and rolled inside the warehouse.

A dozen vehicles sat in the wide space, several little more than automotive skeletons. The burp of pneumatic tools punctured air smelling of petroleum and cigarettes. A short man, bald, his outsized arms blue with tattoos, jumped from the Lexus, eyes widening when he saw Lucas.

"Who the fuck are you?"

Lucas stood and brushed himself off. "I'm looking for Danny or Darryl Hooley. They around?"

The guy yelled, "Intruder!"

In seconds Lucas was surrounded by three men in grease-stained denim, two holding tools, the third pointing a black pistol at Lucas's midsection. The men muttered among themselves as Lucas stood with his hands held innocently out to his sides.

"Who is he?"

"Guy rolled under the door."

"Somebody get Danny."

"He's coming."

A trim, thirtyish man appeared from the rear of the building, pencil tucked behind one ear, cigarette above the other. Red hair flowed from his head. He wore a blue work shirt tucked into denim jeans. A few steps behind him was a younger and skinnier version of the same man, hippie-long hair ponytailed with a blue bandana. His T-shirt touted one of the Dave Matthews Band tours.

"What do we have here?" the older man asked, raising an eyebrow at Lucas.

"It's a bum," one of the grease monkeys said. "I think."

The man with the weapon said, "He said he was looking for the Hooley brothers."

The older man slipped the cigarette from

behind his ear, lipped it, lit it with a chrome Zippo. He blew a smoke stream to the side, his eyes never leaving Lucas.

"What do you want to talk to them about?" he said. "The Hooley brothers?"

Lucas smiled, crossed his arms, returned the man's gaze evenly.

"I want to schedule a presentation," he said.

CHAPTER 11

Saturday arrived, the day of Dani's Channel 14 bash. The Franklin case had overridden the mental circuitry I use for day-to-day transactions, and I'd neglected to rent a tuxedo. I was out gathering materials to build a storage rack for my kayak when I had the memory-jogging fortune to pass a formal wear shop by the University of South Alabama. I know tuxedos as well as I know theoretical physics, and had let a young, spike-haired clerk prescribe one for me.

"Nothing old and stuffy," I instructed, remembering this was a big deal to Dani. "Something classy and contemporary."

At five, I put on the leased tux and headed to Dani's, pulling stoplight stares on the way, a guy in evening wear piloting an eight-year-old pickup painted gray with a roller.

Dani lived at the edge of the Oakleigh Garden District, stately homes from the 1800s. It was a lovely old home and Dani had lined the walk and fronting trees with flowers. A white limo sat at the curb of her modest two-story, the driver leaning back in his seat and reading the *Daily Form*. I parked ahead of the limo, walked the tree-shaded and flower-bordered walkway to her door, knocked, let myself in. Her living room was bright and high-ceilinged, with an iron fireplace at one end and a red leather grouping of couch and chairs at the other. A scarlet carpet bridged the distance. It was cool inside and smelled of the potions women use for bathing.

"Dani?"

She entered from the dining room. Her gown was a rush of red from shoulders to ankles, sleek and satiny and melded to her slender form.

"Helluva dress." I grinned and slid my palms over her derriere.

"Whoa," she said, grabbing my hands and stepping away. "Gotta keep the wrinkles out, at least for a while."

"Of course," I said. "Sorry."

She had a chance to take in my rakish evening garb. I expected delight, instead received a frown.

"Where did you get that thing?"

"Tuxedo Junction. By the university. Très chic, no?"

"It's looks like something Wyatt Earp wore."

I patted the crushed-velvet lapel. "The kid at the store said it's a western cut. Very popular."

Dani closed her eyes and shook her head.

"Popular at high school proms, Carson. Not *adult* events."

I felt my face redden. "I didn't know. Maybe there's enough time to –"

"It's all right," she said, looking away. "It'll be fine."

"What's with the limo outside?" I asked, happy to change the subject.

She ran to the window. "Do you think it's for me? Could you check?"

The driver had been instructed to wait until a DeeDee Danbury was leaving, intercept her, and bring her via the white whale, not taking no for an answer.

"They's a cold bottle of champagne in the back, suh," he added. "Glasses in that box at the side. Cheeses and shrimps in the cooler."

I fetched Dani. The driver opened the door with a flourish and drove off as smoothly as if on a monorail. I poured champagne and assembled plates of shrimp and cheese. Outside, Mobile slipped past and nearby vehicle occupants wrinkled their foreheads trying to peer through the mirror-black windows of the limo.

"Check it out, Carson," Dani said, gesturing at the faces with her champagne glass. "They look like monkeys."

The Channel 14 event was at the Shrine Temple, a high-ceilinged, marble-floored exemplar of baroque excess. Our driver pulled up front, jumped out to open the door. I think he bowed. We stepped into the path of Jenna Doakes, a weekend news anchor my girlfriend dubbed "Prissy Missy High'n'Mighty".

Doakes regarded the departing limo with a raised eyebrow.

"Isn't that a little Hollywood, DeeDee?"

Dani said, "You didn't get one?"

"What are you talking about?"

"The station sent it for me," Dani explained.

Doakes's grin melted into confusion, then fear. She hustled away on the arm of her escort, shooting over-the-shoulder glances at Dani, like she was twelve feet tall and glowing.

The soirée was in the ballroom, entered via a dozen marble steps sweeping to the floor, spotlit top and bottom. The only thing lacking was the monocled guy announcing the arrivals.

We descended to the milling crowd. Soft light fell from above, a sprawling chandelier resembling a wedding cake iced with glass. The edges of the cavernous room were columned every dozen feet, walls of dark velvet. Forty board feet of food waited at the rear: carved roasts of beef, glazed hams, shrimp, crab cakes, cheeses, breads, sweets. A fountain dribbled minted punch. Three ice sculptures rose above the food: two swans and a four-foot-tall Channel 14 logo.

Three bars were at the edges of the room, black-vested barkeeps already pouring fast to manage demand. On the stage, a ten-piece band tuned up.

The round tables were filling fast with employees and clients and guests. I saw a vacant table near the stage. I couldn't figure out why it was empty until close enough to see a tabletop placard announcing, RESERVED. We took a table with staffers from the station.

Unfortunately, I was the only attendee in a gunslinger tuxedo.

The band kicked in and we launched into the mingle portion of the program, Dani moving like a dervish, barking "Hey-yas" and "How-de-dos" and spinning from one clot of revelers to the next. I finally got to meet the news director she adored, a shambling, fiftyish guy named Laurel Hollings. Hollings had missed a button on his shirt, mumbled when he spoke. He kept checking his phone, maybe hoping some major catastrophe might pull him from the event. I liked Hollings from the git-go, even more when he expressed admiration for my tuxedo, saying he wished he "had the balls to wear something like that".

Dani talked shop with reporters, discussed industry trends with home-office types, schmoozed station clients – car dealers, realtors, mobile-home manufacturers, supermarket owners – with either modest propriety or bawdy wit, depending on the client. After a half-hour, she called for a minute off her feet.

The closest chairs were at the still-empty RESERVED table. I set my beer on the white tablecloth and took a seat, gnawing a roll while she slipped off her shoes and squeezed her toes, cursing the inventor of high heels.

"Excuse me, sir," said a voice at my back and a finger tap on my shoulder. I swiveled to a pout-mouthed man wearing a bow tie, purple vest, and a name card announcing EVENT MANAGER.

I set my roll on the table, picked up my drink. "Yes?"

"I'm sorry, but this table's waiting for someone." He pointed to the RESERVED card. I saw his glance take in crumbs of roll on the tabletop and a damp circle from my drink.

"The lady's resting her feet. If the table's owners arrive, we'll move."

"I'm sorry," he said, ice on his vocal cords. "No one can sit here."

"I hate to disagree with you, sport . . ." I said, about to point out we were already sitting. Dani heard my voice shift to the one I use for supercilious assholes. Her fingers tapped my wrist.

"Don't be that way, Carson. There's a table across the way. Follow me."

We moved. EVENT MANAGER signaled for the bus staff to change the RESERVED tablecloth, like I'd left some kind of stink on the table.

The band stuttered to a halt in the middle of a rhythmically challenged "Smoke on the

Water", launching into "Hail, Hail, the Gang's All Here". Heads swung to the door. A party of three men and three women gathered atop the marble steps as two photographers raced to shoot pictures. Behind this nucleus were several other men and women.

Forefront in the vanguard group was a tall, fortyish man with an older woman on his arm. She was the one person in the group who didn't look direct from a *Vogue* eveningwear issue: white-haired, plank-faced, pale, eyes as dark as coal. A large woman, she wasn't obese, but sturdy, a prize Holstein in a designer toga.

The tall man escorted her to the unoccupied table as pout-mouth whisked away the RESERVED placard. Only after she had sat and nodded did the others take seats.

I chuckled at the spectacle. "Looks like Buckingham Palace let out."

"It's the Kincannons, Carson. Surely you've heard of them."

It struck a chord. "There's a big plaque at the Police Academy that mentions a Kincannon something or other. Maybe a couple huge plaques. A program?"

"A grant, I imagine. The family is big on grants and donations and endowments."

I studied the tall man: well-constructed, his tuxedo modeled to a wide-shouldered, waist-slender frame. His face was lengthy and rectangular; had he wished to ship the face somewhere for repairs, it would have been neatly contained in a shoe box. Judging by the admiring glances of nearby women, however, it was a face needing neither repair nor revision. He seemed well aware of this fact, not standing so much as striking a series of poses: holding his chin as he talked, crossing his arms and canting his head, arching a dark eyebrow while massaging a colleague's shoulder. He looked like an actor playing a successful businessman.

"Who's the pretty guy working the Stanislavski method?" I asked. "Seems like I've seen him before."

A pause. "That's Buck Kincannon, Junior, Carson. Sort of the scion of the family."

"How are scions employed these days?" I asked. "At least this scion?"

"The man collects cars and art and antiques. Sails yachts. Breeds prize cattle."

"Good work if you can get it," I noted.

"He also runs the family's investments. The Kincannons have more money than Croesus. Buck keeps the pile growing."

The funds would be fine if they grew as fast as the throng gathering to acknowledge the late arrivals, I thought. An overturned beer truck wouldn't have pulled a crowd faster. Several notables hustled over: an appellate judge, two state representatives, half the city council.

"What's the connection to the station?" I asked.

"The family's one of the major investors in Clarity, part of the ownership consortium. Buck Kincannon's my boss, Carson. Way up the ladder, but the guy who makes the big decisions."

Clarity Broadcasting owned Channel 14 and a few dozen other TV and radio outlets, primarily in the South, but according to newspaper accounts they were pushing hard toward a national presence.

"Who's the older woman?" I asked.

Dani's voice subconsciously dropped to a whisper. "Maylene Kincannon. Queen Maylene, some people call her. But only from a distance. Like another continent. Buck's the oldest of her kids, forty-one. Beside Buck is Racine Kincannon and his wife Lindy; Racine's thirty-eight or so. The guy closest to Mama is Nelson Kincannon, thirty-four, I think."

"Who are the others with them?"

"Congressman Whitfield to the right, beside him is Bertram Waddley, CEO of the biggest bank in the state, next to Waddley is –"

I held up my hand. "I get the picture."

I turned from the hangers-on and scanned the brothers: Buck, Racine, Nelson. Though the angular faces weren't feminine, the men seemed almost *gorgeous,* their eyes liquid and alert, their gestures practiced and fluid.

My eyes fell on the matriarch, lingered. Though her skin was pale and her hair was snow, nothing about her said frail. She looked like she could have wrestled Harry to a draw.

"What happened to Papa Kincannon?" I asked.

"Buck Senior? I haven't heard much about him. He has some form of mental ailment, early onset Alzheimer's or something similar, a disease of the brain. He's alive, but has been out of the picture for years."

"He started the fortune?"

"He had a mind for business. An instinct or whatever."

"You know a lot about the family, Dani."

She looked away. "I'm a reporter and they're a major investor in my company."

"Where's Kincannon's wife?"

"He's single. Divorced years ago."

"Have you ever met him?"

Dani studied her wineglass, drained it. "I met him at a charity event eighteen months back."

"You talked to him since?"

She passed me her glass. "Could you get me another, please? While I climb back into these shoes."

Rather than cross the center of the room, where I might re-meet someone I'd already forgotten, I moved to the shadowed edges and circled toward the nearest bar. My path took me behind the Clan Kincannon. The Buckster was still working the receiving line, his hand squeezed by men, cheeks pecked by women.

Mama Maylene was another matter: it seemed forbidden to touch her, and even the most hand-grabbing, hug-enwrapping, cheek-kissing folks stopped short of Mama, offering a few brief words before quickly slipping past.

When not engaged in long-distance greetings, Maylene Kincannon raked the crowd with emotionless eyes, black as cinders in the whiteness of her face. I watched in fascination as they gathered full measure of the room, every face, every gesture, every contact.

Perhaps she felt my gaze, for her eyes swung to mine. For a moment we stared at one another, until her eyes moved away, restless, scanning. I had the feeling of having been surveyed by a machine, deemed of zero value, dismissed.

There was a crowd at the bar and I got in one of the lines. My position faced me down a service hall to a kitchen door. Surprisingly – and delightfully – a woman's derriere backed from the kitchen, wiggling as it retreated. The owner followed, throwing air kisses and whispering *thanks*. I suspected she was a late arrival not wishing to enter via the cascading steps and glare of lights.

I put her age in the early thirties, slender where she needed to be, ample where she didn't, big lavender eyes augmented with too much shadow, perhaps trying to balance a succulent, lipstick-ad mouth. Her dress was cobalt blue, strapless, anchored by gravity-defying breasts whose origin was dubious.

"Whatcha need, sir?" the barkeep asked.

I reluctantly turned from the woman. "Tall bourbon and soda, light on the bourbon, and a white wine."

"We have three whites tonight, sir. A Belden

Farms Chardonnay, a B & G Vouvray, and a Chenin Blanc by Isenger."

I knew wine as well as I knew Mandarin. I said *uh* several times.

"Go for the Vouvray, Slim," a woman's voice said. "The others are horse piss."

I turned. The woman in cobalt leaned against the column at the end of the bar, a few feet distant. She winked. "Grab me a drink while you're there, wouldya? Double scotch." Her voice was a purr of command, cigarette husky, a voice with more years on it than the woman.

I turned, three drinks in hand. She snatched hers and spun away. I watched her circle behind the crowd, pause against another column, study the surroundings. She belted the scotch. Then she snapped her wrist twice, like flicking paint from a brush. She thought a moment, then repeated the odd motion, more exaggerated this time, like cracking a whip.

She flipped the empty glass into a trash can, snapped on a bright smile, and headed into the crowded room. My eyes kept following her derriere, but the room went dark.

Lucas arrived a half-hour after the Channel 14 soirée had started, parking outside the Shrine

Temple, slipping the used Subaru into the anonymous dark between street lamps. He had been eating granola, spitting stale raisins out the window into the street. It had irritated him that a fucking health-food store would sell granola with stale raisins and he'd considered returning to the store, grabbing the slacker clerk by his Bruce Cockburn T-shirt, dragging him down here and making the bastard lick the raisins from the pavement.

"Those taste fresh to you? You little cocksucking son of a . . ."

He had caught himself. Taken several deep breaths, cleansing breaths. Listened to Dr Rudolnick conjure up clouds.

"Settle into the clouds, Lucas. Let your anger drift away . . ."

Nothing much had happened while he waited; not that he'd expected anything. But he'd read about this soirée in a newspaper column and decided to rub elbows with the swells, even if it was a distant rubbing.

Sometimes things were revealed in small motions. Like the black stretch limo parked in the lot down the block, engine idling, keeping the air conditioning at a precise seventy-eight degrees. Lucas had wanted to knock on the door of the limo, engage the driver in conversation. Maybe leave a warm ass-print in the leather seat, like a dog spraying its territory.

Common sense had prevailed. It wasn't yet time to prod the Kincannons.

After he'd been sitting for several more minutes, calm again, a woman slipped from the doors of the Temple, a sexy woman in a blue dress, large breasts bobbing as she high-heeled down the sidewalk. She was weaving a bit, a sheet or two to the wind. She laughed, flicked her hand in the air in a strange and sudden motion, like a drummer tapping a cymbal. Then she hawked and spat onto the sidewalk, lit a cigarette, and crossed the street to climb into a battered red Corolla. It took two minutes of grinding the ignition before the engine kicked over and the car rattled away trailing a plume of blue exhaust.

The woman was suddenly more interesting to Lucas than a building he couldn't safely enter, and his curiosity made him follow her, just for a lark.

CHAPTER 12

As I crossed the ballroom in the dark, a drink in each hand, the podium turned white with spotlight, signaling the business side of the affair. I returned to the table as the general manager took the dais. He droned industry jargon for twenty minutes: ratings points, targeted growth analysis, revenue streams, optimized asset utilization, and so forth. He was followed by three heads of something-or-other. Finally the GM reclaimed the microphone, burbled a few more comments, then swept his hand toward the Kincannon suburb.

". . . cornerstones of our station and community, ladies and gentlemen, the Kincannons . . ."

The family members smiled and waved. Buck Kincannon elevated from his seat. A balcony spotlight centered him, and I figured it had been aimed beforehand. The crowd applauded Kincannon like it had applauded everyone, solid, polite; then, after a few seconds, started to wane.

A voice yelled, "Speech."

Several men at a front table stood, hands clapping, calling for words from Kincannon. Folks at adjoining tables followed, checking side to side as they rose, concert-goers uncertain whether the music was that good, but everyone else seems to think so. Applause thundered from the front table. They reminded me of cheerleaders in tuxedos. Or, less politely, shills.

Dani stood and pounded her palms together. Kincannon took the dais with a laugh line, apologizing for disturbing "everyone's reason for being here: free food and drinks", then segued into more business-speak. To my untrained ear, it seemed fifty per cent jargon, fifty per cent bullshit; the trick, perhaps, to discern which was which. Or perhaps it didn't matter.

After several minutes, Kincannon reverted to English.

". . . nowhere is professionalism more evident than in the news department. No news team won more awards in Alabama last year than Channel 14 Action News . . ."

Applause from the audience at large.

"We've heard from some of those fine folks this evening, but there's someone else needs to say a few words. I'm talking about the hard-charging investigative spark of the team . . ."

"I didn't expect this," Dani said, touching at her hair. "How do I look, Carson?"

"Like you. Only dressier."

". . . gives me *great* pleasure to introduce a present star and future superstar of Clarity Broadcasting Network, a woman with more in her future than she knows . . ."

Dani grinned, shook her head.

". . . I give you DeeDee Danbury . . ."

Kincannon lifted his arms wide, the Pope blessing St Peter's Square.

"Come on up, DeeDee."

Applause rang out as Dani jogged to the dais. Buck Kincannon extended his arms and she walked into them, his wide hand rubbing her bare back. They traded smiles and a few words and Dani stepped to the microphone as Kincannon moved back a step, but still in her light.

She cleared her throat and mimed opening

an envelope, blowing into it, reaching inside. The crowd went silent, wondering what she was doing.

Dani plucked an invisible card from the invisible envelope, held it distant as if to better see the words.

"And the winner in the category of best employer is . . . Clarity Broadcasting Network!"

The crowd laughed, applauded, whistled. I clapped as well, fighting the notion that I'd seen her pander to the audience, to her employer. I felt embarrassment, but didn't know for whom. Then I realized I was as naïve to the ways of broadcasting as I was to the rental of formal wear. *This is what they must do at these bashes,* I thought. *Kiss ass and march in rhythm. Relax.*

Dani's speech took two minutes. It was humorous. Smooth. Rich in praise to Clarity Broadcasting and the Kincannon family. And, like her allusion to the Academy Awards, seemed more act than sincerity.

Kincannon grabbed the mike, yelled, "Let's hear it for our own beautiful DeeDee Danbury!" He waved his hands in a *Bring it on* motion. Again led by the group at the front table, the audience jumped to its feet as if Dani were a figure skater who'd just completed a quintuple something-or-other.

The soirée broke up at eleven. Since Dani's effusive blessing by ownership, she'd been surrounded by sudden friends. Outside, I waited as she chatted with others, enjoying the limelight. With little to do, I wandered in the warm night. I stepped around the corner and saw Racine and Nelson Kincannon and their wives waiting for transportation. It was a service entrance and I figured people like the Kincannons didn't queue with the riff-raff.

I leaned against a lamp a hundred feet distant and watched, just me and the Kincannons. No one in the family spoke to anyone else, their eyes flat and expressionless. It was like the show was over, everyone could turn off their faces and go home. Racine Kincannon was drinking, carrying glasses in both hands.

Nelson said something. I couldn't hear what. Racine spun, threw one of the drinks in his brother's face. Racine threw the other drink on the ground, grabbed his brother's lapels, pushed him away hard. The wives stepped a dozen feet away and looked into the night sky, bored. The two men seemed about to square off when I heard a voice like broken glass.

"Stop it, now!"

Maylene Kincannon exploded from the building like a rodeo bull from a gate, Buck Kincannon at her side. She thundered up, finger jabbing, tongue lashing. I heard the anger, but not the words. Her two squabbling sons looked at their feet. The wives remained turned away, like nothing was happening.

Then Buck Kincannon leaned toward his mother, said something. Whatever it was didn't agree with her. She slapped his face so hard it sounded like a gunshot. No one else seemed to notice or care.

A black stretch limo rolled into view. The family grouped together as the chauffeur emerged to open the doors. The black beast pulled from the curb. I saw an impenetrably dark window roll down. A male face, contorted in anger, yelled, "Get a life, asshole."

The curtain fell.

It was almost midnight when our driver returned us to Dani's, the night drenched with haze and lit by moon glow, the air perfumed with dogwood and magnolia. Arms linked, we walked to the porch as a night bird sang from the eaves. She shook her keys free of her purse, opened the door. The cool, clean air felt good after sharing the exhalations of three hundred others for two hours. I looked at her phone, a red LED blinking.

"You've got a message."

She went to the kitchen to rattle the lock at the back door, the habitual checks of a woman living alone. "Probably Laurel Hollings twitting me for the speech. He does that kind of thing when he's had a few. Punch it on while I look out back."

I heard the kitchen door open, the screen slam, as she went out to check the back porch door. I tossed my jacket into a chair, walked to the phone, pressed Message.

"It was great to see you this evening, dear DeeDee. I meant everything I said about the bright future. And by the way, that red dress was fantastic. I'll talk to you soon."

Four hours earlier I wouldn't have recognized the voice. But now I did.

Buck Kincannon.

I closed my eyes and wondered what to do, then diddled with the reset button on the phone. Dani returned a minute later. I stood in front of the hall mirror, fiddling with the button on the vest.

"Crap," I snarled.

"What?"

"The button's snagged. Wrapped in a thread."

She looked at the phone, the display blinking like it had never been touched.

"You didn't check the phone?" she asked.

I glared at the button. "If I tear the damn button off they'll probably charge me thirty bucks. There still scissors in the bathroom?"

She nodded and I hustled to the john, closed the door. I stood in the dark with my racing heart as she checked her message. My straining ears caught Buck Kincannon's voice again roaming through Dani's house.

It was a business call, I told myself; Buck Kincannon was the *capo di tutti capo* of the Kincannon family and Clarity Broadcasting. He probably called all the station's speechgivers, made them feel part of the team. It was just business.

I returned a couple minutes later, vest in hand. Dani was in the kitchen moving dishes from the dishwasher to her shelves.

"Can't that wait until tomorrow?" I asked.

She shrugged; put on a smile. "Just felt like doing something. Excess energy or whatever."

"The message, was it your jokester from the station?"

Her eyes wouldn't meet mine; she turned and slid a dish into place, spoke into the cupboard. "Nothing important. A friend wanting to talk when I have a chance."

That night we lay in her bed, but neither made motions toward making love. Lightning flashed at the windows and filled the room with shadows, but rain never came. Just past dawn I arose without waking her, penciled a note explaining I had a busy day, and fled into a day already breathless with heat.

CHAPTER 13

Harry shoved aside a file of forms on his desktop, set a new stack in its place. He paused and stared at me.

"You all right, Cars?"

"Sure, Harry. Why?"

"You've said maybe three words since you got in this morning. How was the big kick-up for Channel 14? Dancing and prancing with the swells? That was this weekend, right?"

"It was fine."

I realized if I didn't go into detail, Harry's antennae would register my distress. I gave a brief synopsis of the evening: impaired music, great eats, first-class beverages, lots of chatter in biz-speak.

"Plus I even got a look at upper-crust Mobile: a family called the Kincannons. They were so –"

Harry broke into my recitation. "You meet Buck?"

I stared at my partner like a plumed hat had appeared on his head.

"What?"

"Buck Kincannon. You get a chance to say hi?"

"How the hell do you know Buck Kincannon?"

"Back four or five years ago I was working with a civic group in north Mobile, by Pritchard. Maybe you remember?"

"I recall a couple months when all your nights seemed locked up. Weekends, too. Something about a ball league?"

He nodded. "The group's big push was getting inner-city kids into sports, baseball. Kids from ten to fourteen years old. Keep 'em on a ball field, not the streets. We were beating our heads against the wall, scratching up third-hand equipment. We'd been trying to get the city to let us use an abandoned lot as a practice field, but they kept whining about liability. Mardy Baker, the director of a social services organization, sent letters to all the big civic and charitable organizations, trying to scratch up money. No go."

"Where'd Kincannon fit in?"

"One of the letters had gone to the Kincannons' family foundation. A philanthropic deal. Kincannon himself showed up at our next meeting, checkbook in hand."

"Keep going."

"Suddenly our ragtag kids got Louisville Slugger bats, Rawlings gloves, uniforms. It wasn't just money, it was influence. Like he walked into City Hall with a shopping list and said, 'Here's what I want.' Two days later all permits are in order, insurance isn't a problem, nothing's a problem. The old field got resodded, sand and dirt trucked in to fill the baselines, build a pitcher's mound. Stands went up so parents could sit and cheer for the kids."

"So you sat around while Kincannon waved a magic wand?"

"The group was moms mainly, plus a couple of community-activist types. They made me designated hitter for dealing with Buck, me being a big, important cop and all. We went to lunch, him laying out plans, me nodding and going, 'Sure, Buck, sounds good.'"

"What'd you think of him – Kincannon?" I sounded casual.

Harry flipped a thumbs-up. "From setting the city straight to setting the timetable, he took over. You don't think of people with that kind of power and influence getting down in the gritty, and he's cool in my book."

I stopped listening, put my head on nod-and-grunt function as Harry continued enumerating the angelic feats of the Holy Buckster.

". . . opened that field and you should have seen the kids' eyes. Buck later said it was one of the highlights of his . . ."

Nod. Grunt. Nod. Grunt.

". . . all the local politicos showed up like it was their idea, standing next to Buck and getting their pictures taken . . ."

Nod. Grunt.

". . . guess you can do anything, you got the money to do it."

I was between grunt and nod when I remembered I wanted to call Warden Malone up at Holman and get a status report on Leland Harwood. I headed toward the small conference room to get some quiet, but Harry followed, still singing the glories of Buck Kincannon.

"Good-looking fella, too. Probably has to shovel the ladies out the door in the a.m. . . ."

We went to the small conference room. I dialed the prison, ran the call through the teleconference device, a black plastic starfish in the center of the round table. Malone was on a minute later.

"Leland Harwood died two hours after he was stricken in the visitors' room. Never regained consciousness."

"Poison?" I said.

"A witch's brew of toxins. Organophosphates, the report says. I'd never heard the term. Pesticide, herbicide, some industrial chemicals." I heard paper rattling in Warden Malone's hand as he read from the page.

"Where did all that stuff come from?" Harry asked.

"All available inside, Detective," Malone said. "Cleaning supplies, rat poison, roach paste, paint thinner. They're kept tucked away, but . . ."

"So someone squirted a bunch of stuff on Harwood's scrambled eggs and he drops dead later?"

"The docs say it took some mixing of compounds to get the right effect, the maximum bang for the buck, to be crass."

"Harwood got banged hard," I noted. "He have any enemies?"

"I've checked around and the answer is, not really. He was a smart-ass, but managed to stay out of major confrontations. Wanting to appear angelic for the parole board will do that."

"Got any poisoners up there?" Harry asked.

"Several. But we keep them real far from the pantry, so to speak. The docs said anyone with access to the right supplies could have mixed the brew . . . with a little help from someone with bad thoughts, the right formula, and high school chemistry."

"Info that could have come from outside."

Malone laughed without humor. "Imagine a couple guys in the visitors' room. The one on the outside says, 'Soak twenty roach tablets in alcohol, let it sit two days, mix in . . .'"

"Got the point," Harry said.

We asked Malone to keep us in the loop. Harry clicked the starfish off. He closed his eyes and shook his head.

"The next time I decide to race Logan to a scene, how about you strangle me."

"I was just thinking that. Where from here?"

"Let's check into Harwood some more, call up the man's sheet. Talk to folks that knew the deceased. Maybe figure out Taneesha Franklin's interest in a guy like Leland."

I sat at the computer, pulled up overviews on the incident as Harry leaned over my shoulder, reading ahead.

"Bernard Rudolnick was Harwood's victim," Harry said, frowning at the computer screen. "*Dr* Bernard Rudolnick."

"Killed in a bar, right?" I scrolled the screen to the correct info as Harry recited particulars.

"The Citadel Tavern. A low-life joint. Got into a scuffle at the bar, the men went outside. A gun goes bang in the night. The shooter lit out, but Mobile's finest grabbed Harwood a few hours later."

I studied the screen. "Doctor? Like in M.D.?"

"Psychiatrist," Harry said. "Bet they didn't get a lot of shrinks at the Citadel. A pity the one they had didn't last the night."

Time for me to pick up the prelim from Taneesha Franklin's autopsy. I took the stairs, looked into the second floor, and saw Sally Hargreaves sitting at her desk, staring blank-eyed at the wall. Sally was a detective handling sexual crimes, a tough gig on the best days. I continued down the flight, realized Sally wasn't the wall-staring type. I climbed back up, went to her desk.

"What's up, Sal? You look like your cat got sucked into the vacuum cleaner."

She turned, brightened. Pushed strands of auburn hair from her eyes. Smiled with false bonhomie.

"Hi, Carson."

"You OK?"

She looked at a report she'd been filling out. Shook her head.

"I just got back from the hospital. A rape victim. Among other things. Jesus."

"Tough one?"

"Ugliness through and through. Bizarre."

I rolled up a chair for the vacant desk beside Sal's. The desk had belonged to her former partner, Larry Dayle. Dayle had resigned after four months on the Sex Crimes unit, moving his family to a mountainside in Montana and stringing the perimeter with razor wire.

The floor – Sexual Crimes, Crimes Against Property, Vehicle Theft – was quiet, most of the detectives out. I took Sal's hand.

"Want to tell a friendly face about it? I can go get Harry."

She laughed, and the laugh cracked into a

sob. She caught herself. Brushed away a tear. It was Sal's empathy that made her so good at what she did. The downside was what poured back through the door.

She said, "A woman, twenty-five. Student. Got grabbed off the street just after dark last night. Picked up bodily and jammed into a vehicle. She was taken somewhere – a barn or stable, she thought, by the smell. Afterwards she got pushed from a moving vehicle into a hospital parking lot. That was one a.m. this morning. I was with her most of the night."

"Strange. She was raped?"

"And beaten. Her face . . . it'll be a long time before the surgeons make it a face again. She wanted children. That's gone. Her insides were . . ."

"Easy," I said.

"The guy who did it, while he was punching her, doing all the things he did, he kept laughing, yelling, 'Look at me, bitch, can you see me?' Then he'd hit her, scream, 'Look at me, tell me what you see.'"

"She got a description?" I asked.

"No."

"The perp wore a mask?"

Sally shook her head. "No."

"What?" I asked.

Sally buried her face in her hands.

"Oh, Carson. She's blind. Been blind since birth."

I thought about the rape-abduction as I drove to the morgue. I'd never worked sex crimes, though as a member of the Psychopathological and Sociopathological unit had studied sexual predators. The actions as Sal described them seemed to combine the power-assertive, or entitlement, type of offender with a sadistic, or anger-excitation, type of behavior. The first behavior type humiliates the victim to increase the perp's sense of self-worth and self-confidence. The second is brutal, often involving a high level of physical aggression, including torture.

I had no idea what to make of the anomalous gesture of dropping the woman at the hospital.

The Crown Vic started to feel crowded and I lowered the windows to let fresh air blow out too many dark thoughts. I parked in the morgue lot beside Clair's sporty little BMW, worth more than my annual pay. Clair's former husband, Zane Peltier, was a bona fide member of Mobile society, the old-money contingent, and some of that largesse had rubbed off on Clair during the divorce proceedings.

It hit me that Clair would certainly know of the Kincannons, maybe even know them personally. I might get a question answered, maybe two, if I could sneak them into a conversation.

Clair wasn't in her office, so I checked across the hall in the main autopsy suite. She was gowned in green and standing against the wall as Lula Baker mopped the floor beneath the autopsy table. Lula was a former housekeeper in New Orleans, one of the vast army of transplants.

"Hi, Lula," I said.

"Morn', 'tect Ryd'," she said. Lula was thirty or so, white, skinny, and had the ability to edit most words to a single syllable.

"The prelim's out front, Ryder," Clair said, looking up from a copy of the CDC's *Morbidity and Mortality Monthly*, required reading for pathologists.

"I wanted to ask you something else."

"And?"

I shrugged. "I forgot."

Clair pulled off her reading glasses, studied me with the big blue miracles.

"Maybe because you're not getting enough sleep. You've got dark circles under your eyes."

"It's the Franklin case. Nothing's moving ahead."

"Take vitamins and eat right. Remember to sleep."

"Thanks, Mom."

She frowned, but said nothing. I turned to leave, then tapped my forehead, like I'd been hit with a sudden thought.

"I was at a Channel 14 party the other night, Clair. Formal, all the bigwigs. I half-expected to see you there with the social types."

"If I never see another champagne fountain it'll be too soon. Out of your element, weren't you?"

"If I never see another tux it'll be too soon. You wouldn't know a family named Kincannon, would you?"

Her face darkened. "Why?"

"People treated them like royalty. I've never seen so much bowing and scraping."

Clair turned to the housekeeper. "That's fine, Lula. You can go."

"Be bact'mar."

Lula rolled the mop and bucket out the door. Clair set the CDC report on a counter.

"The Kincannons have money, Carson. It equates to power: lots of money, lots of power. Some people have an automatic reflex when they get near power. Their knees bend."

"A lot of politicos were there, too."

"Political knees bend further and more often. *She* was there, too, wasn't she: an older woman, white hair, chunky, aloof?"

"Yes. May-bell-line?"

"Maylene. Yes, she would have been. She'll always be there, in some way or another."

I heard something off-key in Clair's voice, anger maybe, or resignation.

"Some way or another?" I asked. "What do you mean?"

She looked at her watch, frowned. "I've got two pathologists down with the flu. I've got the day's second post in three minutes. Look, the Kincannons do a lot of giving to the community and the region. Hundreds of thousands of dollars for parks, health-care institutions, schools, law enforcement . . . an incredible amount of money."

"And so . . .?"

"The Kincannons . . . well, only some of the truly wealthy can give with both hands, Ryder."

Her words seemed cryptic; Clair was rarely cryptic.

"You mean the Kincannons have so much they can shovel it hand over hand into the community?"

"Think about it. But elsewhere, please. I've got to get to work."

I sucked in a breath, said, "How about Buck Kincannon?"

"Is there a specific question there?"

"No," I admitted. *There are about a hundred.*

Clair picked up the phone on the counter, asked for the body to be brought to the table. She turned to me.

"Buck Kincannon is the current golden boy of the family, forty-eight karats of flawless Kincannon breeding. Last month's *Alabama Times* magazine listed him as one of the top ten eligible bachelors in the state."

Not what I needed to hear.

"*Current* golden boy, Clair?"

"Maylene Kincannon runs that family like a competitive event. Next month it may be Nelson on the pedestal. Or Racine, unless he gets blitzed and slips off. Race likes women and liquor, probably not in that order. Now, unless you're going to assist, it's time to skedaddle."

I nodded, headed for the door. I was stepping into the hall when she called my name. I stopped, turned.

"The Kincannons, Ryder. They haven't stepped outside any limits, right? You're not investigating anything, anyone?"

"Just natural curiosity about a lifestyle I'll never know."

She gave me the long look again. "It's mostly fiction. Stay away from those folks, Carson. There's nothing to be gained there."

I picked up the report at the front desk, then stepped into a day more like August than June, heat rippling from the asphalt surface of the parking lot.

Stepped outside any limits . . .

Walking to the car I revisited Clair's phrase, a curious assemblage of words. And that throwaway line about staying away from the Kincannons . . .

Was that some kind of warning?

You're losing it, I thought, slipping behind the wheel. The only warning here is to keep your imagination in check.

CHAPTER 14

Mrs Kayla Rudolnick was the mother of Dr Bernard Rudolnick, Harwood's victim. A thin woman in her late sixties, she wore a brown pantsuit and pink slippers, holding a cigarette in one hand, a glass ashtray in the other. She'd apologized for having her hair in curlers and led us to a couch with antimacassars on the back. The room smelled of Ben-Gay and nicotine. She switched off the television, a soap opera.

"It was just a phone call. But I recall her saying she was a reporter."

"Taneesha Franklin?"

Smoke plumed from her nostrils. "The Taneesha is what I remember."

"What did Ms Franklin want to know?" I asked.

Mrs Rudolnick's eyes tightened behind a wall of smoke. "I told her to leave me alone. Bernie was gone. Never call me again."

Mrs Rudolnick plucked a pink tissue from her sleeve, lifted her bifocals and blotted her eyes.

"He was a good man, my son. Brilliant mind, good heart."

"I'm sure."

"He had his problems. But we all do, don't we?"

I shot Harry a glance. We'd come back to that.

"The doctor wasn't married?" I asked.

"When he was twenty-eight, again when he was thirty-six. Both marriages lasted under two years. He couldn't pick women, they both cleaned him out like a closet. Two times he started over."

A photo sat on the table beside me: Rudolnick and Mama maybe a half-decade back, his arms around her from the back. Like his mother, Rudolnick had sad Slavic eyes and a nose-centric face. His hair was black and thinning, brushed straight back. His white shirt was buttoned to the Adam's apple, the collar starched. He looked like he could have been dropped into the 1950s and no one would have noticed.

Harry and I had hoped a wife might provide insight into Rudolnick's behavior and patterns. But the good doctor had been five years gone from marriage and lived alone. I said, "So his last wife might not be able to tell us much about his life."

"Shari? He met her at a bar. You don't meet decent women at bars. She moved to Seattle four years ago. Probably found herself a new bar and a new Bernie."

"You mentioned Bernie having some problems, Miz Rudolnick," Harry said.

She tapped ash into the tray and looked away. "You know, don't you?"

"No, ma'am, I never met your son."

"It's in the records. You didn't look?"

"I don't know what records you're referring to, Miz Rudolnick."

"The records down where you work."

I finally made sense of what she was saying. And maybe why she'd been spooked by a reporter.

"Your son was arrested?" I asked. "When?"

She looked away. "Four years ago. He had some problems."

"Can you explain, please?"

"After Shari left he became depressed. Sometimes – not often – he took things to help him cope, calm down. He was always high-strung."

"Drugs?"

"He was a doctor. He used it like medicine."

"Of course."

"One day he came here. He was crying and I was terrified. He said there was a hospital worker he'd been buying some of his medicine from, and the police had been watching the hospital worker. Bernie was purchasing something. He was sure it would come out in the papers, his career would be over."

She looked from my face to Harry's. Though her son was dead, the episode printed fright and humiliation across her face.

"It's all right, ma'am. We don't need the full story."

I figured we'd get it from the arrest report, save the poor woman the retelling.

She said, "He stopped taking those things. What happened with the police finally made him stop."

"How was his behavior before the end?" I asked. "Normal?"

A grandfather clock in the hall chimed. We waited until it fell silent.

"About a month before . . . that day, he seemed depressed again. He came over to see me less. He was quieter, like he was deciding on something."

"Could have been something with his work? Unhappiness?"

She walked to the mother-and-son photo. Touched it with reverence. "He loved his work. He was born to help people get better. He consulted in the region's best facilities. Bernie was on the board at Mobile Regional Hospital. He had a private practice."

It was a good place to take our leave, on the high note of her son's achievements. As we moved to the door, I asked one final question.

"Excuse me, Mrs Rudolnick. Did your son have a specialty?"

She exhaled a plume of smoke, spun a tobacco-stained finger at her temple. "He worked with tormented minds."

Psychotics? A bell rang in my head. Had Rudolnick known Harwood earlier? I wondered. Did they have a history? What if Harwood had been a patient, or part of a study?

I said, "I don't suppose he ever mentioned patients by name."

She crushed the cigarette dead in the ashtray and set it aside. "He was absolute about privacy."

Harry said, "The records your son kept about his patients. All gone, right?"

"They were in his house and I didn't know what to do with them. I keep them in storage. I don't know why."

"Would it be possible to look at them?"

She held up her hands, waving my words away. "No. It's all confidential, a bond of trust."

Harry stepped close. Gathered her hands in his, held them steady. I could never do anything that simple and perfect. "It might be helpful, Miz Rudolnick," he said quietly. "It would never go further than Carson and me. And it might be our key to finding who killed your son."

Her eyes shimmered with tears and her mouth pursed tight. "It was that filthy Harwood animal, scum. Piece of dirt . . . piece of *shit*."

"I wish that was true, ma'am. But Leland Harwood was just a tool, a hammer. The man who swung the hammer is still out there."

She shook her head. "No. It can't be. It's not right."

"Detective Ryder talked to Leland Harwood

an hour before he died, ma'am. He thinks Harwood was sent to harm your son."

She looked at me. "Is that true?"

I nodded. "Leland Harwood was an enforcer. He always worked for others."

Her face tightened in anger, turned to Harry.

"You'll respect the confidentiality of my son's files?"

"You have our word on it," Harry said.

Kayla Rudolnick looked into Harry's eyes until she found something she needed to see.

"The storage facility is on Cottage Hill Road. I'll get you the key."

There were eight white boxes in the facility, rows of locked cages in an old warehouse; a guard had been alerted to our visit. We took the boxes from the cage rented by Mrs Rudolnick and stowed them in the trunk of the Crown Vic.

Picking up the last of the boxes, Harry nodded through the grid at the adjoining enclosure. I saw a crib, boxes of child's toys, stuffed animals, posters pulled from walls, the tape at the edges brittle and yellow. A small wheelchair. A red bicycle with training wheels. Even under dust, the bike looked unused.

I suddenly knew what used-up prayers looked like. Harry sighed, shook his head, and we tiptoed away like thieves.

We dropped the files at Harry's house, then returned to the station. I tapped Rudolnick, Bernard, into my computer, expecting an arrest record. Mitigating circumstances allowing Rudolnick to pay a fine, perhaps, slip past punishment if he enrolled in a program and stayed clean.

The computer whirred and beeped, and came up blinking:

NO RECORD.

I tried again. Same effect. Harry stared at the screen.

"Either the bust never happened, or it got wiped totally clean. And the second option takes some doing."

Ms Verhooven gestured for Lucas to follow her. There was no furniture in the room and the realtor's high heels banged on the parquet floor. Ms Verhooven was as bright as a new trumpet: blonde hair, yellow dress, white shoes. Bright teeth moving behind glossy pink lips. Long legs sheathed in silky hose, rising up past the knee-high hemline toward . . . Lucas felt himself hardening and looked away, knowing such notions had to be *sublimated*, to use a term from Rudolnick's world.

Ms Verhooven pushed open a door and gestured grandly, like a woman on a TV prize show.

"Ta-da!" she said.

Lucas stared at a toilet. "Ta-da?"

The fixture was cream colored, just like the adjoining countertop. Ms Verhooven bent over the counter, stroked it like a kitten.

"Granite countertops in the restroom, Mr Lucasian. Real, honest manufactured stone. Over at Midtowne Office Estates the counters are only Corian."

Lucas nodded, though he had no idea what she was talking about. He was most interested in the sink.

Note to self, he thought, *buy bath towels.*

There was a faux baroque gilt-framed mirror on the wall. Lucas glanced at a slender and clean-shaven man with a neat part in his short and trendy, red-highlighted hair. His suit was dark and conservative, like the blue shirt and muted tie. He looked young but affluent. A success-driven young man, a starry-eyed entrepreneur with backing from Daddy, ready to make it on his own in the world. There were plenty of them out there.

Lucas winked at the entrepreneur, then turned his attention to the sink, turning the hot water on and off.

"The neighborhood seems quite nice, Ms Verhooven, a warren of free enterprise."

"This is mid-Mobile's most prestigious mercantile complex, Mr Lucasian. An address here has *cachet*." She pronounced it catch-hay. "You're lucky. This location did have an interested party and a hold on the space for several months. But something fell through and it's now available."

Lucas almost laughed. They used to be office parks, now they were mercantile complexes. With catch-hay, nonetheless. He looked through slat blinds at several small clusters of offices, red-brick buildings, the tallest four stories. The grounds were nicely landscaped, myrtle and dogwood and circles of hedge. A few magnolia bushes, the ever-present azaleas.

Lucas looked across the street at the nearest building, a hundred feet distant. The top floor, fourth, was large and sparsely populated offices, a quiet little kingdom of teak and brass. On the next three floors, cubicle drones could be seen shuffling papers and talking on phones. There were four levels, but only the top floor interested Lucas. The space Ms Verhooven was showing was on the fourth floor as well, but the building was on a slight rise, putting Lucas above the level of the fourth floor across the way. The angle allowed Lucas to look down on the facing building, which tickled him.

"You're in a wonderful business community, Mr Lucasian," the rental agent chirped, seeing his eyes scanning the neighborhood. "Accounting firms, brokerages, financial advisors, that sort of thing. Four or five doctors. Two corporate headquarters, three legal firms . . ."

Lucas wandered through rooms smelling of fresh paint and cleanser. He struck several poses he found particularly businesslike: holding his chin and nodding out the window, clasping his hands at his belt and arching an eyebrow at the ceiling, crossing his arms and leaning against the wall. Lucas cut a glance toward the building across the way, marveling at the luck of his location. Or had this perfect site been arranged by the man upstairs, divine guidance?

"It feels very businessy," he said, pushing from the wall. "A place to call home. Where does one park, Ms Verhooven?"

"Around the back of the building. It's a little out of the way, but –"

"No. That's just perfect," Lucas said. "Couldn't be better."

Ms Verhooven beamed. "What is it, basically, that your firm does, Mr Lucasian?"

"I'm in securities," Lucas said. He chuckled at the wonderful double entendre: *insecurities*.

"Is the space to your liking, Mr Lucasian?" the agent trilled. "Everything you need?"

"Yes, Ms Verhooven," Lucas said. "Everything is absolutely perfect."

After catching up on paperwork and calls, we returned to Harry's. I was eager to look at Rudolnick's records, Harry less so.

My partner lived in a small enclave a couple miles west of downtown. The yards and houses weren't large, but compensated with charm. There were trees aplenty, old live oaks and pecans and thick-leaved magnolias. Whenever I pulled into the neighborhood in summer, the shade made my soul feel twenty degrees cooler.

Harry's house was a compact single-story Creole with a full gallery and a magnolia in the front yard. The paint was coral with mauve accents which, for Harry, showed restraint. In the setting, it looked just right, a contented house.

I felt as much at home as if I'd stepped into my own living room. Harry's walls were red, the woodwork a light green. He had several pieces of art on the walls, primitive paintings of musicians picked up at the Center for Southern Folklore in Memphis. The art was my influence; I fell in love with art in college, passed my enthusiasm on to Harry.

In return, he introduced me to jazz and blues. When we first started hanging out, he asked my musical influences, shaking his head at most. He'd pulled a vinyl of Louis Armstrong from its jacket, set it on the turntable, dropped the needle on a 1929 rendition of the W. C. Handy tune, "St Louis Blues". It was like nothing I'd ever heard, bright and alive and flowing like a stream, and I was a convert before sixteen bars had passed.

"Let me put on some tunes," Harry said, kneeling by a stack of vinyls beside his sound system, his sole luxury, eight grand worth of electronics. Ferdinand LaMenthe – better known as Jelly Roll Morton – started a piano solo in Harry's living room.

I sat cross-legged on his living-room floor,

Bernie Rudolnick's professional life surrounding me in white boxes. It might have been a breach of doctor-patient privilege to have such records, and I was uncertain of the legalities. We weren't about to ask, ignorance being, if not bliss, at least more comfortable than knowing we were in violation of something or other. Thus we took the records to Harry's instead of the department.

Harry said, "How about I unbox, unbundle, and stack each box's contents in its own area, and you check what's inside?"

I shot a thumbs-up and surveyed materials at random. Harry grabbed a couple of beers to set by our sides. Having spent a fair portion of my six-year college career in the Psych department, I was familiar with the language and methodology involved in Rudolnick's materials. I thumbed through several case histories, and found Rudolnick to be a good note-taker and clinician.

"What are we looking for?" Harry said. "There's a half-ton of files here."

"Anything pertaining to Leland Harwood. Or the penal system, halfway house, prison or jail consultations. We're casting a wide net."

Harry studied the mountain of boxes. He made a sound like wounded bagpipes.

CHAPTER 15

Harry and I studied records until our eyes crossed, about four hours. I ran home, grabbed some sleep, was back at it in the morning, coffee replacing the beer. After two hours Harry tossed a pile of pages on the floor.

"I can't take shrink-jarg for four hours at a stretch. Let's go beat the streets."

I rubbed my eyes, stretched my back.

"How about we divide up what's left, work on it solo every day? Half-hour minimum. We'll get through it in a week to ten days."

We hit the streets, reinterviewing everyone in Taneesha's phone book, talking to her family, tracking down our snitches to offer money for anything they could dig up. At five, we headed home. My path took me a few miles out of my way, passing by Dani's place on the edge of downtown.

I walked to her porch and rang the bell. There was no response and I considered letting myself in with my key and waiting.

"Carson?" I heard my name called in a quavering female voice. I turned to see Leanna Place, Dani's elderly next-door neighbor. She gestured me over like I was a servant.

"Come over, Carson. Look what's here."

I sighed, not in the mood for Ms Place. She thought a cop too coarse for Dani, below her station. Ms Place always pretended to be solicitous of my health and welfare, all the while launching small, backhanded missiles.

I followed her inside her tidy home, was overcome by the smell of flowers. Beside the threshold was a huge vase of blooms. At least I assumed a vase was beneath the explosion of color and scent. Roses and tulips and carnations reached to my waist.

"It's for DeeDee," Ms Place said. Like most, she used Dani's television name. "The flowers came an hour ago. DeeDee wasn't home so I took delivery. Aren't they gorgeous?" She gave me a wry eyebrow. "I wonder who they're from."

It rankled that the old shrew thought me incapable of sending flowers.

"Me, maybe?"

She puffed the blooms like a pillow, then tapped the small envelope wagging from the vase. "The flowers are from Jon-Ella's, Carson. I'd guess three hundred dollars' worth. Not something one gets on a *policeman*'s salary."

Jon-Ella's was Mobile's most hoity-toity florist, over in Spring Hill. I once priced a half-dozen roses at Jon-Ella's, gasped, got them at Winn-Dixie for a quarter of the price.

I avoided telling Ms Place that euthanasia's not such a bad idea and toted the flowers back to Dani's. I let myself in, set the massive arrangement on her dining-room table. The sender's card fluttered before my eyes, a small dot of tape holding it closed.

I left it untouched.

I made it all the way to the bottom of the porch steps before turning back. The tape peeled loose with ease and I slid the card from the envelope to my sweating palm.

Dearest DeeDee . . .
The beauty of these flowers pales beside your beauty.

Love and Hot Kisses,

Buck

I left the flowers in the small vestibule outside the front door, where a delivery person would set them. I don't remember driving home.

I was sitting on my deck in the dark, clothing optional this time of night, nearing midnight. The wind had picked up, a hot breath keeping the mosquitoes at bay. Far across the water a drill rig flamed off gas, orange fire pressing indigo sky. There was a high whine in the back of my head.

My dining-room table was filled with my half of Rudolnick's files. I'd put in a half-hour of reviewing, pushed them away, come outside to think about nothing, Dani included.

My cellphone rang from the table beside me. Dani, her voice a tight whisper.

"Carson, I think someone's been in my house."

"A break-in? Are the cops there?"

A hesitation. "I didn't call them."

"Why not?"

"It's that there's no . . . that is, the alarm didn't go off."

"Where'd they get in? Door? Window?"

"It's not that there's actually, uh . . . I'm scared, Carson. That much I know. Can you come over?"

When I pulled to the curb in front of Dani's house, I saw her at the window, backlit, the curtain pushed aside. Her outline was hauntingly beautiful, and I felt an ache simultaneously within me and far away. She opened the door as I stepped to the porch.

"Thanks for coming so fast."

I brushed past and left her hug hanging in the air. Her front closet held the alarm center. No lights were flashing to indicate a breach.

"You haven't reset anything, have you?" I asked. "Moved the parameters higher?" The detection modes set to thresholds so the system didn't dial the cops every time mail dropped through the door slot.

She shook her head. "Haven't touched it."

"No windows open, doors unlatched?"

"No."

"Might I ask why you think someone's been inside?"

She beckoned me to follow her upstairs. Passing her bedroom, I glanced inside. An unmade bed, the covers a tangle, a big tangle.

It seemed I could smell flowers coming from the room.

Dani led me to her office, shelves of books and magazines, a couple of billowing ferns beside the window, a ceiling fan. The space was centered by a large teakwood desk. There was a credenza behind it, a chair between them. She pointed an accusatory finger at the chair.

"Someone was at my desk."

"How do you know?"

She sat, turned to the computer monitor. "I touch-type about seventy-five words a minute. I focus on the screen, watch the words. Because I never take my eyes away, everything's set up to grab it efficiently. Like a blind person, maybe. Watch."

She opened a blank screen, began typing, her eyes riveted to the monitor. I stood beside her and watched the words race across the screen.

I'm writing a story, Carson, but now I've decided I want to make a note, so I reach for a pencil . . .

Her hand reached out to a mug of pencils. Two inches past her fingertips. She drew her hand back, kept typing.

See? Too far away. I'm back writing my story. Uh-oh, I need to confirm some facts with a source. So I reach for the phone . . .

She reached. This time her hand was an inch or so to the right.

Suddenly I decide I need a telephone number. It's in my PDA. Still banging away, I reach behind me to its usual place, right on the corner edge of the credenza, but . . .

Her hand swung behind her, fingernails tapping the edge of the credenza, the PDA a book's-width away. She turned to me.

"See?"

"Maybe you were having an off day. About an inch off. I'm not trying to be funny."

"I've been working like this for eight years. My office at the station is set up the same way. Someone was here, moving things."

"You've checked your files? Anything missing?"

She opened the bottom desk drawer. A few hanging folders, scant pages in them. "Nothing I can see. No active stories. No names of people or companies being investigated, no secret meetings, no incriminating papers. All I have here are outdated notes. What should I do?"

I cleared my throat. "There's no evidence someone's been in here. It's based on . . . ergonomics."

Her pink nails clacked on the credenza. "You don't believe me, do you?"

"I'm not sure what I believe anymore, Dani."

She frowned. "That's a strange thing to say, Carson."

"Where are the flowers, Dani?"

A pause. "What flowers?"

"You haven't seen Ms Place, I take it? I stopped by earlier. She accepted a few hundred dollars' worth of posies. I brought them over here."

"Uh, they're in my bedroom. They were from the station. Uh, because of me being made an anch—"

"Save yourself some lying. I read the card."

All color drained from her face. "Carson . . ."

"I heard your phone message the other night, too. When did you start fucking Buck Kincannon? Recently? Or all along?"

She closed her eyes. Swayed. At that moment I would have let her fall.

"We, Buck, and me . . . were dating before

you and I met. It was over a year ago, obviously. What you're thinking, it's not . . ."

I mimed pulling a card from an envelope, like at an awards show. Or from a florist's delivery.

"And my final question is . . ."

"Please don't, Carson."

"Have you been to bed with Buck Kincannon recently? The past month?"

Her fists balled into knots. Tears streamed down her face. "Carson," she whispered.

"ANSWER ME!" I screamed.

She closed her eyes. Took a deep breath.

Said, "Yes."

"You've got some items at my house, Ms Danbury," I said. "I'll leave them on your porch in a day or two."

CHAPTER 16

By two-fifteen a.m. I had all Dani's possessions in a green garbage bag. I set the bag in the kitchen, but that didn't feel right, so I put it on the deck. That felt wrong, too. The same with the stoop. I finally carried it downstairs and jammed it in the little cold-water shower beneath the house.

I tried to sleep but pictures clashed in my head and feelings banged into feelings in my heart. The internal warfare kept me awake until four, when I went outside and fell asleep at the edge of the water. The sun woke me at daybreak. I stood, brushed sand from my clothes, and went inside to shower and make coffee.

Though it was barely half past six, I decided to head into the department, get a jump on the day. I was still ten miles south of Mobile when I saw a plume of smoke rising above town, a brown smear against the crystal-blue sky. I flicked the radio to the fire band, heard the cacophonous mix of voices that indicated a bad burn.

"Jeffers here, on the east side. We've got flames from the fourth-story windows."

"Get a hose on it."

"All the high-volume hoses are working the south side."

"This is Smith. We're losing pressure from the Corcoran Street hydrant. Get us a tanker, fast."

"Jeffers. I've got a woman says there's people on the fourth. She heard screaming. Wait . . . I got a man at a window. Elderly. Jesus, he's getting ready to –"

I stuck the flasher on the roof, pushed the accelerator to the floor, aimed the truck at the plume.

Eight minutes later I was weaving through the crowd of gawkers at the periphery. I pulled onto the curb a block away, staying well back from the firefighters. The last thing they needed to deal with was a vehicle blocking a needed path. I flapped my badge wallet open, stuck it in my pocket, jogged toward the scene. The air was oily with the smell of smoke and steam.

I knew the place, an old apartment building, four stories, maybe a dozen units per floor. The rent was inexpensive, but not so cheap the place became a haven for junkies and derelicts. I'd been on a few calls there as a patrolman, a couple domestic beefs and picking up a hooker on a bench warrant, no big deal. Back when I was working the streets, there were one or two hookers who lived at the place, out-service types, not streetwalkers. They tended to keep low and stay out of trouble and we pretty much left them alone, having a lot worse to deal with than call girls.

I saw a firefighter buddy of mine, Captain Rawly Drummond, standing beside a truck and shedding his air tank and yellow flame-retardant coat. He shook off his gloves and wiped sweat from his forehead.

"Hey, Rawly."

He turned, showed a smile beneath a red handlebar mustache that would have looked at home on a gold-rush prospector.

"Yo, Carson. You here to see how real civil-service types work?"

"I was looking for a doughnut joint, took a wrong turn. How's it going?"

"Tough at first, but we're getting it knocked back. Lotta combustibles in that building."

"I caught some radio traffic. People in there?"

The mustache turned down. "Don't have a resident count, but it seems most people got out. An old guy panicked, dove from a window. Another two minutes and we could have had a ladder to him. They took him to the hospital, but it was over."

"Any idea what caused the fire?"

"I had two guys made it deep into the building, back toward the heart of the burn, the start point. They thought they caught a whiff of gasoline, even with the masks."

"Arson."

"Some materials put off a smell of gas when they burn, so maybe not. Still, that place was cooking when we arrived, heavy involvement on two floors, starting on a third. Asphalt from the roof was a burning river."

The danger to surrounding structures had passed and Rawly was out of the fight, another engine company working over the active flames at the far end of the building. We shot the breeze a couple minutes, telling fishing lies combined with enough truths to keep each other off balance.

"Captain!" a guy yelled from the corner of the building. "Got a body."

"Oh, shit," Rawly said. He ran toward the guy and I followed. We rounded the corner. A ladder truck was beside the building. Between the truck and the structure was a body on a collapsible stretcher, two young firefighters staring at the form. Judging by their eyes, it was their first dead body. The guy who'd called Rawly over had the name "Jeffers" printed on his helmet. A slender guy with some years on him, Jeffers nodded toward the younger guys.

"Wills and Hancock found the body, hauled it out."

One of the young firefighters said, "Maybe we should have left it. It was just that . . ."

The kid couldn't finish. I stared down. The corpse was charred beyond recognition, a wet briquette in semihuman shape.

Jeffers saw my badge. "You're a cop? Maybe there's a reason you're here."

"What are you talking about?" I asked.

"Roll it over," Jeffers said.

Faces averted, the young guys turned the corpse from supine to prone. I saw two black twigs, arms, stretching behind the dark mass.

And on what had once been wrists, handcuffs.

Rawly hunkered beside the corpse and thumbed ash from the cuffs. Underneath, they were stainless steel. The lock mechanism was sturdy, the link forged. Good cuffs, pro quality.

Rawly frowned. "I think the arson probability just jumped a notch, Carson. I'll call Forensics."

Jeffers said, "There ain't much left of the room it was in. The body was on the third floor, but started out on the fourth. It was in a huge bed judging by the frame. It all fell through when the fire ate away the floor joists."

"Think this'll be one of yours, Carson?" Rawly asked.

"Someone else'll get the case. My dance card's full."

"Wanna take a look inside anyway? I can't say the area will stay secure. Too many feet stomping around."

The fire was pretty much knocked back on our side of the building, a few rooms at the other end still spewing black smoke as firefighters aimed thick ribbons of water through the windows.

I looked at Jeffers. Said, "Lead on."

We climbed the ladder to the third floor, crept in the window past jagged teeth of glass.

I pushed back my borrowed helmet and looked up and saw sky, the floor above and the roof gone.

"Stay close to the edge of the room," Jeffers said. "The floor's bad in the middle."

I found myself in a brick-walled box of ruination. There were bits of furniture, mostly the metal parts. I saw the melted remains of a television and computer. Near the room's center lay the twisted box springs and mattress springs of a large bed, larger than king size, it seemed, most of the fabric burned away in the center of the springs, blackened fabric at the edges.

"The body was in the middle of the bed?" I asked.

"Dead center." He grimaced at his words, said, "Sorry."

I studied the floor, a mess of charred flooring from above, wires, and shattered glass. I kicked at the glass. It was everywhere in the ash.

"I'm working on my fire investigator's certificate," Jeffers said. "I've got a teacher who'd say the burn patterns are suggestive of an accelerant poured on the body and the bed. I'm also picking up a background scent of a petroleum-based chemical, gasoline maybe."

"What would you conclude?" I asked.

"Right now I'd conclude I'm just a student."

I took a couple steps forward, the charred flooring crunching like ice.

"No further," Jeffers said, grabbing my arm.

I backpedaled. "You don't have to tell me twice." I reached down and brushed aside detritus, lifted a piece of the ubiquitous broken glass. I blew off ash, saw my face in my hand.

"It's a mirror," I said.

Jeffers knelt and brushed at the floor.

"A lot of mirror. Must have been a biggie." He inched across the floor to the bed.

"The springs are full of mirror, big pieces." Jeffers stared up at a non-existent room. "What's that make you think, Ryder?"

I studied the wreckage. Now that I knew what to look for, I saw mirror fragments everywhere.

"A mirror above the bed. Or on the wall. But probably both."

"Probably says a little something about the lady," Jeffers said.

CHAPTER 17

I walked into the detectives' room just as Harry was hanging up the phone. He looked at me, nostrils flaring.

"I smell smoke."

"There was a fire at the apartment building at Corcoran and Hopple. I stopped to look."

Harry nodded. "It was on the news. Sounded pretty big."

"They've got it tamed. Two dead I know about. Some poor old guy got spooked and flew out the window. I was there when another body came out. The arms were behind the body's back. Handcuffed in place."

"Uh-oh. His wrists or her wrists?"

"Couldn't tell; female by the size. It looked like the body came from a room full of mirrors."

"It was that four-story yellow-brick apartment at Corcoran and Hopple, east side?"

I nodded.

"Used to be a few out-service gals in that building, maybe some inside work, specialty stuff. Bondage, sado-maso. Role-play weirdness. Maybe one of the specialists lost control, had to cover some tracks fast."

"They're covered. Any trace evidence in that room is now floating somewhere in the troposphere."

Harry shrugged. "Someone else's case, thank God. Listen, I just got a call from Lincoln Haley at WTSJ. He found some pages from Taneesha Franklin. Our name appears on something."

"Let's go take a look."

When we walked through the door, Lincoln Haley was talking to the receptionist. He gestured us to follow to his office. I heard James Brown over the ubiquitous speakers, wailing *Baby, baby, baby* in a voice like a scalded ocelot.

Haley said, "Teesh did some work as a copywriter. Commercials. Not much after she started in news, just whenever our regular writer got jammed up. Teesh didn't do the ad writing at her regular desk, but in the sales office." Haley tried a smile. "I think she felt writing commercials at the news desk sullied the newsroom."

We entered his office. A desk, couch, couple chairs. A shelf with various memorabilia, photos of music celebrities, three autographed baseballs, an autographed glove. He pointed to the chairs and we sat. Haley followed, picking up a sheaf of papers on his desk.

"Our regular copywriter, Sharie Dumond, was cleaning old files off the computer and found a file Teesh created. It's a small file, just a few pages, titled 'Danbury'."

I sat forward. "Danbury?"

"I think I mentioned Teesh met with DeeDee Danbury a few times, the reporter on Channel 14. The file appears to be her notes from the meetings. I figure Teesh finished writing commercials one day, decided to transcribe handwritten notes into the computer. They're a little hard to decipher – she transcribed direct and in her own shorthand."

"Our names are in the writings?"

"They resemble class notes, like Ms Danbury was lecturing and Teesh was writing. Here's the page . . ."

I leaned and took the page from Haley's hand, read the reference.

MPD Protec's: Det C Ryder, Det H Nautilus. If trbl. // also SP, Arn Norlin.

"Anything important, Carson?" Harry asked, peering over my shoulder.

I shook my head, feeling the letdown. "Not really. I'm sure the message simply means should Taneesha have any trouble with the MPD, her protectors would be you and me."

"Trouble?" Haley frowned. "Protectors?"

"It's not like it sounds," I said. "It's names to drop if she was being given a runaround, maybe needed a little access. Some cops shut reporters out as a hobby."

Pace Logan came to mind. I hoped he wasn't passing that trait on to Shuttles. You don't hand the press the store, but treat them right and it comes back in one way or another. I'd learned that much even before dating a reporter.

"How about the other name?" Haley asked.

"Same things, different jurisdiction. Arn Norlin's with the state cops. He's a good guy, Dani's had an in with Arn for years."

"Dani?"

"Ms Danbury," I said. "Her name's Danielle, thus the DD initials and nickname."

"You know her?"

Cornered. "I, uh, she's my . . ."

Harry winked. "Ms Danbury is my partner's significant other, Mr Haley, if that's what it's called anymore. Cop and reporter, oil and water. Somehow those two have been together for a year."

Haley smiled. "Congratulations. From what Teesh told me about your girlfriend, you're a lucky man."

I tried to affect a courteous smile, but it felt like I was baring my teeth. Haley said, "Sorry I brought you up here for nothing, but I thought it might be important. I wanted to call before I headed out of town tonight."

"Vacation?" Harry asked. I stood and turned away, my face beginning to ache from not screaming.

"My brother lives in Atlanta. I'm visiting for a couple days, take in a game. Take my mind off things a bit."

"Braves?" Harry said. "You a fan?"

Haley nodded. "I played ball in college, outfield. How about you?"

Harry pushed up from the chair, juiced. "Love the game. But my experience is Little League, kind of. Know that ball field on the west side of Pritchard? I helped get it running a few years back."

Oh Jeez, not that story again . . .

Haley shook his head. "Don't know the field. But I'm not usually out that direction. Hey, you want copies of Teesh's notes? Just to have them?"

"Sure," Harry said. "We'll add them to the case file. You ever at a game when Aaron was playing?"

"Let's go, bro," I said, grabbing him by the elbow.

"The kids were hoping for a scoreboard, Carson, nothing fancy, slap up numbered cards for runs, outs. Be nice if that happened."

"Umph," I said.

Harry slid the cruiser across three lanes, oblivious to the angry horns behind us. He glanced in the rear-view and waved, *thanks for letting us in*. The baseball conversation with Lincoln Haley had restarted my partner's soliloquy about creating a ball field with Buck Kincannon.

"Hey, Cars, let's take a detour, check it out."

"Check what out?"

"The ball field. I never get over this way. Take ten minutes."

I can leap from the car, I thought as Harry cut

the wheel toward his field of dreams. *Open the door, scream "Geronimo"* . . .

Harry drove a few miles, slowed, craning his head side to side. Modular buildings surrounded by fences and barbwire, a metals-processing operation, a school bus graveyard. Even with windows tight and the AC on recirculate, a hard chemical smell seeped into the car.

"It's been so long I don't remember where it was. Things have changed. I'm all turned around."

Harry pulled up in front of a bone-skinny guy wearing nothing but a loose pair of raggedy jeans. His face was patchy, like mange, and he looked in his forties.

Harry rolled down his window. "Say, bro, you know if there's a little ball field nearby?"

The guy stumbled toward us. His face grinned with something like recognition and I saw he had meth mouth: gums dissolved away, blackened teeth showing to the bleeding roots.

"Haa-i-eeee," the guy keened, grabbing at Harry's elbow. "Haaa-i-eeeee."

Up close, looking past the ravaged mouth, the guy was maybe eighteen. Smoking crystal methedrine was like gargling with muriatic acid. Plus users scratched their skin apart trying to get at the bugs crawling in their veins. Weight loss left skin hanging like wet cloth.

"Uh, thanks anyway." Harry drove away, shooting glances into the rear-view. The guy kept yelling, "Haaa-i-eeee."

"That was instructional," I said.

"It was around here. I know it was."

"Maybe Buckie airlifts the field to Minnesota this time of year, where it's cooler."

"What?"

"If you can't find it, you can't find it. Let's head back."

He tapped his fingers on the wheel, thought. "One more stop."

"Harry . . ."

We pulled into a rough neighborhood of decaying buildings and dead-eyed people. We passed a school, windows grated. The businesses were typical for the neighborhood: check-cashing outlets, bars, pawnshops, bunkerized groceries where clerks cowered behind bulletproof glass.

Harry stopped in front of the only festive storefront on the block, a hanging sign proclaiming, DreamCenter Social Services. The façade was a colorful mural, faces of white and brown, tree-lined streets, a man grilling hot dogs, children swimming in a pool, a friendly yellow sun watching over everything. It was as incongruous as Oz in downtown Nagasaki, 1946.

We checked twice to make sure the car was locked, and headed in the door.

A woman's voice trumpeted our entrance. "Harry Nautilus? Harry-damn-Nautilus!"

Mardy Baker was a big woman, taller than my six-one but shorter than Harry's six-four. She wore baggy khakis and a T-shirt emblazoned with the words, JOIN THE COMMUNI-TEAM! Improbably, she wore pink high heels, backless and toeless. Her nails, up and down, were painted with gold glitter.

Ms Baker's ebullience seemed proportionate to her size. She wrapped Harry in a hug the size of a truck tire, then stared at his bemused face.

"Lord have mercy, Harry-damn-Nautilus. Whoops, is that blasphemous? I see your name in the paper now and then, Harry. Ain't you something."

Harry introduced us. We were bustled into an office, desk and chair and lots of shelves. Ms Baker thundered down the hall for coffee. I studied the surroundings: upbeat posters on the walls, stacks of handouts advising people to get tested for AIDS, avoid alcohol during pregnancy, obtain a GED, and so forth. There was a colorful rug in one corner, toys on it; where kids could play while she counseled parents, I supposed.

Ms Baker returned with a carafe of coffee on a tray, creamers, sugar packets. She leaned against the wall and studied Harry.

"What brings you here, Harry? Just in the neighborhood?"

"I was talking to Carson a few days back, the old ball-field project came up. We were nearby, so I thought I'd show him. I can't seem to find it."

Ms Baker blew out a breath.

"Maybe because it's under a warehouse."

Harry's shoulders fell. "After all that work, equipment, the improvements? What the hell happened?"

Mardy Baker turned to the window and looked out over the streetscape. "My recollection of those days might not be precise, Harry. Biased, maybe. Not for public consumption." Her voice seemed to balance resignation and resentment.

"We look like the public to you?" Harry said.

She went to her desk and sat, both hands clasping her coffee cup. "Things went along great for the first year. Money arrived as promised, the teams grew, maybe seventy kids. The next season came close to rolling around . . ."

Harry turned my way. "I had to bow out after things got cruising. I'd just moved from Vice to Homicide. It was a bloody summer, new gangs springing up, gunning and running. I was working three drive-bys at once."

Ms Baker continued. "Harry'd set everything in motion, made the connections."

"What changed?" I asked.

"I went back to the well, drew up a formal budget request, called Mr Kincannon. I could never get him on the phone: on vacation, out of town, in a meeting. One day a lawyer type showed up, buttery smooth, polite as Miss Manners. He had some suggestions for the upcoming season."

"Like?"

"The teams had names like Panthers and Gators and Bears, names picked by the kids." Ms Baker smiled. "Of course, they really wanted names like Stone Killers, Bloody Warriors, and Ninja Mutants, but we gave them a list to pick from, a bit less extreme."

"The lawyer guy wanted Stone Bloody Ninjas?" I wondered.

"He suggested company names like Panorama Advertising, Magnitude Construction, Clarity Broadcasting."

I nodded. "All names of Kincannon investments, I assume. Still, if they're fronting the money . . ."

"Sure, corporate sponsorships. I said, fine, we'll re-name the teams. A few days later, there was another suggestion." She paused. "This one a bit more . . . intrusive."

I raised an eyebrow.

Ms Baker looked at Harry. "Remember when the city wanted to put the industrial waste transfer point over by the Saylor Street projects?"

"Bitter fight. The company handling it didn't have a rep for integrity. Chem-Tron?"

"Chemitrol. The lawyer guy showed up with charts and graphs suggesting the transfer station was a great opportunity for the neighborhood: jobs, training, education . . . money spreading out like a tsunami."

Ms Baker took a sip of her coffee and frowned. I didn't think the frown came from the taste of the coffee. She continued.

"I dug around. Discovered the specifications we weren't given. The projections. The amounts of chemicals traveling our streets. I read up on the industry itself, similar installations. Guess what?"

"Facts were slanted a bit?" I suggested.

"A dozen people could handle the duties of the station, four needing degrees in chemical engineering. The others answered the phone and filed."

"Eight minimum-wage jobs," I said.

"It was the usual bullshit: all frosting, no cake."

Harry leaned forward. "What went down from there, Mardy?"

"Mr Lawyer showed up with all these fancy-ass fliers in favor of the transfer station, wanted the kids to distribute them in the community."

"Warm and fuzzy," I noted. "A good photo op."

"Mr Lawyer suggested organizing a parade for the station. All we had to do was show up, moms and dads and kids and aunts and uncles, get the cleanest people we knew to come . . ."

"The cleanest people?" Harry said.

"Not a second thought about what he was saying."

"Scumbucket," Harry whispered.

Ms Baker said, "All parade permits would be handled, all news media in place. Mr Lawyer even had scripts. 'A step ahead for our children,' 'Children are the future when parents have jobs,' 'Chemitrol Means Community Control.' Our *clean people* were to chant this lying shit like fucking parrots – pardon my French. I told the guy he could wrap his fliers with barbwire and stick 'em where the sun don't shine. A little more politely than that, maybe. Not a lot."

"The money dried up?" I said.

"The field got padlocked. Within a week it was all over."

"You never heard from Kincannon?" Harry's voice was a rasp.

"I thought about making a stink. But then I realized they could point to a bunch of bats and gloves and uniforms and we'd come off like whining ingrates. Of course, the uniforms got dirty and torn, the equipment fell apart. And without a decent place to play, the kids lost interest."

Mardy Baker closed her eyes, rubbed them with her fingertips.

"I thanked God a thousand times for sending

such good-hearted people here. The next year they were at the door with their hands out, our payback time."

"I understand something," I said to Harry. "Clair said few of the truly wealthy give with both hands. I thought she meant the Kincannons were exceptions, using both hands to ladle out the lucre. She really meant one hand passes out the goodies, because the other one's busy grabbing something back."

Ms Baker looked at me over her coffee.

"One hand gives, the other hand takes," she said. "Damn if that don't sum it right up."

A deflated Harry retraced our route in, passing by the warehouse, a cheap frame-and-metal structure squatting on two acres of asphalt, the cyclone-fenced lot now home to industrial equipment – trailers, crane assemblies, scaffolding. He stared as an equipment truck pulled from the building, a small dozer trailered behind, Magnolia Industrial Developments painted on the truck's door.

Harry pointed. "There's where it was, the field. Know who owns Magnolia Developments?"

"The Kincannons," I ventured.

"Bastards."

Harry drove down the street where the meth head had stood, doing ten miles an hour, looking back and forth, stopping to scan down alleys.

"Looking for something in particular?" I asked.

"The meth-head guy, the kid with the mouth like cancer. Haaa-i-eee. I figured out he was trying to say my name. He must have been one of the ball players from back then, one of the kids. It's the only way he could have known me."

"I'm sorry, bro," I said.

"I swear if Buck Kincannon was in front of me right now, cop or no cop, I'd nail that son of a bitch to the side of a barn, stand a hundred feet away, and teach myself how to shoot a bow and arrow."

I had been trying to figure when and how to tell Harry about Dani. This seemed appropriate.

"Harry?" I said.

"What, brother?"

"Ms Danbury's getting screwed by Buck Kincannon."

I saw Harry's hands squeeze tight on the wheel, like choking it.

"Lotta that going around," he said.

CHAPTER 18

Harry and I returned to Mobile and silently pored through Rudolnick's records. Our simmering funk made us a threat to others, set off by an errant word or gesture – one of Pace Logan's wise-ass remarks, for instance – but since we'd both been wounded by Buck Kincannon, we were safe with one another.

After an hour of reading psycho-terminology, Harry pitched a stack back in the box. "How about we get Terry Baney to talk to the trucker, get a sketch made to pass out on the streets?" he suggested.

Terry Baney was the departmental artist. "Sketch? The perp doesn't have a face to draw, Harry. We got one eyewitness, right? According to our wit, the perp looks like a Wookiee. Or maybe a yeti."

"If you saw a yeti walking down the street, you'd remember it, Carson. Right?"

An hour later we were in the flower-lined hospital room of Arlin Dell. He'd been disconnected from most of the machines. The truck driver scowled, thinking our request strange.

"All I saw was hair, like I told you," Dell said. "Remember Cousin Itt on *The Addams Family*? Draw him, just leave off the top hat."

"It was a bowler hat," Terry Baney corrected. He sat in a chair beside Dell's bed, a drawing pad in one hand, a thick pencil in the other. Harry and I leaned against the wall.

Dell rolled his eyes. "Bowler hat, top hat, whatever."

Terry Baney was forty-three and looked like a man more at home with actuarial tables than drawing materials – slight, bespectacled, pomaded hair, a pink hue to his scrubbed cheeks. He wore a suit fresh from K-mart's bargain rack; his only artsy touches were a bolo tie and silver belt buckle dotted with turquoise. But the man had a gift, an ability to coax fragments of recollections from witnesses, transforming them into representations that held not photographic exactitude but something almost better: emotive content.

Baney drew three shapes on his pad, a flattened circle, a circle, and a vertical oval. He turned the pad to Dell, tapped the drawings with his pencil.

"Which of these was the basic shape of the perpetrator's head?"

"Come on," Dell scoffed.

Baney smiled nonchalantly, kept the drawings in front of the trucker.

Dell thought a moment. "The middle one. Maybe more square, like a box."

Baney ripped the page off, tossed it to the floor. He drew a squarish circle, began adding lines indicating hair shape.

"The hair, did it fall straight down like this?" He scribbled vertical lines from the oval. "Or did it fluff out to the sides, more like this?" Baney radiated lines out at an angle, creating a delta form.

"That one. It was fluffed out."

"Did it fluff out straight? Or was it curly hair, the boingy stuff, like this?" Baney drew curling lines.

"No, the other way. It was straight."

Baney ripped the page away and started on a fresh sheet.

"The guy's eyes, Mr Dell. You said they were like holes in the middle of all that hair."

Dell reached for the switch controlling the bed and raised himself higher. "Just holes. And they were kind of deep. Like his eyes were pushed back."

"Let's talk shape. Round holes like this?" Baney drew his perceptions. "Or were they more like this?" His hand flashed over the paper, drawing, smudging, shaping. The result suggested prominent cheekbones and deep-set eyes.

Dell jabbed a finger at the pad. "That. I remember a white triangle above his eyes. Skin. Shaped like a tent from the front."

"That indicates hair parted at the top," Baney said, tossing aside a page, beginning fresh. His pencil skipped over the paper, a blur. "Right in the middle. That's what makes the, uh . . . tent effect. Can I use that in the future, Mr Dell? Tent effect?"

Dell grinned and nodded, pleased with his invention.

"The hairy man's deep eyes," Baney asked. "Small, large?"

Dell closed his eyes, thought. "Small. Or maybe they seemed that way because the guy was . . ." The trucker's eyes popped open. "Angry. Scowling." Dell frowned hard at Baney, indicating the look.

Baney nodded, kept working. "So, if I take a skinny basic face, add the cheekbone effect around the eyes, keep the hair straight but full, and put a part in the dead center, make his eyes tight with anger . . ."

Baney seemed transported, drawing, smudging, shading. After a minute he turned the pad to Dell.

"This remind you of anyone?"

The trucker's eyes widened and his mouth fell open.

"It's him. How the hell did you do that?"

Harry and I headed back to the department to photocopy the drawing, take it out on the street to show people and run through our snitch network. We dropped the drawing on Harry's desk, headed toward the coffee urn. When it sputtered and went dry, we headed downstairs to steal from the urn in Crimes Against Property.

When we returned, the drawing was on the floor beside Harry's desk. The closest dick was

Pace Logan, leaning against a column and studying a sheaf of papers. Shuttles stood beside him, looking pained.

"You got it wrong here," Logan was lecturing Shuttles. "Plus your spelling is screwed. It's *perp-e-trator,* not *perp-a-trator.*"

"Sorry, Pace," Shuttles said. "I'll re-do the report."

"Somebody mess with my desk?" Harry growled, staring at Logan.

Logan looked over his reading glasses. "Don't have a meltdown, Nautilus. I looked at your silly-ass picture. I was walking by and couldn't figure if it was Charlie Manson or Grizzly Adams."

"How about getting it back on the desk next time?"

Logan shook his head and turned away, walking back to his cubicle. Harry muttered "two more months".

We showed the pics around, gave several out to snitches and told them to call if they saw the guy. Of course, if he'd cut his hair and beard – odds being heavily in that direction, unless he was a total lunatic – it was useless.

When we ran out of pics, we headed to Flanagan's to grab a beer and bowl of gumbo.

Harry shot me an occasional glance that I felt but didn't see. He pushed aside his bowl.

"What you gonna do, Carson? About Da— Ms Danbury?"

"It's already done."

Harry clinked the spoon around his empty bowl. "You're sure about her and Kincannon? I mean, she really was –"

"I flat-out asked, Harry. She admitted she was boinking Buckie."

Harry nodded. He shot a glance over my shoulder, grimaced. I turned to the TV above the bar. Dani was anchoring the six p.m. news slot, doing the papers-on-the-desk bit. She launched into a story on the morning's fire.

". . . man jumped before firefighters could reach him and was pronounced dead at the hospital. A badly burned female body was found in the rubble, identification held pending notification of next of kin . . ."

"How about you switch that to another channel," Harry called to Eloise, our waitress.

"Keep it on, Eloise," I said. "And turn it up a bit."

Harry shot me the eye.

"I have to get used to it," I said, staring at the screen.

Harry cleared his throat and leaned close. "Uh, Carson, you ever think about, uh . . ."

I turned from the TV. "Messing with Buck Kincannon? Waiting outside Dani's until I see them coming home one night, ripping out Buckie's eyes and kicking them up his ass so far he's staring at what he had for dinner?"

"Yeah. You ever think about stuff like that?"

"Never."

"That's good. I've got to head home. My ass is worn out." He slipped on his jacket, tossed a few bills on the table, walked to the door. He turned and came back.

"What now?" I said to Harry's looming form, hands in his pockets.

"You know if you ever lit into a guy like that you could kiss your job goodbye."

"I know, Harry."

"Good."

He turned away. Paused. Turned back around.

"Your job would be gone in an hour, Carson. No, a finger snap."

"I realize that, bro."

"I know," he sighed. "I'm just making sure I do."

CHAPTER 19

I slept some that night. It was between 4.15 and 5.45, I think. The rest of the time I stared at pictures forming and re-forming on my shadowed ceiling. Listened to words tumbling through the darkened air.

She'll betray you. They always betray us, don't they?

The words were my brother's. Jeremy was, by all measures of the human mind, insane. Driven mad by our father's relentless punishments and beatings, Jeremy had at age sixteen killed our father. Over the years he had killed five women. In his twisted mind he was avenging himself on our mother for never protecting him.

But she was blameless, little more than a

child herself. It was the three of us against my father, a trio of Chihuahuas caged with a rabid Doberman.

Jeremy was incarcerated at an institution west of Montgomery. I was a hesitant visitor every four months on average. Last year I had taken Dani with me to visit Jeremy. He hated women, and the visit had not gone well, ending with him forecasting my relationship with Dani would end in betrayal.

His senses were uncanny. Had he seen something I had not? Or was it just his usual anti-female ranting?

I had planned on visiting my brother soon, was overdue by a month, in fact. But when he would ask, as he always did, *How's your little love-muffin, Carson? Has she betrayed you yet?* I did not want to admit the truth: that she had tried me for a year, found me wanting, and had taken up with a man who could deliver her the world wrapped in ribbon and served with a split of champagne.

I decided to postpone my visit this time around. Take a break from Jeremy. He wasn't going anywhere.

I stumbled from bed at six, turned on National Public Radio, and fixed coffee. Figuring

I needed the caffeine, I used four tablespoons per cup, drank four cups, buzzed off to the department.

Harry showed up with a half-dozen ham biscuits, correctly figuring I hadn't eaten. We chomped biscuits and shuffled through phone slips from the previous day, hoping for points of gold glittering in the mud. Harry read a slip, reread it. Snicked it with a fingernail.

"Something here, maybe. Lemme make a call."

Harry got up and went to the conference room to phone, returning a call to a snitch. When we told a snitch no one was listening as they talked, we told the truth. Maybe it didn't mean much, but that's the way we played it.

Harry was back a minute later, eyebrows raised.

"You know Leroy Dinkins?" he asked.

I searched my memory and saw nothing but an amorphous blob wriggling in a doorway. It took me a second to realize my mind was showing me Leroy.

"Met him once when I was in uniform," I said. "A shoplifting beef. Leroy got stuck when he tried to run out the back door of a grocery downtown, the back door being a lot smaller than the front. He was about eighteen, if I recall."

"That's blubber butt himself," Harry said, scowling at the slip. "I got this snitch hangs with Leroy Dinkins sometimes. He says Leroy was cadging drinks at a bar when a guy looking like our drawing comes in. They talk in private, the hairball leaves. Suddenly Leroy's ordering from his own pocket."

"The hairball gave Leroy some money," I said.

"That's the way my snitch saw it."

"Why'd your snitch tattle on his buddy Dinkins?"

Harry laughed. "Leroy drank all night and didn't buy anyone else a single pop. My snitch got pissed off, dropped the dime."

"Leroy should learn to share," I said. "You know where blubber butt lives?"

"With his mama," Harry grinned. "Where else?"

Leroy Dinkins was easy to spot: a hulking mass on a porch. Harry knew Dinkins better than I did, filling me in as we drifted into a space in front of Dinkins's house, a tiny frame bungalow.

"Leroy's the original fraidy-cat, Carson.

Placid, flaccid and lazy ass-ed. Hangs at the edge of the street scene, too lily-livered to get in any serious trouble. Scared to death of doing time."

I nodded. There were guys in the can who'd rather see a fat guy than a slim woman. Harry continued his assessment. "Leroy's not real bright, but he's all over the 'hood, and he's got two big fat ears that suck up information that he sells. Who's got the best reefer, where the upmarket hookers hang. He's less a doer than a connector."

"How should we approach him, bro?"

"Like he's about twelve years old."

Dinkins was testing the limits of a lounge chair, lying back. He wore a kinte cloth-pattern shirt the size of a bedspread over voluminous jeans and orange plastic flip-flops. He tensed as we pulled up, looked stricken when we headed up the sidewalk.

"Howdy, Leroy, remember me?" I asked. "Here's a hint, the front half of you was outside Packy's EZ Mart, the back half was inside."

"Dunno what you talkin' about."

Leroy Dinkins was sucking a forty of Coors Light and nearing the bottom of an industrial-size bag of cheese puffs. A wide circle around his mouth was orange with cheese-puff dust, like clown makeup.

Harry gave Leroy the hard eye. "Rumor has it you were at a joint called Lucky's a few days back."

"So wha'? I go to Lucky's two–three times a week. They got good po' boys and cheese fries."

"Plus Lucky's has wide doors, right?" Harry said.

"Why you botherin' me? Bein' nasty an' all?"

Harry leaned close. "We're looking for a guy. You might remember him, looks like King Kong maybe? Face that's all fur."

Dinkins pushed himself up from the chair, the Goodyear blimp filled with Jell-O and struggling to get aloft. "I got to go inside and fix my mama's supper. She has to eat same time every day."

I stepped between him and the door. "Come on, Leroy, you're not in a jam. Did you sell this guy something?"

"I don't know nobody look like that," he whined. "I gotta go inside."

The door pushed open behind me and bumped my ass. I turned to a petite woman in her late sixties wearing horn-rim glasses, the frames adorned with rhinestones. She was leaning on a cane. I figured she'd been behind the door trying to hear our conversation.

"Leroy, you didn't tell me you had company."

"They salesmen, Mama. They just leaving."

She looked at me, squinted. "What you boys selling?"

Harry stepped in front. "Actually, ma'am, we're with the Mobile Police Department, here asking about someone Leroy might have seen."

"Lee-roy?" she asked. "Who you seen?"

"Ain't nothin', Mama. They got the wrong guy."

She turned to Harry. "Who you axin' about?"

"A fellow with a big beard and long hair."

She looked at her son. "When that boy here last, Leroy? Didn't I see him out here four–five days ago?"

Dinkins's face plummeted. "I don't remember, Mama," he moaned. "I don't think so."

"Sure it was. I saw him clean as day. You two was in the front yard. I thought that fellow had his back to me at first, all that hair, then I saw eyes an' a mouth."

"Mama!" Leroy whined.

"Thank you, ma'am," Harry said.

"I need my chicken tonight, Leroy. Wit' biscuit. You comin' in soon?"

"Right now, Mama."

She nodded at us and tottered back into the house. Dinkins tried to slip in behind her, but Harry's hand found Dinkins's chest. "Walk us to the car, Leroy," Harry said. "We'd enjoy your company."

"I gotta *go*," he wailed. "Mama needs her chicken."

Harry took Dinkins by a blubbery bicep and guided him out to the sidewalk.

"We need to know details about Fur-face, Leroy. No holding back."

"You guys'll twist up my words, make me go to jail." Dinkins looked like he was about to start bawling. Dinkins knew something, but was scared it could cause him trouble. Street advice was if you shut up and pretended ignorance, it all went away, cops included.

"Stand here," Harry said. "I'll be right back."

Harry parked Dinkins in the middle of the sidewalk, then grabbed a stick of yellow chalk from the car. He inscribed a large square on the sidewalk. Harry paused, studied the square, grabbed Dinkins by the arm.

Dinkins's eyes went wide. "What's gonna happen to me?"

"Shhh," Harry said. He walked Dinkins to the square, set him dead in its center. Dinkins stared down at the yellow outline.

Harry said, "It's a free space, Leroy. Anything you say inside the free space is not official. Nothing can be used against you. In fact, it's not even like you saying it. It's just a voice in the air."

"You're makin' that up."

Harry produced his badge, held it out like a small bible on his palm. "Take the free-space pledge, Carson."

I put my hand over Harry's badge. "I, Carson Ryder, detective, hereby solemnly certify that full and bona fide free-space privilege be granted one Leroy Dinkins." I stopped, then added, "So help me God."

Harry said, "You're in a legal free space, Leroy. Safe from anything you say, forever and ever."

Dinkins peered down. "No shit?"

"Don't step out of it," I cautioned.

Harry leaned against the Crown Vic, crossed his arms. "Now, tell me anything you want to about the guy at Lucky's. What was his name, how did you meet, and what did he want?"

Dinkins shrugged, sending waves jostling through his fat. "He just came in the door, sat at the bar, looked around. He ate a samwich, talked to people. He finally talked to me."

"About?"

Dinkins started to shrug it away. Harry pointed to the ground. "Free space, Leroy. Use it while you got it. They don't have free spaces down at the station."

"He had some cars to get rid of, but there were a couple problems with the paperwork. Lost in a fire, he said."

"Stolen."

"Sure, the cars was hot. He was just talking in code."

"What was his name, Leroy?"

"He din't say. That's the truth."

"What'd he look like up close? Solid guy, kind of square, the fur face?"

"All I could see was his eyes. They were brown, I think. But he wasn't square. He was . . ." Dinkins held his hands about a foot apart, moving them up and down.

"Slender?" I said.

"Shaped about like you. And about how high. Maybe more. That's all I remember. He showed me a big bunch of crisp money."

Crisp like fresh from an ATM, I figured. The cash Mrs Atkins had been forced to withdraw.

"What was he wearing?" I asked.

He shrugged. "I dunno. Jeans and a shirt. Blue shirt? The usual stuff."

"Did you give him what he wanted?"

Dinkins looked like a man on a jittering tightrope.

"Come on, Leroy," Harry said. "Use the damn free space."

"He said he was paying a thousand dollars for the right information. A place to unload the metal."

"A thousand dollars?" Harry said. "A *grand*?"

"Five hunnert up front, five after the name proved out."

Harry paused. Frowned.

"He came back?"

"Two days later he's out in my front yard, hands me the other five. That's when Mama saw him."

"Who did you give him, Leroy? What name?"

Dinkins looked down, made sure he was centered in the box.

"Uh, there are these two guys, brothers. They got this bidness going on with cars . . ."

"The Hooleys," Harry said. "Right, Leroy?"

Dinkins nodded nervously.

"Hooleys?" I asked.

"Two brothers," Harry said. "Darryl and Danny Hooley. Back when I was in Crimes Against Property they were boosting sound systems, smash and grab. This was eight or nine years back; they were in their late teens." Harry gave Dinkins a skeptical eye. "You know where the Hooleys keep their chop shop?"

"I just gave the hairy guy their names. I mean, they're in the fucking book."

It was probably a lie, Dinkins not wanting to say where the shop was, but location wasn't what we needed. Dinkins eyes turned scared. "This hairy guy did something wrong, didn't he? You'll tell the Hooleys and I'll get beat up."

"Calm down, Leroy," Harry said. "It's all protected by the free space."

Dinkins studied the sidewalk, relaxed. "Oh, that's right."

Harry and I started to the car. Dinkins remained in the box, looking down, fascinated.

"Hey, you guys," he called.

We turned. "What?" I said.

"You sure I can say anything in the free space, not get in trouble?"

"You got it," I said.

Dinkins said, "You fuckers are flat-out goofy."

"Don't press your luck, Leroy," Harry said.

CHAPTER 20

Of the two Hooley brothers, Harry said Darryl was the one to work on, a goofed-out stoner. Darryl lived in a single-story ranch in mid-Mobile, an aging suburb of expressionless boxes, anonymity with a mailing address. Harry parked a block away, lifted the binocs to his face.

"Oh my," Harry grinned. "There is a God."

"What?"

"Darryl Hooley, all by his lonesome. Sitting on the porch and toking on a reefer. Let's park in the alley, come around from behind."

We crept through the backyard, snaked around the side of the house. I jumped up over the porch rail, grabbed up a baggie of pot, tossed it to Harry. Hooley tried to stand but my hand encouraged him to remain sitting. Hooley was a small guy, bony shoulders, soft eyes. He wore faded jeans and a black KISS T-shirt, the band that wouldn't die.

Harry held the bag delicately, his pinkie sticking out, like sipping tea. "Lord have mercy, Darryl, what's this greenish substance?"

"It's fuckin' pot, what the hell do you . . . Hey, Harry Nautilus! Been years. You're looking good, dude, few extra pounds . . ."

Harry reached to the back of his belt for handcuffs. He shook them in Hooley's eyes like ringing a bell. "Let's go, Darryl. You know the routine."

"Huh? You serious?"

"This is an illegal substance, Darryl. A no-no."

"We both know that bag's not going to be heavy enough to get me on trafficking. This is a roust."

Harry rattled the cuffs. "Hands on the house and spread 'em, Darryl. Time for some hooking and booking."

"You're homicide now, right? Why are you doin' this to me? It's harassment." Darryl had a nasal voice and sounded like a kid whining about being fed spinach.

"It's a night in the bag, Darryl," I said. "And

a court appearance. And a shyster to warm your side at morning court. It's pissant bullshit, I know, but it's also a pain in your ass and a drain on your wallet."

"You're right, Darryl," Harry said, "it's harassment. I've got a couple of new hobbies, and harassing you is one of them."

The curtains parted in Hooley's cannabis intoxication. He sighed.

"You want something. Right, Harry? You always wanted something."

Harry laid his hand on Darryl Hooley's shoulder, leaned close. "You got a guy just started boosting for your operation. Has or had Wookiee genes, hairy everything. Am I correct?"

Hooley stared at his shoes, mute. Harry stood back and jangled the cuffs. "Damn, I love a new hobby. The thrill of repeating something over and over until you get good at it. Did I ever tell you how long it took me to learn to play tambourine? Don't think in days, Darryl. Months either."

Hooley shot a glance over his shoulder. His voice became contemplative.

"I'm in a kind of gray area here, Harry, admissions and all that. Might be best to just take the misdemeanor, my man. Don't want to have any translation problems here, find out you're saying one thing, but I'm not catching the meaning, y'know?"

It was the ready-to-deal voice, one I'd heard a hundred times. I winked at Harry.

"You remember me ever lying, Darryl?" Harry said.

"You were always straight, Harry. Hard, but straight."

"Here's the deal: you get a pass on the pot this time around. And anything you say is dust the minute we leave. Guaranteed."

Hooley nodded. "Good enough for me, Harry. Can I sit down, get comfortable? Finish my doob?"

"You get two outta three, Darryl," Harry said. "Guess which two?"

Hooley sighed, turned and sat in the chair, pushed his hippie hair back behind his ears.

"Harry, the guy you're looking for is crazy."

"How about starting on page one, Darryl?"

"It was last week. Guy came by our, uh, establishment. My brother said, 'What you want, my man?' The guy said, 'I want to schedule a presentation.' My brother said, 'A fucking what?' The guy said, 'I think we can work together, a limited partnership.' I thought to myself, *This fucker's crazy.* Danny said, 'Here's how we work together, partner, you bring us merchandise limited to just high-end stuff, we give you money.'"

"You and Danny didn't think he was a setup, a cop?" Harry interrupted.

"The guy was too fuckin' crazy, like I said. Talked weird, used ten-foot words. And he didn't look like a plant. You guys stand out like parrots on a shitpile."

"What happened?"

Darryl Hooley shook his head, a dreamy pot smile on his face. "He came by the next day in a '58 Mercedes, a classic. Handed me the keys."

"What'd he do next?"

Hooley clapped his hands in delight. "Got on a fucking bus. It's morning, Saturday, broad daylight. Comes back an hour later with a 2004 Beamer series. Does it again and brings in a '97 Porsche Turbo. The man had a gift."

"Where is he now?" I asked.

Hooley's face dropped. "He dropped off the Turbo, tossed the keys and grabbed thirty-five big ones. I said, 'What's next?' He said that was it, he was done."

"Done?" Harry asked.

"I said, 'Brother, we can put you on staff, you got a natural talent.' You know what that crazy fuck told me?"

"What?"

"Said he'd made all the money he needed. Who in their right mind has all they need, Harry? See what I mean about the guy being crazy?"

The next stop in our blind passage was Crimes Against Property, Vehicle Theft Division, one floor down. Vince Raines ran the squad, but Vince was out of town and we spoke with Mitch Burdon, second in command.

"A '97 Porsche Turbo, '58 M-B Roadster, a 2004 Beamer-seven?" Mitch said, pecking at his computer. He shook his head. "No hits on those models. Got a few Lexuses, Infinitis, upscale SUVs, Caddys. All gone in the same week you're talking about."

Another dead end. Harry said, "Word is the Hooleys were on the receiving end. That do anything?"

"All that means is efficiency. The Hooleys only take high-end and keep it in hand for less time than it takes most people to sneeze."

"We're sure the cars came from town," Harry said.

Mitch nodded. "A few ways it could happen. Your thief got them from a stash of previously stolen vehicles, from a place where they're stored and not yet missed, or from long-term parking at an airport, and no one knows they're gone yet. I'll stay in touch, guys."

We headed upstairs. Harry stopped to pull a drink from the water cooler and I headed to my desk. There were just a few detectives in attendance. Roy Trent was on the phone asking someone about credit card purchases, following a trail. Larry Barnes sat at his desk with fluorescent pink diver's plugs in his ears, staring at the ceiling and squeezing a tennis ball, his deep-thought mode.

I passed the Logan–Shuttles cube. Logan was at his desk, Shuttles behind him, looking down at Logan's desk. They were studying an 8 x 10 photo. I couldn't make out the subject.

Logan said, "She don't look sexy, but she looks hot, don't she, Tyree?"

"Jesus, Pace," Shuttles said. "That's sick."

"Keep you warm on a cold night, I'll bet. Smokin'!" Logan laughed, a wet gurgle.

I poked my head over the divider.

"What's up, guys?"

Shuttles shook his head. "Pace is losing it."

"Have you seen our latest case, Ryder?" Logan grinned. "Take a look, it's my dear old mummy."

He held up the photo. It was a charred corpse, looking mummified, if that's the way you wanted to see things. It was a morgue photo, after the body had been transported.

"The victim from the apartment fire on Corcoran," I said. "I was there when they brought her out."

"You saw the cuffs?" Shuttles asked.

I nodded. "Find anything out?"

Logan interrupted. "We found out she looked better as bread than toast."

He flipped open a file folder, pulled out another photo, spun it my way. A good-looking woman wearing a theatrical pout, net hose, spike heels, a leather G-string and little else. She held a riding crop. A superimposed URL suggested the photo had been pulled from a website. I hope my mouth didn't drop open like a cartoon character, but I think it did.

"I know her," I said, as Harry walked up. He looked at the picture, muttered an expletive, shook his head.

"I know her, too," he said. "Carole Ann Hibney."

"I found out she went by the name of Mistress Sonia," Logan smirked. "You guys clients?"

In less time than a finger snap, Harry was in the cubicle, his hand pulling Logan upward by his shirtfront.

I jumped between them, dodging Logan's hands as he tried to get them around my partner's neck. There was some thumping around, files tumbling from a desk, a chair skittering into the wall, but between Shuttles and me, we separated Harry and Logan.

"You're a head case, Nautilus," Logan snarled over Shuttles's shoulder.

"And you're the world's shittiest detective, Logan," Harry returned over mine. "You got no respect for anything."

"I got no respect for you. You were a decent street cop, but ever since you got the gold you act like Mr Stinkless Shit."

"Shut up, Logan," I said. "Harry and I seem to have some connections with the victim. How about acting like a detective and making your next question along those lines?"

I heard Shuttles whispering to Logan, telling him to sit, relax, it was all over. Across the room I saw Trent look our way with moderate interest, then go back to his calls. Personality clashes weren't unknown in a detectives' room. Larry Barnes was oblivious, squeezing his tennis ball, studying the ceiling tiles.

Harry and Logan shot each other knife eyes until Logan returned to his chair and Harry retreated to the opening of the cubicle.

Shuttles took the lead. "She was a call girl, is what Pace is saying. A dominatrix type. You really know her, Carson?"

"Bad choice of words," I said. "I saw her at a party at the Shrine Temple last Saturday night, a business banquet sponsored by Channel 14. We spoke maybe four words."

I replayed the memory. The woman in the cobalt dress arriving via the kitchen, asking me to get her a drink, then standing beside a column and scoping the room while banging down the liquor. I recalled her practicing a big, bright smile, like preparing to play a role. Then the lights went dark and I lost track of her.

"Who was she with?" Shuttles asked.

"No one. Now that I know her occupation, I think she was sneaking into the party."

Shuttles said, "How about you, Harry? How did you know Ms Hibney?"

"Or Mistress Sonia," Logan said, his standard sneer back in place.

Harry ignored Logan, spoke to Shuttles and me. "I met her about ten years back. Carole Ann was maybe twenty-three, showed up in Mobile after leaving an abusive boyfriend. She was from some hick town in Mississippi. She was basically bright, y'know? But ignorant, a dropout in eighth grade. She landed in the Greyhound station with a black eye and a suitcase."

"Bad news," I said. Pimps and perverts cruised bus stations like sharks, salivating for the Carole Ann Hibneys of the world.

"One guy got his meat hooks into her, pimp named Sleet Bemis. Nicknamed Sleet because he was so slick. He turned her out three weeks later. Bemis beat her, too. Carole Ann and I met in the hospital after one of those beatings. I had a talk with Bemis, who vacated town shortly thereafter. Then I convinced Carole Ann she was bright enough to go back to school, get her GED, maybe go to a JUCO, but . . ."

Harry shook his head.

"But she was lazy," Logan said, clapping his hands and leaning into the conversation. "Right, Nautilus? I seen it a dozen times. Girl grew up in some white-trash trailer park, never saw anyone get up and go to work. When she found out she could make easy money from the old jelly jar, all that studying and school stuff was just too much work."

Harry glared. Logan shrugged, held his hands palms up.

"Am I right here?"

Harry looked away, sighed. "You're right, Logan. She bagged the school bit. Last I'd heard, Carole Ann was in New Orleans. Guess she got washed back here."

"I wonder what she was doing at the Shrine," I said.

Shuttles said, "I remember a case from a class I took –"

"Oh, Jesus, here we go with the class crap," Logan said, rolling his eyes.

Shuttles continued. "There was a ring of prostitutes, good-looking, expensive. They kept hotel workers on their payrolls. The workers told the prostitutes when a convention was coming up, or a corporate wingding. The girls would put on party clothes and show up, spread the good word, so to speak."

"You think that's what happened?" I asked.

"It makes good sense," Shuttles said. "From

what you said about her sneaking in the place."

"Horseshit," Logan said, rolling his chair forward so fast Shuttles had to jump back to keep from getting his toes run over. "Look at the fuckin' picture. The woman was a beater, a fem dom. Tying up johns and whipping them, snapping clothes-pins on their nips, pissing in their mouths while they jerk off. 'Excuse me, Mistress Sonia, could I have some more ginger ale?'"

Logan laughed at his little joke. I heard Harry growl. It was about time to git.

"Your point, Logan?" I asked.

"Beaters don't solicit at conventions. They use the Net these days. That's where we got the picture. Why go door-to-door, so to speak, when you can put up a website with pictures of titties in leather, get the submissive trade beating a path to your door?"

Logan clapped his hands and laughed again; the beating reference, I guess.

I turned to Shuttles. "I'd talk to the kitchen folks at the Shrine, Tyree. See if anyone there knows how she got let in and why."

"There you go, Shuttles," Logan chuckled, clasping his fingers behind his head and leaning back in his chair. "Ryder's figured out your chore for the afternoon."

Harry and I slumped back to our cube to lash together notes on Dinkins and the Hooleys. I started scratching an outline. Harry stared at the ceiling, as though following Barnes's lead.

"Can I get you some earplugs?" I said. "A tennis ball?"

"What? Oh, sorry. I was zoning out."

"You thinking about Carole Ann Hibney?"

He nodded, sadness in his eyes. "She was basically pathetic, Cars. Born lost in the woods and nowhere to go but deeper in the forest. But there was a spark in her, a brightness. In her world, strange as it was, she felt she had things figured out. Logical, in a way. She decided she wasn't going to be whipped on by men anymore, that it was her turn to do the whipping. She'd had a couple johns who wanted it that way, and realized they were the easiest to deal with and paid the most. That's when she came up with the Mistress Sonia act. She once told me she picked her johns carefully, thought she was safe."

"It only takes the one," I said.

CHAPTER 21

Taneesha Franklin's visitation arrived the following Monday morning. Harry and I were going because perps sometimes attended the services of victims, a compulsion seeming to border on the erotic. We'd spent from Friday through Sunday retracing our steps, and hadn't found any place we'd slipped up, but had found nothing new, either. I was hoping a wild-eyed and hairy guy would walk into the services with I DID IT stenciled on his forehead.

The day was clear and bright, the sky a blue mirror. The funeral parlor was large, with a wide front lawn, a large primary and smaller secondary parking lot to the side. The parlor was bordered on both sides by small shops, the nearest a grocery. Knowing Dani would be at the service, I hadn't looked forward to attending, but it was part of my job and my promise to Taneesha. The events with Dani hurt like hell, but every time the sun came up, I was a day further down the road.

We pushed into the shoulder-to-shoulder crowd, perhaps two hundred folks. The service had been earlier, family only. Harry and I studied the crowd from the corners. Lincoln Haley stood across the room, black-suited, his face somber. He saw us and headed our way.

"Gentlemen, thanks for coming."

"It's actually part of the job, Mr Haley. But from what we've learned about Ms Franklin, it's what we'd want to do anyway."

We stood silently for several moments, sharing the uneasiness of grief. A voice came from behind as a male shape moved past my shoulder.

"Mr Haley? You're Lincoln Haley, sir? I recognized you from your photo on WTSJ's website. I'm sorry for the loss. It must be a tremendous blow to everyone at the station."

I turned to see a guy a bit under my height, paunchy, slope-shouldered. He was dressed in dark pants and a dark sport coat. His short hair was the sort of subdued red favored by folks who want to be edgy, but don't have the type of job permitting blue or green. A silver ring protruded from his eyebrow and there was a soft color to his flesh that was probably makeup. He spoke with a slight lisp.

Haley said, "Thank you, sir. Are you a friend of Taneesha?"

"No, I'm sorry to say. I'm more a friend to WTSJ, my favorite station. I've been listening for years. I remember back when Ms Franklin started, the midnight-to-six slot. I always tuned in and listened. I wasn't born until 1981, but I always loved the funk and Motown of the sixties and seventies. Otis, Sly, Mahalia, Aretha, James Brown . . ."

I tuned the conversation out, scanned the crowd while trying to appear nonchalant. I was looking for wild eyes and an aura of menace. Sometimes the crazies walked right into your pocket.

"She had a great voice," the fan was saying to Haley. "It's a terrible loss. I hope someone pays dearly for what they did."

Haley said, "You heard her in the middle of the night? That puts you in a select audience of a few hundred. You still listen, Mr . . .?"

"Lucasian. Jim Lucasian."

The two shook hands. Lucasian turned to me. "Are you a friend or another devoted listener?"

Haley said, "Detective Ryder is with the MPD. He and his partner are here in a surveillance role."

I winced. "Uh, Linc?" I said.

Haley's turn to wince. "Oh, sorry."

Lucasian held up his hand like making a pledge. "Your secret's safe with me, Detective. I hope you nail the SOB." He sauntered off toward the exit.

I excused myself and wandered to a doorway. I turned the corner as Dani was entering the room. We nearly walked into one another. She stood in the threshold. My breath went shallow. Her fingertips touched my arm.

"Please, Carson, can we talk about –"

"There's nothing to say," I croaked.

"I just want to explain."

I wanted to hear the explanation, to know which of us was wrong. I needed to assign blame. Instead, I shook my head, looked away.

"Did you lie about going to bed with Kincannon?" I said, appearing more interested in a nearby lamp than Dani.

"No. But I need you to know that it wasn't –"

I said, "No is all I needed to hear. We've got nothing more to talk about, Ms Danbury. You want to talk to somebody, talk to Buckie-boy."

Her fingers remained on my arm. I shook them loose and turned away. A few minutes later I saw her leave.

Lucas slipped through the tight crowd and out the door. Time to head back to his insecurities firm. Get a nap, surveil the building across the way. He was crossing the funeral parlor lawn when a voice whispered at his shoulder and a hard object rammed his side.

"It's a gun, Lucas. Don't do anything but walk, just like you're doing."

"Hello, Crandell," Lucas said, stopping, keeping his voice steady. "My, but we're stealthy as ever."

"Keep walking, Lucas."

"Keep moving, Luke, and there's no pain. Stop and they break."

Lucas moved as slowly as possible, but keeping one step ahead of disjointed fingers. The man beside him was six feet tall, dressed in a sculptured gray suit. His physique was boxy and muscular, bowed legs imparting a simian quality. The eyes were small obsidian dots, like button eyes in a doll. Like always, Crandell's hair was perfect: waves of curly blond hair flowing from his temples.

Lucas affected nonchalance. "You saw through my disguise, didn't you, Crandell? I'd forgotten how good you were. My height, right? You were looking at everyone six-one, checking closer? You're amazing, Crandell."

"You've scared a lot of people, Lucas. They're terrified that you're out and doing God knows what. They'll be glad to see you and me together again."

"Plus it's a big payday for you, right?"

"I always have a big payday when we meet, Lukie-boy."

"Let's see, Crandell, the last time you and I got together it was four years ago, beneath a microwave tower in a field." Lucas winked.

"You're a sick boy, Lucas. Delusional. Got anger problems, problems with women. You need help."

Lucas looked away. Took a deep breath.

"I'm not going back. You'll have to shoot me here. How will you fix shooting me in a parking lot?"

"You'll be fine, Lucas. You just have to . . . resume your normal routine."

Lucas heard a roar of an engine and a dark

boxy car jumped from the line of cars and pulled in front of him, braking hard. The door swung open. Lucas bent, smiled, looked at the driver.

"Are you in law enforcement, sir? Crandell likes to employ from its ranks."

Crandell said, "Get in or I'll put you in, Luke. It'll hurt for days."

Lucas shot a last look at freedom. Or at life. No one near. *Wait.* Over there, a hundred feet away . . . walking down a line of parked cars like a man deep in thought.

That cop. Detective . . . What the hell was his name?

CHAPTER 22

I stepped outside to check the lot, happily free of the parlor. I find contemporary funerals stunted and artificial, stage-managed by businesspeople hired to mute death's impact. Quiet reservation is the protocol. We lose our words in whispers and walk softly on silencing carpets. If we avoid dissolving into weeping and wailing and honest emotion, we are lauded for *holding up well.*

When I die, I don't want people holding up well, I want folks shivering and shaking and dropping to the ground like an old-time revival meeting. I want floor-rolling, tongue-speaking, moon-ranting. I want poetry spoken, songs sung, hands clapped. I want people who never met me to hold the hands of those who did.

I want truths told, balanced by beautiful lies.

"Detective Ryder!"

I turned to see the red-haired fan of funk who'd been talking with Haley waving in my direction. He stood beside another man, his square build and tight-curled blond hair seeming oddly familiar. Angled to the curb behind them was a dark sedan, Buick maybe. I turned and walked that way, hands in my pockets. There was a bright smile on Funk Fan's face, but the other man's face looked somewhere between fight and flight. When I was a half-dozen steps distant, Funky sashayed sideways.

I said, "Whatcha need, bud?"

The driver of the vehicle laid on the horn, a piercing blast. I grimaced. Funky laughed and backpedaled faster. I looked into the face of the curly-haired man and immediately knew him from somewhere. He recognized me at the same split-second. I saw motion at his waist, the grip of an automatic in his left hand, the hand beneath his jacket. The gun had a pig snout, a suppressor. The hand began to move. The gun emerged.

He's going to shoot you! my mind screamed as the gun arced upward. My weapon was shoulder-holstered under my left arm. Useless. I had one motion: go for his legs. I dove, hands outstretched, saw legs scrabbling away as I rolled, grabbing at air, at nothing. A door slammed, tires screeched. The stink of burned rubber filled the air. No shot was fired.

Then Harry was beside me, kneeling.

"What the hell's going on, Carson?"

"That guy. In the car. He had a gun. With a damn suppressor." The words were in a voice not mine, a trembling voice.

Harry helped me to my feet. My knees wouldn't hold and I sat back down.

"Who the hell was he?"

I spun my head, looking for Funky.

"The other guy, Harry, where'd he go?"

"I didn't see any other guy. I was inside and heard a car horn blare, came out to check. I see you laying on the ground, a blue sedan smoking its tires down the street, a guy pulling the door shut."

"The other guy was a funk fan, talked to Haley earlier. Haley didn't know him. The guy was talking about Taneesha, the station. I was checking cars. Funk Fan yells my name and I see him standing by a hard-looking blond guy. I walk over and the car horn blows, like the driver saying, *Screw it, let's run.* Funky gets a big grin and splits, and I see the other guy's got a suppressed pistol in his hand. I think he was debating whether to crank off a round. I jumped for the gun man, ended up eating grass."

"I didn't see any of that. Just you on the ground and the peeling-out vehicle."

"Funky used me," I said. "I was diversion for his escape."

An older woman walked by on the sidewalk and shot us a nervous glance, a big black guy kneeling beside a slender white guy reclining on the lawn of a funeral parlor. I stood on improving legs. Harry and I followed the path Funky had taken. We turned a corner and saw a pillow in the middle of the sidewalk.

"This Funky," Harry said. "A chubby guy, right?"

"Not any more, obviously."

We returned the way we came, tossed the pillow in the cruiser. It had a cotton case, soft, not a fingerprint surface.

I ran the scene through my head again, came to one conclusion.

"Funky's our boy, Harry. Taneesha's killer. He came in disguise. And he's got someone else after him."

"Could you ID him again if you saw him?"

I shrugged. "It's the gun-toting guy that's bothering me, bro. I knew him. And I'm sure he knew me. Problem is, I got no name, no place. I just know the face from somewhere."

Harry said, "We're never far from a surveillance camera anymore. Whole goddamn world is growing eyes. Let's go see if any were watching."

The parlor had security cams, but not out front. There was a service station a half-block down the street. The chances its security cams saw anything usable from this distance were nil. Still, it had to be verified. We walked down the street toward the station, passing a ten-foot-wide storefront grocery flanking the parlor's lot. Harry grabbed my arm, pointed at the grocery's window.

"Looky there, Carson."

I turned to the window and saw a sign proclaiming, HAM HOCKS $1.89/POUND.

"You're hungry?"

"Look inside. Right up there."

I looked past the sign. Mounted behind the window in a corner was a small security camera pointing out to the street.

"Odd direction for a camera," Harry said. "Let's check it out."

A bell jingled our arrival. Behind the counter a tall and slender black man in a white apron was cutting slices from a wheel of cheese. He shot us a glance. I put him in his late fifties, a touch of gray in his short natural. Another camera behind the counter watched over the twin rows of shelves running back into the store.

Harry flashed his badge over the counter. "You the owner, sir?"

The guy concentrated on slicing. "Naw, I'm the floor show. The owner don't get here for another hour."

Harry waited it out. Finally the guy turned to us, rolled his eyes.

"Hell yes, I'm the owner, Oliver Tapley. Who else gonna be stupid enough to work here?"

"That camera by the window, Mr Tapley. Odd placement."

Tapley showed us his back again and continued sawing cheese.

"Mr Tapley?" Harry prompted.

Two more cheese slices fell. "I talk better when interruptions turn into customers."

Harry pulled his wallet. "Give us two ham and cheese on rye. Hot peppers on both, brown mustard on one."

Tapley lifted a baked ham from the cooler and set it on the counter. "I got two parking spaces out front. Designated just for this store, sign on the pole says so. People run in, get what they need, run out."

Harry said, "But other people use the spots, right?"

Tapley scowled. "Funeral people, mostly. Fifty-six goddamn spaces in the parlor's lot, and where do people park? On the street in front of my store."

"So you keep an eye out front as well as in the store?"

"If they ain't coming in here, I give 'em a cussin' until they move."

"Does the camera out there record?"

Tapley studied the ham like there was something fascinating on its surface. Harry sighed. "I guess we need some drinks, Mr Tapley; a root beer and a Dr Pepper."

Tapley whittled at the ham and assembled sandwiches. He nodded to a monitor beside the register. We had to lean over the counter to see it: a split screen, half showing the store interior, half Tapley's prized parking slots. The cameras were a cheap setup with low image quality, like the lenses were covered with gray cheesecloth. The image didn't extend to the area where the incident happened.

"You shoo anyone out of your spots recently?" Harry asked.

Tapley wrapped paper around the sandwiches, set them on the counter.

"Maybe a half-hour back. A big-ass car pulls into my spot like it pays the rent on this place instead of me. Just sits there like waiting for something. I chased the bastard off."

"Do you recall what kind of car it was?" Harry asked.

"A blue box, Detroit iron, I think; Buick? Olds?"

"You keep the tapes, Mr Tapley?" Harry asked, barely concealing the excitement in his voice. Tapley turned away and pulled a jar of pickles from the case. He inspected it carefully, turning it round and round.

Harry spun to a shelf at his back, grabbed an armload of items at random, threw them beside the register.

"We'll take this stuff, too."

Tapley went to the rear and returned with

a videocassette. He racked the tape to the approximate time frame, handed us the control, then wandered off to fetch items for an elderly woman. I thumbed fast-forward. On the in-store side of the screen, customers came and went in comedic jitters. Outside the spaces stood empty, vehicles blurring by in the traffic lane.

"There," Harry yelled. "Pause it."

I stopped, rewound. Hit play. Empty spaces in front of the store, an occasional car passing. The blue sedan, a Buick, glided in dead center, hogging both spaces. Nothing to see, the Buick's windows opaque with tint.

We held our breaths as the passenger door opened. Curly slid out, finger-brushed his hair back, walked toward the parlor. He was in frame two seconds, one and a half with his hand between the lens and his face. The image was grainy, blurred.

"Way too brief," I said. "But he's so familiar it's agonizing."

We gave Tapley a receipt for the tape, headed outside, me carrying the cassette and sandwiches, Harry lugging a paper bag. He reached into the bag and produced one of the items grabbed haphazardly from the shelf, a purse-size pack of tampons. According to the package they were "Scented For That Springtime Feel!"

"Lawd," was all he could manage.

CHAPTER 23

We fought the traffic to Forensics, out by the campus of University of South Alabama. Hembree was at a meeting, due out in twenty minutes. I told Harry I was heading over to the morgue and he opted to keep company with a half-full box of doughnuts in the Forensic Bureau's employee lounge.

Clair was at her desk, book in hand, her lanyarded reading glasses in place. She hadn't heard me walking the hall, and I watched her read for a few moments: study the page, lick the tip of her china-smooth thumb, lift the edge of a page, turn the page as she moved the book slightly to the left so as to begin reading before the page was fully flat on the left-hand side of the book. Efficient. She even anticipated the wetting process, pink tongue tip slipping out as her thumb lifted.

After a minute of study, I cleared my throat. Stepped to the threshold.

"Hi, Clair. What's got your attention? A tome on bullet wounds? Blowflies?"

Her neck reddened with embarrassment. Grimacing, she held up a tattered paperback romance novel, the cover illustration of a muscular and shirtless man staring into the eyes of a raven-haired woman in Victorian garb, wind-whipped trees in the background, like a typhoon was blowing through. The title was *A Storm of Passion*.

"Clair?" I asked. "Are you studying meteorology?"

She tossed the book to her desk. It fell front cover up. She quickly turned it over.

"Idiot things. My aunt goes through them like candy, then gives them to me. Not to read, Ryder, to pass on. There are a couple women in the office who scoop them up the second I set them in the break room."

"You weren't reading?"

"I picked it up two seconds before you

walked in. Read maybe a half-paragraph. Infantile stuff. Enough chit-chat, my lunch hour's almost over. What do you need?"

"You did a post on the woman burned in the fire, the one with her hands cuffed behind her back?"

"Yes. Why?"

"I was on my way to work that morning, saw the fire, headed over. I was there when she was discovered, took a look at the scene, what was left. It's just a passing interest."

"She was savaged," Clair said. "There's no other way of putting it."

"Explain."

Clair pushed aside *A Storm of Passion*, snapped a sheaf of papers from her desk.

"Here, you know enough medical terminology . . . read about it yourself."

She handed me the preliminary autopsy report. I sat, flicked on the light beside the chair, started reading. After a long three minutes, I handed the report back. My stomach felt like I'd eaten a sack of cockroaches.

"Whoever did that is a sado-sexual terrorist. Someone who despises women. The word sick doesn't even kick it off."

"The flesh was deeply burned, as you noted.

But the insides could still tell part of the story. Especially the damage to the vagina and uterus, what remained, that is."

"All while she was alive?" I asked.

"While I was performing the autopsy I kept praying she'd passed out at some point, missed the worst. What do you think, Carson? You're experienced here."

I sighed and rubbed my forehead with my fingertips. "From what I know, Clair, it's often the agony that keeps the perpetrator torturing the victim. If the victim passes out, the perp loses interest. Her mouth was probably taped so no one could hear."

"Where do monsters like this come from, Carson?" she asked, her voice a whisper. "Can people be born with broken souls?"

"They're not born, Clair. They're made. And in many ways they're barely a step distant from us."

"Now there's an ugly thought. There was torture with the woman in your case, Ryder. The Franklin woman. Think there's a link?"

"Ms Franklin's fingers were broken. It's sad to say, but on a torture index, she got off much lighter than Ms Hibney. Ms Franklin was in her car, Ms Hibney at home. Ms Franklin appeared to be a crime of opportunity, Ms Hibney's death probably involved planning."

"So they're not related."

"Anything's possible in freakland," I said. "Could be our boy liked sticking Taneesha Franklin with a knife and breaking her fingers. He just cranked it up a couple notches with Ms Hibney. Who showed up at her autopsy?"

"Detectives Logan and Shuttles." She frowned. "Detective Shuttles asked interesting questions, sharp. Kid's got a future. Logan did like he always does."

"Which is?"

"Sit in the chair behind me and stare at my ass."

I returned to Forensics. The doughnut box was almost empty. Harry saw my frown.

"A couple techs gobbled them down. I just had one."

I frowned harder. He said, "Two."

I handed him a copy of Carole Ann Hibney's autopsy prelim in an envelope. Her name was on the envelope. Harry looked at me.

I said, "Save it for later. It's not pretty."

He sighed and reached for another doughnut, solace.

Hembree escaped from his meeting ten minutes later and met us in the main section of the lab: white counters, computers, beakers. There were several vials of fluids, some like colored water, the more disturbing ones resembling stew.

Harry held up the cassette. "We were hoping someone could take a look at this, Bree, maybe give us an enhancement."

Hembree grinned. "Had many lucky days, lately, Harry?"

"None. Why?"

"Because today you caught one."

Hembree led us to the computer-oriented part of the Forensics lab, a recent addition. A long counter held monitors, keyboards, various electronic devices. The guy who'd pseudo-shot Hembree a few days back was sitting on a stool at the counter. Up close he was seventyish, thinning gray hair brushed back, age-freckles on his pink face, reading glasses strung from his neck with kite string. His forehead was large and high, his eyes a jolly green. He wore sandals over white socks below his khakis and a silky aloha shirt, electric-pink seahorses galloping through a fluorescent blue sea.

"Thaddeus Claypool, our new digital cowboy," Hembree said.

I stared. I think Harry was too busy admiring the shirt to notice anything else. Claypool laughed, stuck out his hand.

"I know. The manual says all CGs are supposed to be twenty years old."

"CGs?" I asked.

"Computer geeks."

"I didn't mean to imply that your age . . . ah, that is . . ."

"Got my first pocket protector at MIT in 1957, Detective. Worked on direct keyboard input, associated algorithms. Drifted to Bell Labs in the sixties and early seventies. Went to IBM to make some money in the mid-seventies, felt straitjacketed by the culture. Still managed decent work over eight years. Finished out with twelve years of consulting, running between the two poles."

"North and South?" Harry asked, confused.

"Apple and Microsoft."

Hembree said, "Thad's a Mobile native, returned to be with the kids and grandkids. He volunteers with Forensics twelve hours a week. If we had to pay him based on his consultant's salary, we might afford two weeks a year."

Claypool tapped his bulbous forehead, his eyes sparkling. "You don't keep it busy, your big oyster turns to chowder."

I handed him the cassette. "I suppose enhancing a videotape is a pretty boring project?"

"Algorithms," he exalted. "Numbers dancing with numbers, the enhancement program basing choices on statistical probabilities. I made a few tweaks to the software, tricked it out, as the kids say. I love this cop stuff."

He slipped the cassette into a machine, punched buttons on a keyboard. A monitor came to life, the tape displaying the blond man in one of his few visible frames.

"It's like he's built from shadows," I said. "Anything you can do?"

"Let me establish a balance." Claypool caused a bright square to outline the tire of the vehicle, as distinct as fog.

He tapped a few keys, mumbled to himself, tapped a few more. I saw numbers race across the screen. Claypool nodded at the numbers like they carried a pleasing message. He finished with a dramatic flourish on the enter key.

The tire shape shivered and disappeared. Seconds later it returned, so clear I saw tread and the valve stem.

"I think I love you, Mr Claypool," I said. "How about doing that trick with the guy's face?"

"Faces are more difficult," he apologized as the bright square surrounded the smudge of head. "More choices to make, less definition. And it's not a real facial blowup, it's a statistical assessment of what it might be."

Claypool reprised the triumphant press of the enter key.

"Lawd," Harry said, staring at the result.

I scowled at the screen. Though the face was defined, it remained elusive. But I *knew* it from somewhere.

"How about it, Cars?" Harry asked. "Tell me you're making a connection."

"I can't. But it's so close. Like it's on the tip of my brain . . ."

"Did you see him in the BOLOs?" Harry asked. "Maybe he's wanted."

I memorized hundreds of faces on Be On the Look-Out sheets, put together displays of perp photos to show victims, paged endlessly through mug-shot books.

"It doesn't feel right."

"How about I flip the image?" Claypool said. "Give you a different orientation."

Claypool tapped twice on the keyboard. The right-looking face swooshed into a black dot in the center of the screen, swooshed back a second later, now looking to the left.

I closed my eyes and saw the curly-haired blond man. But not on the walk in front of the funeral parlor. Sitting to my right, looking left. A phone to his mouth. Talking through a Plexiglas window to a hulking, scar-headed monster.

"I know where I saw him," I whispered. "He sat beside me the day Leland Harwood exploded."

CHAPTER 24

Warden Frank Malone fiddled with the VCR in the corner of the room. It was VCR day, I guess. Though I was in the office of the prison's head dog, it felt like a cell, bars on the windows, the pervasive stink of fear and disinfectant. We were hundreds of feet from the nearest cell-block, but the smell rolled through the place like smog.

There was no need for both Harry and me to drive up, so I'd made the run, cutting a big chunk out of the day. What this country needs is a good teleportation system.

Malone pressed a remote to activate the unit. He'd racked up the visitors' room tapes from the morning I'd visited. He fast-forwarded until I saw myself enter the visitors' room.

He looked up and I nodded. This was the start point.

I watched myself talk to Harwood for several minutes before the hulking, scarred convict entered, simultaneous with the arrival of the square-bodied, suited man with the blond hair rippling back from his tanned, blocky face. Though a solid guy, he moved like silk in the wind, a dancer inhabiting a bricklayer body.

Malone tapped the monitor screen. "The huge convict is a serial rapist, Tommy Dane Dowell, known inside as Tommy the Bomb, as in you never know when he'll go off."

Tommy the Bomb swaggered in like he not only owned the prison, he held the mortgage on every other piece of property within a hundred miles. I'd seen that look more times than most people.

"Psycho," I said. "Full blown."

"The guy was a biker with the Iron Rangers, got too psychopathic even for them, was cut loose."

"Too crazy for the Rangers? That's like being too tall for the basketball team."

Malone sighed, removed his reading glasses. "I'm the warden, Detective Ryder. I'm supposed to use clinical terms when discussing inmates. I took courses in psychology in order to make my discussions scientific, rational."

"And?"

"Tommy the Bomb's a true melt-down. Three hundred pounds of fried wiring."

"Terms I can understand," I said. "Think he had a hand in Harwood's poisoning?"

"Inmates do favors for folks like Tommy to stay on his good side."

"Good side?" I pulled my chair up to the monitor, tapped the visitor. "You know this man, Warden? He's who I'm really here to ID."

Malone put on his glasses, started the tape segment again. The guy's back was to the camera, mostly. Harwood blathered at me. After five minutes, he started wriggling, punching at his chest. I noticed the blond guy shooting a couple fast glances in Harwood's direction.

Malone froze the tape. "Never seen the visitor before. The guards say the guy's visited the Bomb three times in the past couple weeks." He slid a sheet of paper my way. "Visitors-log entries from the morning of your visit."

I checked the time against the names, found the only fit.

"C. M. Delbert," I said. "He needed ID to get in, right?"

Malone nodded. "Not many people fake their way into prison. We check the ID, but our major concern is contraband and weapons."

"And we both know any teenager in the country can get a fake ID with the right contact and a pocketful of bills."

Malone said, "Guy signed in as counsel for Tommy. You figure him a lawyer?"

"Long shot. At least not Harvard law."

Malone grunted. "Not too many Harvard types want to sit across from a psychotic monster like Tommy the Bomb."

"Think Tommy the Bomb would talk to me, Warden?"

"Think you'll grow tits and a pussy soon?"

"Doubtful," I said.

"Not a chance."

Malone restarted the tape. Two minutes later Harwood was convulsing on the floor as Tommy the Bomb watched. The visitor retreated from the room without looking back, like walking from a public restroom.

Malone dropped his glasses in his pocket. "Your man doesn't look real interested."

"He knows how the story ends," I said.

* * *

When I returned to the department, Harry was in a conference room, the murder book between his arms on the table. He looked up.

"Tell me you found the golden link at the prison, Carson. That you're about to sit your ass right down in front of me and pull it all together."

I sighed and laid out the story.

"He signed in as a lawyer?" Harry said. "Maybe we should check local legal types, see if they can ID him."

I ran a list of lawyers in my head. Only one got highlighted in yellow. "What we need is a lawyer perfectly comfortable with murderers, rapists, dope mules, and general pukes."

Harry said, "I can't go near Preston Walls, Cars. I already ate today."

"Don't sweat it. I can solo."

Harry stood and yanked the orange sport coat from his chair, pulled it over the blue-centric aloha shirt.

"I wouldn't do that to you, partner. Let's stop on the way over and buy a can of Lysol. I want to spray down before we visit Walls."

D. Preston Walls had an office near the courthouse, tavern on one side, bail bondsman on the other. Location, location, location. A

Porsche at the curb was vanity-tagged LGLEGL. I shouted my name into a metal grate and held my badge and ID to a camera before being buzzed inside.

Walls's secretary, receptionist, whatever, was a torpedo-breasted blonde with bee-stung lips, cocaine eyes, and a pair of handcuffs tattooed on a bare shoulder. She purred that we should sit until her boss was off the phone, then sucked a cigarette and stared at my crotch until I crossed my legs.

Ten minutes later Walls appeared, fortyish, five-seven or -eight, overweight, sloppy brown suit, hair in a ponytail like it made him hip. Diamond stud in one ear. At handshake time, Harry turned away and looked out the grated window.

"Carson, Harry, I'm floored," Walls brayed, indifferent to the slight. "Jeez, I haven't seen you guys since Rollie Kreeg's trial. Last year? Has that much time gone by since . . ." He paused, mouth open like something slipped his mind. "I think I'm having a senior moment, guys. What was the verdict? Who won?"

I gritted my teeth. "You did, Walls. A technicality, if I recall."

Walls grinned. "Technicality, schmecknicality . . . it's all the clash of ideas. Of Constitutional guarantees. Of the collective versus the individual, the safety of the rights of private citizens who –"

Harry stared at Walls. "How safe are citizens from the rapists and murderers you get off?"

Walls raised an eyebrow. "If I get them off, Harry, they're innocent."

I stepped between Harry and Walls and slid a photo from my pocket, a still shot pulled from the VCR at the prison.

"How about this lawyerish-looking guy, Preston? You know him?"

If he glanced at the photo, it was a millisecond. He tried to hand it back.

"Look again," I said. "Longer."

Walls took a perfunctory second glance, seemed to be looking past the photo. He frowned.

"What is it, Preston?"

Walls tweezed the photo between his thumb and forefinger, like it was something he didn't feel safe touching. The picture dropped in my hands.

"Never seen him before. Gotta go, guys. Nice talking to you."

He walked us to the lobby and retreated behind his door. I heard it lock.

We returned to the department. Harry started through the doorway, stopped abruptly, threw his arm in front of me and nodded across the room at our cubicle. Pace Logan was sitting at Harry's desk, leafing through papers. Harry moves fast and light when necessary; a second later he was standing behind Logan.

"Help you, Logan?"

"Oh, shit. Nautilus. I was just –"

I jogged up. Logan had Taneesha Franklin's murder book in front of him, opened to the photo section.

"Just what?"

Logan went into defensive mode. "What's it look like? I'm checking the book. I was there, remember? First, if I recall. I got some spare time, thought I'd see how things were developing. That all right with you?"

"You want to look at things, Logan, ask."

Logan stood, showed teeth. He jammed the book into Harry's chest.

"Fuck you, Nautilus. I didn't know you owned the murder books. Guess I forgot to sign it out from King Dick."

I stepped between them before Harry did or said something that was momentarily gratifying but improvident in the longer run. Logan stormed back to his desk, the smell of tobacco in his wake. Harry blew out a long breath and we sat. I had my usual pile of call slips from strung-out snitches trying to peddle fiction, but a name stood out. Mrs Rudolnick had called. The message was, "Nothing important, just checking."

I picked up my phone, called, kicking myself for not alerting her the moment we'd secured the files, good manners.

"How are you, ma'am?"

"I was just wondering, did the key work?"

"Thank you, yes. Your son's files are safe. No one else will ever see them."

"Are the files helpful?"

"We're still reviewing them. It's a big job."

"Just find the person who caused my son's death, sir."

"We will, ma'am. Thanks for checking."

"Certainly. Oh, by the way, sir?"

"Yes?"

"I had some wonderful moments yesterday. A delightful young friend of Bernie's stopped by."

"Who?"

"I don't trust many people, and I know there are all manner of scams directed at people my age, so I asked questions. He knew everything about Bernie: how his left eye fluttered when he got nervous, how he liked puns. Bernie had a very individual way of walking, fast, spinning on his heel to turn around. The young man mimicked Bernie's walk and we both had a good laugh. It was refreshing, the best I'd felt in a long time. He had such wonderful things to say about my son."

"Who was this young man, Mrs Rudolnick?"

"Frank Cloos. He'd worked with Bernie two years back, at the psychiatric wing of Mobile Regional Hospital. Bernie consulted there two days a week. Mr Cloos had been an MHT – mental health technician."

"What did Mr Cloos look like?"

"About your size, I guess. Dark hair. Piercing eyes. A very good-looking young man."

"You said young?"

"Mid-twenties, I'd guess. A mature bearing."

"What else did you talk about?"

A pause. I heard the grandfather clock bonging in the distance.

"That was a sad part. Mr Cloos had been out

of town for a while, business. He didn't know about Bernie. He'd been trying to track him down, couldn't understand why his phone was disconnected. There aren't any other Rudolnicks in the phone directory, so he came here."

"He didn't know Bernie was deceased?"

"It was the one moment I thought I'd made a mistake by letting him inside my house. When I told Mr Cloos what happened, well, he seemed to disappear inside himself. He closed his eyes. His hands grabbed his pant legs, his knuckles turned white. It seemed like, like . . ."

I heard her struggling for words.

"What, Mrs Rudolnick?"

"It was like he was being torn apart inside, ready to cry or scream or throw things. I was scared, but didn't say a word and it passed. Then he took my hand and asked questions. He was so concerned, so nice. I went to fetch some drinks and sweets and that's when we talked about Bernie, the good things, the happy things. We talked for a half-hour. Then he had to go. He said he'd be back next month, we'd go to dinner, talk longer."

"Did this Mr Cloos tell you how to get in touch with him?" I held my breath.

"Only that he'd call. We'd go to dinner

somewhere nice, somewhere Bernie would have liked."

I resisted banging my head on the desk. When we hung up I called Mobile Regional and confirmed what I already knew: there was no record of a Frank Cloos ever having worked there. I called Mrs Rudolnick back, asked if I could send a fingerprint team to her house, pretty much knowing the outcome.

I started for home a few minutes later, stopping by Sally Hargreaves's desk on the way out.

"How's your progress with the rape and beating victim, the blind woman?"

"I'm feeling better about her, Carson. She's tough, a survivor. She has one minor surgery coming up tomorrow, hopefully heads home by mid next week. She's using her hand again, too. It's improving daily."

It stopped me. "What do you mean, using her hand?"

"She had two fingers broken in the attack, another severely dislocated. The doctors were afraid there might be nerve damage, but apparently –"

"You never mentioned the fingers."

Sally gave me a *so-what* look. "They were the least of her injuries."

"Can I meet her, Sal? Talk to her?"

"She's recovering from horror, Carson. I'm not sure she should relive those moments. Why?"

"I've got a dead girl who had broken fingers, torture, probably. Maybe it's the same perp."

"Can you wait a bit? Let my victim get home, return to familiar surroundings, familiar routine?"

"The perp's a psycho. If he's on the road I think he is, there's another woman in his sights right now."

Sal closed her eyes and shook her head.

"Carson . . ."

"We've got no leads, Sal. The guy's a cipher."

Sally frowned. Fumbled through her purse for her phone.

"Let me make a call."

A half-hour later we were sitting beside the bed of Karen Fairchild. She was petite and Caucasian, dark-haired, with a voice still husky from screaming and being choked. Her face was swathed in white bandages tinted pink at the edges with antibiotic cream. Despite her travails, she greeted me without apprehension, and I gathered Sally had both explained the reason for my visit and presented me in a kindly light.

One of Ms Fairchild's hands was contained in a soft brace, the fingers supported. On the other hand, several fingertips were bandaged from nails tearing off as she'd defended herself. No traces of the perp's blood or skin had been found beneath Ms Fairchild's nails, or anywhere on her body, and Forensics had determined Ms Fairchild had been thoroughly bathed before being dropped – literally – at the hospital.

Like the trip to the hospital, the bathing was anomalous, a moment of careful thought and organization in what the victim recalled as a night of psychotic mania in a barn.

"It wasn't a horse or cow barn," she said, answering one of several questions I'd asked. "It was probably an equipment barn."

"You can tell?" I asked.

"It was part of my training at blind school, Detective Ryder. The teachers would bring us samples of dirt from an animal barn, and we'd have to differentiate it from a barn used for storing equipment."

"What's that supposed to teach you?" I asked, amazed.

The white ball of swaths and dressings laughed through the exposed mouth, jiggling the tubes tracking into her arm. I looked at Sal. She held a laugh tucked behind her hand.

"Ouch, my leg," I said.

The pile of bandages smiled through lips still bruised and puffy from stitches.

"Sorry, Detective. I grew up on a farm west of Movella, Mississippi, know a bit about them. I smelled grease, fertilizer, plain old dirt. Hay was around. But I didn't smell any animals nearby. They have a strong odor, even from a distance. The more I think about it, I suspect the barn hadn't been used in a while, years maybe. There was a smell of mold and decay, like the hay was old."

"And you don't know how long you were held at the barn?"

The laugh disappeared. "Time didn't have any meaning that night."

"Do you remember when your fingers were broken?"

"It was very painful. It was when he was . . . on top of me. He had my hand clenched in his. While he was pushing he kept ordering me to say I loved him. I wasn't saying it loud enough, and he kept bending my fingers further and further backward until I was screaming the words. I finally passed out."

"What do you remember about his voice?"

"A loud whisper, like he was hiding his real voice. Even so, it was an incredibly angry voice."

"You woke up at the hospital."

"When I realized I was alive, I was amazed. He kept telling me I was going to die. Laughing as he said it." She turned her head in my direction. "I'm not complaining, Detective Ryder. You're excellent company. But aren't you a homicide detective?"

"My partner and I are also part of a special team, the Psychopathological and Sociopathological Investigative Team. We deal with disturbed minds. I know it's tough to tell us these things, but, trust me, we learn from each story. It adds to our store of knowledge about such criminals."

"Crazy people," the bandages said, sorrow beneath the voice. "Not just a little crazy, but like from another world."

"Yes."

She looked straight at me as if she had perfect vision and her eyes weren't covered in gauze.

"Then you've smelled it, Detective Ryder."

"I'm sorry. I'm not sure what you mean."

"Smelled insanity."

"I never knew you could smell insanity."

Her voice tightened with the memory. "It's a foul, ugly smell. I couldn't smell it at first, when he was just talking to me, pleasant, almost reasonable. Then he started getting angry for no reason. That's when I noticed the smell. It got stronger as he . . . handled his needs. Like smoke getting thicker."

"What's it smell like?" Sal asked, her voice a whisper. "Insanity?"

Karen Fairchild shook her head.

"There aren't any words for it. You have to be there."

CHAPTER 25

Lucas lay on the floor of his office, blinds drawn, absentmindedly watching his new television. He'd also bought a chair and desk at Staples. The TV sat on the desk with the volume low. The blonde woman with the dead eyes and paste-on smile was gesturing at letters. It seemed she'd been gesturing at the stupid letters most of Lucas's life. He wondered what she'd be like to fuck, figured it would be some kind of appliance, like a toaster.

"Bend over, hon, I need to set you on medium dark."

Lucas chuckled to himself and studied the televised puzzle. The answer on the board was a place name. Someone yapped about buying a letter, a consonant. Lights flashed, letters turned. Four words, Lucas mused, letters numbering three, four, five and eight.

NOO OOOO

OOOOO OXOOONOO

Lucas yawned, mumbled, "New York Stock Exchange." The contestant didn't see it, her mouth open like a cow.

"Moronic bitch!" Lucas yelled. "Retard."

He caught himself. Closed his eyes. Saw a man with a button nose and lopsided grin running through a peaceful woods.

Mumbled, "Sorry, Freddy."

Lucas drowsed through the other channels, wishing he had cable, but that took more complete identity. They'd be watching carefully for him to create identity.

Lucas paused on a group of half-naked people shooting flaming arrows at a coconut, a commercial for another television show. He'd seen the show, people with various personality deficiencies dropped in a jungle and trying to out-think another group of the similarly afflicted.

Everything was so stupid. But some of the women were hotties, one in particular, a blonde who wore a leather thong around her neck, like a collar. She always looked wet and sticky, like she was sweating honey.

I'll make you sweat, hon . . .

Lucas masturbated into yesterday's underwear, then stretched out on his sleeping bag, crossing his arms behind his head. He'd gone to a sporting goods store and bought a sleeping bag and an inflatable mattress. If, for some reason, he had to vacate quickly, the bag would be useful beneath a bridge or wherever he would hide.

It couldn't come to that. This was his game and he had to avoid mistakes. Like attending that damn funeral. But there were protocols to be observed. The Ritual of Condolence. The respect due one who has passed away.

He owed her. She was an innocent.

Lucas owed Dr Rudolnick for many things, but not his life. The psychiatrist hadn't blundered into the fire, but made it his choice. Granted, he'd not had much latitude in his choices. That was the way it had always worked.

Lucas felt anger rising from deep in his groin, heating his belly. Felt his jaw clench, hands ball into fists.

"The clouds, Lucas," Rudolnick said from just behind Lucas's ear. *"Let the anger drift away on the clouds."*

Lucas let the calm wash through him for several minutes. He stood and took his position behind his most important purchase, a Celestron C5 with the 1.25 inch, 10mm eyepiece, the best spotter's scope in the sporting goods store, an optical marvel. It was dark in Racine Kincannon's office, the lights off, a silver flask of whiskey on his desk. Lucas cranked the lens to a higher power. Saw a TV monitor on a credenza, a woman giving a guy head. A porn flick, Racine Kincannon at work.

Crandell would be out on the streets, searching. A humiliated Crandell, not a pleasant thought. It might not be good to go out in the day, but Lucas crept down the back steps, got in his car, a simple Subaru Outback, two years old, bought for cash. He would have loved to keep one of the machines delivered to the Hooleys – or another from the fine selection in the Quonset hut – but the Subaru was anonymous. It had dealer tags; two more weeks before they expired.

Lucas drove to a phone on the outside wall of a convenience store, hoping Racine had finished his business. Probably on the underside of his desk.

"Hello, Race, long time no see."

Silence. Lucas smiled and wished he could make some reference to the porn flick.

"How ya doin', Lucas?" Racine finally said, a theatrical drawl in his voice covering his bewilderment. Just like Racine Kincannon, Lucas thought, always playing the good ol' boy that somehow got stuck in a two-thousand-dollar suit.

"I'm fine, Racine. Nice out here."

"Y'know, Lucas, you still got some treatment coming before you should, uh, be out and running around."

Racine pretending Lucas had a bad case of bronchitis. *"Another week of antibiotics and you'll kick that little problem, son."*

"Gee, I don't believe parts of that, Race. The getting-out part especially."

"This is hard on all of us, Lucas. We should talk. Meet somewhere."

"I saw Crandell recently, you know."

The silence told Lucas that Racine hadn't heard of the event at the funeral parlor. Excellent. Crandell didn't boast of his failures, which was helpful to Lucas's plan.

"When was that, Lucas?" Racine said, a lousy rendition of blasé in his voice.

"Within a day, Race. We spoke for a bit. He's

added a couple pounds, cut a couple inches off his hair, changed his cologne to something heavier. But it was the Crandell of old."

Silence. The weight, hair, and cologne information would verify that Lucas had indeed met Crandell. Lucas could almost hear the gears turning in Racine Kincannon's head. Slowly, as if coated with rust, but grinding nonetheless.

Lucas said, "I guess the next question is, Why am I still here? You know Crandell's success rate. I was asking myself that question. You know what I came up with, Racine?"

"I got an idea or two," Racine said, defensive.

No you don't, Race, Lucas thought. *You've never had an idea in your life.*

"What are your ideas, Race?"

"Why don't you tell me yours?" Racine Kincannon suggested. "See if we're on the same page."

Lucas gave it a moment of dramatic pause. "I think I've got you to thank, Racine. I think you maybe came to a realization. You always were the thinker."

Racine was blindsided. The silence again. Lucas said, "Did you hear me, Race? I said, thanks. If you were a part of things, that is."

Finally, Racine Kincannon said, "We really should talk, Lucas. Maybe it doesn't have to be like this. Sometimes things that look good one day don't look so good the next, you got me?"

"A lot of things look different out here, Racine. Maybe Crandell just screwed up. There were people around. But one second his hand is moving me to the car, the next minute I'm walking away. Coincidence, maybe. But if not, thanks, Racine. I'm thinking maybe you know the potency of a good alliance. Of course, the best alliance is where each partner is a specialist, right? Two talented people taking something to new heights."

"You said two partners, Lucas."

"Dos."

"Huh?"

"Nothing. I'll call later."

"Listen, Lucas, how about –"

Lucas hung up the phone. That would do for now. He jumped in the Subaru and drove back to his insecurities business, slow and careful, don't want the police to enter the equation. He sat at the desk and aimed the Celestron at the office building. The worst thing he could see would be a meeting of all the brothers, Crandell included. That would be a disaster.

Instead, he saw Racine Kincannon at his desk, door closed, pouring a drink from his ever-present flask. Lucas cranked the power up a notch and it was like looking into a flattened version of Racine Kincannon's face from three feet away. Lucas saw indecision, which he'd expected, and fear, which he had hoped for. Then, after ten minutes, he saw a touch of a smile, Racine Kincannon grinding his way to a decision.

"Thank you," Lucas whispered to the man upstairs.

CHAPTER 26

A ringing. I could actually see the sound, like a train bearing down on me. Just before being slammed I opened my eyes and grabbed the bedside phone, fumbled it to my face, turned it right-side up.

"Nmh?"

"Carson, it's Clair Peltier."

"Mmph?"

"You're not awake, I take it?"

I stifled a yawn, shook my head. "What time is it?"

"Six-twenty. Since you're obviously not at work, how about you stop by the morgue on your way in? I've dredged up some interesting information. Bring Harry, too."

I blinked at the clock on the opposite bedside table as it blinked from 6.20 to 6.21.

"Answer me one question, Clair. When do you sleep?"

"I'll sleep when I'm dead, Ryder. See you in a few."

Harry and I walked into the morgue at half past seven, me jamming my shirttails into my pants, Harry in a sky-blue blazer and plum shirt, yellow pants anchoring the ensemble. Muted for the morgue.

Clair walked us to her office.

"It was four years ago. I didn't do the post, Daugherty did. I was out of town, too, a symposium on temperature and humidity's effect on epidermal degradation. Pretty good presentation."

"Were you lead presenter?" I asked.

She smiled.

I asked, "What made you recall the victim, Clair?"

She tented slender fingers beneath full pink lips. "You, in a way. Talking about Carole Ann Hibney, the woman from the fire, got me thinking about torture. I recalled a conversation with Daugherty about broken fingers, checked with him. Bingo."

We drew chairs before her desk. Clair opened a report, pulled some photographs from the file, slid them across the desk. Harry grabbed a half-dozen, I picked up the rest. Autopsy photos, a visual record of visible wounds. There were plenty of photos, but there was much to record.

"The damage looks damn familiar," Harry said.

"Name's Frederika Holtkamp," Clair said. "The body was found by hunters in a shack up by Nenemoosha, at the edge of the Delta. Sixty-three years old. A retired teacher. Unmarried. Lived alone. No narcotics in the blood."

"Look at her hands, Cars," Harry said, handing me two of his photos.

"Broken digits, like with Franklin," Clair said. "Nearly identical wounds and slashes, including the neck wounds."

"When did you say this happened?" I asked, shuffling through the pictures.

"Four years ago."

"The vic's name again?" Harry asked. Clair spelled it out. Harry excused himself, pulled his cell, stepped to the hall to start gathering information.

Harry reappeared a minute later, dropping his phone into his pocket.

"It was a county case with help from the state boys. Unsolved. Never had a suspect."

It was time to move toward Nenemoosha. We thanked Clair for her vigilance. Harry said he'd meet me in the lobby and headed to the restroom. I slipped on my jacket.

"Tough one?" Clair asked.

"Lots of tentacles but no octopus."

Her face softened into concern. She touched my arm. Her fingertips felt warm and dry.

"You feeling all right, Carson?"

"Sure."

"Not coming down with anything?"

"I, ah . . . it's personal stuff, Clair. Nothing major."

I turned away but felt her gaze, as if the intense blue of her eyes had weight and volume. Words welled unbidden from my throat, burst across my lips. "My girlfriend and I are having big problems, Clair. I found out she's seeing another man."

Clair made a sound of sympathy and shook her head. She stepped forward and I found myself wrapped in her arms. Her hands were tight on my back and her breasts pressed warmth into my belly. I felt the beating of her heart. Her hair smelled like sunlight on peaches.

She leaned back and our eyes stared into each other's. They always left me breathless, and now was no exception.

"I'm sorry, Clair. It's my business. I shouldn't have . . ."

"Don't apologize. I'm glad you told me."

"It's been a weird few days."

"Do you want her to return, Carson?"

"I have a feeling I'm noncompetitive. The guy she's seeing has money out his wazoo and looks like Adonis's *GQ* brother."

She brushed hair from my eyes with her palm.

"I worry about you, Carson. Please take care of yourself."

I don't know why, but I kissed her temple. I turned away and stumbled down the hall like a drunk.

Harry had called the County Sheriff's Office to ask about the Frederika Holtkamp case, and was given Sergeant Cade Barlow. Surly on the phone, Barlow was worse in person, treating us like we'd urinated in his shoes.

"The State boys took the case over. You want to know more, ask them."

Barlow stood in the entrance to his office,

no invitation inside. He was a tall, bone-knuckled guy in his early fifties, weather-beaten, bags under crinkle-corner eyes. The broken veins of a serious drinker threaded his nose and cheeks. His teeth were horsy and yellow.

Harry said, "We'd like to see where it happened, the scene."

"It's a distance."

Harry nodded toward the sheriff's office.

"You want me to ask your supervisor if you can take a field trip?"

Barlow stomped toward the door. "Christ. Let's git this bullshit done so I can git back to work."

We followed Barlow for several miles, cut down a tight dirt lane more cow path than road, the Crown Vic bottoming out as we pitched over ruts for a mile or more. Barlow was driving a high-sprung SUV. He stopped near the edge of a sprawling woods.

"This isn't my usual routine," he said. "Babysitting people wantin' to see an ancient crime scene."

Harry stared evenly into Barlow's eyes. "Four years isn't ancient. It's yesterday. And last I recall, there's no statute of limitations on murder."

Barlow grunted and led us to a clearing.

Centering it was a stew of scorched timbers, twisted roofing metal, heat-shattered brick.

"Here's where her body was found."

"I thought it was in a shack," I said.

"Guess it burned down."

I heard my teeth grinding and looked into the distance. Jutting above trees a hundred yards away was a tall microwave tower, a white light strobing at its tip.

"Who was she?" I asked. "The victim."

Barlow cleared his throat, spat. "State cops have that stuff. Teacher. Retired."

"Age?"

Barlow flicked something from his gray teeth, shrugged. "Sixty-something."

"Who was lead on the case, Sergeant Barlow?"

"Some kid was putterin' in it. He ain't here no more."

"This puttering kid was abducted by aliens?" Harry asked. "Fall down a sink hole? Drown in his grits?"

"Moved to Montgomery." Barlow grunted, spat, walked away. He climbed in his cruiser. Harry walked over.

"You always this helpful, Barlow? Or you just being nice to fellow law enforcement?"

Barlow hawked deep, started to spit toward Harry, thought better of it. He swallowed.

"I got four more months to pretend I give a shit. Then I'm retired. You get out the same way you come in."

Barlow drove away in the opposite direction, cutting through a road in the trees.

"Why'd he go that way?" Harry asked.

"I think I know. Follow his tracks."

We aimed our front bumper at Barlow's rear one. A couple hundred feet later we came to a paved road. Barlow's vehicle disappeared in the distance.

I said, "He brought us in a mile across the fields just to bang us around for the hell of it. A local custom, you think?"

"Hick asshole," Harry muttered.

We put Barlow in our Unpleasant Memories file and headed to the local state police post. Luckily, we knew our contact here, Arn Norlin, a pro with twenty-plus years in grade. We called ahead with an outline of what we wanted to talk about. He was ready fifteen minutes later.

Arn looked like a Viking who'd traded the horned helmet for a trooper's Stetson. He had a ruddy face, strong Nordic nose, wide forehead, eyes of diluted blue. His hands were thick and hard, like he'd rowed between Denmark and Iceland. Those same hands painted the most expressive watercolor seascapes I'd ever seen and I was honored to have one of Arn's works in my living room.

"We have part of a file. I think the cold-case folks look at it now and then, scratch their heads, move on to more fertile ground. I'd love to say we've got it front-burnered, but . . ."

"Manpower," I said.

"Every politician talks about putting more feet on the beat, but come budget time, we're hidden in the basement like a crazy aunt."

"Part of a file, you said?"

He shot me a look over tortoiseshell reading glasses. "Pieces disappeared. Misplaced, supposedly."

"When?"

"In the hands of the county folks. Barlow didn't tell you, I take it?"

"A slight omission," Harry said.

Arn leaned back in his chair, laced his fingers behind his head. "I had hopes for a solve on the county side, kept out of it. It was a Pettigrew case."

"Pettigrew?" I said.

"Ben Pettigrew. A young guy, only on the

county force a couple years. Pettigrew was a hot dog, the good kind, bright, curious. It was his first gut-wrencher case, knifeplay, torture. Pettigrew took the case to heart. Went at it with hammer and tongs."

"Good for him," Harry said.

"First thing Pettigrew did was grid the whole area. He was crawling on the ground, pushing through sticker bushes. You see the microwave tower near the scene?"

I nodded.

"Pettigrew climbed the damn thing to get a better lay of the land. He saw where a car had been hidden away and also felt someone had been laying in the weeds at the base of the tower."

"Barlow mentioned Pettigrew moved to Montgomery."

"Got recruited by the city cops up there. Good for a bright, hard-charging guy like Pettigrew to get on with a big-city force. Good for Montgomery to have a guy like that. Bad for the county."

"Because it lost a hotshot?"

"Bet you money if he'd stayed, he'd have nailed the killer by now. That boy was a pit bull."

"Wish Pettigrew was still around," Harry said. "We couldn't get squat from Barlow. The guy treated us like we had airborne syphilis."

Arn picked up a couple of paper clips, linking and unlinking them.

"I don't know what happened there. Barlow used to be a pretty decent cop. A few years back, he suddenly got old and cranky. It was like someone he loved died and he never came back from it. But I didn't catch news of anything like that."

"Years back?" Harry asked. "Like four?"

Arn dropped the clips to the deskpad and brushed them aside. "That'd be about right. Maybe a bit less. How'd you know?"

"It's a time span we're hearing more and more."

Montgomery Police Department detective Benjamin T. Pettigrew leaned back in his chair and set tooled alligator boots on the meeting-room table.

"It was grim," Pettigrew said. "The victim was crumpled inside the little hunter's shack, over two dozen knife wounds."

Even at a steady twenty mph above the limit it had been a two-hour trip to Montgomery, and one we probably didn't need to make. But between the lost files and the burned-out shack and Arn Norlin's description of Pettigrew, we felt it best to cover all bases. And face time beat the hell out of phone calls.

"Fingers broken?" I asked.

He wiggled the appropriate digits. Pettigrew was in his late twenties, sandy hair and a light complexion. He wore a threadbare cotton jacket over jeans, a beaded leather belt. He looked relaxed but his eyes were fully engaged.

"Arn Norlin says you scoped out the scene down to individual blades of grass," Harry said.

"Norlin exaggerates. I did what little I could."

"You really climbed the microwave tower?"

"Wanted to get a bird's-eye view of the field and woods. I did find something interesting at the base of the tower. The grass and weeds had been crushed down. I found blood on the grass, bagged it for Forensics. It DNA'd out as Frederika Holtkamp's blood. The victim."

"A teacher was what Barlow said."

"Special education. Taught retarded and autistic kids. Retired. Seemed to be getting on all right, real nice house, good car. She had more money than most retired teachers I've seen. But we never found out much more. We don't even know where or how she got taken. It was so slick it was scary."

"You mentioned blood around the tower. But the shack was a football field's distance away. How you figure her blood got there?"

"I thought maybe she'd broke loose from the perp, ran to the tower scattering blood from her wounds. But Forensics said it wasn't spatter but soaking. Like a bloody rag left on the weeds. Or clothes."

"The perp rested there, maybe," Harry suggested. "Soaked with blood."

Pettigrew sat forward, picked up a pencil and tumbled it through his fingers.

"I grew up hunting with my daddy and uncle. Deer, wild hogs, anything. Got OK at tracking. A lot of it's looking for subtle indicators."

"Talk *subtle* to me," Harry said.

"I was up in the tower, fifty, sixty feet. It was half past eight in the morning. Ms Holtkamp had been found an hour earlier by two old farmers out squirreling before chores. Sunlight was at a sharp angle and dew hadn't cooked off yet. I saw several trails in the weeds, the dew knocked off, the tiniest shift in color. A camera wouldn't pick it up. The trails met at the base of the tower."

"Arn Norlin said you found evidence of a vehicle."

"Definite tire impressions in the grass, busted-off branches probably used to cover the vehicle." He paused. "There was one thing about the car that never made sense to me."

Harry said, "That being?"

"Tire impressions where it had been driven back into the trees, fifty, sixty feet off the road. There was another set where it backed out. The tread picked up dirt, got faint where the vehicle pulled onto the road, but still discernible. Then the tracks stopped dead."

"Vanished?" Harry said, narrowing an eye.

"Like the car pulled onto the asphalt and disappeared. Never figured it out. Sucked into a Martian spaceship?"

He chuckled at the example, but I could see it still bugged him.

"Your take on the whole scene?" I asked.

Pettigrew put his arms on the table and leaned forward. He spoke near a whisper.

"You guys are the PSIT down in Mobile, right? The guys that get the crazies?"

"It's a part-time gig," I said. "Like twice a year."

"Ever do any conjectures that get a bit out of the box?"

I nodded. "Even when we're wrong, it's the right way to think. Everything's a possibility."

Pettigrew leaned forward and lowered his voice. "My conjecture: the perp brought the victim to the shack, made his kill. He wandered from the scene to the tower – tired? High on something and disoriented? I'll never know. But someone else showed up. More than one someone, I'm thinking."

"Keep going."

"I think someone else caught up with the killer at the base of the tower."

"Who?" Harry asked.

Pettigrew grunted, slapped the table. "No idea. None. Not a damn one."

"What about the car?"

"Two choices: either it belonged to the perp, or his pursuers. I'd think the perp, since it was hidden."

I'd been tumbling a thought through the back of my mind since Pettigrew mentioned the lost tire tracks.

"If the car got hauled away instead of driven away, it might explain the missing tracks."

"I like that," Pettigrew said, narrowing an eye, like squinting across four years. "I like it a lot. Wish I'd considered it then."

"What did Cade Barlow think?" Harry asked.

Pettigrew's nose wrinkled like someone had opened a garbage can under it. "What do you know about Barlow?"

"That he ain't much interested in a murder that took place in his jurisdiction four years back."

I'd seen how Ben Pettigrew looked when he was uncertain. Now I got to see what he looked like angry.

"Barlow should have been trying to get out ahead of me on the case, steal my thunder. It's how he was, a scene-stealer and credit-grabber. I didn't mind, the competition kept me sharp. But on the Holtkamp murder, he threw roadblocks in my way, ridiculed my ideas. I floated my thoughts on the trails in the grass, Barlow rolling his eyes, comparing it to crop circles, asking if I thought extraterrestrials killed the woman. He had higher-ups laughing at my ideas."

"Think he had something to do with the missing case materials?" I asked.

Pettigrew instinctively glanced through the meeting-room window into the squad room, making sure we weren't being eavesdropped.

"I wouldn't be surprised."

I had a sudden thought, one of those errant connections. "You ever see Barlow talking to a guy, square-built, hard-looking, six-one or -two, blond curly hair? Looks kinda like Jerry Lee Lewis if he pumped iron instead of playing piano."

Pettigrew pursed his lips, thought. "Got a photo?"

"I can fax you one."

"Do that, may spark something."

We stood, shook hands, thanked Pettigrew for his time.

"That case sits hard in my craw," he said. "It was tough to leave in the middle."

Harry said, "Arn mentioned you got hired by the Montgomery force. Recruited."

"They needed patrol personnel, had a grant for adding cops, got my name somewhere. Hired me the day of my interview. Got the gold two years later."

"They came looking for you?" Harry said. "Big compliment. I'm impressed."

Pettigrew reddened; for a split second I saw a shy country boy.

"Aw hell, they were just beating the bushes for small-town cops looking for the big-city experience, guys that wouldn't need a lot of training." He shrugged. "I hated leaving cases hanging, but the Montgomery department needed me fast. It was basically jump right then or spend my days dealing with Cade Barlow. I jumped."

CHAPTER 27

We were fifteen minutes above Mobile on I-65. I was lying in the back, trying to make sense of the last two weeks. I felt someone had set a basketball-size tangle of thread before me and said, "Untangle it, but don't use your hands."

The phone rang in my jacket. I spoke, hung up, looked at the back of Harry's head.

"It's your favorite lawyer. Walls wants to talk."

Harry wrinkled his nose. "The scumbucket say what he wanted? He always wants something."

Walls met us at the door, pointed us to his office. Harry pulled out his bandana handkerchief and dusted off the chair before he sat. Walls pretended not to notice.

"Something came to me," Walls said, sitting behind his desk and pinching lint from his shiny silk suit. "The picture of the blond guy. See, I was in my office late last night, working on a client's case, guy named Tony Binker, Tony the Bee . . ."

"Oh shit," Harry moaned.

"Tony's not a bad guy, just a kid who got trapped in the wrong crowd . . ."

Harry said, "Tony the Bee runs a drug gang, Walls. He makes wrong crowds."

". . . when it occurred to me you guys were the investigating officers on Tony's little event. While I was trying to place the guy in the picture, it also occurred to me that you guys could make a positive recommendation to the Prosecutor's Office about Tony. Lighten things up if he goes down."

Harry smoldered. Walls licked his forefinger, scratched something from the lapel of his suit. He rolled whatever it was into a ball and flicked it away.

"In many ways I'm like a social worker, y'know? Giving my life to disadvantaged human beings who take a wrong road. Folk needing a modicum of rehabilitation, probably not half as much as the state deems necessary . . ."

I shot a look at Harry. Disgust blanketed his face. Still, he nodded his head, *Do it.*

I said, "All right, Walls. We'll do what we can with the prosecution side. No promises."

"Harry?" Walls said. "Is that your thinking?"

Harry's lips twitched with the words he wanted to say, finally coming out as, "Yeah, Walls. I'll back it up. See if they can shave a bit. It's the least I can do for such a fine social worker."

Walls beamed. "You boys are aces." He reached out to shake hands on the agreement.

"Your turn," I said, ignoring his hand and holding up the photo. Walls blocked it with his fingers, like he didn't want it in his field of vision.

"First off, Harry, Carson, you never heard any of this from me."

Harry grunted. "We don't take ads out in the *Register* saying where we get our information."

"I'm in deep water here, guys. I don't need to look up and see a shark coming my way."

"This guy's a shark?"

Walls went to his door, looked into the lobby as if expecting an eavesdropper under the carpet. He closed the door, snapped the lock, sat back down.

"He's a king-hell shark. A shark for sharks. Name he usually goes by is Crandell. He's a fix-it man, problem-solver. But this shark doesn't swim at the bottom of the barrel. He swims way up high. Unions, though maybe not lately. Oil companies. Brokerage houses. Big shiny places like Enron."

Harry was dubious. "He kills for them?"

"If it came to that, sure, he'd probably love it, be happy for the chance. But at Crandell's level, killing is a last resort. Too messy, and someone in the hierarchy has to point a finger and say *go*. I imagine Mr Crandell spends most of his time returning lost items to where they belong. Missing art. Misappropriated stocks. Wayward spouses."

"How do I know you're not making this up?" Harry said. "A crock to knock a couple years off your boy's drop."

"I started in a big practice – Barton, Turnbull and Pryce. This was a dozen years back. White-shoe firm, guys who talcumed their fingers to make the tip of their nails whiter. We had a big-ass corporate client. The wife of one of the directors ran off. Wifey was telling tales on the guy, that he was a wacko, sick. It didn't reflect well on the corporation. Plus the lady'd appropriated a fat pile of bearer bonds to finance her new life."

I said, "I can see where that might be embarrassing."

"Legal action was a spotlight no one wanted. Someone in the firm had heard of Crandell, called him. Crandell looked like a successful businessman, a guy who'd started on the loading dock, now ran the firm. Bright smile, intelligent vocabulary, boardroom clothes. See, dealing with a guy like that, your standard white-collar types need to feel they're passing the job over to another businessperson, like, 'Here's a problem in marketing, deal with it.'"

"Just don't tell us how."

"It's business: results are everything. Anyway, I met Crandell, not knowing what he was or did. Most people couldn't tell, but I could."

"How?" Harry asked.

"His eyes. If he looked at you steady, you couldn't see anything off. But now and then I could see rabies sloshing around, like it was pooling behind his pupils. Does that make any sense?"

Yeah, I thought, *if you've ever spent much time around psychos and socios.* Many appeared as innocent as Salvation Army bell-ringers. But turn your back and they'd bite your spine in half.

"What happened?" I asked. "To the problem."

"It all went away. Wifey stopped telling tales, the stack of bonds wandered home, a bit lighter. Happened fast, too. That's all I know."

Harry stared at Walls.

"So what's your bottom line on having Crandell in our midst?"

The lawyer tightened his tie, smoothed down the front of his jacket. I saw the talcum beneath his nails.

"Someone around here's got a problem, Harry. A big one."

We got back to our desks at five. We drew straws – broken pencils, actually. Harry lost and had to run to the Prosecutor's Office to see what he could do about Walls's request.

I grabbed a cup of coffee that tasted like fried paste, sat at my desk and tried to encapsulate the day into computerized notes, e-paperwork: who, what, where. It was a creative exercise to write case notes making us seem smarter and more in charge than two guys jerked back and forth across Mobile County by indecipherable events spanning four years.

A half-hour later I dropped my head to my hands and massaged my temples. I didn't want to head home, didn't want to stay at my desk.

"Beer," said something in my head, and I was forced to obey.

I pushed through Flanagan's door, took the window table beneath the neon sign that hummed. Harry and I always joked that it didn't know the words. The place was almost empty, heavy traffic not due for another couple hours. The juke was silent, praise be. Though there was one song on the box that blew me away, a haunting old piece called "Wayward Wind" by Gogie Grant. Me and a retired sergeant from Records were the only ones who ever played it; he'd get tears in his eyes. I'd get melancholy, too, but the sweet kind. I have no idea why. I'd drop a quarter, play the song, and Harry'd look at me like I was crazy.

I scanned the bar, a few desultory drinkers, one staring at me, a slender, broad-shouldered black guy, young, thoughtful eyes in a café-au-lait face.

Tyree Shuttles.

After a moment's hesitation, he ambled over.

Shuttles had been a detective for four or five months and still looked uncomfortable in plainclothes, absent-mindedly tapping the service belt he no longer wore, the street cop's life-support system: weapon, baton, cuffs, ammunition, radio, pepper spray – twenty pounds of tools for every occasion. I'd worn what some guys called the "Bat Belt", after Batman, for three years. Sometimes in the morning when dressing, my head thick with sleep, I still reached for the damn thing.

Shuttles pulled up a chair and we small-talked cases and street monsters and the revolving-door system, standard cop time-passers. Shuttles was kind of a tech-head, telling me about new gadgets and gizmos in law enforcement.

After a few minutes I asked how things were going with the Carole Ann Hibney case, figuring I'd pass the news on to Harry.

Shuttles looked away. "It's OK. Not much breaking, but we've got some leads."

"Leads like?"

"Cellphone records for one. Regular johns. We're going through them."

"*We're* going through them, like you and Logan?"

"Well, mainly me," Shuttles admitted. "The tough part's the interrogations, like you'd expect."

"Been there. You show up at a house and the john opens the door, with wife, three kids, and the family dog right behind him."

Shuttles started laughing.

"What is it, Tyree?"

"I got a guy aside from his girlfriend, asked where he was on the night in question. He said – and I swear I'm not making this up – 'I think I was tied up that night, Detective.'"

I started laughing, and we traded a few other funny cop stories. I had five more years in the department, so I had more stories, plus the time to develop them, get the timing right.

Twice when a lull arose in the patter, Shuttles started to say something, seemed to think better of it, looked out the window. He finished his beer, said it was laundry night and he had to go shovel quarters into machines. He tried to argue me out of the tab, lost. We knocked knuckles and he drifted out the door.

I looked at his back as he left, wondering what he had been trying to say.

My cell rang as I stood to leave a few minutes later, thinking I'd follow Shuttles's lead, go home and do mindless tasks until I fell asleep. I checked the number on the incoming call.

It was Clair, her cell, not the morgue.

"Hi, Clair. I was going to call you in the morning. Your lead on the victim from four years back looks tied to today."

"I hope it helps. You at home? Work?"

"Flanagan's, about to head home."

"I'm finishing up at the morgue," she said. "Got a few minutes?"

"Want me to call Harry, see if he's available?"

"Just you, please."

"I'll be right over."

I rang the after-hours bell, was let in by a security guard. It was quiet as, well, death, a lone janitor running a mop at the far end of the hall. Clair was at her desk catching up on paperwork. She gestured for me to sit, dropped her lanyarded reading glasses. She brushed aside a lock of black hair and sipped from a cup of hot tea, Earl Grey, judging by the scent of bergamot. Her eyes stared at me through wisps of steam. For a microsecond I felt whatever slender bond held us, a rustling of molecules in the air.

"I've been worried about something, Carson. Debating with myself whether or not to . . . It's never been my inclination to poke into people's private lives."

She picked up a paperweight, a dandelion trapped in a glassy half-round, moving it from one side of her desk to the other with nervous hands, a rarity for Clair. She cleared her throat, took a sip of tea.

"A few days back, after the Channel 14 soirée, you asked about a certain family."

I suddenly felt an odd dread. "The Kincannons."

"Yesterday you mentioned you'd split with your girlfriend, making reference to her taking up with another man, handsome and wealthy."

"The guy's got everything," I said. "And a spare everything in the trunk."

"Is it one of the Kincannon brothers, Carson?"

"Buck," I admitted.

"Close the door, please."

I complied, returned to my seat.

"Do you know much about them?" she asked. "The Kincannons?"

"Until I spoke to you all I knew was the name. I've seen it on some plaques down at the Police Academy. But something came to light: Harry worked with Buck Kincannon and the K-clan foundation a few years back, building a little ball field for underprivileged kids. Then the Kincannons wanted favors in return. Big ones. They thought they could buy people's integrity. They were dead wrong in this instance. But the kids lost their field, teams, everything."

"Not unprecedented," Clair said. "Unfortunately."

"You'd know because the Kincannons were part of your old blue-blood crowd, right? The two hundred or four hundred or whatever constitutes the social register?"

Clair tented her long white fingers, poised her chin at the apex.

"Lesson time, Carson. There's a social order in Mobile, of course. Old money at the core, old names. If it weren't for many of those folks, the symphony, museums, all manner of cultural events would suffer. Many are honorable people, generous with time and money, others are insufferable prigs."

"The latter being the Kincannons?"

"They're not part of this group, *sassiety* types, as Harry calls them. Behind their façade, the

Kincannons are coarse and crude. Pariahs. True society types go out of their way to avoid them."

"I saw all manner of folks squirming after the Kincannons at the party, Clair. I didn't see much avoidance."

"You saw politicians and sycophants, Carson. Old-line Mobile families wouldn't invite the Kincannons to a weenie roast – not that they have them. That may even be a part of the problem."

"Not having weenie roasts?"

"The Kincannons are shunned. In a coldly civil way, but ostracized nonetheless. It's made them insular, self-absorbed. They pass out money hoping it will buy respect and acceptance, but they're so heavy-handed and self-serving it only makes the insiders loathe them more. The public, of course, sees none of this."

"Negative publicity isn't big with these folks."

"The family employs the biggest PR agency in the state, the toniest law firm in town, the caterer du jour does all their events, a photographer documents their every turn . . ."

I held up my hand. "I don't care for the clan. But I have a hard time picturing them being as malicious as you're implying."

"The Kincannons have been playing at being

benevolent and likeable for so long that they may even believe that story themselves. They abide social and legal compacts for the most part. Until something threatens their world. Then you see the dark side of their souls, the broken side. You never want to deal with that side."

"You're saying they can be dangerous?"

"When threatened. Or denied something they want."

"Clair, they're just rich, selfish shits. Maybe you're making too much of their power to –"

"Shhhh. Listen to me. This girlfriend. Do you still care for her?"

"I'm having a hard time telling her, but . . . I think so."

A strange moment of sadness or resignation crossed Clair's face. "Warn her away from Buck Kincannon, Carson. From all the Kincannons."

I sighed. "I'll do what I can, Clair."

She studied me for a few seconds, then turned away. I pushed to my feet and walked toward the door. At the threshold, I turned, remembering the other day, wanting to thank Clair for holding me in my moment of desolation.

Her back was turned to me. She was looking

out the window. I saw the reflection of her face against the night, like a white moon in a sky as lonely as a Hank Williams song. I started to speak but my heart jumped in the way.

CHAPTER 28

The next day, Wednesday, was a day off rotation. I'd arisen at eight, late for me, and spent an hour in the kayak, cutting hard through a low surf. I'd followed the kayaking with a three-mile beach run. I had to force myself to sit at the dining-room table and do a brief stint with Rudolnick's papers. I'd put in a boring fifteen minutes when Harry called.

"I'm thinking about running over to the Mississippi line, Carson, that little bass lake over there. You in?"

I'd given a lot of thought to Clair's warnings. I wasn't convinced Dani was in true personal danger unless rising so high and fast in the Clarity chain gave her a nosebleed. Still, Clair was not given to cry-wolfing, and I figured

I could combine some lax time with some learn time.

"Thanks anyway, bro. I'm thinking about just getting out and driving. Maybe in the country. Roll down the windows and let the air blow my head clear, at least for a while."

I heard suspicion in Harry's voice. "Where in the country? Not up by where Ms Holtkamp was killed?"

"That was northeast," I corrected. "I'm thinking more to the northwest side. Farm country."

"You being straight?"

"What? You don't trust me to simply take a drive?"

Harry grunted and hung up.

Farmland lay as far as the eye could see, melons and cotton and groves of pecan trees. I passed piney woods, trees rising straight as arrows pointed at the heart of the sky. The green smell of pine perfumed the heated air.

Then the landscape changed, the woods at my shoulder becoming meadow wrapped with whitewashed plank fences, the land studded with water oak and sycamore, here and there a slash pine looming like a spire. The land seemed cool with shade.

I had once passed through central Kentucky, the horse farms east of Paris and Cynthiana, where fences stretched to the horizon and thoroughbreds grazed in the lime-rich bluegrass. Only here in north Mobile County the champions were cattle, Brahmas, with minotaur-heavy shoulders and gray hides as sleek as seal pelts.

Kincannon raised prize Brahmas. I figured I was close.

I passed the hub of the husbandry operation, a half-dozen barnlike outbuildings, open doors revealing tractors and livestock trailers. There was a vehicle carrier with a small Bobcat-type dozer on its bed. I saw a feed silo, pens, food and water stations.

I drove on, crossing a rise. Below was a stone arch like a segment of Roman aqueduct, a massive iron *K* affixed to the keystone. A guard house stood behind one of the pillars, almost hidden. The main house was a good quarter mile from the road, white brick, massive, plantation-style. White fence bordered the lane to the house. In the center of the sprawling lawn was a larger-than-life sculpture of a Brahma bull, golden in color, an outsize Kincannon *K* branded on its flank. The bull held a fore hoof aloft and glared toward the road like a challenge. The sculpture seemed an amazing exercise in hubris and I shook my head.

I looked again and noticed a second house on the property, as large as the closer house, tucked back in the trees a quarter mile distant. I blew past the entrance, continued for several hundred feet, turned on a dirt road to the right. It appeared to be the western border of the property, white-fenced to the right, thick woods to the left. I lumbered to the side of the road and stared into the woods. The main structures would be on the far side of the trees, perhaps a quarter mile.

I pulled field glasses from the glove box. Ten seconds later I was over the white fence and moving into the woods. I wasn't sure of my motives, only that I had to see more, as if I could find a sign or symbol on the vast property explaining who these beings were. And why, having so much, they demanded still more. I pulled the glasses to my eyes and saw a snippet of the white house through the trees. I continued walking, then froze at a voice ahead, high and giggly.

"You can't find me."

I slipped behind a slender oak, put the

binoculars to my face, tried to isolate the direction of the voice.

"You're getting warmer," the voice said.

A sound pulled my glasses to a large and chubby child crashing through the growth. He was perhaps two hundred feet away. I heard a small engine kick in.

Then an adult voice, male. "Where's Freddy at?"

"You can't find him! You're getting colder now."

A game of hide-and-seek. The engine sputtered, moved nearer. "Where has Freddy gone?" said the adult voice, verging on anger, tired of the game.

A childish giggle. "Over here!"

The engine came closer. I dropped to the ground, wriggled beneath branches, flipped leaves over me as impromptu camouflage. The engine was loud and unmuffled and close enough to smell the exhaust.

The machine stopped two dozen feet away. I saw a tall and lean man on a four-wheel ATV. He wore a nondescript brown uniform like that of a security guard. A semiautomatic pistol was holstered at his side. If he looked in my direction, there was no way he'd miss me.

"You're real cold," the child's voice giggled in the distance.

"Fucking moron," the guy muttered. He cleared his throat, spat, put on a playful voice. "I'm coming to get you, Freddy."

"You'll never find me."

The guy cranked the throttle, and tore away. I let my breath out, stood on shaky knees, and began my retreat. I was halfway to the road when I heard a burst of laughter and returned the glasses to my face. Through the leaves I saw the man on the ATV, the chubby child at his back, holding tight with stubby arms, laughing. They were moving slow, puttering along.

I focused the glasses tighter, saw a beard line on the child. *Not a child, an adult.* His face was small and round, his mouth wide with delight. I turned to the road and my foot caught a fallen limb. I crashed hard to the ground, a dry branch cracking like the report of a .22.

The ATV engine revved hard, clanked into gear, started my way. I ran the last leg, clambered over the fence, jumped into the car. I fishtailed away, looking in the rear-view. No one at the fence line. But anyone caring to look would note the scrabbled-up leaves where I'd built my impromptu hidey-hole.

Three miles down the road from my escapade I pulled into a small grocery store, thirsty. The clerk was a heavyset black woman in her forties, hair bleached yellow. Her name tag said Sylvia.

"You're pretty close to the Kincannons' place here," I said, snapping a package of beef jerky from the rack.

"Yep," she said. She shot me a wary glance. "You know them?"

"Heard of them's all. Hear they're big with charities, that kind of thing."

"I guess."

"They ever stop in here?"

"Some a the workers do. I saw a Kincannon once, the one called Racey."

"Racine?"

She nodded. "He come in wit' a bunch a his buddies. I think they'd been shootin' birds or somethin' by how they was talking. They'd been drinkin', I smelt it soon's the door came open. One says to the other, 'I don't care. If my bag's empty after an hour, I gotta ground-shoot something.' Then they all took to laughing and slapping backs."

"What'd they come in for?"

"Pick up a couple six-packs, get rid of a couple others." She nodded at doors toward the back, *Restrooms* hand-painted above.

"Good to know rich people use the john like the rest of us," I said, walking to the counter with my purchases.

"Mebbe not like the rest of us," Sylvia said.

"How's that, ma'am?"

"They pissed ever'where but in the commode. Floor, walls, in the sink, acrost the stack of paper towels. Cleared out they noses on the mirror, too."

"Maybe really rich people think that's funny," I said. "Ones like Racine Kincannon."

Sylvia handed back my change. Her eyes were tired. "Devil puts his money where he gets the most back."

When I got outside, a blue truck was sitting next to my truck, a dual-track monster idling like a diesel-powered dragster. A *K* in a circle was painted on the door, the same *K* I'd seen over the stone entranceway and on the sculpted bull's flank. The man at the wheel was on the far side, a big guy in a uniform. The guy in the passenger seat was the raw, bone-hard guy from the ATV.

I walked between the vehicles to get to my door. The rawboned guy stared at me with small hard eyes. The patch on a muscled shoulder said Private Security. I nodded, just a guy loading up on snacks. The guy kept up the cold-eyed glare. He reminded me of a coiled rattlesnake.

He said, "I just see you on that single-lane dirt road a couple miles yonder?"

"Must have been someone else," I said. "Why?"

"That's my bidness. Not yours."

I tapped his door panel with my knuckle, said, "What's the *K* stand for?"

"Keep your fuckin' hands off the truck."

"Have a nice day," I responded, climbing behind the wheel.

My next stop in the Kincannon pilgrimage was an office park, a multiacred expanse of rolling, neatly tended grass with square brick office buildings every eighth mile or so. The buildings were auburn; from a 747 the campus would resemble red dice on green baize.

Every tributary from the central road held a brass sign pointing out address ranges and directions. I wound past two large ponds complete with high-spraying fountains in the center and white ducks on the shoreline, pulled beside a red box with coppery windows. A sign beside the entrance said KEI, Kincannon Enterprises, International.

There was a parking lot, but it was closer to park on the street, walk to the building. I pushed through a tinted glass door into a cool lobby smelling of plastic and rug shampoo. A building receptionist sat behind a U-shaped desk. A beefy security guard stood in the corner. He looked me over hard, hair to shoes, like he was expecting someone but wasn't quite sure who.

"I'm looking for the building directory," I said to the receptionist, a young woman who thought it would be ultrasophisticated to combine a British and southern accent.

"May I awsk what firm y'all looking for?"

"Just a building directory."

The security meat moved over quick. "Help you with something, sport?"

He didn't expect to be shown a gold badge by a guy in raggedy cutoffs and a shirt from a Key West fish joint.

"Directory?" I repeated.

"Why you need to know?"

"Am I hearing the beginnings of an obstruction charge here?" I said.

"The top floor is the KEI executive offices. The third floor is KEI administrative offices. Clarity Broadcasting is the second floor. The first is Magnolia Development." He said it like it hurt to move his mouth.

"There. Wasn't brain surgery, was it?" I said, heading out the door.

Lucas finished the last of the moo shu pork, tossed the carton in the trash bag. He rubbed his eyes, yawned, then stood and bent to the floor, relaxing his spine. He opened the window blinds an inch and peered at the building across the way, corner office, top floor, Buck Kincannon's office. Racine Kincannon's office was to the right of the corner, Nelson Kincannon's to the left. From this angle he could see only into Buck and Racine's offices and, down the hall, the conference room.

A week ago his world was a bed and a room. Now he had his very own insecurities firm. Lucas leaned against the wall and struck a pose that had always amused him, arms crossed, head canted, mouth stern with decision-making. He started laughing, and the laughter brought a memory.

Why are you laughing, Lucas?

Because it's all so funny, Dr Rudolnick.

What's funny?

How much I scare them. How much IT scares them.

What do you mean by IT, Lucas?

Shall I do some calculations? Would you like a brief analysis of pork bellies?

Lucas stepped from the wall, looked outside, saw nothing interesting. It was night when things got exciting, when the other people came and went, sometimes in a frenzy. Watching them was glorious to behold, jackets off, sleeves rolled, ties pulled loose. They spread maps on the conference-room table. Vehicles came and went in the lot below. Sometimes a cop car floated past, stopped briefly.

The faces of the participants were always dark with worry. Even Crandell's. Everyone was playing a role in response to the roles played by the others. But behind the roles . . . I, Me, Mine.

The night before, the whole crew had been in the conference room – the war room, in Lucas's self-amusing terminology. He had used his new microwave to make popcorn, then sat in the dark and watched events like a movie. It became quite dramatic near midnight, a fistfight breaking out between Nelson and Racine, the others pulling them apart.

The blame game with no one to name. Or everyone.

He'd also seen something of consummate interest, the sort of thing his mentor had suggested would be occurring. In his current role of primary family mouthpiece, Buck Kincannon was often absent from the firm. No one could enter his office but his personal assistant, a prim and efficient woman, middle-aged, pear-shaped with a plain face and heavy ankles. The very same pair of ankles he'd seen above Nelson Kincannon's ass two afternoons running, the couch sessions lasting six minutes. Lucas wondered what fantasies Nelson conjured to keep his equipment engaged. It would take some major sleight of mind.

It was thus no surprise that Buck's out-of-building experiences were followed by his assistant scampering into Nelson's office with a file in her hands. Phone calls and message slips, he supposed. Nelson shuffled through, made a note or two, the assistant returning the file to Buck's office. Buck would keep personal e-mails private and password protected. But the call slips would be a good indicator of his activities and intentions.

A call to Buck would be slipped to Nelson via his plain-faced loverette. The duplicity thrilled Lucas.

He crept to the window and looked out into the bright sunlight. On the road below was a gray truck that looked like it had just driven in from Guadalajara. The driver, a white guy in scruffy clothes, was pulling it away. A janitor type, maybe. Not interesting. But it was a beautiful day. Maybe he'd go sit in the back lot, out of sight, just for a few minutes of sun.

Do you think they'd let me outside today, Doctor?

You disappointed them the last time, Lucas.

We learn from our mistakes, Doctor. I'll just go sit by the window and watch Freddy play outside. I like to hear him laugh.

CHAPTER 29

"I got the photo you sent, Detective Ryder. Pretty fuzzed-up by the time it came across our fax. The fax machine's ancient, coal-powered, I think."

The next morning I started by calling Pettigrew to see if the augmented photo of the man called Crandell had struck a chord. I didn't expect it to, but everything had to be tried. I used the conference-room phone, Harry listening from across the table. I hadn't told Harry about my trip to the two Kincannon sites. He wouldn't have been pleased.

I said, "The pic was fuzzy to begin with, Ben. It spark anything?"

"Four years have passed. Sorry."

Dead end.

I said, "Thanks for trying, Ben. For Barlow to know Crandell was a long shot. Your knowing anything would be longer."

"Crandell? You never mentioned the name," he said.

"The name mean something?"

I heard Pettigrew shift in his chair and pictured him leaning forward, elbows on the desk, phone tight to his ear.

"Not long before I left for Montgomery, Barlow crept around to the side of the headquarters, nothing there but weeds. He was talking. I wouldn't have heard him with the windows tight, but I don't like too much AC, so I keep my window open a few inches."

"Barlow met someone out there?"

"He was on his cell. I figured the call was one of his girlfriends, a scary bunch. Then I got caught by how polite he was being, deferential, saying yessir and nossir. That's not Cade Barlow."

"He was talking to Crandell?"

"I remember him saying Mr Randall, but . . ."

"Awfully damn close," I said.

"Barlow came back into the building grinnin' like a shitbird. That was strange, too. Even before Barlow turned nasty he didn't smile much. I think he's sensitive about them corn-colored chompers."

Harry leaned in. "After that time . . . Barlow ever come up with any interesting property or money?"

"How'd you know? Just before I moved he started riding a big ol' vintage Harley panhead. Fifties-era, heavy custom work. I figured thirty grand minimum."

"This has been a real good talk, Ben," Harry said.

We hung up a minute later. Harry pushed the phone device out of the way.

"Barlow ain't just nasty, Cars, he's dirty. I smelled it on him. This clinches the deal: Rudolnick, Taneesha, Fur Face or Funky or whoever, Frederika Holtkamp, the pressed-down grass beneath that microwave tower, Barlow. It's all the same case – find out something about one, we find out something about the others."

It was a daunting array of investigative possibilities. "What do we do next?" I asked.

"Taneesha, Ms Holtkamp, and Bernie Rudolnick are dead. Barlow's alive. Let's drop the photo of Crandell in front of him. Out of thin air. See how he reacts."

I ran the scenario in my head. "Barlow's a

cop, Harry. Good at the stone face. He might not give anything away if we just drop a picture in his lap."

"You got something better?"

"How about we come at Barlow with an angle, something that confuses him just enough to mess with his response mechanism?"

A half-hour later I was bending over a paper cutter, Harry handing me copy paper a dozen sheets at a time. For the first time in two weeks, the air felt refreshing to breathe, like it had gotten a jolt of new oxygen.

"How much, you think?" I asked, tapping the stack of paper rectangles.

Harry lifted the stack, riffled it like money. "Gimme another half-inch, Cars. I want Barlow's fingers to touch it and get horny."

We finished, headed to Forensics, and found Thaddeus Claypool in the ballistics section, banging on computer keys and muttering about apogees and parabolic decay and whatnot. He wore an aloha shirt with blue macaws on a field of green. His jeans looked field-tested at Woodstock. When Claypool saw us he jumped up and created an ad hoc group hug. It took a few seconds to disentangle.

"Remember that tape you cleaned up for us, Thad?"

"Sure. I played with the program a bit after that, squeezed a couple bugs out. I talked to a game developer buddy of mine, got input on spatial modeling. What you do is map a grid of floating points on the –"

"Want to try a project?"

"Whatcha need?" His earnest eyes sparkled behind scarlet reading glasses.

"You still got the tape of the suited guy?"

"Sure."

"But he's looking to the side, right?"

"I've got two frames where he almost moves to three-quarters."

I reached in my pocket and pulled out a photograph taken last fall at Bellingrath Gardens. Harry and I are standing in front of a tumbling wall of azalea, Dani between us. We're grinning at a camera held by a ninety-year-old tourist from Bath, England. Her name was Mabel Hodge and we ended up taking her to a gumbo joint where she out-ate the three of us. I set the photo in front of Claypool. He looked at me, raised a questioning eyebrow.

I told him what I needed. He did a little dance and said to come back in an hour.

Barlow lived in a brick split-level, nothing spectacular. The garage door was open and we saw that the sergeant liked big toys, including a tri-wheel ATV, a couple of dirt bikes, and the vintage Harley panhead Pettigrew had mentioned, a low-slung hog encrusted with chrome.

We pulled into the driveway and got out, Harry carrying a bucket of fried chicken from Popeye's. He fished out a drumstick, set the bucket on the hood. We leaned against the Crown Vic and ate chicken until a drapery twitched, followed by the front door banging open. Barlow stepped to the stoop and looked at us in disbelief. Harry waved his drumstick in greeting.

"Howdy, Cade. Join us for lunch."

Barlow pointed down the road.

"The dump's a mile thataway. Take your fuckin' picnic there."

Harry made a point of scoping out the house, the bike. "Nice digs, Cade. Cool ride, too. What's a scoot like that cost, twenty-five grand? Thirty?"

Cade strode off the stoop, walked to us, his eyes dark with anger.

"Get off my property."

Harry held the drum at Barlow like a microphone.

"Where's the material from the Holtkamp case, Cade? Remember her, the teacher got killed on your watch? You didn't tell us the case materials got mislaid."

"Don't remember you asking. I want you off my driveway. I got nothing to say to you."

Harry bit off the tip of his microphone, fished around in the bucket, pulled out a biscuit.

"You implied the state cops had all the materials. They have bupkus. Where'd it go?"

"How the hell would I know? For all I know, it got picked up by a maintenance crew, tossed in the trash."

Harry studied his biscuit like he was deciding something. He came up with a packet of honey, squirted it over the biscuit. He started to take a bite, paused, looked at Barlow.

"We talked to Pettigrew, Cade. In person."

I saw Barlow freeze. But a split second later he was smirking. "Pettigrew ain't been around here in four years. He ran off to Montgomery to be a big shot. What's he know about anything?"

Harry took a bite of biscuit and chewed with his eyes closed. He smiled, like the honey had been the answer.

"You saying you don't know jackshit about the Holtkamp murder? Never went near the evidence?"

"You fuckers are big-time crazy. That's my answer."

"Say it again," Harry challenged.

"Glad to: You're crazy."

Harry made a show of looking at me and raising an eyebrow, as if weighing something. I looked back, nodded, like I'd come to the same conclusion. Harry turned to Barlow and applauded.

"Chill out, Cade, m'man. Have a piece of chicken. You earned it."

Barlow looked at Harry like my partner had lapsed into Gaelic.

"What the fuck are you talking about?"

"Like they say on TV, this has been a test. You passed."

"Make sense, dammit."

Harry said, "We were sent here to make sure the past stays buried."

Barlow's eyes flickered at the word *past*.

"I got no idea what you're talking about."

"Which, as I said, is the right answer. And the right answer just won you a little something for your silence. A bonus for passing the test."

Harry pulled an envelope from his pocket, flipped it to Barlow. The county cop trapped the package against his chest. His fingers danced over what was probably a familiar rectangular shape inside the envelope.

"Where'd this come from?" Barlow said, squeezing the package.

I slipped my hand into my jacket pocket, fished out my own envelope. I said, "Is a picture worth a thousand words? Or is it a photo?"

I slid the photo from the envelope, shooting a final glance at Claypool's computer handiwork as I passed it over: Harry and me at Bellingrath Gardens, between us a manipulated photo of Crandell. We were all grinning. Shadows weren't exact, and Claypool had blurred everything a notch to help conceal the problems, but for a one-shot roll of the dice, it was damn good.

I passed it to Barlow. He looked down and froze, his eyes wide.

"You mean you guys know Cran—"

It was the wrong thing to say. Barlow knew

it one second too late, eyes trained to spot forged registrations and licenses finding the photographic discrepancies. He threw the photo to the ground. Kicked it away.

"I don't know who that is."

"You think we're stupid?" Harry said. "You just said the name."

Sweat beaded on Barlow's forehead. His left eye ticked and he swallowed hard.

"You're running a game on me."

"Crandell who?" Harry asked. "Crandell what? Crandell where?"

"I never saw him before."

"Am I going to have to get my chalk, Barlow?" Harry said. "Make you a free space?"

"What?"

"Why'd you mess with Pettigrew's investigation?" Harry shot.

I said, "What are you hiding?"

"What'd you get paid?" Harry asked.

Barlow's eyes bounced between Harry and me like a rabbit between two wolves. He rubbed his palms down his thighs to dry them.

"Who the hell are you?" he said. "State? Federal?"

Harry stepped whisper close, narrowed his eyes. "We're just two cops who have you figured out, Cade. And when we get to the bottom of what's going on, your ass is mulch. Want to talk about it?"

"Get out of here." Barlow's voice quivered. "Now."

Harry shot me a look. We'd done all we could. I grabbed the chicken from the hood, Harry headed back to the driver's side. He turned, looked at Barlow.

"We heard you used to be somebody. A good cop." Harry flipped one of his cards to the ground. "Call me when you make the right decision, Cade. When you remember what side you represent."

We drove away. When I turned, Barlow was as still as a statue, torn envelope in his hand, white paper the size of money fluttering at his ankles.

We needed time to make sense of all we'd seen and heard in the past few hours. Then decide how to proceed. Flanagan's was too public and distracting, my place too far, so we went to Harry's. He poured the coal into Ellington's "A Train". The chair in Harry's living room held a box of Rudolnick's case histories, so he pulled a ladder-back chair from the dining room and sat it backward, facing me on the couch. He was in lecture mode: I'd seen it at the Police Academy when he taught classes there.

"There are a fair amount of cops like Pettigrew around, Carson. Bright and talented hotshots in quiet burgs. Some get press, nail someone from the FBI's most-wanted list, take down a major pedophile, talk a jumper off a building in the glare of TV lights, that kind of thing. Pettigrew was first-rate, but probably never made any splash that would have carried to Montgomery. Why was he selected? What even got him noticed?"

"I don't know, but it sure seemed like he was plucked away just in time to keep him from the Holtkamp investigation, good cop or not."

"I don't believe in coincidence anymore," Harry said. "Not on this case. I want to know exactly why Pettigrew flew the coop."

"Call him and ask."

Harry shook his head, *not an option.* "Pettigrew told us the outside details. I want inside details. Plus, I ain't trusting anyone involved to tell us the truth. Not even Pettigrew."

"That leaves us high and dry. I couldn't get

that kind of political info from the MPD, much less Montgomery's force."

Harry stared at me. It was uncomfortable.

"You've been dating an investigative reporter for a year and don't know how it's done?"

"I don't know what you're suggesting."

"We need a top-flight investigative type from the Montgomery area. A guy with deep connects on the political side, where everything happens."

"I don't know anyone like that, Harry."

"You know someone who would."

"Dammit, Harry, I can't call Dani and ask her to . . ."

Harry went to the stereo and snapped off the speakers. The room filled with silence. He leaned against the wall and crossed his arms.

"She messed you over. She knows it. She'll have the guilts and be vulnerable. Use it, Carson. She goddamn owes you."

"You want me to call her? Just say . . . what? I'd like to come over, we need to talk?"

Harry's voice got quiet.

"I've got a little experience in this area, bro. She wants to talk. She needs to talk. All you got to do is aim what she talks about."

CHAPTER 30

I stood in the center of Dani's living room and held her in my arms, looking over her shoulder. I had never seen so many flowers in a room where there wasn't a corpse. Explosive bouquets in vases. Crystal tubes holding lone roses. Sprawling vats of carnations. Kincannon seemed to have some kind of flower fixation. I enjoy the scent of flowers, but her house reeked with the damn things.

I'd arrived five minutes earlier. We'd engaged in a tentative fashion, stilted *Hellos*, and *How you been*s, broken sidelong glances, and finally, touching.

The full embrace with failing words.

Then, finding the words. The explanation.

She leaned back, her eyes red and wet and swollen, blonde hair matted to a damp cheek.

"I didn't mean to hurt you. Buck just happened. Buck and I dated several months before I'd met you, stopped. Then he came by last month, just to float the notion about my becoming an anchor. It started out as dinner."

"But you fell into . . . old ways."

She looked away. "Yes."

"I was always working, Dani," I said. "I wasn't there for two months."

I admit distraction. I admit stupidity. I had taken our relationship for granted for weeks. But I also knew she'd had only to grab my hair and tell me her feelings, and I would have changed the situation.

Or so I wanted to believe.

I said, "Are you serious about him? Kincannon? Is this relationship everything you want?"

Something changed. Her eyes turned to a dimension far away. She looked like she was stepping through a door with one chance to retreat before the door closed.

"Yes . . ." she said, the word hissing away.

"Then everything will be for the best."

She put her hands on my chest. Agitation shivered through her face.

"He's very caring, Carson. He calls every hour at least. Look at all the flowers. He's going to teach me to sail. I've never –"

I felt a rush of anger. "You don't have to sell him to me, Dani. I don't like Buck Kincannon. And I'm not going to change."

She dropped her hands loose to her sides, stared at the scarlet carpet.

"Of course."

She walked across the room. A realization came to her eyes.

"This is the last time you'll ever be here, in this room. In my house."

"Yep."

She turned away, dropped her face into her hands. "What have I done, what have I done . . .?"

I went to her, held her shoulders. She remained hunched over, tucked into herself.

"What have I done . . ."

"Dani? Are you sure you're all right?"

She spun, took my face in her hands. "Oh God, Carson, I'm so sorry. For my stupidity. For everything. If there's anything I can do . . ."

I pulled her close.

Be careful around Buck Kincannon, I could have said. *Watch yourself. Clair Peltier thinks they're dangerous, unstable, unhappy people capable of . . .*

Instead, I put on a sad face and a bewildered voice and said, "I dunno, Dani, maybe there's something on this you could help me with, just a name. It'd save me a week's work . . ."

I left Dani sprawled on her couch, sobbing. Inconsolable. In the last few minutes she had fallen into a world where her grief was within some private internal domain. I took one last look at Dani's home, knew my hours there were over. I stepped outside and pulled the door shut.

"Excuse me, who are you?" a voice said.

I turned to face Buck Kincannon striding up the steps. In the drive was an automobile that looked fresh from a wind tunnel. His cologne moved in advance of his body, something light, almost feminine. Kincannon wore a gray linen suit, blue shirt, lavender tie with a small hard knot. Not a wrinkle anywhere. I wore a coffee-stained thrift-store jacket over faded jeans, and was too many miles from my morning shower.

"I'm Carson Ryder."

Neither of us made a move toward shaking

hands. He nodded, made a show of waggling his forefinger at me, a remembrance.

"Right, I recognize you from the party. I liked the cowboy getup, something different, funny. You're just leaving, right?"

The last line he delivered double entendre, the slight smirk at the corner of his lips saying, *You're history, loser.* The bright teeth sparkled with innocence. I made no answer as we moved past one another in the disengagement dance. I was walking away, he was moving toward the door.

He paused, snapped his fingers.

"You're a detective, aren't you? I've heard a few things about you."

He hit the word *few,* like I was a guy who stopped by every couple of weeks to mow the lawn.

"Really?" I said. "I've heard a lot about you."

He canted his head, grinned, raised an imperious eyebrow. It looked like a pose for a menswear catalogue.

"From DeeDee?" he presumed.

"From Harry Nautilus."

Kincannon pursed his lips. Shook his head. "Sorry. The name doesn't ring a bell."

He dismissed me with his back. Started to

knock on the door. I said, "You worked with Harry Nautilus on a project a few years back, a sports venture."

He glanced over his shoulder. "Bringing Tiger Woods to town for the Magnolia Open?"

"Putting together the little ball field up in Pritchard. The one for the poor-as-dirt kids."

He froze before his knuckles knocked the door. Turned to face me. The glittering eyes had gone flat. I looked into frosted black marbles.

"I'm afraid your friend must be mistaken. I don't recall it."

I gave it a two-beat pause.

"That's strange, Buckie. Folks up there remember the incident. Which probably doesn't bother you a lot because they're poor. But I also hear the bluebloods of Mobile wouldn't wipe their asses on a Kincannon. Enjoy your evening."

I winked and walked to my truck without looking back, feeling Kincannon's mute, blind hatred every step of the way.

It felt good.

Twenty minutes after leaving Dani I sat on Harry's gallery. Harry was in the glider sipping a beer. He'd traded work garb for a tie-dyed tee heavy on the red, lavender shorts, size-14 leather sandals. He'd moved the red-frame sunglasses to the crown of his head.

I reached in my pocket, pulled out a slip of paper.

"Guy's name is Ted Margolin," I explained, passing the slip to Harry. "He's local, with the *Mobile Register*. But he handles state politics, and that means Montgomery. Good and fast and connected, according to what I could get from Dani."

Sobbing as she wrote Margolin's name and number. Apologizing again and again. Our year-long relationship exploding around us and I'm lying to wangle information.

"Connected to the cops?" Harry asked. "The administration side, people with access to records?"

"As much as any reporter could be, I guess. Dani says the guy's almost sixty, worked the beat a long time."

"Who's opening the lines of communication?"

"Ms D said she'd call the guy tonight, pave the way."

If she could pull herself together. If she hadn't

told Kincannon my request, him saying, screw the cop, let him get his own information. Or maybe she'd already forgotten about it, busy romping with the Buckster in a house stinking of flowers.

Harry said, "You tell her anything about what we're –"

"Just the fake story, Harry. She wasn't really listening. I got the feeling her life's a bit complicated."

"Complicated how, Carson? She's keeping her toesies warm with . . ."

I raised my hand like a Stop sign and said, "Enough." Buck Kincannon was history.

For the moment.

I declined Harry's offer of supper and started for home. The moments with Dani ached in my belly, a physical pain, like being punched. Then I remembered a kind and generous offer that had been made to me, and cut across town, heading west. It was nearing seven p.m., the shadows long, the air hazy and golden.

Before her divorce two years back, Clair Peltier and her husband had lived in a piece of high-money real estate on the eastern shore of Mobile Bay. It seemed more museum than home, centuries-old furniture, art on marble pedestals, glittering chandeliers. A gilded harp, for crying out loud.

The lust for ownership had belonged to her husband, Zane Peltier. Clair preferred experiences to objects. Reading, cinema, the symphony, travel . . . all stirred her pot harder than a fancy car or an armoire by Louis the something or other. When divorce loomed, Clair found herself in the enviable position of having a husband with both money and a need to avoid news coverage. Today she lived in a small but elegant house on a woodsy acre in Spring Hill, the champagne section of town.

Driving down her street, I saw Clair in her front yard. She was painting the mailbox, brush in hand, a small paint can at her feet. The methodology was pure Clair: dip brush, remove excess, carefully paint one square inch of mailbox, repeat.

I pulled into her driveway, leaned out my window. "I didn't know women in Spring Hill could paint anything but their nails."

"Don't give up your day job for Second City, Ryder."

She finished another perfect square inch, set

the brush on the can, walked to the truck. She wore jeans and white running shoes and a long-sleeved khaki shirt with tails nearly reaching her knees. A blue bandana held her hair back. After her divorce she'd gotten into yoga and health-type foods, getting lithe and limber and losing twenty pounds.

"What brings you to my driveway, Ryder? You lost?"

I slow-tapped my thumbs on the wheel. "Listen, Clair, uh, you said that if I ever needed someone to talk to . . ."

"Let me put away the paint, clean my hands –"

"I didn't mean now. But thank you."

She put her hand on my forearm, concern in her eyes. "If something's bothering you, please, let's talk."

I said, "I know you're busy with society things, pathology things, a heavy social schedule. Tell me what's a good time for you."

"I've done all my society things for this month, Ryder – a fund raiser for the symphony. Pathology I do at work, not home. As for . . . what was the third option?"

"Your social life, like dates and whatnot."

"I've got two guys hitting on me, Ryder.

One's a banker who waxes rhapsodic about money market funds, ugh."

"The other?"

She made a purring sound deep in her throat, winked. "A hottie, I think is the term. A charming and intelligent man, self-made multi-millionaire, one home in Mobile, one in Provence, a pied-à-terre in Manhattan. We were out together last night."

"Oh."

"I'd be real interested if he wasn't eighty-four years old. What are you up to Saturday, Ryder?"

"My new routine: nothing."

"Want to come here? Or my office at work? I can close the door, we can talk as much as you want."

"How about my place?" I suggested. "We'll sit on the deck, watch the dolphin-tour boats go back and forth."

She turned and walked back to the mailbox, her hips graceful beneath the denim. She dipped the brush in paint, poised it over the mailbox.

"You sure know how to show a girl a good time, Ryder. How about sevenish? That work for you?"

CHAPTER 31

I pulled away from Clair's and aimed my truck for Dauphin Island when my phone rang: Harry. I pulled to the side of the road.

"You at home, Cars?"

"Still in town, Harry. I was just talking to Clair."

"You're at the morgue?"

"I stopped by her house for a few moments."

A two-beat pause. "After you took off I nuked some leftover Chinese. Then I sat down and pulled out a stack of Rudolnick's cases to scan while I ate, plow through another half-inch. There was a magazine mixed in with them, a psychiatry thing. Some pages fell out."

"Pages from the magazine?"

"Pages tucked inside the magazine."

"Those are subscription forms, Harry."

"Whatever pills you're taking, Cars, they're working. These ain't subscription forms. They're notes in the doc's handwriting. Comments on a case, I think, but this is the kind of thing you know more about."

"How about I stop by in the a.m., eight or so?"

"There's something about the notes, Carson. I'd really like you to look at them now."

I was sitting on Harry's gallery in minutes. It was verging on dusk, but the gallery was well lit and the skeeter truck had been by minutes earlier. I had no idea of the chemical composition of the gray fog that poured from the mosquito-control truck, but like everyone who lived near coastal marshland, I didn't care as long as it kept the bloodsuckers at bay.

"Here's how it was when I grabbed it up, Cars."

Harry handed me the spring issue of *The Journal of American Psychiatry* from two years back. It was Rudolnick's personal issue, sent to his home address. Harry handed me the magazine by its spine, pages open toward the floor. Several pieces of white typing paper fell to my lap. Six pages, I counted, held at the upper-right edge with a paper clip.

There was only one small block of text on the front page, typewritten:

This commences a special project. The undertaking is my own; independent study would be the term, I suppose. I am in this instance merely an eye. But I believe there are behaviors to be observed and catalogued.

This will be a record for reference.

"Get ready for an interesting trip," Harry said.

I turned the page. Handwritten notes, sparse, some simply a line or two. There was no name, only "Subject".

The pages were dated, the dates starting three and a half years back. I read the first entry.

Subject agitated. He paces behind me during my visit. There's no doubt he wishes to get my attention (though I'm uncertain whether he himself has this realization). He complains of feeling "depressed" and "out of sorts". He laughs, says, "Maybe it's the surroundings."

I lead him to a discussion of visualization techniques as foci for relaxation. I provide suggestions: waves, birds in flight, scudding clouds. He becomes agitated and demands I not treat him as I would one of my "fucked-up patients".

I assure him that visualization techniques are commonplace, used daily in the home and workplace. His suspicion abates and he indicates interest. Like many, he selects clouds as his preferred setting, and we spend a half-hour working with techniques to calm his mind.

I continued reading, wondering if Rudolnick had stuck the pages in the journal for later transcription and forgot where he had put them. The entries were sporadic, averaging six weeks between each. Most were three or four lines, much in the vein of an entry the second year:

Subject calm, a good day. He sits by the window, hands folded, and gazes into the trees. He watches Freddy playing.

The next entry, a few months later, was longer. And more foreboding:

I must be very circumspect, not a shrink, but more a – what? Friend? He has no friends, not in a usual sense. I must provide him with relaxation techniques without seeming to prescribe them. Or anything else I might suggest without seeming to make suggestions. If I appear to prescribe, he will believe I think he is sick. If he thinks I think he is sick, there could be dire consequences. Mirrors within mirrors. How did I get myself into this?

Two more mundane entries – the subject seems to enjoy watching "Freddy" playing outside – then, a month after, a bit of an insight into whoever is described:

He can be absolutely charming, humble. An interesting person to be around, normal, relaxed. Moments later he is demanding, dictatorial. His changes are mercurial and, I am beginning to think, difficult to control, though still contained. He sublimates his impulses exceptionally well, especially what I perceive as an anger toward women.

I doubt the sublimation can continue.

I read, fascinated, a brief entry occurring two months later.

Today he asked me, "Do people really taste like chicken, Rudolnick?" A minute later he was striding forcefully across the floor, appearing to make business decisions. Then he sat and read several of the magazines lying around, general-interest. Later, putting the magazines away, I discovered he had scratched the eyes blank in the photographs of several women, probably unconsciously.

There were more observational visits, Rudolnick commenting on the patient's(?) state of mind. The doctor's observations seemed circumspect, veiled, almost as if watching from behind a glass window. The next long entry was the penultimate entry. I noticed the writing was looser, less controlled, as if written in a hurry or in a stressful situation.

When I arrive, he is waiting. His first question: Do I think women's blood differs from men's blood? I am becoming a magnet for him. He needs me, but does not realize it. I cannot fathom what will happen if he develops a dependency. He asks me to walk in the woods with him. I am reminded of photographs I have seen of leaders at Camp David, slow-walking down paths bordered with trees, heads bowed in discussion, hands folded behind backs. Except instead of discussing world events, all he discusses is sex and control and death. Not philosophy, but methodology.

I lie – what are my choices? – and assure him his thoughts are normal, and as a psychiatrist, I am perfectly qualified to make such assurances – everyone has such thoughts.

He talks of "escaping" without going into detail; though several meanings can be inferred, none good. In the best of all possible worlds I would be allowed to medicate him. Forestall what I feel is the inevitable.

It is not an option.

For a few moments he becomes agitated and angry. There are clouds in the sky and I point upward and remind him of the relaxation techniques. I never know what creates such moments. It is like walking beside a normal and respected person who has decided to become a suicide bomber, never knowing when he will grasp the plunger.

Then, a week later, the final entry:

This marks the last of this series. I have made my decision to extricate myself from this situation. Everything is a spinning mirror and my share of the blame is large and horrendous. I suspect the subject has come to see me as an enemy. How do I know? He is nicer to me than he has ever been, solicitous of my health. Gentle.

I smell his hand on the plunger.

I must get out.

Five weeks later, Rudolnick was dead.

"What do you think?" Harry asked when I had finished reading.

"I think there's a decent chance he was treating our killer," I said, a cold knife tracing circles over the base of my spine.

"I figured you'd agree," Harry said.

Near midnight, I got a call from the reporter, Ted Margolin. Dani, bless her, had contacted him. She had told Margolin two local dicks were wondering how certain political procedures worked in Montgomery.

"Naturally," Margolin said, "it intrigued me."

"We're interested in a former Mobile County officer, Benjamin Pettigrew. He is not – repeat, *not* – the subject of any form of investigation. We'd like to know, in general, how Pettigrew got hired."

"I got a real good source for that kind of

stuff," Margolin said. "I'll need time to make some calls, maybe wait until a friend can get to some locked files. How about we get together late tomorrow morning?"

I didn't try to hide my surprise. "You'll have it by then?"

"If it's have-able. Oh, Detective Ryder?"

"Yes?"

"I haven't talked to DeeDee in a few months. She sounded pretty down. She all right?"

"She's fine," I said. "Something to do with the change in the weather."

After wrestling with the notion for several minutes, I decided to call Dani, thank her for the assistance. Maybe buoy my conscience. Her number was still first on my speed dial.

Tap. Connect. Ring.

"Hello?" Her voice tentative. "Carson?"

"It's me, Dani. I just wanted to let you know that –"

"Buck's here," she whispered.

I clicked the phone off and stared at it for several seconds. I pulled up my call list and deleted her number.

CHAPTER 32

Harry and I went to the office in the morning and caught up on every bit of paperwork the case had generated. We had the feeling that something was due to break. We wanted to be caught up if the shit got delivered to the fan.

The Crandell character had come to light and we were using it to leverage Barlow. A four-year-old murder appeared to have been done by Taneesha Franklin's killer. I suspected Dr Bernard Rudolnick had treated – or at least observed – the perpetrator. The man who killed Rudolnick had been poisoned after being interviewed by our primary victim, Taneesha. It was a rat's-nest of tangles, but we were picking it apart a twig at a time. Something was going to bust loose on one of the angles.

At ten forty-five we headed to Harry's house, where we'd arranged to meet Margolin. The day had turned too hot for sitting outside, so we paced in the living room, Harry north to south while I went east to west. After a few crossings we got the rhythm right. At eleven thirty we heard a car door slam and Harry went to the window.

"He's here."

Margolin strode into the living room with a black leather bag over his shoulder. He was a small, fit guy in a blue seersucker suit and white shirt, no tie. His eyes were dark and electric, his steel-gray hair buzzed short. He moved like a Jack Russell terrier, fast and choppy. The guy looked closer to fifty than sixty, investigative journalism must have agreed with him.

We did introductions. Margolin took the couch, Harry and I pulled our chairs close.

"What you got?" I asked.

Margolin reached into the bag, dug out a folder, set it on his lap.

"First off, don't get the idea I jump like this for anyone. Cops especially. I'm doing this because DeeDee told me to. I do mean *told,* like an order. I owed her one for a tip she passed on last year. This is me paying back."

"Understood," I said.

Margolin snapped open the folder, put on reading glasses.

"Pettigrew, Benjamin Thomas. Started with the Montgomery force four years back. Patrolman second grade, the rank owing to three years experience as a county cop. Made detective one year later. Nicknamed 'Bulldog' because of his investigative tenacity. A perp once found out Pettigrew was on his case, came in and surrendered. Actually, I think that's happened twice."

"Pettigrew's not a guy to give up," Harry said. "And known for it."

Margolin looked over his glasses. "If you're looking for a downside to Pettigrew, I never found one. This boy's all silver and no tarnish."

"Actually, we're more interested in how he was selected," Harry said.

Margolin shuffled through his papers, reviewed one for a few seconds.

"Pettigrew got lucky, actually."

"Lucky how?"

"The city got a special grant to add cops that year. I mean, like the week before. Over a half million bucks drops in from a KEI grant –"

Like touching me with a live wire. I jerked

forward, waving my hands in the *time-out* motion. "Wait a minute, Ted. KEI?"

"Kincannon Enterprises, International." Margolin's reporter sense kicked in. "I say something interesting, guys?"

Harry said, "Keep going, Ted."

"KEI tossed big money on the table, special one-time grant – use it or lose it. It was a little out of KEI's range to provide funds for direct hiring, but welcomed by the city, of course."

Harry said, "Would folks at KEI have any sway over who was chosen?"

"If the Kincannons had a candidate for a cop position, the candidate would get heavy consideration. No, he'd flat-out get hired."

Harry said, "What if the Kincannons wanted a guy out of their hair? They'd do the same, right? Have him plucked away by Montgomery?"

Margolin started to reply, but his eyes turned cautious. He looked between Harry and me.

"I'm late for an appointment. That's all I know about Pettigrew. I do know the Kincannons are rumored to have inroads into law enforcement." Defiance in his voice, and veiled anger.

Harry held up his hands. "Wait a minute. You think we got you here under false pretenses? Maybe dope out your view of the Kincannons?"

Margolin picked up his bag, slung it over his shoulder, stood. "Nice talking to you fellows."

Harry reached out and snatched the bag from Margolin's shoulders.

"Hey!" Margolin snapped.

Harry slid the bag over his cannonball shoulder. Margolin looked between his bag, Harry's shoulder, and Harry's face.

"Have a seat, Ted," Harry said. "Please," he added.

The reporter sat warily.

"You need a quick history lesson," Harry said. "Buck Kincannon helped me create an inner-city baseball team. A year later, when the team's mentors wouldn't play dirty political ball with family interests, Kincannon deep-sixed the dreams of about fifty kids I cared about. I'd personally like to rip Kincannon's face off and shit in it."

Margolin studied on that for a moment, then looked my way.

"I have my own story," I said. "It isn't his face I want."

Harry said, "Someone we know described the Kincannons as using one hand to give while the other takes. Everything's quid pro quo. Fit anything you know, Ted?"

"The old Kincannon quid pro quo . . . I got one: the Montgomery Chamber Orchestra. The Kincannons were trying to schmooze their way into Montgomery society, wanted to impress the social register types. They approached the symphony and donated money to create a chamber orchestra. Three months later, music."

"And?" I said.

"You can't wash stripes off a skunk. The Kincannons can't bear giving without getting. Every time the family had a bash for their political ass-kissers up in Montgomery – and they have a lot of 'em, bashes and ass-kissers both – the MCO was expected to perform gratis. After a year of freebies, the musicians rebelled. The funds quietly dried up over the next couple years."

Margolin shifted his gaze between Harry and me. "That's a funny story and no one was hurt. I've heard other stories, never verified, that weren't funny, you get my drift. I've always wanted to put a tight lens on the Kincannons. Maybe it's time."

Harry slipped the bag from his shoulder, handed it back to the reporter.

"Watch your back," Harry said.

Margolin winked, said, "One of the things I do best." He skittered out the door, all sauce and energy.

I turned to Harry. "Pettigrew is checking into the killing of Ms Holtkamp. He's got a rep as a guy who finds things out. Suddenly the KEI dumps a shitload of the big green jizzle into the kitty in Montgomery, says hire some cops. And by the way, there's this guy in Mobile County . . ."

Harry nodded. "Pettigrew is called to the big city. Barlow slides into place and becomes a wrecking ball."

"Crandell arrives on the scene and works some kind of magic," I added. "Problem solved."

"Four dead bodies, a funky Wookiee, and a high-level fixer. What the hell have we stepped into?"

Harry's cell went off in his pocket. He fumbled it free, looked at the screen for the incoming number, didn't seem to recognize it. He put the phone to his face, brightened.

"Hi, Arn, what's up?"

Harry paused. Leaned forward. "What? When?"

He listened with his hand on his forehead. Grunted a few times. Hung up. Turned to me.

"Cade Barlow was found in his garage this morning. He shut the door, cut the gas line to his water heater in the garage. Then he sat on his shiny Harley and rode into the sunset. Or wherever."

I slammed my fist on my thigh. "He leave a suicide note?"

"Nothing but a body on a bike, the asshole."

I thought for a few moments.

"He was already dead, Harry."

"What do you mean?"

"Arn Norlin said Barlow was a decent cop until four years back. That's when he got odd. Arn described Barlow as seeming like he'd lost someone he loved. Maybe he traded his integrity for thirty pieces of silver. Or chrome, in this case."

"Barlow lost himself when he sold his honor? That's what you're saying?"

I shrugged. "It fits."

Harry leaned back in his chair with his mouth open and tapped a yellow pencil against his cheek. It made a hollow sound.

"Wonder who bought it?" he said. "Barlow's honor."

CHAPTER 33

Rather than second-hand Clair's take on the Kincannons, I wanted Harry to hear it from her own lips. I had a growing sense that our complicated journey was about to take us into the realm of the Furies.

She didn't sit behind her desk, but in a wing-back chair in the corner of her office. Harry and I sat close. Clair wore a cream pantsuit tailored to the millimeter, a bright silk blouse, lavender. She crossed her long legs and leaned forward, aiming the big blue headlights at Harry and me.

"Here's the condensed story, Harry: money is power. The only restraint on power is personal morality. That's not innate, it's learned. Trouble is, the Kincannons never had that on their lesson plan. If they had a coat of arms, it would say

Me First. If you had to characterize the family as a single entity, it would be a devious child."

Harry said, "Why do people bend at the waist when they hear the name?"

"The Kincannons spend vast sums to appear like benevolent royalty, to be adored by the public. It doesn't hurt that the boys look like movie stars."

Harry said, "Carson told me about the one hand giving, the other taking. It sounds like, if they had a third hand, it'd carry a knife."

"Don't gamble that it doesn't, Harry. Do you actually think they, or one of them, has something to do with your case?"

"There's no hard evidence," Harry said. "But the circumstantial pile is growing."

"There's nothing to go after them with?"

Harry rubbed his temples and shook his head. "We've discovered some things from a reporter, but we need personal insights. Not how many lawyers or PR people they have, not how many millions they keep in the Caymans. Something about them as people. History. Personalities. We need to know if they have any ghosts in the machinery we can leverage."

Clair stood, brow creased in thought. She walked to her window and tapped her nail against its surface as she gazed into the day, her graceful form backlit by filtered sunlight. I felt my breath catch and turned away.

"Ory Aubusson," she said, turning.

"Roy Orbison?" Harry said.

"Ory Aubusson," Clair corrected, going to her desk. She picked up her BlackBerry, tapped the keys. "Ory was Buck Kincannon Senior's best friend years back. Ory's got money, but nothing like the Kincannons. Ory married a woman who made him slow down. Buck Senior married one who pushed him into hyperdrive."

"How do you know Aubusson?" I asked.

"He was part of a crowd I hung with when dating Zane. Ory's a piece of work, in his seventies now, bawdy, cantankerous. Smarter than he looks, one thing to keep in mind."

"You think he'll talk to us?"

Clair picked up her phone, a slim finger poised over the keypad. "If I ask him to see you, he will. If he decides to kick you off his property two minutes later, he'll do that, too."

The call got through. Clair chirped, purred, told a couple of stories. Then slid us in the door. She hung up.

"He'll see you tomorrow morning. I'll get you the address."

We headed for the door. Clair got there ahead of us, pushed it shut. She leaned against the door, her eyes tense.

"If you're wrong, if you screw up, the Kincannons will tear you to pieces, hound you with lawyers, get you kicked off the force. Even if you're right, it could happen. And you don't even know if you're right."

"We're right," Harry said. "Still doesn't negate any of the other possibilities, though."

Clair stepped aside. Harry started down the hall, pulling out his cell to check for messages. She turned to me, her voice low.

"Are you all right, Ryder? With your personal upheaval?"

"Keeping busy. I think it's the answer."

"Too busy to get together and talk? That was tomorrow night, you know."

"Sevenish, if I recall."

She put her hand on my shoulder. Gave it a gentle squeeze. Said, "Stay safe, Carson."

The door reopened and I followed after my partner, a bell-like ringing in my ears.

Harry had to go to the Prosecutor's Office to straighten out a time line on an upcoming trial, and I envied him a few moments thinking about something else, even if it was another murder. I dug out our mass of paper and started at the beginning, the Wookiee jumping from the Mazda and running into the truck's headlamps. The knife in the rainy gutter. The oddities with the extra water in Taneesha's car.

After a half-hour I dropped my head to my hands and rubbed my eyes.

"I know that look," said a voice at my back, Tyree Shuttles. "Frustration, pure and simple."

"This isn't simple frustration, Tyree," I said. "This is the new and improved frustration – a hundred per cent more for no added charge."

"Grab a bowl of gumbo at Flanagan's?" he suggested.

"Anything to get out of here."

Like the last time we'd spoken, Shuttles had silent lapses where he'd seem far away, making a decision, or mulling his own set of problems. He pushed his bowl away, stared into my eyes, seemed to make the choice.

"You were one of the last guys in the department to make detective, Carson. You remember how it was to be new, right?"

"It's a whole 'nother world. Something not fitting right yet?"

He looked down at his hands. "It's Pace and

me. There's something not working in our chemistry. It's keeping me awake at night. Maybe I'm not up to his . . . expectations or something."

"Expectations? Pace Logan?"

Shuttles rubbed his face. "Not me personally, I hope, but more like new school versus old school. I'm college, he's not. I had criminology courses, profiling, tactics, strategies, psychology, sociology – you name it, I took it."

"Damn," I said, impressed.

"I had a scholarship, made it easy. But Pace, well . . . he's just got the street experience. The hard-fought smarts, doing things in ways I don't quite get. I respect his years of experience, and want to learn from it. You know Pace, he's a doggone good guy and, uh, he knows people and, uh . . ."

"He's great with children and loves his mother dearly," I said.

"What?"

"You've got a helluva start on Logan's retirement-party speech, Tyree. But hard to miss that Logan wants to get his gold watch and get gone. He can do a little or a lot before he leaves, and a little's a lot easier."

I admired Shuttles's protection of his partner,

trying to not diss Logan. But Tyree had a future in the department while Logan had only a past, and it was time for Shuttles to start cutting his own piece of the pie.

I said, "Everything you learned, everything you've seen . . . does it suggest Pace Logan is a good detective, or a mediocre one? And, for the record, what we say doesn't reach past here." I knocked the edge of the table.

"For sure?"

"'Til death do us part. What's wrong?"

Shuttles leaned forward, his voice a whisper. Fear in his eyes. "I soft-pedaled what I think about Pace. He's getting paranoid. He thinks I'm trying to undercut him, just because I'm interested in contemporary techniques and equipment, the latest in forensics, that type of thing. Plus he's got a fixation with Harry. Like that night with the Franks woman."

"Franklin. And what fixation?"

"When he heard Harry and you were heading to the scene, it was like we were in this big competition, he had to race over and grab the case."

I grunted. "First case he ever grabbed, I imagine."

"Then there's the things on the Hibney case, remember our burned woman?"

"Hard to forget. Things like what?"

"Like telling me I'm keeping stuff from him. He doesn't get out of the car to interview anyone, just pisses on me whatever I come back with. Like he's angry with me. He ever work with a black partner before?"

"I don't think it's that, Tyree. I think he's just a miserable human being."

"For sure. Plus he's getting weird this last couple months. I hate to say it, but I'll be glad when he retires. He worries me."

I thought it over. "I've seen old-guard types getting ready to retire before. Some can't wait, others get depressed. Maybe he's just getting the blues, taking it out on you. Just wait it out, Tyree. And thanks for letting me in the door."

Shuttles leaned back and let his shoulders slump in the chair, like he'd just set down a wheelbarrow full of bricks.

CHAPTER 34

Morning came and Harry and I headed to Ory Aubusson's place in Baldwin County. I studied the MapQuest sheet.

"It should be right up around the bend."

The road curved; ahead and to the right we saw an imposing yellow house with at least five acres of front lawn, a couple of live oaks per acre, the oaks garnished with Spanish moss. The house was plantation style, a full gallery to the front. I saw a solitary figure sitting on the gallery.

"Should be Aubusson," I said. "He told Clair he'd be waiting outside."

Aubusson was in his late seventies. He was in a huge antique wheelchair, an oaken throne with wheels, a marble table beside him, cane propped against the table. He'd once been a large and robust man, I saw, but age had bent his back, gnarled his hands, and turned his hair to smoky wisps of gray. Aubusson wore belted khaki pants and a white shirt, a neat scarlet bow tie below his strident Adam's apple. His daughter stepped out the door, a sturdy, handsome woman in her late forties. She pulled on the back of Aubusson's chair.

"Come on, Daddy. Let me get you out of the sun."

"Leave off, Ella. I got company. Bring me out a whiskey."

"It ain't close to noon, Daddy. And you're not even supposed to . . ." She stared at the old man with a look that was supposed to be anger, but held too much fondness. She shrugged, turned toward the door.

Aubusson aimed a long finger at chairs set before his. "Put some cushion under your butts, boys. You're cops, surely you know how to sit."

He laughed, a wheezy caw. His daughter brought a heavy crystal tumbler of amber liquid, set it down, shook her head, and retreated inside. Aubusson took a long drink, wiped his chin with the back of his hand.

"See, what it is is a generation thing. I came

up before all this stuff – whiskey, tobacco, fatted-up food, pussy – was supposed to kill you. So it don't. Ever' time one of my friends decided to start eating right and exercising, they tipped over in a year."

He lifted the tumbler, drank. I smelled a scent like flint and barley; high-end scotch.

"Why didn't Miz Swanscott come along?" Aubusson asked. Swanscott was Clair's maiden name.

I said, "She's working. She sends her regards."

His eyes got wistful. "Miz Clair Swanscott, or Peltier, as she goes by now, was as fine a piece of young womanhood as I ever laid eyes on; far too fine for that worthless ex-husband and, unfortunately, far too young for me." The eyes switched to the present and turned to me. "Clair said you wanted to talk a bit about Buck, the old days."

I nodded. Close enough for now.

The old man shook the ice in his glass. A heavy brown wasp buzzed before his eyes, hovered. Aubusson backhanded it away.

"Buck Senior and me's about the same age, came up the same place, over by Bay Minette. We stayed tight for years, made money pretty young, starting with timber, pulpwood. Ol'

Buck kept going, dee-versified, as they say. I always figured dee-versified meant to cut off part of a poem."

Light tickled in the old man's eyes. He knew we hadn't expected the wordplay.

"You ran with him how long?" Harry asked.

"We stayed thick up through his courting and early part of his married life, Maylene dropping babies like a brood mare. I swear that woman's pussy musta growed so loose you could –"

"How many kids she have?" I asked.

"Six or seven. Not all of 'em made it. Sickly, I guess. There was a couple miscarriages. A stillborn kid."

Harry said, "What was she like? Maylene?"

"You ever meet her?" Aubusson asked.

I said, "I saw her once at a company party. She wasn't real conversational. Or very happy looking."

He cackled. "She became what she was meant to become, a tough, mean old woman showing the world that, by God, she's built a family people have to respect."

"Family," Harry said. "That's Buck, Nelson, Racine, right? You know them, I take it? From when they were growing up?"

Aubusson seemed to straighten in his chair, become taller. He looked hard into our eyes.

"Why are you people really here? There's no reason for anyone to talk about Buck Senior. He's up there on that spread, in the back house. I saw him seven-eight years back. Walkin' around in his jammies and grinnin' like a kid on Christmas, 'cept kids know how to wipe their mouths. Had a negra nursemaid followin' him around, doin' for him. He looked at me and farted, started laughing. Basically, he's dead. I'm gonna ask again: Why are you here?"

I leaned forward. "We're not sure why we're here, sir. We may never be sure. But we think there are some strange goings-on that might center around the family. To be frank, I'm talking the possibility of murder."

"Ella!" the old man bayed. He thumped his cane on the floor of the gallery. The door banged open. I could already hear the coming words: *Wheel me back in the house, Baby, and kick these people off our propity.*

The daughter arrived. Stood beside her father.

"What is it now, Daddy?"

Aubusson held his glass high, glinting in the summer light.

"Hit me again, girl. I got to tell some funny stories and I need my throat wet to do it."

Lucas had purchased a desk, a simple and non-involving task. He went to a Staples, paid cash for the desk and the delivery. It was not the company's largest desk, more mid-range. Lucas thought of it as a practice desk. He pictured the desk with training wheels and started laughing.

A chair accompanied the desk, ergonomic, with a handle like a turn signal under the seat. Lucas twiddled and adjusted until his legs fit perfectly beneath the desk and he was well supported from all angles. He had also purchased a pack of pens and some writing paper. He set the pad on the desk and centered the title atop his page in bold strokes.

$$C(S,T) = SN(d1) - Ke\ (-rt)\ N(d2)$$

For the next hour he wrote beneath the title equation, adding subsets and refinements and a doodle of a dog puppet he found particularly amusing. At the bottom of the page, he wrote, *Buck: Run this by someone who knows about money.*

He made another trip to the phone outside

the gas station, sitting in his little green Subaru and waiting for a heavy man with a greasy mustache to finish talking. Lucas was two miles from the KEI offices and knew Crandell would have people wandering within that perimeter, several photos of Lucas in their possession, both the hairy Lucas and the clean Lucas. The clean-shaven Lucas photos would be dated, and wouldn't show him in a suit and tie, like he'd taken to wearing.

Practicing.

Lucas hunkered down in his seat. The fat man yelled something into the phone about a busted differential and waddled away. It took a minute to get through to Buck Kincannon's duplicitous secretary. He assured her that he knew her boss. When she asked his name, he came up with "Mr Lucas Runamok", carefully spelling it for the woman.

"R-U-N-A-M-O-K. It's an Icelandic name," he offered. "Like Reykjavik."

"Hello?" Kincannon said after the call had transferred, suspicion in his voice. "Who is this?"

"How's it hanging, Buck? There's a fax coming your way in precisely one hour. I suggest you be there to receive the transmission."

Lucas dropped the phone to the cradle and

revisited Staples. He paid to have a fax sent at a specified time, tipping the clerk twenty dollars. Lucas returned to his office and practiced tying and untying his tie.

At five minutes before the appointed hour he leaned into the Celestron scope. At thirty seconds after the hour, Buck Kincannon raced into his office, fax page in hand. He closed the door, then crossed the room and closed the blinds.

It didn't matter, Lucas thought, snugging another four-in-hand knot to his throat. He knew what would be going through Buck Kincannon's head. And that a record of his call would secretly move to Nelson Kincannon as soon as the lusty little assistant with the fat legs got the chance.

Lucas pulled his tie loose and thought a moment. He decided to try a Windsor knot.

CHAPTER 35

"The DuCaines?" Harry asked the old man. "That was Maylene's family?"

"Family ain't the word. Carnival? Sideshow? That works better, the DuCaine sideshow. They lived over in Fairhope, had lived there since, I don't know, the whole place started up."

"First a social experiment, then an artists' colony," Harry said.

"The whole DuCaine family was a social experiment. How we hooked up with them was me and Buck Senior was in our thirties, prime beef, thinking it was time to do some planting."

"Start a family?"

"Man needs something behind him besides money. I was partial to this girl about twenny-five, Coralene, lived down the street from the DuCaines. Nothing ever come of it, 'cept me, a few times. Payoff wasn't worth time invested."

"Daddy!" Ella said, coming out the door with two sweet teas she'd brewed for Harry and me, plus Aubusson's refill. Ella set down the tray, shook her head, retreated to the house. Aubusson grinned, turned back to Harry and me.

"But a couple times Buck had gone over to Coralene's with me and he'd seen this sassy little piece of fluff out walking. Stuck-up type, nose way up like she's sniffin' air the rest of us ain't allowed."

"Maylene?"

"She let herself turn into a fat ol' bulldog shape today. But back then that hoity-toity bitch had a butt like twin melons bobbin' in a tub. Lord, that woman had a shape. So we started going over to the DuCaine spread: four acres a few blocks from the bay, big house in the middle. One of those places with rooms sticking out every whichaway, added as needed. Coralene never went over to the DuCaines', called it a nuthouse. She wasn't the only one thought that."

"A strange place?" I asked.

"You've heard about the crazy aunt in the attic? The DuCaines had one. You'd be over there and hear her upstairs – howling, laughing, cussin' like a sailor. One time when I was there, she came screeching through the house, naked as a jay, feet slapping, titties flopping, and ran through the door to the porch. And I mean *through* the door, leaving the screen flapping in the frame. A couple of the servant types wrestled her down, but not before she kicked two teeth outta one of 'em."

"The aunt went off a lot?"

"That wasn't nothing. Most of the family seemed tore up in some way. One of Maylene's brothers didn't do nothing but sit in a chair and look out the window, his eye blinking like sending Morse code. Had a sister, young, already taking after Auntie – running in circles, ripping at her hair, pulling fits in the middle of the room. Had another brother who'd built a house in one of the live oaks, pretty much lived up there. When he came down it was to make fires. I never saw much of him. There was a retarded sister who just kind of walked around town touching things."

"The mother of the family. Where was she?"

"She was an ar-teest. Spent most of her time painting things, carrying around one of those painting racks –"

"Easels?"

"That's it. All she did, paint. By the bay, mainly. One time she'd paid a bunch of folks to frolic nekkid in the water, sat there painting away; 'figure studies', I remember she called them. The police come and suggested maybe she'd do better to study at home with the blinds shut."

"The father?"

Aubusson tapped his temple. "Smart. The brittle kind of smart that comes to a point at one thing. He sat around all day figuring out hard problems that use letters instead of numbers . . ."

"Physics, maybe?"

Aubusson nodded. "He was too brittle to work with people, but places sent him things to figure out. Like the government . . . which-away rockets will head, stuff like that. Got paid good money, which kept the whole circus afloat. He never seemed to notice anything but the stuff in his head."

"And Maylene invited people into this place? Her home?"

A wicked grin. "Oh Lord, no. We'd just show up. It was cruel, I guess, but Buck and me'd come pecking at her door, say we was thirsty, could we have a lemonade please, Miss Maylene? Then we'd hang around and catch the show: Brother drooling in his lap while his eye ticked like a clock, Sissy fighting with the servants, Auntie racing around with her bush showing, Tree-house Boy shoutin' down from the branches. It was better'n anything Hollywood ever invented."

"I've seen situations similar to that, Mr Aubusson. Where everything's out of control. Sooner or later . . ." Harry let the words float in the air.

"Yep. Bad things catch up, don't they? The retarded sister disappeared one day. Police found her lying in a bare lot in Bayou La Batre, all cut up, messed up inside, too. She lived, but you couldn't tell by looking at her."

Harry looked into Aubusson's eyes. "Finish it out."

Aubusson leaned forward and put his elbows on his knees, looked into the distance.

"Tree-house Boy . . . Jimmy? Jerry? I don't know much but rumors that come to me years later. There were some problems around the

DuCaines' household. Dogs disappearing in the neighborhood, found all chopped up in the woods. Then the kid got whipped up, started fights, big yellin' and screamin' things. One day he took off in one of the cars. He stayed gone for a few weeks. It gets real clouded here."

I leaned forward. "I'm used to the weather."

Aubusson shot a glance toward the door. Lowered his voice. "It was said he killed a woman who'd once done gardening work for the DuCaines. Guess he'd gotten an obsession on her or whatever. Went at her real bad with a knife, then burned down her trailer. Nothing ever came of it – if it happened – and Treehouse Boy was never arrested that anyone noticed. But he was never seen again. And nothing was ever tied to the DuCaines."

"No publicity," Harry said. "No nothing."

"Like it never happened," I said. "Money can do that."

Harry turned to Aubusson. "All this happened over the span of what, in terms of years?"

"All during the time Buck was courting Maylene. No matter what'd happen around us, she'd get up to get us another drink, whatever, keep them melons dancing. She knew what she had, she knew how to work it – she melted him into something she could shape like she wanted. Buck was her key out of crazy town."

"A happy marriage?"

"Buck needed someone to run him, but she flat ran over him. Do this, do that, talk like this, dress like that. Took over every second of his life. All their lives."

"Turned an out-of-control youth into a life of absolute control," I said.

Aubusson clenched a fist until his knuckles turned white, held it up. "Control like this," he said. "She finally got to shape the world like she wanted. A closed place, ain't many invited inside."

I said, "Daddy Kincannon isn't even there anymore."

Aubusson took a long drink of his whiskey, his face hidden behind the glass.

"I think maybe he found his own way free."

"Pardon me?" I said.

"I don't think he got the Alzheimer's like they say. I think he let hisself go crazy 'cause it was a better way to live than with her."

Aubusson shook the ice in his glass, empty. He set it aside. I figured he was about talked out.

"Tell me more about Maylene's children, Mr Aubusson," I said.

"Never held much hope for the kids, myself. I remember being over there one time. One of the kids' birthdays was going on in the other room, kid was eleven or twelve. Racine, or maybe Nelson, took a bite of Buck's cake when he wasn't looking, grabbed a forkful. I see Maylene motion Buck to her side, whisper in his ear. He turns and sees the missing bite. A minute later he marches over and flat-out punches his brother in the mouth."

Harry made a noise like a deflating balloon. "Don't let anyone take from you. Not even your brother? That was the lesson?"

Aubusson sipped from his glass. "Or maybe Maylene just liked winding him up and setting him loose, her little soldier. Wasn't no favoritism. Next time around it might be Nelson set loose on Buck."

"I'm surprised they didn't get in trouble growing up," Harry said.

"They got in scrapes, but nothing too bad. A little money cured the problems. Strange thing is, for all their weird-ass upbringing, the kids are boring. The older ones, that is. No spark. Put you to sleep just listenin' to them a few minutes. But Lucas had sparkle from the git-go. A fire in him."

"Lucas?" I said, shooting Harry a glance. "Who's Lucas?"

"Miss Maylene's last boy. Came as a surprise when she was in her forties. Strange kid. Born too late to be a hippie, but had that hippie thing, you know? Questioned everything, argued about everything, hated everything. Took streaks where he'd get pissed off, yell about having to live with a bunch of capt'list pigs, run off across the country. Got all the way to California when he was fifteen, Maylene had to send private investigator types to bring him back."

"Lucas sounds like trouble," I said. Or, perhaps, decompensating: falling apart mentally.

"He was ten handfuls of trouble when he wanted to be, but everybody agreed he was whip-smart. Had his granddaddy's brains, but didn't get the brittle. Helluva lot brighter than his puddinghead siblings."

"Puddingheaded?" Harry said. "I thought the Kincannon brothers were business geniuses, growing the empire and all."

Aubusson grinned. "A lotta folks assume

that, but like the old song says, it ain't necessarily so. Take young Buck. Boy's not an ignoramus, he just ain't sharp. Buck knows things about business . . . number one being what phone numbers to call for advice. The Kincannons hire the best advisors, best financial consultants, best lawyers. It's hard to make money, a lot easier to hang on to it."

"Let's get back to Lucas," I said. "He had a destructive side?"

"I know he busted some stuff up around the house. But the boy could be a charmer if he wanted, sweet. Even when he was ten, twelve years old, he could carry on a conversation better'n most adults. I liked the little monster, myself, even though he once called me a running dog lackey for the system, whatever that meant. At least he had a personality."

"Where is Lucas now?" I asked, keeping my voice even.

Aubusson drank the liquid from melting ice, flung the ice into the yard.

"I'd heard he was calming down, but nope. When he turned eighteen, he up and left. Ran as far as he could and won't have nothing to do with the family, hasn't been heard from in – what's it been? – about four years now. Got himself chopped clean out of the will, probably what he wanted. I hear he's up in Canada or Alaska, living in the mountains, doing things with beads."

"Or maybe not," Harry said, so quietly only I heard.

CHAPTER 36

Harry and I entered the department through the back door. Vince Raines from Vehicle Theft was in the hall sipping coffee and tacking a page to the bulletin board. It was in-house stuff: folks selling a car or boat or had a litter of kittens to dispense.

Vince saw us, nodded. "You guys don't need a jon boat, do you? Just put one on sale. Two years old. Cost thirty-five hundred with a ten-horse motor. Yours for twelve hundred even."

"I got a kayak," I said. "And an aversion to motors."

"I got an aversion to seasickness," Harry said.

"Just thought I'd . . . hey, I just got back from vacation. Mitch Burdon told me you two stopped by, looking into something."

"We were trying to track down some stolen cars," Harry said.

"Find 'em?"

"Mitch checked by make and model," Harry said. "Some upscale machines that weren't in the system. Mitch thought they might have been yanked from the airport, owners still out in Hawaii or whatever."

"Like what?" Vince asked.

"A '97 Porsche Turbo, '58 Mercedes Roadster, a 2004 Beamer, I forget what."

Vince's forehead wrinkled in thought. "I dunno. I got kind of a weird call last week. I was working alone. Got a call that some fancy cars were missing from a place off Highway 45. 'Fancy', that was the word the caller used. Went to a Quonset-type warehouse, climate controlled, a collection of cars in storage."

"There'd been thefts?" Harry asked.

"That's the strange part. The guy that called – a guard or something – was all worked up. Scared. He said to get there quick. I got there about a half-hour later. The guy, a big goofy hick, said it was all a big mistake. His boss, the guy who owns the vehicles, had sold some and the guy didn't know. So that was that."

Harry said, "I'd sure like to take a look at

this place. Mind if Carson and me became vehicle-theft cowboys for an hour?"

"Saddle up, boys. Lemme draw you a map where this place is."

The address led us to a defunct single-runway airfield between a melon field and scrubby woods. I think the KEEP OUT signs outnumbered the TRESPASSERS WILL BE PROSECUTED signs, but not by much. The only action nearby was an old strip-mall cum flea market about a half-mile down the road. A twelve-foot cyclone fence surrounded a gray Quonset structure, a small guardhouse in front. An industrial-size air-conditioning unit sat beside the hut, and I heard it running. The security was an electronic lock keypad that seemed to control the main gate. I saw a second keypad unit by the door of the hut, two dozen feet away.

The guardhouse looked little used: weeds growing from pavement cracks, the door half ajar. There was a phone in the guardhouse, a sign on it saying, 'In case of emergency, call . . .' such and such.

Harry looked at me. "You got an emergency?"

"I have to take a leak pretty bad."

"I'll phone it in."

Harry dialed the number. I wasn't lying, and crouched between the car and guardhouse to lose some coffee.

"Someone's on the way," he said. "Ten minutes."

We leaned against the Crown Vic and watched heat shimmer from the old runway. Eight minutes later a pickup truck pulled into the lot, kicking up gravel.

The driver jumped out, a heavyset guy, thirties, knock-kneed, belly drooping over a too-tight belt. His face was wide, his cheeks as red as if rouged.

"What's the emergency?" he asked, looking worried.

Harry and I flipped out the buzzers. I said, "We're following up on a report about some stolen cars."

"That's all cleared up," he said. "Over a week back."

"Oh shit," I said. "The report got filed wrong again."

Harry slapped his forehead. "What?" the guy said.

"We got a new girl sticking reports in the wrong box. We pick it up, see the address, head out. What happened?"

"It was a mistake. The cars got sold."

Harry laughed, clapped his hands.

"Come on? Really?"

The guy grinned, happy to tell the story again. "See, what happens is I come by ever' morning to do a look-see. I'm s'pose to check inside, make sure the temperature and humidity are set right. I opened the door and saw empty spots where three of the cars had been. Nothin' there. I called the cops, told them. Then I called out to Mr Kincannon's office, told his people about the cars bein' gone."

"You mean like Buck Kincannon?" I shot Harry the eye.

"The one. Got a helluva collection of cars in there. Great to be rich, huh?"

"What happened next?"

"Mr Kincannon came over. Buck. Mr Nelson, too. I was outside and I heard Mr Buck inside having a real shit fit. Just yellin' and screaming and throwing things. But when he come out he was smiling and said the cars was sold a few days before and he was sorry he'd forgot to tell me. Then he took off back to work. Then the cops come about ten minutes later and I explained it all."

"Why do you think Buck Kincannon was yelling?"

The guy shrugged; it didn't fall under his purview.

"I got no idea why rich people do the way they do."

We returned to the department. The detectives' room was pretty much deserted, with Roy Trent and Clay Bridges back in the conference room laying out files on their own mean-ass case, two biker gangs going toe-to-toe to carve out drug-sales turf. They had three bodies and no leads, biker types not prone to ask for police assistance.

I filled Harry in on my conversation with Tyree Shuttles.

"Fixated on me? Logan?"

"I don't really know what that's all about. Shuttles was pretty shook. I told him to relax, wait it out. Logan's out of here in around a month."

Harry drummed his fingers on his desk.

"Two times Logan's been wandering around in our area. He said he was back looking at the Wookiee drawing that time."

"I remember. It was on the floor."

"The second time he's sitting on my chair and says he's reading the murder book."

We sat at our desk and looked at Logan's area, twenty feet distant. Like our arrangement, Logan and Shuttles had abutting desks in a tri-walled cubicle.

"What's the saying about turnabout?" Harry asked. "It's fair play?"

Harry walked over to Logan's desk, sat. I followed, stood behind him, and kept an eye on the door. Logan was, strangely enough, a tidy kind of guy. Harry lifted a stack of papers, looked in files, checked in Logan's desk drawers. He lifted Logan's calendar, then his desk pad.

"Guess they didn't slide into the trash by mistake after all," Harry said, pulling out the two crime-scene photos missing from the Franklin book. Taken by the Forensics team, one photo was a wide shot of the Mazda and fifty or so feet surrounding it, rain-wet sidewalk, water running down the gutter. The other was basically the same, except the photographer had climbed the side of Arlin Dell's truck cab to get the wide downward angle: Mazda, background. A dozen feet ahead of the car I saw the yellow marker indicating where the knife had been found.

"Why in the hell would Logan want these?" Harry said. "They're location setters, not close enough to show anything important."

He slipped the photos back under the pad and returned to his desk shaking his head.

"Souvenirs, maybe? The last scene he never worked? Shuttles is right, the son of a bitch is weirding out."

Harry headed to the Prosecutor's Office, a final meeting before the trial on Monday. Harry would be on the stand a fair amount, grilled by a defense lawyer, and everyone wanted to get their acts down. I was just happy the PO preferred Harry to me on such cases. But I had a tendency to ramble when questioned whereas Harry kept his answers brief, to the point, and had the presence of Thurgood Marshall in a room full of Munchkins.

I had an idea we hadn't yet considered: having sketch artist Terry Baney do a drawing of Crandell. We concluded he was running his operation from a rental house, somewhere with land around the dwelling, so he could remain anonymous and not make neighbors suspicious with what would probably be comings and goings at all hours. But he'd still have to be near Mobile.

We could put a sketch on the air, accompanied by a "wanted for information" type of line. I made a phone call, but forgot it was Saturday; Baney worked standard hours, wouldn't be in until Monday.

I scrawled my usual reminder – *Call Baney: Drawing of Crandell* – set it front and center on my desk. I spun a few times in my chair.

I looked at my watch. Clair was stopping by tonight at seven, and we were finally going to have our talk. I wiped my palms dry on my jeans and went home to sweep the sand from my floor.

CHAPTER 37

At six fifty-nine, Clair Peltier's little red Beamer crunched across the sand and shells of my drive. For a moment I thought I'd forgotten to brush my teeth, recalled I'd brushed them twice this hour. I finger-combed hair from my eyes.

I heard Clair walk up my dozen wooden steps, pause on the stoop. When I opened the door, Clair's knock was still gathering in her hand. I bowed flamboyantly and gestured her inside. She took a tentative step, then crossed my threshold. Clair wore a simple lavender blouse, a slender silver necklace across her flawless skin. She had on shorts, white, mid-thigh. I'd rarely seen her when not wearing slacks, or dresses with mid-calf hemlines. I glanced down, smiled up.

"My gosh, Clair, you've got legs."

"I, uh . . . thank you, Ryder."

She passed by, studying my décor of shells and driftwood and pieces of art I'd scrimped to acquire, bright and whimsical pieces of folk art. I felt dizzy, like the air around her was suffused with a gentle intoxicant.

"Can I get you a drink, Clair?"

"Wine available?"

"If you wish. Or I can mix up something with more . . ." I almost said *sexiness*, changed it to "sizzle".

"Such as?"

"I worked as a bartender in college, at least when I felt like working. You enjoy rum?"

"When I've had it."

"Ever had a Caribbean Lover?"

She touched a forefinger to her chin, batted her dark eyelashes, did Scarlett O'Hara.

"Mista Rydah, now that's puh-sonal."

"Rum, pineapple juice, O.J., amaretto . . . Whoops, I don't have any amaretto. No Caribbean Lover. How about a zombie or a mai tai?"

She thought a moment, her lips pursed tight as a fresh rose.

"I've tried them. Give me something I've never tasted before."

I opened the cabinet, removed several little-used bottles and a cocktail shaker. I dug around in the fridge. Clair went back to gazing at my art while I measured and mixed. Two minutes later I handed her my concoction and poured one for myself.

"My take on Barbados Punch," I said. "Triple sec, lime, pineapple, dark rum and a pinch of cinnamon and clove."

She took a sip, tasted her lips with her tongue, a flicker of pink. She winked her approval.

We walked to the deck doors, stepped outside. The water was aquamarine, turning deep blue a half-mile out. Gulls screeched and tumbled in the air. A blue heron eyed us warily from a seagrass-covered dune in my front yard. The white Bertram I'd been seeing lately idled past, just outside the second bar. Clair walked to the railing and looked seaward. The breeze played in her hair.

"It's an incredible place, Ryder."

"When my mother passed away she left me four hundred and eight thousand dollars. I had every intention of buying a twenty-thousand-dollar trailer out in the county, living off the interest of the remaining money."

She turned. "I can see you doing that. I can't see you being happy for long. What changed your mind?"

I tumbled backward in time, to one of the most haunting moments of my life. For a moment I was frozen in the memory.

"It might sound strange, Clair." I tried to put a laugh in my voice, but it came out raspy.

"Try me."

I turned and pointed to the surf.

"One night I drove to Dauphin Island to go fishing. I was right out there in the water, waves at my waist, a sky full of stars. The moon was full. It made a white line on the water that reached to the horizon. All of a sudden everything seemed to stop moving. I felt I could step onto the moonlight and walk to the horizon, gather the sky in my arms like silk. I could feel everything, Clair: sky, stars. Even the moonlight on my skin. It was the most peaceful moment I'd ever known, and I wanted to stay in that moment forever, never leave the water."

I expected an amused smile. Clair's eyes balanced concern with approval.

"One more thing, Clair," I added. "When I headed back to my car, I passed this house, saw a FOR SALE sign. Guess what it cost?"

"Four hundred and eight thousand dollars, of course."

"I've never known if I should have been delighted or scared. Do you think it was coincidence? Synchronicity? Fate?"

She moved beside me, her shoulder pressing my arm.

"You had a moment of light, Carson."

"What do you mean?"

"It's beyond words. The moments can't be described, only felt. We don't have the language or system of reference for any form of description. The world works in ways we find mysterious, forbidding. But only because we can't see beneath the surface. We sense shapes moving down there, feel ripples as they glide past. It's logical and orderly. But we can't explain why, or what powers it all, since . . ."

"It's outside our frame of reference," I finished. For a moment we looked into one another's eyes. She swallowed and looked away.

"Have you told your ex-girlfriend to watch out for the Kincannons?"

"Not yet. I want to study them first. Closely."

"Don't take long. They're like quicksand. She could get sucked into something she doesn't understand."

"Ms Danbury looks for things she doesn't understand and throws herself into them. It's what made her a good investigative reporter. If I'm going to tell her to stay away from her new boyfriend, I'm going to have to explain why."

Clair spun the cocktail glass in her fingers for a few seconds, stared at the action, mulling over a thought.

"I always wondered why you never introduced Ms Danbury to me."

"I always meant to, Clair. I don't know why I didn't. I'm sorry."

She studied the glass again. Set it on the railing. "It bothered me that you didn't introduce us. A lot, to tell the truth."

"Why?"

Something shimmered in her eyes. The breeze slipped through her hair as she stared toward the horizon.

"It's ridiculous," she said. "Nonsensical."

"Tell me, Clair."

She turned to me. I realized her eyes weren't blue. They were beyond anything that simple.

"I felt left out," she said.

"Left out?"

"I said it was stupid. It's just that . . . we've been through some strange events together,

Carson. Two years ago, when my life was falling apart, you were there. If we hadn't talked in my garden on that terrible day, I would never have faced my vanity and insecurities, the forces that had moved me for years. I might still be trapped in that life."

"It had nothing to do with me, Clair. It was you that stood up to –"

She put her finger against my lips. "I could have retreated into the known and the safe, or jumped across the divide to a new world. I only jumped because you expected me to, Carson. I jumped because you believed I had the strength. I'm here now, safe on another shore, because of you. There was a reason you were in the garden that day."

"There's a reason we both were."

She started to respond, but I saw her mouth falter, not finding the language, the point of reference. Her lips were exotic petals drifting in water. My hands started to rise to her form.

And like Clair's lips, my arms faltered, drifted back to my sides. I turned my eyes from her face, mumbled, "Can I get you another drink?"

"No thank you," she said, rubbing her eyes, like they were worn. "I didn't realize I was so bushed by the week. I think I'd better go."

"Of course," I said. "We've both had some long days."

"We can finish our talk later. Maybe get together for dinner next week. A nice seafood place."

"That'd be good."

I followed her inside. She picked up her purse, slung it over her shoulder, went to the door. I remained in the center of the room, hearing a roaring, like the waves had advanced fifty yards and were breaking against the pilings of my home.

Clair turned. Her eyes took a moment to rise to mine.

"Goodbye, Carson," she said. "Take care."

"Later," I said.

The rains gathered in the west on Sunday, what one forecaster called "the last blast of spring", set to roll through. I saw the system on the weather radar, lines of storm cells rolling in from south Texas and Mexico like ragged green ghosts. I lay in bed most of the day, half-heartedly poring over Rudolnick's pages. Harry called at six; he'd been doing the same.

"I finished my look-see on Rudolnick's case histories. No more pages tucked into magazines.

Nothing more on the guy that scared him. Nothing on Harwood."

"I got about a quarter of a box of Rudolnick's files left over here, Harry. You're free to read through them, you want."

Harry grunted.

"How about you finish them up and I'll drop by later to grab them. Get 'em back into safe-keeping. If I never read another psychiatric case history it'll be too soon."

I glanced out the window: chop in the waves from the wind, but little more than scudding cumulus above. Larger pleasure boats were out; the big white Bertram rolling slowly a quarter-mile out. I wondered if it was a charter. Tourists loved dolphin cruises. My body felt the need for a tour across the water, but via kayak.

First though, there was my homework. I sighed, unboxed the last of Rudolnick's files, set them on my table. Pressed my palms against my temples and read.

Harry arrived close to eight, brushing mist from his hair. I'd finished my Rudolnick files and found nothing else exciting. I had just changed into swim trunks. The rough weather was predicted to last several days and I wanted to get a last run in before the storm arrived.

Harry looked at my swim gear.

"You just got in, I hope."

"Heading out. I need it."

"Carson . . ."

The local cutaway popped on the tube and I made a final check of the Doppler, studying the direction of the clouds on the time-lapse replay.

"I've got to get out there for a bit, Harry, clear my head."

"Look at the damn clouds, Carson. They're a wall."

I looked through the deck doors to the horizon. It looked like war being waged between earth and sky, vertical mountains of indigo smoke lit by jitters of internal lightning. I'd be cutting it close, but I needed the water and the exertion. I'd awakened at three a.m., thinking of my conversation with Clair, and had almost gone to the kayak, sense finally prevailing.

"They're moving almost parallel to the shore right now, Harry; trouble for Florida, not for me, at least not for another hour. I'll be back and on my second beer by then."

Harry shook his head. He would have made a good Daniel Boone, a lousy Thor Heyerdahl.

"I'll have a scotch here; keep an eye out. When you get back, I'll take the files to storage."

"I'll be fine, bro," I assured him. "Go home and play some tunes, blow out the jets."

A murmur of thunder blew in with the wind. Harry grunted, headed for the door, flicking a goodbye wave over his shoulder.

I fought hard past the breakers, putting burn in my shoulders, a rasp in my breathing. Salt stung my eyes. Flying fish jumped my boat. A half-mile out, I stopped paddling and stretched my back.

The breeze shifted direction, carrying the scent of rain and ozone, and I knew it was time for that beer. Twilight had almost deepened into night, and I spun to the pinpoint light of my deck. After a dozen strokes I became aware of a light at my back, behind it the burr of a wide-open motor.

I saw a bow bouncing. Bearing down on me.

I cut at a right angle, but seeming to sense my evasion, the craft angled my way. I waved the paddle above my head like a pennant, idiotically yelling, *"Stop!"*

I dove overboard and pulled hard toward bottom. The thud of the boat hitting my kayak reverberated through the water. The screw slowed as the craft spun in a tight circle. I surfaced, stroked to the side of a thirty-foot Bertram.

Light struck me, a circle of white. I looked into its brilliance and turned away. A rope ladder tumbled over the side. I pulled myself up the ladder, light blazing in my eyes, the boat rocking in the waves.

"Easy with that light," I said, climbing into the craft. "It's blinding me."

"I was afraid we were going to miss you," said a voice from the helm.

"Miss finding me in the water?"

"Miss hitting you just right. I haven't driven a boat in a while."

I froze and looked into the face of the man at the helm. A videotape honed into resolution: Crandell. He was grinning.

"Howdy, Carson," said a voice beside me, strangely familiar. I turned.

Tyree Shuttles.

I spun to dive from the boat, but an arm encircled my neck and threw me to the deck. Something burned hot in my bicep and my mind turned to water and washed me down a hole in the deck.

Crandell's grin followed, like the Cheshire Cat tumbling through the dark.

CHAPTER 38

"I'm not going to believe it," Clair Peltier said. "You people are simply mistaken."

Her hand shook as she let the curtain fall back into place. She walked to Ryder's bedroom, closed the door. Outside was a Coast Guard truck, a battered and bent red kayak roped in the bed. It was ten a.m., the succeeding bands of storm now in their thirteenth hour.

"Where was the kayak again?" Harry Nautilus asked.

"Washed up on Fort Morgan beach, just south of the point." Lieutenant Robert Sanchez was twenty-seven and wrote left-handed on a clipboard. "It was a strong storm, Detective."

"He was an expert in the things. Kayaks."

"Did he wear flotation, sir?" Sanchez asked. "On a regular basis?"

"No," Harry Nautilus admitted.

"We have a team scouring the area, walking the beach. We had boats out, but weather made us pull them. The choppers were grounded as well."

"Are you looking for a swimmer? Or a body?" Nautilus's voice was matter-of-fact, a professional talking to a professional.

"The wind might have blown him across the mouth of the Bay, toward Fort Morgan. Into the ship channel. There were several freighters in and out of the bay last night. Currents at the point are powerful. I once heard a diver describe them as freight trains under the water. There's debris down there, wrecks, things to get hung up on."

"I see," Nautilus said, his voice a whisper.

Sanchez cleared his throat. "Pardon me, Detective, but why would your friend go out in a kayak knowing a storm was blowing in?"

"He made it through his childhood. Sometimes it made him think he could make it through anything."

Sanchez nodded politely, like he understood. A blast of wind shook the house, screamed across the windows. The lights muted to brown, flickered, returned.

"As soon as the storm lets up, we'll go back out, Detective. There's another heavy storm fifty miles out, but we might get a chopper up for a half-hour."

"Thank you," Nautilus said, wondering if the search was little more than a formality.

"Would you like for me to leave your friend's kayak, sir?" Sanchez asked. "Or I can haul it away, if you want."

"Leave it," Clair Peltier said from behind the bedroom door, her voice breaking. "And get that goddamn helicopter in the air."

CHAPTER 39

I had been swimming underwater for days, through green-black water so mossy it abraded my skin. Occasionally I'd see wobbles of light on the surface and swim that direction. Once there, the surface bent from my outstretched hand as I tried to thrust myself into the world of light and air. Yet I found I could float just beneath the luminous gel, hearing snatches of conversation from the air world . . .

How long will he be here?

He'll be gone soon.

What do we tell the others?

Who gives a shit?

After the voices had floated away in the current, I again reached to the glimmer. My hand sunk in to the wrist, then elbow. Inch by inch, like climbing from a wet shroud, I wriggled from the sea, then lay for what seemed hours trying to catch my breath.

When I opened my eyes, I saw a pink balloon floating above my head. It bobbed back and forth. The balloon had a balloon face and the face was smiling. It was a happy balloon.

"Where am I?" I asked the balloon.

"You're in heaven, mister," the balloon answered.

Harry Nautilus stood at the threshold of Carson Ryder's home, hand on the knob. He heard rain on the other side of the door. He turned to Clair Peltier, a question mark in his eyes.

She shook her head. "I'm not leaving. I'm going to wait right here." She walked to the window yet again.

I missed something, Nautilus thought, studying the distraught woman from the corner of his eye. *Or maybe it was so recent . . . There was always something between them. A subcurrent.*

He said, "It's a good idea, Doc. Waiting."

"I read about people who've floated for days, hanging on to something. Remember last year, the guy whose boat went down? He got picked up by a freighter. But the freighter was heading to Galveston. It was two days before the guy got back to land."

Nautilus saw Clair Peltier realize Carson's rescue would trigger an immediate radio call advising of his safety.

"Shit," she whispered.

"All sorts of things can happen," Nautilus said. "Good things."

Clair walked to the deck doors. The next line of storms gathered at the horizon, purple clouds dragging tendrils of lightning. Wind blew in hot bursts, the waves gray and ridged with foam.

Clair's eyes went wide. "Someone's at the door, Harry."

She ran to the front door and yanked it open. Nothing but rain in rippling sheets.

"I know I heard it. Knocking."

Nautilus said, "It's the rain on the roof."

Then Nautilus heard it. Faint, at the edge of hearing. Coming from outside. He followed the sound into the rain, down the steps, under the stilted house. Nothing. Then the wind gusted and Nautilus saw the red kayak, curved, scarred, rocking in its rack with the wind.

"Harry," Clair yelled from the stoop.

"It's nothing," he said. "The wind." He stared at the kayak.

A minute later he was standing in the rain, trying to push the boat as far into his old Volvo wagon as he could manage, binding it to the passenger seat with a rope. It protruded six feet from the rear gate, but was secure.

"Harry!" Clair called from the door. "What are you doing?"

"I'm not sure."

He climbed into the car and drove into the whistling gray.

I had closed my eyes against the vision of the balloon and tumbled beneath the surface of the green water, deliriously happy. Down here, below the surface, was where I knew Clair. A world where everything would make sense had our minds the language to comprehend its logic and order.

Choonk . . . choonk . . . choonk

A rhythmic sound caught my attention. I kicked and spun in the depths, trying to localize the sound. No . . . not a sound. A sensation. Something tapping on my knuckles. I opened my eyes carefully, half-expecting them to flood with seawater. But they opened into air, dry and cool.

The tapping on my knuckles again.

My head seemed to rotate on an axis, and a round pink face floated into view. The eyes were blue and interested. There was a smile that seemed slightly off-kilter. It was the face of a child. My vision sharpened, saw a beard line; not a child, a grown man.

"Who are you?" I asked. My words seemed to come from somewhere beside me. From the edge of a pillow, its case white and crisp.

"Freddy. What's your name?"

"Carson." It was the only thing I could say with certainty.

"Want to meet my friend, Carson?"

"Give me a minute, Freddy. I'm just waking up."

"Miss Holtkamp said a minute is sixty seconds. One . . . two . . . three . . ."

I took several deep breaths, noting my chest wouldn't expand completely. With each breath my awareness seemed to rise, as if air drove out the dark. What is happening? Where am I? *Think. Analyze. Survey.*

"Fifteen . . . sixteen . . ."

A room. Blue walls and ceiling. Fifteen by

fifteen or so. Wide door leading out to a hall. Green tile floor. A window to the side. Are those bars? Daylight. A smell of disinfectant . . .

"Thirty-one . . . thirty-two . . ."

Chest restrained somehow. Belt? Rope? Hands, feet, no motion. Sense of pain at the wrists, compression at the ankles. Mouth dry. *Oh God, there's an IV shunt in my hand! Fight the fear . . . study, measure, analyze . . .* Music in the air, low volume. Electric piano, sax. Heavy bass line. Then a blare of horns. Funk music, Bootsy Collins maybe.

"Fifty-nine and sixty! Want to meet my friend, Carson?"

Friend? I shot a puzzled eye toward the door; no one there.

"Uh, sure, Freddy."

The guy pulled his arm from around his back. There was a cloth puppet on his hand, worn almost bare, a nondescript and cartoonish dog with floppy brown ears, plastic eyes with floating, black-button pupils, and a lolling felt tongue. Freddy made wet sounds, opening and closing his hand on my arm, like the puppet was gnawing or licking.

"Puppy likes you."

"That's great. Can you help me, Freddy? My arms are tied or something. Can you untie them?"

The puppet stopped licking and disappeared behind Freddy's back. He frowned. "That's not green. It's red."

"What?"

"When your arms are like that it's because you did something red. They don't come loose until you're green again."

Red equals bad; green, good?

"Is it, uh, red to have a drink of water, Freddy? I'm very thirsty."

He shook his head and giggled, like I'd just told a great joke.

"There's no color in drinking, Carson; it's just drinking." He padded away, leaving me alone with the music, just at the edge of hearing. Freddy returned seconds later with a plastic cup held in the puppet's mouth.

"Puppy brought you Kool-Aid. Purpleberry."

I found I could wriggle a little bit higher, and the head of the bed was elevated several inches as well. I opened my mouth.

"It's raining purpleberry," Freddy said, dribbling sugared water into my mouth.

"Thanks, Freddy."

"You're welcome, Carson."

"Freddy? Could you tell me where I am?"

He told me. It was the second time I'd heard that answer today.

CHAPTER 40

I drifted off again. My dreams were dark and inchoate, whether the result of my situation or drugs, or both, I could not tell. I dreamed of two balloons bobbing in an indigo sky, one light, one dark. They floated above and around me. I knew I was an object of interest.

"What do you suppose will come of this?"

"We can only give him so much."

"What do we do?"

"Wait and watch."

Later – no idea how long – I heard metallic clattering and opened my eyes to a black woman pushing a cart into the room. She was five-nine or -ten, slender and strong, her fore-arms dancing with muscle as she jockeyed the cart across the threshold. Her hair was pulled back. Her skin was dark and luminous, her face high-boned and classical, Egyptian. I read her age as early sixties. She wore a lime-green nurse's uniform of jacket and skirt. White hose hissed over her legs. Towels were stacked on the cart beside a box of something called Steri-Wipes.

The cart bumped my bedside and she snapped a towel open; no, not a towel, an adult diaper. She whisked the sheet from my body, naked save for a white bunching at my waist. I smelled urine.

"You been sleeping past your bladder calls. I need to make a change so you don't get the rash. Lift yo' butt in the air."

The whole incident was so incongruous I couldn't speak, but could lift a few inches. She removed a wet diaper, cleaned me off with a wipe, taped on a fresh diaper. All in under thirty seconds.

"Where am I, ma'am?"

"You're in heaven." She said it like she'd say *You're in a shoe store.*

"What?"

She flapped the sheet back over me. "It's the only name we're allowed to call it, and the only answer you're gonna get."

"Where the hell am I?" This time my voice was angry.

"I got others to do for," she said, checking her watch. "There's a schedule."

"What's your name?"

"Folks call me Miss Gracie. That's always been enough for the others."

"What others? Where am I?" I called at her retreating form. But all I heard back was the clatter of the cart.

Lucas sat crossed-legged against the wall, the *Mobile Register* in his lap. It seemed Detective Ryder had met an ugly fate.

He read from the paper.

> *. . . confirm that Ryder was an avid kayaking enthusiast who enjoyed rough waters. Records in the Mobile Bay Pilot's Office indicate three freighters entered the bay during the period Mr Ryder might have been in the water, the* Argentine Star, *the* Lady Hannah, *and the* Bali Pearl. *The kayak, recovered on Ft Morgan point, was bent and scarred, the markings of a craft dragged beneath a barnacle-laden hull . . .*

Convincing, Lucas thought. But Crandell was an expert in convincing others of false events. Lucas closed his eyes and his head flooded with memory. Comets turning to flashlights. A strobing white light high above. Voices through a pre-dawn fog.

"I saw something at the base of the microwave tower. It should be to your left; can you see the tower light blinking above the trees?"

"Be careful. He's . . . resourceful."

Resourceful? Hardly. But one learns from mistakes . . .

Lucas shook the past from his head. Even if Ryder had died in a natural accident, things would start moving fast now. And if Ryder were alive somewhere, albeit temporarily? They'd move like a whirlwind.

What was the advice his mentor had provided? His beloved teacher?

"When a shitstorm starts blowing, cover your ass and figure a way to get your enemy to walk into it."

I heard a car pull close outside, tires crunching over gravel. Two minutes later Crandell entered the room, shutting the door behind him. He wore khaki Dockers and a polo shirt. A heavy gold watch wrapped a thick wrist. His arms were pelted with golden hair. He was broad-chested, tanned, powerful looking.

"Hello, darlin'," he sang in a raspy baritone.

I stared at him.

He said, "Now, I didn't mean that as an endearment, Ryder. It's a line from a song that goes –"

"Spare me, Crandell. You have any idea of the prison time you're racking up?"

He clapped his hands and laughed like I'd shared my favorite joke. "What's the sentence for abuse of a corpse?"

"What?"

He leaned close. "You're missing and presumed dead, Ryder. You were blown by a storm into the path of a freighter. By the way, your little pointy boat confirms the story; it's in real bad shape. Sorry 'bout that."

His breath was disgusting, like something in him was rotting. I turned my face away. He picked up a pencil on the table, began pricking my cheek with the point.

"Question time, if you get the point. What do you know about Lucas?"

"Lucas?"

I felt the pencil point break my skin.

"Ouch, Jesus."

prick

"I'm moving up to your eye next."

prick, prick

"He's one of the Kincannon brothers," I said. "The prodigal son, or something. He's a psycho."

Crandell pecked the sharp lead randomly on my face as he talked: forehead, chin, nose, cheek.

"Where is he?"

prick, prick

"How the hell would I know?"

prick

"What did Taneesha Franklin give to DeeDee Danbury?"

"What?"

Crandell swung the pencil in a roundhouse arc, like driving a knife into my right eye. I gasped. He stopped an inch short. I stared at the pencil point above my pupil. Crandell's hands were absolutely steady. My heart hammered in my chest. Crandell set the pencil back on the table. He reached to his pocket.

"I'm showing you two photographs. Tell me what they represent."

"I don't know what you're –"

"Shhh. Two pictures. Ready?"

He pulled a photo from his pocket. "Number one."

A long shot, Dani and Taneesha Franklin in the front window of a Waffle House, coffee on the table, pages spread between them.

"If I recall, they're discussing reporting techniques."

Crandell retrieved a second photo from his pocket, held it before my eyes. It had been taken in late afternoon, the shadows lengthened. Taneesha Franklin stood on Dani's porch, handing her a small parcel.

"What is Miss Franklin handing Miss Danbury?" Crandell asked.

"A copy of *All the President's Men.*"

Crandell tucked the photos back in his jacket, then jangled the change in his pocket.

"I want to know what Danbury got from Franklin. And where it is."

"It's a fucking book. A gift. Have your boss ask Ms Danbury. Buckie-boy's your boss, right? He hired you to put loony brother back in his pen?"

Crandell grabbed the handles at the foot of the bed and whisked me from the room.

"Come on, Ryder. I want you to meet a friend of mine."

I was propelled down a tight hall off the main room.

"Who might that be?" I asked.

He grinned and licked his finger.

"Mr Ampere," he said, touching his wet finger to my bare toe. *"Buzzzzt."*

Harry Nautilus stood in the covered loading dock of the Alabama Forensics Bureau and watched two interns pull the kayak from the Volvo.

"Easy," Wayne Hembree said. "Kid gloves."

"Kid gloves?" an intern laughed. "This thing is beaten like a . . ." He saw Hembree's eyes. Said, "Where do you want it, sir?"

Hembree gave instructions, then turned to Nautilus, his voice somber. "Harry, we're all devastated. Carson was like a –"

Nautilus put his hand on Hembree's shoulder, squeezed.

"Not right now, OK?"

The interns set the kayak on a table that reminded Nautilus of an outsize autopsy table, a bank of lights overhead. Someone flicked a switch and the kayak was bathed in white light. The boat was bent like clock hands indicating 4.00. Hembree reached out and stroked the craft with a fingertip.

"I've never dealt with a kayak before."

"You got one now, Bree. Learn."

Hembree looked across the room at one of the techs, a young guy with an intense look, like he was doing math in his head and being timed on the results.

"MacCready, you know polystyrene, right? Polymers?"

The guy scowled. "I love plastics. Plastics are my life."

"Drop what you're doing and give me a hand," Hembree said. The guy walked around the boat until he found the manufacturer's name. Aimed the scowl at Nautilus.

"They still in business? The manufacturer?"

"I guess so. The boat's pretty new."

Nautilus tumbled through time, recalling when Carson had purchased the boat. He'd had a party, like a housewarming, except for a kayak. Carson set the boat in the living room on sawhorses, hung leis and Mardi Gras beads over its pointy tips. Everyone at the affair, thirty or so friends and neighbors, had to put a hand on the boat and offer a blessing of some kind.

There was a fair amount of drinking and most benedictions were funny. Nautilus recalled being dragged to the center of the room by Danbury, his hand pressed against the boat.

He'd never been good at speeches – hated them – and mumbled some things about winds and tides and friendship.

No one laughed like they had at the other little speeches, everyone getting quiet. Several people wiped away tears. A tipsy Carson had hugged him. It was embarrassing and Nautilus had slipped outside to walk on the beach. When he returned the kayak was in the street, upside down on the shoulders of a dozen people, Carson riding it like a horse as folks waved tiki torches in the dark.

What if those nights were over?

". . . tensile strength and resistance and we might be able to . . ."

"What?" Nautilus said, jolted into the here and now.

"Talking to myself," MacCready said. "I'll give the manufacturer a call. They'll probably have specs on tensile strength, resistance strength. Or can put me onto someone who knows."

Hembree looked at Nautilus, said, "I'll call you when we have something."

Nautilus was almost out the door when Hembree called after him. Nautilus turned.

"Get some sleep, Harry," the moon-faced

technician said, his eyes quiet wells of concern. "You look ter— pretty tired."

Nautilus pulled the Volvo from the loading dock. He drove six blocks before realizing it was raining and turned on his wipers. His stomach grumbled from not eating in over a dozen hours. A small seafood restaurant appeared in the rain and he pulled into the lot.

"It'll be a few minutes, babe," a hefty, fiftyish gum-chewing waitress said, scribbling his order on her pad. She tossed the ticket to the cook behind the counter.

Harry Nautilus put his elbows on the table and dry-washed his face with his hands. The restaurant was quiet and his thoughts loud, overwhelming.

"You got a paper around?" he called to the waitress. "Something to read, anything?"

She reached beneath the cash register, came up with a handful of newsprint, brought him the *Register*. He snapped it open. A page one headline read, *Mobile Detective Missing, Believed Drowned.*

Nautilus pushed the paper away like it was on fire, threw a twenty on the table, ran out the door.

* * *

My forehead turned cold and I opened my eyes. My guts felt like they'd been removed, beaten with jellyfish tentacles, stuck back inside. Miss Gracie was wiping my head with a cool, damp cloth. It felt wonderful.

"You feelin' all right?" she asked, looking into my eyes.

"No."

She wrung water from the towel, refreshed it from a bowl of ice water on the bedside table.

"Why are you doing this?" I asked.

Miss Gracie patted the towel against my forehead, then folded it and left it laying.

"Used to be they'd send people here to test us. Fakes. If we told them things we wasn't supposed to, it could be real bad. If you were fake he wouldn't have done that to you. I can't do much, but I can at least give you a clean head."

"Where am I? And please, don't tell me –"

"You're in a story. An' I think it may be ending. Least the way it is now, the way it's become."

"Story?"

"I'll come back later. Maybe you should know a few parts of the story. Sleep now."

I closed my eyes beneath the cool towel and

drifted off. The next time I awakened, my pain had subsided and my vision was clear. I was still in bed, but someone had pushed me into a different room. Smaller. There was a steel door, closed, a slat at eye-height, also closed. The walls were covered in a thick, coarse-woven fabric, like old-time mats in high school gyms. A light was recessed into the ceiling, criss-crossed with bars.

I was in a padded cell.

Footsteps outside the door, slow and careful. *No more electricity,* I thought. Not now. Leave me alone.

The slat slid open and eyes searched the room, found me on the bed. I saw a sock puppet beside the eyes and sighed with relief.

"What are you doing, Carson?"

"I'm resting, Freddy."

"You shouldn't be in there, Carson," he chided.

"Why's that?"

"That's Lucas's room."

I heard a sound of hard-sole footsteps and Freddy scampered away. The door squeaked open. Crandell stepped into the room, his face bright with false bonhomie.

"Whoa there, Ryder. You look like you been

out partying all night long. You got to crank it back now and then, boy."

I mumbled curses his way. It made his smile brighter.

"You was yelling some things while we were playing. Trying to make like you had it all figured out. It was fun to hear."

"I'm pulling some pieces together, Crandell. Like why you're here. And what you're protecting."

He walked to the side of the bed, raised a questioning eyebrow. "And just what is it I'm protecting, Ryder?"

"The family's reputation."

"Interesting theory. Make it go somewhere."

"Lucas was falling apart, decompensating. I'm talking four years back, when he was eighteen, when these sorts of problems usually present. The family knew about it, knew Lucas got the bad seed. He had a crazy uncle, Treehouse Boy or whatever. Insanity repeating in the family. But intervening in Lucas's madness would mean . . . what? Committing him? Embarrassment? Bringing up sordid bits of Maylene's history and humiliating her all over again?"

The breadth of Crandell's smile was unsettling.

"Hang on a sec, Ryder . . ." he said, jogging from the room, returning seconds later with a chair. He sat it in reverse, arms crossed on the chair back.

"I got to sit, Ryder. Listening to your theories is better than a movie. OK, keep going."

I glared at him and continued. "Then one day Lucas does the big wig-out. Kills Frederika Holtkamp. She was Freddy's teacher. Freddy mentioned her name the other day."

Crandell nodded. "She was Fred's teacher for years. Brought that boy a long way, I hear."

"The Kincannons knew Lucas was about to flip out, knew the signs well enough to stay on Lucas's trail. They were too late, finding him under the microwave tower, covered with Holtkamp's blood." I lifted my head from the pillow. "Was that when they called you in for the dirty work, Crandell? To co-opt Barlow? It was your idea to pull Pettigrew to Montgomery, get him off the case, right?"

"What'd make this movie perfect," Crandell leered, "was if I had me some Milk Duds."

His grin was maddening. I said, "I know about Rudolnick, Crandell."

"Oh my. Do tell."

"I figure Mama K thought her boy could be

brought back from the brink of madness. Rudolnick's drug problem was probably known in a small circle. You found out, set him up for a fake bust. From that point on, he belonged to the Kincannons. Rudolnick consulted at Mobile Regional Hospital, right? The Kincannons give big bucks to MRH. Carrot and stick. One hand has money, the other can slip an arrest report into the system. Easy when you own cops like Shuttles, right?"

Crandell clapped his hands. Stomped his feet on the floor. "You ever think of renting out as an entertainment center, Ryder? You're amazing."

"Rudolnick wanted out, conscience maybe. But that couldn't happen, could it? Leland Harwood handles the disposal. He takes the fall, but a paid-off group of witnesses sends him on a light flight. He gets promised big compensation when he gets out. But he's a loose end, a talker. You drop Tommy the Bomb on him."

Crandell shook his head, sighed. "I wish you hadn't been at the prison that day, Ryder. This could all have been avoided."

"We would have dug you up, Crandell. Just from a different direction."

"Not a chance."

"Answer me one thing, Crandell: why did Lucas kill Taneesha Franklin? Miss Gracie keeps the music on during the day when no one's here. WTSJ. Did Lucas form a bond by listening to her?"

Crandell stood, picked up the chair. He was leaving.

"Come on, Crandell," I yelled. "Give me something."

He turned, a big smile on his face.

"You got a couple things right, Ryder. But you ain't near the core."

"What's the core?"

He winked. "This whole shitaree ain't nothing more than a little family business. That's all." He checked his watch. "Got to be going. Business calls. Enjoy breathing, Ryder. You got about a dozen hours of it left."

CHAPTER 41

Nautilus started to put music on, sorting through a stack of recently played CDs, nothing feeling right. He knelt to a shelf of vinyls, flicked through the titles, the musicians: Armstrong, Bechet, Beiderbecke, Coltrane, Johnson, Monk, Parker, Rainey, Spanier, Teagarden . . . a century of jazz and blues. Nothing sounded right. For the first time he could ever remember, there was nothing he wanted to hear. He fell into the couch and willed his head to stop thinking. *Wait on the call from Hembree.*

An hour later his phone rang. He checked the incoming number: Forensics.

"What you got, Bree?"

"You don't live too far do you, Harry?"

"I'll be right there."

Hembree was alone with the kayak when Nautilus arrived, the skinny Forensics expert standing with his hand on its surface. Hembree looked up, saw Nautilus.

"We spoke with the kayak's manufacturers, Harry, WaveDesign out in San Diego. They're big on engineering, their niche in the market. They do impact tests, strength tests. Drop the things from cars going sixty miles an hour, slam them with big boats, little boats, jet skis. They float them in front of oil tankers to see what pops up in the wake. They've even devised a torsion test where they –"

"Bree . . ."

"Sorry. We e-mailed WaveDesign photos of the kayak, close-ups, full-lengths, micros. They called back with more questions, wanting additional photos from other angles. MacCready talked their lingo, made it easier. The WaveDesign folks were fascinated by the problem."

"And?"

Hembree looked side to side. All the other staffers were gone for the day or in other parts of the building. He lowered his voice.

"Were you guys working on anything dangerous?"

"It's possible. Why?"

"From everything the folks at WaveDesign could ascertain, the kayak's been run over by a vehicle. Several times."

"Tire marks?"

"None, but all someone had to do was drop a heavy-duty tarp over the surface. Damage without tracks."

Nautilus scratched his fingernail over the gouges in the surface of the boat.

"Faked, you're saying?"

"Someone may have wanted this thing to look like it'd been plowed under by a big-ass ship. Nothing's washed ashore?"

"Let me get an update." Harry dialed the Coast Guard, asked for Sanchez, held his breath.

Sanchez came on. "It's not quite what I expected. We've had a wind shift. Wind's been running with the current for ten hours. When the wind and current are at cross purposes, so to speak, a, uh, floating object might lay motionless in the water, pushed toward shore by current and waves, pushed out by wind. With the conditions as they stand, I expected we'd see something by now."

"It's rare to not see something?"

"I still wouldn't be hopeful, Detective

Nautilus. Not after this much time. It pains me to say that."

"Thank you." Nautilus clicked off, dropped the phone in his pocket.

"Not so much as a scrap of cloth, Bree."

Hembree thought a long moment. "What should I do with this information, Harry? There's no investigation number for the kayak on the books. It's not official."

"Let's keep it that way for a while."

Hours passed. The door opened. Miss Gracie stepped inside.

"The only people watching are outside waiting for someone who ain't coming yet."

She kicked off the brakes on the bed and grabbed the push bar, wheeling me out into the common area. The lights were lowered and the room was suffused with amber light, like candlelight. The shades over the windows were drawn tight.

Low music drifted from hidden speakers, an old Motown piece I couldn't identify. A radio station, WTSJ, I assumed. Miss Gracie spun the bed to angle me down a wide and dark hall jutting from the large room. She stopped at the door. I saw Freddy asleep on a large bed, the broad, flat face, button nose. Beside Freddy, on the pillow, was the dog puppet.

"That boy won't sleep right unless he can touch the puppet," she said. "It's real to him."

"Freddy has Down syndrome?"

"He don't know what he's got, what he don't got. Of everything, Freddy got the best."

"Excuse me?"

"He's got the run of the place in here. That's the rule. He's allowed outside."

"I saw him outside last week. With security."

"Freddy gets what he wants. He just asks. That's what's supposed to happen; people get what they want."

"Heaven."

She looked away.

"He's a Kincannon child, isn't he?" I asked. "Freddy?"

She stared the ancient eyes at me, like weighing my soul for a journey.

"He Miss Maylene's third boy, born between Mr Racine and Mr Nelson."

I looked at Miss Gracie, let my eyes ask the question.

"He got born," she said. "Not long after, he died. Leastwise, that's what people got told."

She pushed me to the next doorway. I saw

a gray-skinned, goggle-eyed apparition with a head like a pumpkin. The bars of the bed had been wrapped with foam to protect the head. The mattress was thick, as if puffed with air. The man's eyes turned to mine and I took an impression of inestimable sadness.

"Who is that, Miss Gracie?"

"Mr Johnny."

"What's wrong with him?"

"He come out with the water on his brain and some other 'flictions."

"Hydrocephaly."

"He ain't much work. Miz Kincannon always gets the best medical things, just got new beds to fight the sores. We had a problem with sores for years. It's fixed now."

"How old is Mr Johnny?"

"Thirty-nine."

We passed another door. Inside, curled in a tight ball, was a man with mocha skin. I noted his mouth had been repaired, a cleft palate, I assumed. Stunted fingers jutted from flipper-like hands. The floor was padded, soft. There were toys in the corner, simple ones, a ball, inflatable blocks, an elementary jigsaw puzzle.

"Who's that?" I asked.

"Tyler."

"He looks young."

"Tyler's just turned twenty-two."

Tyler's eyes opened and he made wet sounds that seemed to express happiness. His nose was running. Miss Gracie stepped into the room and pulled a tissue from a box at the bedside, gently wiped his nose. She stroked his dark hair and cooed in his ear for several minutes and his eyes softened back into sleep. I saw her fingers brush his arm before she turned back my direction.

We rolled onward for a few feet and stopped. She turned her face away, shame in her voice. "They ain't nothing I can do to help you. It will come back to hurt others. I can't do it. I thought you should know."

"Thank you for telling me."

She took the bedrails and wheeled me onward.

"How many people are here, Miss Gracie?"

"Five lives here. Four, I mean, with Lucas gone."

"Freddy, Johnny, Tyler . . . three. That leaves one."

The ancient eyes studied me again. "We'll get there soon enough."

I went fishing for information. "I met Lucas briefly. I hear he's very bright. Is that true?"

She walked slow and her stockings hissed with every step. It put a soft rhythm behind her words as we moved through the halls of the building.

"You could see the smart pour off Lucas like heat. He was real different that way. The Kincannons, well, most of them are good-looking people."

"But not real bright?"

"Ain't much in them but vanilla pudding. Not dumb, but not smart, neither. Except for Miz Maylene, but her smarts are for jerkin' people the way she needs. The boys know about making money, but ever'body knows money pulls money, so it's no big deal. They all got a meanness they try and hide 'cept when no one's looking. But a person always ends up what they are."

"They come here? The brothers?"

"Mr Buck comes the most. He lives across the way. Miz Kincannon lives near, too. Mr Buck only comes ever' now and then. I think Miz Kincannon makes him."

Buck lives across the way. I was in one of the houses on the sprawling Kincannon estate. At least I now knew that much.

We came to an elevator. She inserted a key

and pressed a button. I heard the whirr of a descending elevator. Miss Gracie waited with her arms crossed, watching the closed door. The years fell away in the subdued light, and I saw what a beautiful woman she must have been in her youth, the Egyptian features time had highlighted, not diminished.

The door hissed open. We ascended to the next floor, a soft *bing* announcing our arrival. I was rolled into a ballroom-size open space, a surprise, given the classic external architecture of the house.

The space was masculine, with slatwood floors, heavy wood and leather furnishings, oak wainscoting rising half the distance to fourteen-foot-high ceilings. The windows were large, with flowing scarlet drapes. There were plush carpets and brass lamps. There was a massive stone fireplace at the far end of the room. The air was cool and comfortable and smelled of bay rum and wood polish. The lights were dim, but the space seemed suffused with its own internal illumination.

The area facing the elevator was an office setting. A massive burled-wood desk centered an oriental carpet of red and gold. A green banker's lamp cast a soft glow across the desk.

Behind the imposing desk, in a high-backed chair, sat a white-haired old man. He was small, lean and compact, with shoulders unbent by time. His face was pink and calm and neatly shaven, his eyebrows full, his hair unshorn for years, flowing like a snowy mane. He wore a red velvet robe. Beneath the desk I saw blue pajama pants, leather slippers over bare feet.

The old gentleman was writing in a tablet with a fountain pen. His hands seemed delicate, the nails manicured. He worked with diligence, writing a few words, pursing his lips over what he'd written, continuing. He seemed oblivious to our presence.

"What you working on, Mr Buck?" Miss Gracie asked.

The old man looked up. It took several seconds for our presence to register.

"The answer to everything," he said, his voice dry and faint. He returned to his work.

"May we see?"

His hands shook when he wasn't writing. He licked his lips and hoisted the page for us to view. Meaningless scribbles. He giggled, a strand of drool falling from the side of his mouth. Miss Gracie made comforting childlike noises in his direction, returned me to the elevator. The doors hissed shut.

"Buck Kincannon Senior, right?" I said. "He looks healthy. Glowing."

"Mr Buck wear a diaper. He sleep fifteen hours a day. Half the time, I spoon food in him. Car's all shiny, but the motor's burned up."

The whole second floor was a sham, I saw, a theatrical set to give Daddy Kincannon a sense of place after all his years in business. The elevator door opened on the first floor.

"Why did you show me Mr Buck?" I asked.

A long pause. "He wanders, like Freddy. If you see him moving around, it's best you know he ain't tryin' to hurt you. You understand?"

I found her tone discordant, almost imploring. I said, "I understand." But I didn't.

Miss Gracie wheeled me down the hall, again passing the occupied rooms.

"Lucas is kept in the red room?" I asked. "The padded room?"

"Sometimes."

"When he's bad? When his madness presents?"

Another pause. "Mr Lucas go in there when his mama come. She can look at him through the door. It's how she's been told."

"To keep her safe from him?"

"To keep something safe for someone."

A sleepy voice came from behind us. "Carson? Is that you?"

Miss Gracie spun the bed. Freddy was at his doorway, watching. The puppet hung from his hand.

"What you doing up, Mr Freddy?" Miss Gracie asked. "You supposed to be sleeping."

"I saw Carson. Puppy and I want to play."

"You get right back in that bed. I'm takin' this fella on a look-see an' we don't need any company."

"No fair."

"Get yourself in bed now, mister. You can play when it's morning."

Freddy grumbled and pouted back to his bed. He jumped in, pretended to fall asleep, growling out fake snores. He half-opened one eye and winked at me, like he'd put a big one over on Miss Gracie.

She sighed as she pushed me past the room. "That boy think he's so cool."

"Boy? He must be nearing his forties."

"He still a child, always be one." She looked at her watch. "I got to make checks, change diapers, make sure Freddy got his butt in bed.

If that boy don't get a full eight, he's cranky all day. I'll be back once more 'fore I turn off the lights." She started to the door, stopped. Turned her head to me, her eyes dark with mystery.

"You don't say nothin' to no one about that little ride you took, that's the way, right?"

"What ride, Miss Gracie?"

CHAPTER 42

I stared at the slatted door and replayed what I'd learned during Miss Gracie's tour. I now knew my location. I knew who was in here with me, and perhaps a bit of why.

I tried to mesh the information with what Crandell's questions had suggested. I'd repeatedly told him Taneesha and Dani's relationship was no more than brief mentoring on Dani's part. But his insistence and the direction of his questions led me to a conclusion: Crandell was sure that whatever Taneesha had uncovered or been looking into had been shared with Dani.

"Buck Kincannon is Danbury's boyfriend," I remembered screaming, the pain a blazing rope stretched from my groin to my brain. "Have that bastard verify it."

"Buck got the bitch off the street," Crandell had replied. "That's his end of it for now."

Off the street?

I repeated the phrase in my mind. Had Dani's promotion from investigative reporter to anchor been a scheme to pull her inside, keep her busy with new tasks to learn? Kept under watch? The methodology fit: move the potentially troublesome piece to a new board, as with Pettigrew.

Dani's insistence that someone had been in her house now seemed likely. Buck Kincannon had taken her out that night so Crandell or some lock-picking subcontractor could get inside, search for notes, for some tie between Dani and Taneesha.

But the suspicions of Dani's potential involvement demonstrated a lack of knowledge about journalists, their ferocity in protecting stories. The rush-hot pinnacle of the craft was breaking a fresh story, the celebrated exclusive. Even a fledgling like Taneesha Franklin would have kept her cards tight to her bosom.

Crandell had not believed me: I could have been screaming that the earth was flat.

The door pushed open. I held my breath. Miss Gracie clattered the cart into the room, snapped open a diaper. She dropped it into the wastebasket beside my bed. I raised an eyebrow and she tapped the bag slung on the IV holder.

"The bottle got muscle-relaxing dope in it. Keep you too loose-kneed to walk if you manage to get up. I messed with the tubes a bit, got it dripping onto a diaper in the waste can. Unless you want me to keep the IV in for the pain?"

"No!"

She snapped her finger to her lips, frowned. "Shhhh. I never know when he gonna walk in, checking."

"Crandell?"

She closed her eyes, her face a mask of sorrow.

"Craziness. Jus' like it was four years back. Last year, too. Ever' time that nasty man's here, the world fall into hell."

She reached for a second diaper, snapped it open. I arched my back and let her perform her tasks.

"Tell me more about Lucas," I said. "His youth. Did you know him back then?"

"Mr Lucas was a crazy type, wild notions. It was like everyone else was running on little batteries and Lucas got plugged into the full two-twenty volts. He'd take angry fits: yellin' at parties, saying what a bunch of fakes they all were, stomping away wishing he lived with a normal family. One time he started a big fire. Lift yo' butt."

"Fire?"

"There was a family gathering. It was like usual. Ever'one came to Mr Buck's. Someone said something and Mr Nelson ran outside and began beating on Mr Racine's new car with a lamp. Them folks never stop fighting. There was a big howling set-to until the fire started. You can set your butt down now."

"Lucas set a fire in the house?"

"He splashed charcoal lighter on his mama's flowers, tossed a match. Then he put on another of his big screaming shows, calling ever'one names, saying what a bunch of hypocrites they all were."

An earlier mention of Lucas and fire made me suspect pyromania, one of the major markers of a serial killer's pathology. But the pyromaniac is generally elusive and secretive: setting fires in abandoned buildings, off-hours construction sites, parked cars. The setter often retreats a short distance and watches in anonymity as clamor ensues.

Behold my power.

"Lucas didn't run off?" I asked.

"He stood there watchin', jumping up and down, screaming what a bunch of idiots they all were, how he wished they were all dead. Miz Kincannon was bad upset, I heard. Crying. An' that woman never cries."

It stopped me: Maylene Kincannon crying?

I figured it took incredible emotional turmoil to evoke tears in someone devoted to absolute control. I wondered if Lucas's behavior had plunged Maylene Kincannon into her past? Made her terrified that her shrieking, fire-setting son was transmogrifying into a maniacal killer, like the sad and savage brother in her dysfunctional family.

What could someone do with that kind of fear? I wondered.

A motion through his window caught Harry Nautilus's eye, headlights moving slow down the street, one light dimmer than the other, ready to fail. A minute later, the same car passed again.

Nautilus went outside to sit on the porch.

The car made a third pass. The brake lights flashed and the car slid to the curb. Pace Logan got out. He shot a nod at Nautilus, started up the walk, hands in his pockets. Logan stopped at the steps to the gallery. He looked uneasy, blew out a breath.

"Listen, Nautilus, I wanted to say I'm sorry. About Ryder. I, uh . . ."

"It's all right, Logan. Thanks."

Logan looked into the street and cracked his knuckles one by one, then toyed with his watchband. *He wants to say something,* Nautilus thought.

"Can I get you a drink, Pace?"

Logan looked surprised at the offer, or the use of his first name, or both.

"That'd be nice . . . Harry. Bourbon and water, if you got it. Thanks."

Nautilus returned a minute later with the drink. Logan took a sip of bourbon, spun the glass in his palms. His cowboy boots tapped his nervousness.

"I was always happy as a street cop, Harry. It was good work that needed doing. Sometimes you had to think fast, but you didn't have to think deep, y'know? I was comfortable with that. But then, time goes on. When you meet people, tell 'em, 'I'm a cop,' they're like *so what?* Or, *Hey, can you get a ticket fixed for me?* But tell 'em you're a detective and suddenly they're seeing *Kojak* or *Law and Order*. It was an ego thing, the chance to make like something more'n a guy that drove around knocking heads and standing between people yellin' at one another."

Logan spun the glass a long moment.

"I'm not a very good detective, Harry. Not like you. It eats at me, sometimes."

"Pace, you don't have to –"

"It goes back to that night in the rain, Harry. Taneesha Franklin. That's why I'm here, I think. To tell you a story."

Nautilus felt electricity sparkle up his back. Said, "I'm listening."

"Shuttles likes to cut me down like I'm a relic, telling me how law enforcement's becoming so scientific . . . Did you know *this* about latents, Pace? Did you know *that* about DNA? Did you know satellites can track a car from a hundred-whatever miles up? Did you know the *new* generation of cruiser cameras can read license tags from four hundred feet away?"

"I didn't know that," Nautilus said. "Maybe I'm a relic, too."

"Shuttles loves talking about all the new crime-solving hoo-hah: computers, cameras, geo-whatever locators – anything that makes me come off like a dinosaur." Logan cleared his throat. "I say this so you'll know I don't like Shuttles – I hate the cocky little prick, Harry – but I don't think I'm letting it mess with my judgment."

"I believe you, Pace. Go on."

"I was seeing a lot of the same scenery that night. Shuttles was driving and just cruising one quadrant of our beat. I said, 'Come on, Tyree, move it around some.' So he moved a couple streets over. I thought, Fuck it, the kid's like a stuck needle. Then he told me how you'd been talking behind my back about what a lousy cop I was for screwing up that one case."

"Pace, believe me, I never said a thing like . . ."

Logan held up a broad hand. "I know, Harry, leastwise I do now. Then the call came, you and Carson heading for the scene. But after all Shuttles's goading I wanted to get there first, grab it from you."

"But after you got there, you turned the case over to us, Pace. Why?"

"When I saw what had happened in that car, I knew you guys would do better than me and some fresh-from-a-uniform kid."

"I'm not sure what you're trying to –"

"I been thinking about that night, Harry. After you and me had our little scuffle, I was leaning against the Mazda to catch my breath. Then I saw a plastic bag floating in the gutter, riding high as a sailboat, just starting to get pounded under by the rain. It was about then Shuttles found the knife. Am I crazy, or does that seem strange?"

Nautilus thought a few seconds. Saw what Logan was getting at.

"It could mean a whole lot, Pace. Depends on the rain flow and where Shuttles was standing."

Logan sipped from his drink. "A couple weeks back I slipped two pictures out of the murder book. I wanted to refresh my head on the lay of the land. The rainwater was rushing away from where Shuttles had found the knife."

Nautilus looked at the aging detective, raised an eyebrow. "What you planning on doing with this observation, Pace?"

Logan smiled sadly, slapped Nautilus on the knee. Stood and shook stiffness from his legs.

"What I just did, Harry, hand it to someone who knows more than me. I'm probably just imagining things, but I had to get it off my chest. Thanks for the time and the drink."

Logan stepped from the gallery, headed down the walk toward his car. Logan got inside, fired up the engine, pulled away. *I blew it,* Nautilus thought, watching the retreating taillights. *I looked at Logan's bumbling and fumbling, filed him under Lazy, filed him under Dimwit. Instead, I could have said, "Pace, sometimes this stuff gets complicated; here's an idea you might want to try . . ."*

CHAPTER 43

It seemed late when Crandell stepped into the room, but it was closer to dawn. I hadn't slept, thinking all night. He checked my restraints and I saw his watch: six a.m. I did the dopey-eyed look, moved slow as my heart beat fast. It had been hours since Miss Gracie had disconnected the IV tube, now running beneath the sheet and cover, dripping not into my blood, but the waste can beside the bed. Yesterday I had felt like a head attached to a rotting log. Now I felt muscles, ligaments, life and motion beneath my neck.

"Figure anything else out, Ryder?" Crandell asked, tapping the half-depleted IV bag, letting his finger trail along the tubing. He started to push aside the sheet and check my shunt.

I snapped my head his way. "This is all a setup, right? A major league piece of sleight of mind. Lucas isn't a psycho."

It got his attention. He dropped the sheet and raised an eyebrow.

"You've been thinking, Ryder."

I babbled a free-association of ideas stewing in my head for hours. Anything to keep his eyes on my face.

"Lucas was acting out, a high-strung kid in a family of self-absorbed greed mongers. He may have taken youthful rebellion to the limit, but he wasn't pathological. The brothers' problem was Lucas's brain. If he calmed down, Maylene might think Lucas was the one to hold the reins of the family businesses, not Buckie or Nelson or Racine, a trio of puddingheads."

Crandell winked. "Those puddingheads are smart enough to call me. Made me a rich man."

I said, "I know about the DuCaines, about Tree-house Boy. The family precedent for homicidal psychopathology."

Crandell shrugged. "It was a fucked-up family."

"Lucas's brain threatened the brothers. So you or someone killed Frederika Holtkamp.

Told Maylene that Lucas did it, that he had an obsession with Freddy's teacher."

"If you found out about her killer brother, you know the old gal knew a bit about obsession."

"After Lucas escaped, you killed Taneesha Franklin . . . just in case Lucas made his way to Maylene and tried to convince her he wasn't a maniac. Taneesha's dead body said otherwise."

Crandell's smile faltered.

"Ms Franklin got wind of some of the dealings, little stuff. She played junior reporter, going to the KEI offices and asking questions. What a dumb bitch. We used one of old Buck Senior's knives, a family heirloom."

"Lucas's prints on it, of course."

"Easily done. Shuttles got us a picture of the murder weapon from a Forensics report. We showed Mama Kincannon the family knife in a photo on official Alabama Forensics Bureau stationery and she fainted dead away. She truly thinks Luke is the incarnation of Tree-house Boy."

"You killed Taneesha somewhere else, drove the car to the scene."

Crandell clapped his big hands and grinned.

"Did it in an ol' barn. Franklin talked and talked. She didn't know squat, as it turned out, a waste of time. I made the car look like a robbery, drove it across town on a hauler, waiting for Shuttles to get there and plant the knife with the prints."

Just like a car hauler had picked up Lucas's car after he'd been set up for the Holtkamp killing, Pettigrew's tracks to nowhere. Crandell had taken a drug-addled Lucas to the field, made sure he was soaked with Holtkamp's blood, then arranged for Lucas to be caught beneath the tower. He and the car were spirited away, and Lucas became a prisoner of the family. I recalled another discrepancy. The trucker Dell had described the Wookiee figure as apelike, but Leroy Dinkins had described Lucas's build as tall and slender. Crandell was wide-built, with short and bowed legs. A simian body.

I said, "It wasn't Lucas the trucker saw."

Crandell patted at the sides of his head.

"Ten-dollar Halloween wig-and-beard combo. Lucas never shaved in here, more youthful rebellion. When Mama read the police reports, she figured it was her boy indulging himself again."

"And you're going to bring him back."

"It won't take long. He'll stay close. Mama's still talking about keeping him here, putting more locks on the doors or whatever. But no more pussyfooting this time, Ryder."

"What are you talking about?"

His grin went to a thousand watts. His eyes glittered with the wonder of himself.

"Lucas is going to kill one more time, Ryder. But no more holiday at the Ritz. Mama's gonna finally allow a complete lobotomy on Lukie-boy. We already got a Mexican doctor to do the digging."

Disgust roiled in my guts. The three older Kincannon brothers were going to turn Lucas Kincannon into a vegetable, ending the threat of his superior mind.

"Who's Lucas going to kill?" I said.

Crandell gave it a two-beat pause. He looked carefully into my eyes, loving the moment.

"Buck Kincannon's girlfriend, Ryder. A pretty little blonde newslady. Ever met her?"

Nautilus walked through the door of the Police Academy at eight in the morning. He'd been up until three, then grabbed a few hours of sleep, knowing his head had to be ready for what he might have to create. What was needed was confirmation, a sign that pulled it all together.

These days the Academy was run by Major Dominick Purselli. Dom Purselli had been Shuttles's training officer and might be able to fill in details on the kid, make sense of Logan's story. Purselli knew Logan, the two were buddies, actually, and had been partners years ago. Like Logan, Purselli was something of an old warhorse, he just had a lot better temperament.

Nautilus opened the door to Purselli's office. A squat woman with wiry hair sat at his desk.

"Hey, Alice, Dom in?"

"He's on vacation this week."

"Vacation?"

"Somewhere up in Canada, moose country. Due back in a week. You teaching a class again this year?"

"Trying not to."

"We'll get you." Her face fell suddenly. "Harry, about Carson . . ."

Nautilus waved her words off.

She said, "I know. Tough to talk about."

Nautilus jammed his hands in his pockets and walked past the Hall of Heroes, photos of officers who'd died in service to the force. There was a space for the next picture, the hanger already in place. He closed his eyes as he passed by, opened them as he passed twenty feet of displays honoring those who'd made some form of contribution to the Mobile Police Department, headed for the door.

He snapped his fingers and spun, jogging back to the display case. There were plaques, photos, newspaper clippings. The items were arranged chronologically. *When did Shuttles start?* Nautilus checked dates, found the most recent. He saw a big wood-and-brass plaque with a photo of Nelson Kincannon mounted on it, the photo and a newspaper clipping coated with acrylic. Kincannon was canted toward the camera, eyes squinted above a big toothy grin.

Nelson Kincannon was shaking hands with Tyree Shuttles.

Feeling sweat prickle on his back, Nautilus read how, a few years back, Tyree Shuttles had been a recipient of the KEI scholarship for law-enforcement excellence, a recognition paying for all his college courses, and any living expenses incurred, and granting him a "Merit Endowment" of fifty thousand dollars.

One hand gives . . .

CHAPTER 44

"You're a liar, Crandell! Kincannon wouldn't let you kill his girlfriend!"

Crandell's hand fell over my mouth. His smile was a mockery of humor, a twisted sneer, poisonous. He put his lips to my ear, whispered, "It was Buck's idea, Ryder. Buck's got a dark side like you wouldn't believe. It'll make Mama think old Luke's taken a turn for the worst."

Crandell removed his hand from my mouth.

"Turn for the worst?" I said. "Maylene thinks Lucas killed two women. That's not bad enough?"

Crandell chuckled, a hollow sound. "A spinster schoolteacher and a black junior reporter? To Maylene, that's deer on the highway. By this time tomorrow, Lucas will appear to have killed Buck's high-profile girlfriend in Buck's house, way too up close and personal for Maylene. She'll beg for that Mex doctor, get Lucas's head roto-rooted so this nastiness never happens again."

"When is this supposed to happen?"

"Tonight, Ryder. Lucas strikes again."

The door closed and I fought my restraints to no avail. I cursed myself aloud and repeatedly. I remembered Rudolnick's hidden records describing a madman, a concealed sociopath on a downward spiral.

> *It is like walking beside a normal and respected person who has decided to become a suicide bomber, never knowing when he will grasp the plunger.*

I'd figured Rudolnick was surreptitiously observing Lucas.

He was observing Buck.

"You want what, Harry?" Claypool said. He was wearing a tie-dyed ball cap, purple jeans, tire-tread sandals, and a black shirt with bold white lettering: ELECTRONS GIVE ME A CHARGE.

Nautilus explained his needs.

"That doesn't take any thinking," Claypool said, "but it sounds like fun. Lemme grab a soldering iron."

"Maybe some of the bubble-wrapper stuff, too," Nautilus added, "like it just came out of a box. You folks got any of that?"

Claypool looked about to swoon with delight and promised to send the package over within an hour. Nautilus made his office by nine. He wrote a few lines on a scrap of paper, then called Glen James from Tech Services.

"That's strange, Harry," James said, studying the lines. "But I'll be glad to help."

Nautilus went to the windowed conference room off the detectives' room and unhooked the monitor and pushed it to the side, like it was being replaced. He saw an intern from Forensics wandering the floor with a brown package in his hand, waved him over. He set the package from Claypool on the table, then dialed Shuttles at his desk.

"Hey, Tyree, this is Harry. I'm in Conference room A. Got a minute?"

"Sure, Har," Shuttles said, excitement in his voice. "Be right there."

Har, Nautilus thought. He recalled the movie

All That Jazz, Roy Scheider popping a couple pills to kick off his day, smiling in the mirror, saying, "It's show time."

"Show time," Nautilus whispered.

Shuttles bounced in the door and took a seat. Nautilus figured Shuttles had to be thinking the two would be paired as a team. *It's a terrible thing about Carson, Tyree, but I need a new partner, and I think we'd work well together . . .*

"What's up, Har?" Shuttles was trying hard to hold in the grin.

Nautilus kept the smile. But shifted his eyes to the ones he used for interrogations. Black rockets, someone once called them. Nautilus aimed the rockets through Tyree Shuttles's pupils and into his brain.

"Did you really think you'd get away with it, Tyree?"

"Uh, what are you talking about, Harry?"

Nautilus picked up the package prepared by Claypool. He pulled out an object protected by bubble wrap.

"What's that, Harry?" Shuttles asked.

"You'll know when you see it."

Nautilus removed the tape securing the wrap. A small slip of paper fell out, INSPECTED BY NUMBER 57, underscored by a line of bar code.

Beautiful, Nautilus thought. He owed the multitalented Claypool a big dinner. Nautilus revealed a small assemblage of metal, plastic, and circuitry surrounding a tube like the front barrel of a rifle sight, a large optic glinting from the center. There was a mounting bracket. A cigarette-pack-sized control panel with buttons and LEDs. The ad hoc contraption looked like a sidearm from a *Star Wars* movie.

"Now do you understand, Tyree?"

"I don't know what that thing is, Harry." Shuttles couldn't keep the scared out of his voice.

"One of the new cameras for the detective cars."

"*What* cameras?"

"Like the ones in the patrol cars, but the next generation. Pace never told you?"

"Told me *what*?"

"Pace and me met with the chief a few weeks back. We discussed who'd get the first one, the test camera. Brand-new super-high-resolution cameras, fifteen grand per. It was scheduled for your car, Pace having the most seniority. But Pace didn't want the camera. So Carson and me got it installed in our car."

Sweat beaded on Shuttles's forehead. He had the dry-mouth swallow.

"Pace doesn't tell me anything. He probably forgot. The asshole doesn't care about this kind of stuff. He won't even use a computer."

Nautilus went to the door, opened it, yelled, "Where the hell's the monitor I asked for?"

Glen James was standing across the room talking to Lieutenant Tom Mason, the head of the department. James glanced down at his cupped palm, reading from the script Nautilus had prepared.

"On its way, Harry. Settle down. We can't use a regular TV, it's got to have the special screen. Like HDTV, where you see the pores on people's faces. They'll have it here in a few minutes."

"Hurry the fuck up."

"You gonna watch a porn flick, Harry? You'll be able to count twat hairs, that much I can tell you."

Glen James, improvising.

Nautilus slammed the door, sat back down. He rarely swore or slammed doors, making it that much more effective.

"I don't give a fuck about cameras, Tyree. What would I want with a picture of Taneesha Franklin's car as we pull in? No one even looked at the tape until this morning. Hell, I didn't even want to test the camera that night, all the damn rain, but you know Carson. He was playing with the thing like a toy."

"Franklin?" A tinder-dry whisper.

"I want you to explain something to me, Tyree. Something that doesn't make a damn bit of sense. The camera's on, it's switched to extreme night vision, something to do with lux rating or whatever. A regular camera wouldn't show jackshit, all that rain, distance. But this new camera is taking in everything."

Nautilus glared through the window into the detectives' room, like he was angry the monitor wasn't there yet.

"It's maybe fifty feet from our cruiser to you in the shadows behind the Mazda. What does supercamera show when we slow the playback, Tyree?"

The kid was too scared to speak.

Roll the dice, Nautilus thought, about to make the jump suggested by Logan's observation. *Here's where I win or lose . . .*

"It shows you pulling a plastic bag from under your rain gear, Tyree. You open it, take out a knife, drop the bag into the gutter. Then you start yelling, 'Knife.'"

Shuttles's mouth made shapes, but no words came out. Nautilus said, "Why'd you bring the murder weapon to the scene in a plastic bag, Tyree?"

"It wasn't my idea, I swear . . ."

"You never cruised more than eight blocks from the murder scene. How long were you supposed to wait for the Franklin car to be found? All night?"

Shuttles pressed his hands to his eyes, as if blotting out reality. Tears fell from beneath his fingers.

"Harry, I . . ."

"Then you tried to convince Carson that Logan was messing up the Carole Ann Hibney investigation. But it was really you throwing wrenches into the works. That idea come from Crandell? Or setting Logan up as paranoid, so if he voiced suspicions about you, it'd seem part of his paranoia. Right, Tyree? Have I got your sorry ass nailed?"

Shuttles pitched forward on the table, buried his face in his arms.

"They gave me so much, Harry, but they wanted so much back."

CHAPTER 45

"Good morning, brother," Lucas said into the phone. "Did you get my fax? My equations? Did you have a professional read it?"

Lucas listened for a minute, shook his head.

"You showed it to who, Buck? Of course he didn't know what it was, he's a pissant banker, a schmoozer. It's the Black–Scholes equation for modeling stock-option prices. Economics 101, for crying out loud. I simply took the '76 Ingerson adjustment regarding assumption of zero taxes and transaction fees, removed CIRs per Merton, then added my own twist regarding . . ."

Shit. It was like talking business to a fish. Lucas shook his head, then relaxed. Remembered his mission.

"Forget the fax, Buck. Listen, in the long run . . . does it matter?"

Lucas watched a dark-haired young woman walk past the phone booth, tight pink jeans, her hips moving like a polka, *one*-two, *one*-two. He'd be there soon enough, he thought, a bed full of metronomic buttocks he would pluck like fruit from a yard-high tree.

"What do I want to do, Buck?" Lucas said. "Shit, you know that. It all comes down to what your gut instinct tells you is the profitable course."

A smile crossed Lucas's face, but he didn't allow it to enter his voice, his business voice.

"That's what I thought you'd say, Buck."

Lucas hung up and returned to his insecurities firm – never more aptly named than today. He ran up the stairs, arriving in his office panting, part from exertion, part from the rush of adrenaline. Lucas swiveled the spotter scope to the KEI offices. Buck Kincannon was in his office, door closed, feet on desk, thumbs twirling around one another as he mulled over the phone conversation.

He hadn't shared the call with the others. Buck was sitting there thinking *I, Me, Mine*.

Every brother was thinking *I, Me, Mine*.

Perfect.

* * *

Nautilus watched Shuttles walk out, a uniformed cop on each side. In his first burst of fear, Shuttles had answered questions, but once he realized how deep the water was getting, he'd started mewling about a lawyer. Shuttles even had the temerity to ask if he could make his exit without the bracelets. Nautilus told the little shit to be happy he wasn't cuffed to a kayak and floated in front of a supertanker.

Nautilus headed to Forensics, stopping at the morgue first. He'd debated whether to tell Clair Peltier anything at this stage, but she'd been in since the beginning and deserved to know.

He stepped into her office, closed the door. The woman looked used up, eyes red, face drawn and sleepless. The fresh flowers normally changed every third day were limp as dead birds. A tear rolled down her cheek and she blotted it with the back of her hand.

"I left Carson's. I didn't want to, but I had work to finish."

"Listen, Doc," Harry said. "Some things have come to light. There's a chance – slim – that Carson might be alive."

Her mouth dropped. Nautilus held his hands up, cautionary.

"I have no idea where he is if he's being held. If I make noise, get cops running everywhere, I think he'll fall down a hole forever."

"Oh Jesus . . ."

"I just uncovered a rotten-apple cop owned by the Kincannons, except the family will never be implicated. They've got too many layers between them and the act, especially one named Crandell. I'd love a search warrant for the Kincannons' homes, offices. But that takes probable cause. I have nothing but circumstances and hearsay."

"How about Carson's old girlfriend, Harry? She's going with Buck Kincannon now, correct? Do you think she could help with anything?"

Nautilus felt guilt sweep through his gut. Danbury had called him a dozen times, left distraught and tearful messages, begging him to call her back, help her understand.

It had bothered Nautilus that his partner had gone through such bullshit with Danbury. She'd behaved poorly. But people stumble, make bad decisions. Get conned by professional liars.

He recalled a call Danbury had left on his phone after Carson had been reported missing:

"I convinced myself that I was so important I deserved the kind of man who was followed by

cameras and reporters and had politicians hanging on his every word. I betrayed myself by betraying Carson. I screwed up, Harry, and I lost something I can never get back."

She wasn't talking about Carson, Nautilus knew. He pulled his cellphone from his jacket and called the station first. The operator said Danbury wasn't scheduled for work for four days. He tried her home, got the answering machine.

"I'm out for a few days," Danbury said, "but will answer your call when I return."

Her voice was flat and abrupt. Used to be Danbury's messages sounded chirpy as a bird, all how-de-do, and call you right back, and always a funny little joke.

Strange. Like maybe life wasn't all she'd been expecting.

"Danbury's not around," Nautilus said.

He told Dr Peltier to cross her fingers, pray, and burn candles, incense, whatever it took. He headed to Forensics wondering if Claypool knew anything about e-mail?

Thaddeus Claypool looked up from a keyboard, a glass of orange juice at his elbow. He wore a white shirt with twin banjos on the front, the instruments made of sequins.

Nautilus said, "We nailed the son of a bitch, Thad. But I need a touch more magic. Know anything about tracing e-mail?"

Claypool blew out a long breath. "Depends on how much misdirection the sender put into staying hidden. It's not like following a thread to someone's house."

Nautilus set the computer retrieved from Shuttles's apartment on the counter in front of Claypool. The tech had it running in under thirty seconds, the e-mail program open.

"Start about month back," Nautilus said. "A few days before Taneesha Franklin was killed."

Claypool popped the e-mails on the screen in chronological progression. The sender – Crandell? – was not given to excess verbiage.

Phone call coming to location C (5–7pm on 20) re patrol Monday. Note this a special activity, a 50G ME.

Nautilus noted the message jibed with what Shuttles had told him about the night of Taneesha's death. He was to find the knife at the scene, making sure the fingerprints remained intact. The "50G ME" Nautilus figured was a "Fifty Grand Merit Endowment". Also noted:

the main details would come via phone. Shuttles had a list of six pay-phone locations, A–F. That night's calls would be at location C from five to seven p.m., the calls repeated every twenty minutes if Shuttles had a problem getting to the phone. Everything seemed to be considered. The next in the series was self-explanatory:

Need all reports concerning Franklin. Scan and e-mail ASAP.

Keeping tabs, Nautilus thought. Whatever was going on, the folks behind it wanted to see how the investigation was progressing.

Need reports on the suspect in TF case. Understand a drawing is on streets. Need drawing immediately. Talk location B, (2-4 pm on 15)

Basically an update and street contacts talking about the drawing. Verbal orders would follow via phone.

Need all reports of stolen cars activity from 4.21–4.23.

Nautilus noted it approximated the time of the activity with Vince Raines at Vehicle Theft, probably a checkup to assure the phony story about the cars having been sold was believed, no further action taken.

Need official photo(s) of knife from Franklin incident, accompanying paperwork, proof fingerprint(s) recovered. Scan and e-mail ASAP.

If a photo of the murder weapon was needed, why wasn't one taken before it was planted? Unless a police version was preferred. That fit with the request for official reports on the case.

Nautilus opened the most recent e-mail, sent last Sunday just past noon.

Ryder kayaking 2 of last 4 nights late, try tonight. Boat leaves at 6p.m. Be there. If Ryder not on water, we grab at home. Pln on 7hrs to get job done. This is additional 50G ME . . .

They'd been lying in wait for Carson since a bit after six. If he hadn't kayaked, they were going to abduct him from home. Another fifty grand for Shuttles; the scumball business was booming. Nautilus read to the last line, and his heart jammed in his throat.

Plan on being seen by target – don't worry.

There was only one reason for that line: Carson would never get the opportunity to make an identification.

"How's the tracing possibility look, Thad?" Nautilus asked, his voice quiet.

"Not good," Claypool said, shaking his head at the routing codes. "There's more misdirection than at a magicians' convention. Maybe if I had a Cray I could brute-force the phony information, but . . ."

"It's OK," Nautilus said. "I got a backup plan. Is the machine hooked up? Like to the Internet?"

Claypool nodded. "It thinks it's at Shuttles's apartment."

Nautilus perched his hands over the keys.

"What are you going to say, Detective?" Claypool asked, holding his breath.

"When in doubt, tell the truth," Nautilus said. "Parts of it, anyhow."

He started typing.

TROUBLE! MY PARTNER LOGAN SAW THINGS. KNOWS I BROUGHT THE KNIFE TO THE SCENE. HE WANTS 50G TO STAY QUIET. HE'S PUSHING HARD. HELP! WHAT DO I DO?

Nautilus hit Send.

He studied the message, realized he'd put Logan in Crandell's sights, picked up his phone. Ten rings later, Logan answered.

"Pace, this is Harry Nautilus. You were right about Shuttles. He's rotten. I got him to admit he planted the knife."

"Son of a bitch," Logan grunted.

"But Shuttles got a shyster and clammed up tight. Listen, Pace, I'm trying to work a scam on the guy pulling Shuttles's strings, goes by the name of Crandell, a big hard guy, square built, curly blond hair. You ever see him, like Shuttles was driving, maybe stopped to talk to a man like that, said he was a friend?"

"I'm sorry, Harry."

Nautilus pulled his handkerchief, patted sweat from his forehead.

"Why I'm calling, Pace. I just sent a fake message from Shuttles telling this guy you dug up all the ugliness, are pressing for a cut."

"You knew where to send the message?"

"E-mail, Pace."

"Oh shit, of course. Listen, Harry, it makes me feel stupid that all this went down and I never saw anything."

"You saw the bag floating in the gutter. That opened the door. But Crandell thinks you're messing with his plans. He may want to take you off the board, and he can do it. You're at home, right?"

"Watching the tube."

"Get out now. Go somewhere. A motel, Pace. I'll pay. Go there and hang out until tomorrow."

"Harry, what can I do to help? I'll do anything. Tell me how to help you track down this Cran—"

"There's nothing to do but get out of there, Pace. Now."

"What are you trying to accomplish, Harry? Clue me in."

Nautilus sighed, time wasting.

"Someone's life may depend on me finding Crandell. I figure he's got a place away from things. But close enough to town to keep his hand in the action. Pace, get off the phone and git."

"What are you going to do, Harry?"

"I don't know, Pace. Listen, I got to hang up."

"Shuttles is slick, Harry, the little bastard is one –"

"Get out!" Nautilus yelled and slammed down the phone.

CHAPTER 46

Miss Gracie stood by my bedside. Her hand rested on the sheet an inch from mine. I had a feeling she wanted to touch my hand, make contact.

She said, "I been told to take the night off."

"Who gives you your orders, Miss Gracie?"

"Him. Cran-man. It's like always when he comes. If it ain't done his way, he won't take the job."

It made sense from what I knew of Crandell. He'd want absolute control to lessen the chance of error. I rattled my wrists in the straps.

"Miss Gracie, can you help here?"

She turned away.

"He's out there now, a bunch of the security folks, too. They're sure Lucas is trying to get to Miz Kincannon. They say he wants to kill her. I don't know what to believe anymore."

"You're not sure Lucas is psychotic?"

"I been told that a thousand times since he came here. That he's sick. Not to trust him, he lies, pretends to be well. I think he was all mixed up as a kid is all."

"How about Dr Rudolnick? What did he think?"

Her eyes closed. "He wrote up papers they gave to Miz Kincannon, saying how Lucas had to be kept here for his own safety, the safety of others. The doctor got told what to say before he even met Lucas. Dr Rudolnick was a troubled man and they had hold of him in some way. It's what they do, hold."

"But Ms Kincannon . . ." I let the words hang in the air.

"She wanted the doctor to check on Lucas every month. See if he could get better. The doctor came to see things as they really were. It made him sick at himself, his part in the lie."

And eventually made him dead, I thought. Had the decompensating Buck grown paranoid over Rudolnick? Or was the doctor simply another loose end?

I looked at my strapped wrists. "You can't undo my arms, legs, Miss Gracie? Give me a chance?"

"If *he* found out I did that, if *they* found out . . ."

"You'd be gone. And your son, too. Tyler."

An intake of breath. Eyes shimmering with sudden fright.

"You know?"

"Tyler's too dark-skinned to be one of the Kincannon children. And you would have told me if he was, like you did the others."

Miss Gracie turned away, fear and shame in her voice. "Tyler'd have to go to a charity hospital, a ward. He wouldn't get nothing like he gets here. Tyler don't know much but love, and I can give it to him here. And I get to be with him all through his life."

"I understand."

She reached to the cart, held up two IV bags. She began slipping them into the holder. "I got told to put these in you. One's the muscle relaxer. The other's a tranquilizer. That man wants you fuzzy-headed. He says make it drip slow so it lasts 'til midnight."

"He's coming for me."

"I can't tell the future. But I'll do the same

as I done yesterday. I'm gonna let the tube drip in the waste can."

Miss Gracie disappeared out the door.

Crandell showed up a half-hour later, mining his canines with a toothpick. He looked freshened, alert, happy with his life and choices.

"You'll be by yourself tonight, Ryder. I sent Auntie Jemima packing. If you gotta crap, you'll have to fill the old diaper. Must be nice to roll over and shit when you want, like the old burnout upstairs, like most of the whatevers in this place."

I turned my head his way, a drowsy smile on my face, a man drifting in a sea of muscle relaxants and tranquilizers.

"Who say what?"

"Must be nice floating around in there, Ryder. Just checking before I go to work. Buck's got your former juice hole coming to his place around nine and I got to get the stage set."

"Unh-hunh. Sure was."

"Just for your records, Ryder, wasn't me killed Holtkamp and Franklin. Buckie volunteered for the job. He needed to work them girls over. Ain't life a bitch, Ryder? Guy looks like Buck Kincannon, and he's all screwy about women."

"Screwly wha?"

Crandell grinned and flicked the toothpick at me. It hit my nose and I looked a foot left of his head. He dusted his hands together.

"I'll be by later. I got to rip up your clothes, splash 'em with your blood, drop them where they'll roll up on a beach. Probably scare hell out of some tourists from Wisconsin. There's a hole in a barn floor about ten miles from here. It's a lonely hole and needing company."

I batted my eyes, like trying to stay awake.

Crandell said, "Now I got to deal with your old buddy, Shuttles. Remember him? Got a little problem over on that side. Pain in the ass, but I just keep repeating, Rio de Janeiro."

"Whuff?"

"You're no fun when you're like this, Ryder. But we'll have a few final laughs before you hole up tonight, I gar-on-tee."

"Incoming," Nautilus said twenty minutes after he'd sent the message. Claypool ran to Nautilus, leaned over the detective's shoulder.

> *Hang tight, help on way. Meet loc B 11 p.m. Tell partner he'll get his payoff. Cash. Respond when you get a chance, ASAP.*

Nautilus said, "He probably thinks Shuttles is with Logan right now."

"Where's location B?" Claypool asked.

"That's my next problem," Nautilus said, rising from the computer and running out the door.

Hearing the outer door close, I started fighting my restraints. The leather was four inches wide, twice as thick as a belt. It was like fighting cast iron.

Freddy walked by in the hall, talking to himself, his puppet held high.

"Rowf! Rowf! Shhh, don't be so loud, Puppy. Carson is sleeping."

"I'm not sleeping, Freddy. I'm just laying here."

His head spun to me. He raced into the room.

"Want to play, Carson? Puppy just woke up, too. He takes an after-supper nap with me."

We played, which meant Freddy licked the puppet over me while I chanted, "Good boy, nice Puppy."

A few minutes passed.

"Freddy, could you do me a favor?"

"You want a drink? More purpleberry?"

"I'm interested in what's going on outside.

It's kind of a special night. Now and then could you check at the window up front for me, tell me what you see?"

"What I see where?"

"At the house across the way."

"Uncle Buck's house?"

"That's the one," I said. "How about taking a look now."

He tottered away, the puppet face dangling off his hand, returning after a couple of minutes.

"There's just one car at Uncle Buck's, Carson. It's the one that belongs to that man I don't like."

"Which man is that, Freddy?"

"That man that comes around sometimes. He fired Miss Holtkamp, my teacher. Then he came and fired Dr Rudy, Lucas's teacher."

"Fired them?"

"That's what Uncle Buck said. It means they had to stop working here. Dr Rudy only came once in a while, but I liked him. I loved Miss Holtkamp. She taught me words and numbers."

"The man you don't like . . . You're talking about Mr Crandell?"

Freddy dropped his eyes to the floor. "One time when no one was looking he stepped on

Puppy, asked me if that hurt him. When I said yes, he laughed and did it again."

"Freddy, I'm going to tell you the truth. There's going to be some trouble outside. Something bad is going to happen if I can't go help a friend of mine."

He frowned. "What's that mean?"

"I've got to get these belts off my arms and legs. They're holding me down. Keeping me from helping my friend."

"They're tight, Carson. I don't think you can."

"I know. That's why I need for you to help me. You can take them off, Freddy. Unbuckle the belts."

He shook his head.

"I can't, Carson."

"Because it's red?"

"I don't do red things. That's what Lucas does."

"You've got to help me, Freddy. I need to get off the bed. It hurts. Do you want a friend of yours to hurt?"

"Lucas says things like that when he's in the red bed and the red room. He asks me to help."

"And you help Lucas, right?"

"I'm not allowed."

It was a simple statement of fact, without moral judgment or sense of consequence. He'd been told not to unbuckle someone under restraint, thus he wouldn't.

"Please," I said.

"Let's just play, Carson. Puppy wants to play. He likes you."

"I don't want to play, Freddy. I need to GET THE HELL OUT OF THIS BED!"

His face screwed up and he started crying.

"You're acting like Lucas does sometimes. I'm leaving."

He turned and stomped toward the door. I called at his back.

"Freddy, I'm sorry. I'm distraught."

He turned, wiping an eye with a finger. "What's distroffed mean?"

"It means I like you and want you and Puppy to stay."

Freddy's smile was wet and lopsided. He ran to the bed. I let the puppet lick my face, bounce on my belly, bark at my toes. Freddy worked the puppet up my leg.

"Walking, walking, walking the doggie . . ."

I said, "Could you take another look outside for me, Freddy?"

His bottom lip pouted outward. "It's way over on the other side of Heaven, past the rooms where Miss Gracie lives. Do I have to?"

"It would make me happy."

He sighed. "All right, Carson."

He scampered away, returning moments later. He held up the puppet like it was talking. "*Rowf!* There's no cars over there now. Puppy says it's empty."

I wondered what time it was. Crandell had mentioned Dani going to Buck's place near nine p.m.

"Do you know how to tell time, Freddy?"

He stared at the ceiling, remembering. "Miss Holtkamp said there are two hands on a clock, like on a person. The big hand –"

"Why don't you look at a clock if there's one around?"

"There's one in Tyler's room."

"Let's see if you really can tell time. I'm thinking you can't."

"Betcha I can."

He was back in a minute. He held his arms out to indicate 6.40. "It's six and forty, ha ha. Here comes Puppy, Carson."

It was getting annoying, trying to think with

the puppet slapping across my arms, chest, and face.

"How about you give Puppy a break for a few minutes, Freddy?"

Freddy kept up the licking and gnawing motion.

"I can't stop him, Carson. Watch out."

The sock puppet gnawed on the bedrail, licked my arm. I started to again ask Freddy to stop, but heard his words repeat in my head: *I can't stop him.*

Was Puppy an independent entity? Cold sweat prickled on my forehead. I kept my voice light and even and smiled at Freddy. I had one final shot at life, the strength of the fantasy of a retarded man.

"You've been told not to unbuckle the belts, right, Freddy?"

"Yup. Puppy's licking your shoulder, Carson."

I giggled, a happy guy. "You're right not to unbuckle the belts, Freddy. But if you hadn't been told not to unbuckle the belts, you could unbuckle the belts. Isn't that right?"

"I was told not to do it. And like a good boy I do what I'm told. Lick, lick, lick."

I took a deep breath.

"Freddy?"

"What?"

"Has Puppy been told not to unbuckle the belts?"

CHAPTER 47

Nautilus thundered into the jail. He looked in the holding cell where he'd last seen Shuttles; empty.

"Where's Shuttles?" Nautilus yelled to a turnkey sipping a cup of coffee.

"Interrogation."

Nautilus ran down the hall. He saw Doria Barnes, an assistant DA, sitting on a bench and sorting through papers. "I need to talk to Shuttles," Nautilus said.

Barnes rolled her eyes. "Good luck. Mr Shuttles is with his new attorney."

"Who's that?"

"Preston Walls."

Nautilus growled and pushed through the door of the interrogation room. Shuttles was sitting in a chair at a small wooden table, Preston Walls beside him, nodding.

"Hey, Harry," Walls said. "How you been keeping yourself?"

Nautilus ignored the attorney and stuck his face in front of Tyree Shuttles.

"What do you know about a location B?"

Walls put his hand on Shuttles's back. Patted it. "My client has nothing to say, Harry. Sorry."

"Shuttles just call you, Walls?" If Crandell knew Shuttles was in jail, it was all for naught.

"Minutes ago," Walls said. "Evidently Mr Shuttles knows of my expertise with the wrongly accused."

Nautilus put his palms on the table, glared into Shuttles's eyes.

"If I don't find out where location B is, Carson could die. How's that, Shuttles? There a glimmer of conscience in there anywhere?"

Shuttles looked away. Walls leaned back in his chair, flicked the tassels on his shiny Italian loafers, shoes as sleek as eels.

"Maybe we can come to a deal, Harry. Mr Shuttles, if I'm given to understand the problem, was an unwitting pawn in someone else's game. He might have unknowingly mishandled evidence, but that was accidental. In return for anything he might tell you, my client wants immunity from prosecution."

Nautilus glared at Shuttles. "I doubt he knows where location B is anyway, Walls. He's low level, a gofer."

Shuttles nodded to Walls. The attorney walked over, listened as Shuttles whispered in his ear. Walls straightened.

"He believes he may know pieces of what you need. He knows them inadvertently, of course, not as part of any crime or conspiracy. Maybe someone from the Prosecutor's Office could talk deal? I believe Ms Barnes is in the building."

"I don't think so," Nautilus said. "I'm done here." He walked from the interrogation room with Walls in his wake. He stopped at a water cooler a dozen feet down the hall.

Come on, Walls, come on . . .

The lawyer parked himself a few steps behind Nautilus, his voice wheedling. "Harry, we can make a nice deal here. The kid made some kind of mistake. He's not even sure what. You got weight with the DA . . ."

Walls bargaining without even knowing what had gone down.

"Bye, Preston." Nautilus wiped his mouth, started away.

"Harry, we can do something good here. I know it."

Nautilus paused. "Do you know what Shuttles did? Who he's working for?"

Walls puffed out a righteous chest. "My client asserts his innocence. And that, Harry, is all I need."

Nautilus started down the hall. A dozen feet away, he turned his head over his shoulder, said, "Crandell." Nautilus got three steps before Walls was in front of him.

"Christ. What did you just say, Harry?"

"The Kincannons have a pipeline into Shuttles for various ongoing necessaries. But Crandell's calling the shots on this gig. You ratted Crandell out to me, Walls, remember?"

Walls looked seasick. "Harry, I did no such –"

"I'm in contact with Crandell by e-mail. I'm gonna go write him back, remind Crandell of his old friend Preston Walls from Barton, Turnbull and Pryce. 'Rabies sloshing under his pupils.' That's what you said about him, right?"

Walls's flesh had turned the color of lard. Sweat peppered his forehead.

"You can't do this."

Nautilus clasped the attorney's shoulder, gave it a gentle squeeze. Lowered his voice to a whisper. "If Crandell doesn't come to me, Walls, I bet he comes to you."

Walls said, "Let me go talk to my client. Perhaps I can –"

"Lie to him, Walls. You know how it's done. I'll be right here."

Five minutes later, Walls came through. Shuttles, apparently thinking he was showing good faith for a deal agreement, wrote a return message on a slip of paper.

Loc B cnfirm. 11 PM cnfirm. IO 50G to man in? Route per rehrsl. 90 min. Don't frgt: IO 50Gs.

A confirmation of location B at eleven tonight, two hours; "I owe 50 grand."

Shuttles also passed along driving directions. Not far, just on the north side of Mobile. Nautilus called Forensics, had Claypool send the message from Shuttles's computer. He took out his service weapon, checked the clip, patted the two extras in his pocket. He'd get there early, scope out the territory. Wait.

He checked the weapon a second time, a Glock 17. Then raced back to the department to pick up the .380 in his locker, a little something to tuck down the back of his pants. Maybe he'd check out a shotgun as well.

I petted Puppy after he'd liberated me – *Good dog, good dog* – then told Freddy his pet needed a reward. Freddy wandered to the kitchen area to fix Puppy and himself a snack. I followed, drank a glass of milk and jammed a slice of pizza in my mouth, fuel, then started searching for a weapon and a way out.

I heard a rumble in the distance, and my heart froze. Crandell coming up the drive?

The rumble again, this time clearly thunder.

There was nothing equivalent to a weapon in the kitchen, only soft plastic implements. A closet by the door provided a pair of men's painter pants and a woman's dark blue raincoat – Miss Gracie's, I assumed – better than the loose pajamas I had been dressed in upon arrival.

Shoeless, shirtless, the raincoat flapping in my wake, I set about finding my escape.

The windows were barred and wired: breakage would trigger some form of alarm in the security detail's offices, I assumed. All doors were steel and secured by electronic locks. No phones.

Everything seemed designed to keep Lucas inside if he ever breached the confines of his two-room Zenda.

That left the second floor.

I found a staircase to the second floor: tiny windows, steel doors locked tight. The elevator was turned off. I searched closets and cupboards to locate a pry bar, finally discovering a utility mop and bucket. The mop handle was hardwood, tipped with a steel attachment to fasten mop heads in place. I tossed the mop, kept the handle, jogged to the elevator. Passing a room off the kitchen, I saw Freddy eating from a bowl in his lap, raptly watching a videotaped cartoon.

The attachment on the mop handle slid between the brass-plated elevator doors, and I tried to jimmy the doors without breaking the handle. The doors opened several inches before the handle slipped and the door slammed closed. Sweat streamed down my forehead, burned into my eyes. I gripped the handle tighter, going for brute force.

The doors separated four inches and I

jammed my bare right foot between them, laying my full weight into the task. With a sound like a gunshot, the mop handle snapped. I fell forward, my foot wedged between the doors. I heard a second gunshot from my ankle. Pain exploded up my leg and I fought my way to standing. I jammed my elbow between the doors, roared with agony. Pushed with everything I had. The doors widened until I tumbled into the elevator.

The doors closed behind me. My ankle was on fire.

A hard knocking at the door.

"Carson?"

I tried to still my breath. "What, Freddy?"

"I heard you yelling real loud. What are you doing?"

"Exploring. I'll be back in a while."

"What are you exploring?"

"The elevator."

"Can I come in and explore, too?"

"Of course, but later."

His slippered feet slapped away. I struggled upright, put weight on my leg. It answered with searing pain. Something had given way, a bone or ligament.

Feet returned to the elevator doors.

"You know that man, Carson? The one that was mean to Puppy?"

"Yes."

"He's outside with another man. He's coming in, I think."

I wanted to throw back my head and scream. Crandell would have keys to everything. All he had to do was open the elevator, pull once or twice on the trigger. My final hope was exploding outward on my one good leg, hoping Crandell would be directly outside the door. I might get my hands to his face, rip my nails across his eyes, blind the bastard . . .

Footsteps approached, slow and measured. I held my breath, ready to dive through if he could open the door.

What if he just fired through the door?

Footsteps, footsteps . . .

Bang! A hand smacked hard against the door. Again.

"Carson? He didn't come inside. They drove away."

I leaned against the door. My head swam. Each of my heartbeats sounded like a kettle-drum.

"Are you sure, Freddy? Crandell's really gone?"

"He drove away in that special truck, Carson."

"What special truck, Freddy?"

"The one Uncle Buck uses to carry his cars around. Uncle Buck has lots of cars."

CHAPTER 48

Trees whipped by the sides of Nautilus's cruiser, the country lane tight. The meeting spot was one Nautilus was familiar with, an old strip center serving what had once been a rural community, now just a couple miles from the edge of the growing city. Nautilus figured Crandell lived nearby, the site, as he and Carson had figured, out of the city, but still allowing fast access anywhere in Mobile.

The meeting location was a pizzeria in the center, A-Roma Pizza. The closer he came, the more he became convinced he should let the county cops in on his plan. This was Mobile County, and he knew several guys on the force, not a Cade Barlow in the bunch. Nautilus waited to pass a slow-moving trailer on the road ahead. He was about to accelerate when the trailer swerved erratically, slid from the road, ground to a hard stop.

Nautilus had dropped back a hundred yards, thinking the trailer or truck pulling it had blown a tire. He passed the rig slowly, checking. It was an extended-cab truck with a vehicle hauler behind it. The hauler was empty.

The cab of the pickup exploded open and a man dropped halfway to the ground, clawing at his chest, the seat belt trapping his body. Nautilus braked hard and stared in horror, his headlights framing the grisly scene.

Don't get out of the car, a voice said from the back of his head. *Call it in, but don't get out.* His hand reached for the radio, was stopped by the flashing red light in his rear-view: a vehicle with an emergency flasher stuck atop the roof, volunteer fireman. Hopefully the guy had some medical training.

"I'm an EMT," called a voice from the vehicle behind as the door opened, feet started his way. "What happened?"

"Looks like a heart attack," Nautilus yelled back. "I'm a cop. I'll call it in. You got a defibrillator?"

"No," a voice whispered. "But I have one of these."

Nautilus felt something hard press his ear. Caught the smell of gun oil. The voice said, "How's about you keep your hands off that mike and right up there where I can see them."

The man hanging from the truck suddenly slipped to the ground, somersaulted to standing, brushed himself off. Nautilus saw a patch on the guy's shoulder: Private Security. He was a tall, raw-boned guy with tight eyes. He grinned at the Crown Vic, then ignited two road flares. He tossed one behind the Crown Vic, another in front. Anyone passing would think car trouble.

"All right, Rafe," said the voice at Nautilus's shoulder. "You earned yourself a double bonus tonight. Drop the ramps and let's get this circus to another town."

Nautilus said, "Crandell, right?"

"Sssssh," the voice said. "Stay relaxed and we'll all go home tonight."

Like hell, Nautilus thought.

Headlights filled the scene as another vehicle slowed, a couple teen guys in an old Camaro with a bad muffler.

"Sssssh," Crandell said to Nautilus, leaning to hide the gun. "One word and the kiddies don't get any older."

"Y'all need some help?" the passenger in the Camaro said.

Private Security smiled, shook his head at the Crown Vic. "Thanks, man, but we got her. Tranny stripped out in second gear. We'll get 'er up on the trailer, haul it to the garage. Hey, you guys want a beer?"

The guy in the Camaro waved it off. "Thanks, bud, but we're set." He held up a six-pack of Schlitz Malt Liquor, grinned stupidly, and the pair roared away.

Private Security hustled to the back of the hauler, dropped the ramps to the road. That was all the time it took for Crandell to have Harry Nautilus on the rear floor of the cruiser, handcuffed to a steel D-ring.

"And before I forget . . ." Crandell slipped his hand into Nautilus's jacket and snatched out his Glock.

"And a shotgun, too? My, we did come prepared, didn't we? I'll just take that with me."

Private Security jumped in the door, backed up the Crown Vic, angled it, then ran the Crown

Vic onto the hauler. He slipped a chrome .44 revolver from his belt, set it in his lap.

"What next?" he asked Crandell.

"Stay in there and keep an eye on our company. You'll have to lay across the seats, stay below the windows."

"No problem." Private Security nodded at Nautilus. "What do I do if he acts up?"

Crandell thought a moment, said, "Put one in his knee."

Lightning flashed on the horizon. Nautilus felt the wind shift direction. It suddenly smelled of rain. Private Security lowered his voice to a whisper.

"I hate cops and I hate niggers. I do believe you're gonna act up once we get under way."

Nautilus felt a cold squirming in the pit of his stomach. Crandell leaned in the open passenger window.

"You're going to behave, right, Detective?"

"I doubt it'll mean much," Nautilus said.

"You'll be good to our guest, Rafe?"

Private Security chuckled. "Unless he acts up, like you said."

"Detective Nautilus, I want you to turn to Rafe and promise you'll be a good boy." The jab with the barrel again.

Nautilus craned his head upward to the leering face of Private Security. Lightning exploded and a small dark dot appeared in Private Security's forehead. The man frowned, waved at something in front of his face, like troubled by a fly, then slumped sideways in the seat.

Nautilus looked to the window. He smelled burned gunpowder and saw a smile on Crandell's face. Crandell reached in with the gun.

Lightning exploded inside Harry Nautilus's head.

Climbing through the hatch in the ceiling of the elevator was easier than expected, relying on arm and shoulder strength rather than my ankle. I was hobbling around atop the box. The ceilings in the house were fourteen feet high, the elevator eight. Combined with the space between floors, it put the second floor a foot above my head, a second set of doors to outwit.

I had no leverage, and even if I did, no way to apply it.

I held on to greasy cables to keep the weight off my foot, trying to make sense of a metallic cocktail of bars and springs, gears and latches.

My only light was from below, beaming weakly through the two-foot-square hatch. I studied the assemblage beside the door and above my head. *Think. Analyze. Deconstruct.* Elevator doors would be inoperable unless the car was safely behind the door, or folks would be dropping down shafts with metronomic frequency.

But would the unlocking mechanism be electronic or mechanical? How did elevator repairmen deal with these situations?

I squatted below the mechanism, pushed upward on one leg, grabbed a steel bar hooked to the door, and pulled myself up until I was staring into greasy metal components. I studied the mechanism holding them shut, saw a servomotor beside the bar holding the door. There was a red button on its side, just the size of my thumb. I pressed it.

Bing. The doors withdrew.

Soft yellow light drifted into the elevator shaft. I pulled myself through the opening. My chest crossed the threshold, then my belly, and finally the whole of me was squirming face-down on the floor. I could hear the pain in my ankle, a high red whine. I forced myself to look down: swollen with fluid.

"Hello?" a wavering voice said.

The old man was sitting at the desk as if he'd never moved from it, a strained look on his face, trying to understand my appearance in his world. I crawled to a leather-upholstered chair, pulled myself to standing, hopped to his desk.

"Phone!" I yelled. "Where's a phone?"

He stared at me like I was a life form never before encountered, his mouth opening and closing like a boated fish. A floor lamp stood behind the desk. I hobbled over and tore off the shade, used the pole as a crutch to the window. Barred, the glass threaded with wire.

I turned and saw Daddy Kincannon at the open shaft, looking down with a sense of wonder.

"Get back from there, Pops!" I yelled.

He shuffled his feet backward in a decrepit moonwalk. I thumped past chairs and tables and love seats to the chimney; too narrow to slip through. The old man sat on a couch and picked up a copy of *Forbes*. He held it upside down, occasionally shooting me puzzled glances above the pages.

A small bedroom was off the sprawling main living area. I tore through a closet, not knowing what I was looking for, finding nothing but casual clothes and robes. No, there in a back corner, a cane! An old man's bentwood cane, leather handle, rubber tip. Maybe the old guy had bouts of gout.

Think. Analyze.

The old man had been there fifteen years, or was it twenty? Surely in all that time someone had planned for an emergency, fire, tornadoes. This was the Prime Buck, numero uno, tucked away but provided exceptional care. Had he ever been prepared for a problem, drilled until the response lodged in his frizzled brain cells?

"There's an emergency, Mr Kincannon," I yelled. "Is there a way out?"

He wiped a strand of drool from his mouth. I thumped across the floor, got down on one knee, took his hand in mine, like proposing marriage.

"What do you do for fire, sir? Have you been told?"

He looked at me with expectant eyes, like I was judging his answer and he wanted a passing grade.

"Sir?" I prompted.

"Hot spots and piss pots. Climb inside, hide and ride."

Piss pots?

I thudded to the bathroom. It was the size of my living room: bath tub, Jacuzzi, multi-headed shower. I yanked open a closet. Empty, the size of a phone booth. I smelled rain and warmth, outside air. It seemed to be wafting up from the floor of the closet. I stepped inside, hands patting the walls. My fingers found a wooden latch. I turned it and began falling, a controlled drop. I heard a counterweight rising with my descent.

Not a closet, a converted dumbwaiter.

The booth slammed hard and I crumpled, boxed tight, surrounded by total darkness. I pushed on the sides of the booth. A door popped loose like a hatch and I found myself with a faceful of the azalea bush concealing the small door. Lightning flashed, a bomb burst of white across the vast rolling carpet of lawn. The house loomed above. I pictured Buck Senior returning to his desk, reading an inverted magazine, vaguely recalling a limping visitor from years ago.

I crept from an azalea bank the size of a truck, rain pelting me like stones. Even with the cane, my ankle felt like white-hot thorns had been driven through it from every angle.

Lightning shimmered between boiling clouds and I saw Kincannon's house in the distance, perhaps a third of a mile. It seemed forever far away.

But I'd just been granted a reprieve, and whether it had been through pure luck, or something underlying the realm of language and human capacity to understand, I was going to get there if I had to drag myself every inch. Knock on the door of the goddamn *scion* of that goddamn family.

Hello, Buckie, remember me?

CHAPTER 49

Nautilus awoke to a roar in his ears and the smell of blood and excrement in his nose. His head ached and something dry filled his mouth. A gag, he figured, consciousness swirling into his head on a blaze of fear and adrenaline.

He was still tight to the floor of the Crown Vic, moving. Occasionally the interior of the car brightened from lightning or passing cars. Private Security slumped sideways, head between the front seats, trails of blood draining from his nostrils. Rain whipped in the open passenger window. Nauseated, dizzy, his head throbbing, Nautilus still managed to figure that was how the extra water had filled the floor of Taneesha's car.

The truck slowed and turned and the ride

became bumpy, like on a rutted dirt road. After a few minutes they stopped. Nautilus heard Crandell get out of the truck. The dark turned to a hazy light.

Crandell opened the door, freed Nautilus from the D-ring, reattached the cuffs, the weapon never straying from Nautilus's head.

"End of the line," Crandell said, yanking tape from Nautilus's mouth, followed by a wadded rag.

Nautilus gasped, sucked in air, his tongue dry as sandpaper. They were inside a barn, yellowed utility lights casting shadows across bales of hay, an ancient tractor, and a miniature backhoe. Beside the backhoe's bucket was a trough seven feet long, three wide. A mound of fresh dirt was piled beside the ditch.

Lightning flickered outside the barn, doors open at one end, thunder hitting seconds later. Crandell jumped to the ground. "Step on out of the car, Detective Nautilus. Sorry about your head. It was a light tap, you've been out under ten minutes."

Nautilus looked at the ditch, then at Crandell, polo-shirted, hands in the pockets of his Dockers, muscles rippling in his forearms as he jingled coins in his pocket, looking like he'd just finished an excellent supper.

Nautilus said, "Why should I get up just to lay down in the hole in the ground?"

"Because ends can come fast, or they can come slow. I have an hour or so to kill – pardon the pun – and it can be a fast hour for you, or it could be agonizingly slow. If I put a couple slugs in your hip bones, I guarantee it could feel like days. Do you really want to spend days with me, Detective?"

Crandell popped open a utility room at the side of the barn, pulled out two wooden folding chairs, snapped them open, set them beside the trough.

"How'd you know I was coming, Crandell?" Nautilus said, looking at the thick barn rafters above. "Someone tip you off?"

"Shuttles did."

"What?"

"You're a star, big boy. Celebrated member of the MPD, big-shot detective. You and Ryder got reputations of going against the grain, a pair of hot dogs. But you always get 'er done, right?"

"What are you talking about?"

"Before all this got set in motion, Shuttles

and me worked out a simple code to ID the potential problem types. A person's initials plus a letter. For instance if it was Ryder, the code was DS. What's Harry Nautilus?"

"IO," Nautilus said. "Like in the note Shuttles had me send you. IO was in there two times."

"Shuttles is a bright boy."

Crandell gestured to the chairs he'd set up on the barn floor beside the trench. "Come keep me company, Harry," he smiled. "Who knows what might happen?"

Nautilus wriggled his back against the seat, felt the hard shell of the leather holster in his waistband. The .380 was unbuckled; if he could knock it loose of the holster . . . He struggled from the cruiser, hands cuffed at his waist.

Crandell jumped up on the flatbed, pulled Private Security out, slipping under the body, steadying it on his shoulders. He jumped the four feet from the trailer to the ground, his knees bending but not collapsing. Power-lifter strength, Nautilus noted as he stumbled down the ramp to the ground.

Crandell went to the trough, shouldered the body into the earth. It landed with a thud.

"Seven feet deep," Crandell said. "What happens is I fill in the hole later, dump your car in a big ol' swamphole in the delta, then return the backhoe to Buck's spread about ten miles down the pike. It's gonna storm all night . . ." Crandell raised his eyebrows, waiting for Nautilus to catch his drift.

"And barns get struck by lightning," Nautilus said. As if cued by a Hollywood director, a lightning flash lit the barn. Rain dripped through the roof, pooled in the dirt.

"Old wood, all this hay. It'll collapse into a big pile, and no one will ever know what's sitting in the basement, so to speak. I do love a good fire."

Nautilus shrugged. "Seems like a waste of a good barn."

"The property is owned by the Kincannons, but not used. Not used much, I should say. Sometimes Buck'll bring someone here."

"He have barn dances?"

"If that's what you want to call it. He brought a blind girl here a couple Sundays ago. I been keeping extra tabs on Buck, and by the time I got here, the lady was about danced out."

Nautilus recalled Carson's story about the blind girl who'd been savaged.

"Why'd Buck Kincannon take her to the hospital?"

"He didn't. I figured her as more trouble dead than alive. Not like she's gonna make anyone from a lineup. So I washed her up real good and made her somebody else's problem."

Nautilus frowned across the floor at the shadowy trench. "My partner down there?"

"Not yet."

"Will I see him tonight? Alive, I mean."

Crandell paused as thunder shivered the barn. "That would mean leaving you here by yourself. Even if you're trussed tight, I can't take that risk. Come have a seat, Harry. Get comfortable. I've made it easier."

Nautilus studied the rickety wood chairs beside the trench. They faced one another from a six-foot distance. Crandell's chair was two steps away; he could head-butt the bastard. Nautilus visualized the moment: roaring, diving, wiping everything from his mind save that his head was a battering ram. He had teeth, too. Use everything. Do a Tyson on Crandell's ear. Or bite one of his eyes out.

Harry Nautilus sat.

Crandell picked up his chair, folded it shut. He walked to the far side of the ditch beside the dirt mound and reopened the chair. He sat, smiling with his teeth.

"You didn't really think I was going to sit across from you without a moat, did you, Harry? And by the way, if you're still a bit dizzy to notice . . ."

Crandell reached in his pocket, pulled out Nautilus's .380, letting it dangle by the trigger guard.

It's over, Harry Nautilus realized, listening to the rain drumming the roof of the barn. *I'm being written out of the Big Play.* He was amazed at how little fear he felt. Only a sense of sorrow that his death would be at the hands of a sociopathic subhuman like Crandell.

Nautilus had never romanticized dying in the line of duty. He figured it would be nice to eat a grand meal, drink a few ounces of hundred-buck-a-bottle scotch, put on Duke Ellington playing "East St Louis Toodle-Oo", then close his eyes and fly away as the muted horn closes the song.

And be a hundred and ten years old at the time.

Nautilus shot a glance into the trench, one of Private Security's arms flung above his up-looking head and propped against the trench wall like he was trying to backstroke through the earth. Though the night was hot, Nautilus shivered at the thought of his meat rotting into that of a malignant peckerwood.

But Carson would be in the grave as well, Nautilus suddenly realized. They'd outflank the peckerwood.

"Jesus, was that a grin?" Crandell asked.

Nautilus didn't answer. But he had a few questions of his own.

"My partner saw Carole Ann Hibney at the Shrine Temple, Crandell. What was she doing there?"

"You mean Mistress Sonia? You'd have to know the Kincannon boys. They're playful, in their own way. Buck needs an occasional visit to a Mistress Sonia type to level out or something. I don't pretend to understand the snakes in Buck's head. The boys try and keep tabs on one another."

"You mean like spying."

"It's a grand family tradition. Nelson found out about Mistress Sonia, paid her a couple thousand to show up at the party."

"To do what?"

Crandell's eyes danced with glee. "Simply walk silently in front of Buck and pretend to crack a whip. Nelson convinced leather lady it was Buck's birthday party, and Buck had requested Mistress Sonia do the gig, as an inside joke. Nelson knew it'd about make Buck crap his pants, his mama by his side as Whip Woman walked past."

Nautilus felt the bottom drop from his stomach. "Buck didn't think it was funny, obviously. So he took it out on Carole Ann. Do you have any idea what your employer did to her, Crandell?"

Crandell shrugged. "This is my last job for the Kincannons. Buck's getting worse. The wrappings are about to tear loose."

"Pity. I'll bet you've made a shitload off the family over the years."

"Enough to retire on. I only came back to put a little extra gravy on the taters, so to speak."

"Not out of a perverse loyalty? Help in their time of need?"

Crandell wagged an admonishing finger at Nautilus. "Loyalty is not a word the Kincannons understand. If they were sure they'd never need me again, I'd be dead."

"They'd Crandell their Crandell. Where would it stop?"

"I don't want to know. That's why I'm checking out and heading to Rio. Time for me to learn to samba."

A cellphone rang from Crandell's jacket. He slipped it from the pocket of his blazer, looked at the incoming number.

"What, Race?"

Crandell stood and walked to the shadows in the corner of the barn. "What the hell are you talking about, Race? How the hell did you get that idea? It's fucking ridiculous. No, don't call Nelson. Here's what you do, open another bottle of scotch, call one of your girlfriends over, relax. What? Racine, calm down, buddy."

Crandell flicked the phone off, stuck it back in his pocket. When he returned, he was holding a semiautomatic aimed at Nautilus's heart.

"Dealing with this family truly is herding cats, Nautilus. Racine's drunk and babbling about how I'm fired or something. Typical. I'm sorry to cut our evening short. If you come stand here at the head of the ditch I'll make it clean, you won't feel a thing."

Nautilus took a deep breath and spat across the trench, his spit falling short, landing on Crandell's loafers.

Crandell cocked the weapon. "I like a man with spirit. But if you don't get up here, I'm gonna put one through your knee."

Nautilus leaned his head back and laughed, real and full and loud.

"You're a sick and sad little boy, Crandell. I expect I can deal with it."

Crandell stared in disbelief. He shook his head and raised the gun.

Three hard reports echoed through the barn.

Crandell seemed to lift from his feet for a split second. He staggered three steps backward, slammed into the wall of the utility room, then crumpled to the ground. The weapon tumbled into the ditch.

Nautilus stared wide-eyed at the door. Lightning flashed and he saw a form crouching at its edge. There was a gun in his hand, the muzzle scanning the barn's interior.

"Racine?" Nautilus called. "Racine Kincannon?"

Pace Logan crept into the barn, his service weapon trained on Crandell's writhing form.

"Jesus, Harry. What'd you get yourself into? Who's that crazy fuck? Who's Racine?"

Nautilus sat with his mouth agape, unable to find words. He stood, and his head swam and his knees wobbled. He sat down again. Logan advanced toward the supine Crandell, moaning, rocking side to side, the front of his shirt turning to a scarlet swamp.

Nautilus managed a breathless whisper. "What the hell are you doing here, Pace?"

"You sounded bad worried when you told me how you were looking for a curly-haired blond guy Shuttles might have met up with." Logan nodded toward Crandell. "Him?"

"Him."

"It got me started thinking. You know Dominick Purselli was Shuttles's training officer?"

Nautilus said, "I tried to talk to Dom a couple days ago. He's way the hell up in Canada."

"Dom's a good buddy of mine," Logan said. "I had his cell number, called, got lucky. I asked had he ever seen the guy you described. Turns out that four years ago, when Shuttles joined the force, the two of 'em did some stuff together. Shuttles told Purselli he knew a guy came to town now and then, always stayed at this old farm on about thirty acres, would Purselli like to go squirrel hunting there?"

Crandell's mouth opened and closed like a dying fish gulping air from the surface. His eyes rolled back in his head. Logan knelt and put a finger against Crandell's throat, feeling for a pulse. None. He turned back to Nautilus.

"Purselli said when they got to the farm, they announced themselves at the house. It was a blond guy at the door, curly hair, strong-looking, square as an outhouse. A hinky kind of guy, like he didn't want to be seen, and that's why Purselli remembered him."

Logan stood, holstered his weapon at his side, walked to Nautilus.

"Purselli said Shuttles drove. Dom couldn't remember where the farm was. But he'd walked all over it hunting, and described a rectangle of land with a barn about half-mile from the road, a white house on the far side of a windbreak, two decent-sized ponds toward the back of the place, a creek cutting between the ponds."

Logan pulled a handcuffs key from inside his jacket. "Guess what happened then, Harry?"

"I couldn't begin to guess, Pace."

"I remembered Shuttles babbling about this place on the Internet where you saw aerial views of just about anywhere, pictures from a geo-satellite or something. Purselli knew the basic area, low on the delta and east of Chickasaw. I went to the library, got a library lady to help me get on the doggoned Internet, Harry. Me."

"You found this place from *above*?"

"It was wild, Harry, like I could fly back and forth over the area – go up and down, too – and I just kept looking at all the ponds up there. Then I found a couple ponds with a creek between them, saw the roof of a house and barn a hundred yards apart . . ."

Nautilus held up his bound wrists. Logan slipped the key into the cuffs, popped them loose.

"You did all this in under three hours, Pace?"

Logan showed a wistful smile and shook his head.

"I'm almost gone and maybe I'm beginning to figure things out, Harry. Jeez, now there's an epitaph, right?"

CHAPTER 50

Each step toward Kincannon's house felt like putting my foot into a canister of hornets. Trees studded the long trek between the houses, and I made my way from trunk to trunk, leaning to catch my breath and wipe rain from my eyes. Lightning turned the Kincannon grounds into a series of spectral snapshots.

With less than a hundred yards to go, I dove to the ground as headlights swept up the drive from the road below, hoping the dark coat would keep me invisible on the grass. I watched the lights outline the huge Brahma bull sculpture near the road, continue up the long lane, stop in the circular drive in front of the house.

A white Audi. My heart stopped.

It was Dani.

She hustled out, opening an umbrella, jogging the two dozen steps to the porch. I wanted to yell out her name, scream, *Get back in the car, drive away!*

Buck Kincannon walked out the door. He moved to Dani with outstretched arms, tried to hold her umbrella for her. She avoided his touch. There was a minute of conversation before Kincannon gestured toward the house. They walked up the steps to the porch, Dani slow, seeming reluctant.

They went inside.

I limped, fell, crawled. Lightning slammed a tall longleaf pine a hundred feet away, sending a flaming branch spiraling to the ground like a hobbled comet. But I made it. The huge house had a wraparound porch. I climbed to the side and crouched around the corner. The porch was fifteen feet deep, the front side holding several large wicker chairs and wooden rockers, two tables, a bench like a church pew. Oversize carriage lamps bookended the wide front door, throwing light the color of honey and laying deep shadows behind the furniture.

"I'm leaving!"

Dani's voice. The front door banged open. Dani crossed the wide porch, her arms tight to her chest. She wavered on the top step, arms crossed. Kincannon stepped outside.

"Please, baby, come back. I'm sorry I grabbed you. I just want you to stay, discuss your future. Come on, baby, don't hurt me like this."

Kincannon was pleading, making kissy sounds, like a little kid. Maybe that was the voice he'd used with Carole Ann Hibney.

"I'm not staying, Buck. And when I say not to touch me, I mean it."

"Of course you do, DeeDee. I was just hurt by your wanting to leave."

"I don't think it's working out between us, Buck. That's what I came to say."

Get out, Dani . . .

"DeeDee, please, give me a chance. Just stay for dinner."

"I can't, Buck. Don't keep asking."

"I have a surprise for you, DeeDee, why I asked you here tonight. I want to give you Houston. Houston! We're buying a station there, making major changes. You'll be lead anchor, start at three hundred grand a year. Houston's one step from New York, LA. Finally, the big time . . ."

She took a step forward from the edge of the porch. Kincannon held his distance, but kept the pitch going. He'd moved from pitiful child to wheedling businessman, running his full inventory of games.

"You're thirty-two years old, DeeDee. Middle age in this biz. You don't jump now, you're gonna be chasing two-bit local politicos the rest of your life. You should be on *Washington Week in Review, Meet the Press.* You've got the talent. I can make it happen."

Don't listen to him, Dani, my head screamed, *get away.*

Instead, she turned to face Kincannon.

"Houston?"

He held up his hands. "It's over between us as a couple. I accept that. It'll be easier, because you'll be in Houston. But we can still be friends, right? Amigos. Even apart we can work together to make Clarity Broadcasting number one in the country."

"I . . . guess we could do that, Buck."

He stood in the door and swept his hand toward the interior of the house, a thousand-watt smile on his face. "Come in and we'll seal the Houston deal over dinner."

She took a step toward Kincannon. Closed her eyes, shook her head. Stepped back.

"I'll call tomorrow, Buck. We can talk then."

She turned and started toward her car in the circled drive. I let my breath out. When Dani was safe I could slip to the road and flag down help.

It wasn't to be.

Kincannon strode to Dani, grabbed her arm, swung her into the house like she was a rag doll. The door slammed. I heard Dani screaming. A crash of falling furniture. A sound of thunder, like a body driven to the floor.

Another scream, cut off by a slap. Then all I heard was the beating of my heart and the pounding of the rain. My mind raced through possibilities, found *Diversion*. I wadded up the raincoat, then slid the cane across the porch, a rattling sound.

"Who's there?" Kincannon called from inside the house. "Crandell?"

Footsteps behind the door, tentative. I heard the door open and edged an eye from behind the chair. Kincannon bent to retrieve the cane, confusion in his eyes.

"Daddy?" he said, the child's voice back as his eyes searched the dark beyond the porch. "Daddy, is that you?"

I leapt from behind the chair and flung the balled raincoat at his face. He flung up his hands, tearing it away just as I dove into his body, yelling and raking at his eyes. He shrieked and pushed my face away, kicking. A kick hit my ankle. I howled and my hands fell loose. He stumbled into the house and I tumbled to the floor.

I crawled through the door on hands and knees. There was no sign of Kincannon, but Dani was on the far side of the room, pushing herself from the floor, blood streaming from her nose and mouth. She saw me. Her hand came to her mouth.

"Carson?"

"Come on, Dani. We've got to get out of here."

I heard Kincannon in another room, raging to himself, cursing and yelling nonsense. It sounded like he was upending furniture. Dani wobbled to her feet, pushing hair from her face, came to me. She bent and I pulled myself to standing, arm encircling her neck.

"He's insane, Carson. It's like something in his head broke."

"It's been bending for years. Let's get to your car."

We were nearly to the door when the shade of a Tiffany floor lamp behind our heads exploded in a thousand pieces. I clutched at Dani and we fell hard.

Buck Kincannon strode into the room with a shotgun in his hands, racking the slide.

"It's PARTY TIME," he screamed. "No one is going ANYWHERE!" He fired another blast and a curio cabinet beside us dissolved. We scrabbled backward on the floor, Kincannon sweeping the muzzle of the weapon across us, his eyes no longer human.

Dani and I slithered toward a large desk in the corner of the room. Buck Kincannon fired a shot up the wide staircase, turning a chandelier into a shower of glass.

"I NEED A PARTY!" he screamed, following it with a ragged peal of laughter.

Kincannon went to the open front door and looked outside, as if inspired by the lightning raging through the treetops. He took a deep breath, madness and fear and triumph all tumbled together in his face. He shook his head as though something jogged in his memory and his eyes refocused on Dani and me, a dozen feet away on the floor.

I could smell his insanity.

Buck smiled and trained the weapon on my eyes. The world turned to slow-moving shapes on a shadowed stage: Buck laughing with no sound coming from his mouth, the weapon raising, a single crystal from the ruined chandelier falling like a teardrop, the muzzle of the shotgun a dark and sudden eye set to wink . . .

The wicker chair exploding through the vast front window, skidding across the polished floor past Dani and me, glass shards tumbling in its wake.

"Down boy," Buck said to my eyes, the shotgun not wavering an inch, like a chair through a window was as common in his life as lunch. "That you, Race?" Buck yelled at the glass-toothed hole in the wall. "Or is it Nelson? Come on in, guys, we're having a *party*."

"You son of a bitch," Nelson ranted, thundering through the foyer into the living room, face bright with anger, finger jabbing at Buck's eyes. "You teamed up with Lucas, right? Or was it you and Racine? Guess who reads your faxes and phone messages, asshole? It ain't gonna hap—"

Nelson was fully in the house now, nose smelling cordite. His eyes took in the shattered lamp, broken furniture, destroyed chandelier. The shotgun in his brother's hands. Nelson's eyes found Dani and me cowering beneath the table. He froze, only his eyes moving.

"Uh, what's going on, Buck?"

"A night of love, Nelse."

"Love?" Nelson whispered.

"I get her," Buck said, jabbing a finger at Dani. "You can have him. It's fun, Nelson. They never love you more than when you own their souls. They scream their love."

Nelson stared at Buck for a few seconds, seemed to understand. Then Nelson regarded Dani and me with accusatory eyes, like he'd become a participant in a nightmare, and it was our fault.

Nelson, Dani mouthed. *Help us.*

My hand crept forward on the floor, picked up a jagged shard of glass, a razor-sharp triangle no larger than a postcard. I slid it beneath me.

"Here you go, brother," Buck said, handing Nelson the shotgun. "Let the party begin."

Nelson Kincannon held the weapon away from his body, as if it might bite him. Sweat beaded on his forehead. He shot glances toward the door.

"Just blow off his foot or something, Nelson," Buck suggested. "Then we can take time with things. The night's still young."

Nelson looked from my face to Dani's, back to mine. Buck leaned against the wall and crossed his arms.

"What's the matter, Nelson?"

Nelson Kincannon made a point of pulling up his cuff to check his watch. He sighed, shook his head, handed his brother back the shotgun.

"I've got an early meeting, Buck."

Nelson Kincannon turned away and walked out the door like leaving a conference room, already scheduling his alibi for the evening. The shotgun turned back to us and the mad fire rekindled in Buck Kincannon's eyes.

"More cake for me," he said. "Yummy."

I knew what he wanted. I looked at him and started crying. Sobbing. It wasn't hard.

"Don't, Buck. Please don't hurt me. I'm begging you, Buck . . ."

"Oh yessss," Buck Kincannon whispered.

"Please, Buck. I don't want to die. Let's just be friends, can we do that? Please, Buck . . ."

"Louder," he said, taking a step closer.

"I'll work for you, Buck, be your eyes and ears on the police force. You'll own me. Whatever you want, Buck, it's yours, just let . . . me . . ."

I put my face on the floor and began blubbering. I heard his footsteps creep closer, one step, two steps.

"LOUDER!" he railed.

"Don't kill me, don't kill me . . ." I begged, tucking the glass into my palm, feeling it razor into my flesh. Buck stepped forward. I felt the muzzle of the shotgun against my temple.

"I OWN YOU. I COMMAND YOU TO LIFT YOUR FACE AND SPEAK!"

"Buck, pleeeease . . ." I wailed, bringing my hands to my face as if in terror. Then I lunged forward, upward, knocking the gun aside with my forearm, putting everything into my bad leg, rising, slashing at his hands on the gun, feeling the glass sever gristle and tendon. He howled like an animal as I tumbled over him, dredging the glass through his face, across his eyes. I kept slashing, as if trying to slice my way into his brain, shut it off forever.

And then Dani was pulling at my back, and we were up and running through smoke-thick air as Buck Kincannon writhed on the floor, hands pressing into the blinded ruination of his face, one cheek flapping loose like a thick red washcloth.

"Crandell," he moaned. "Help me, Crandell."

Dani and I stumbled out the door as Nelson Kincannon's headlights reached the end of the long driveway, screeched away down the road, escaping. Dani dragged me to her car.

Halfway down the lane, she screamed, "Oh God," pointing to a car careering from the main road onto the drive, swerving, accelerating at us. She whipped the wheel, skidding sideways on the wet pavement. We were slammed in the side, spun. Her car broke through the fence lining the lane, white slats banging off the windshield. The engine stalled. I jumped out, held myself up on the open door. The other car stopped two dozen feet distant, headlamps shining through rain and steam from a busted radiator.

"Lucas?" the driver bawled. "Is that you, Lucas?"

Racine Kincannon lurched from his car. Lucas Kincannon and I were the same basic height and build. Racine squinted through swirling steam, his drunken voice shrill and desperate.

"Lucas. It's you and me, brother. I fired Crandell. Fuck Nelson and Buck. It's us, a team. That's what you meant, right? RIGHT?"

"Racine Kincannon," I roared, "you're under ARREST!"

Racine made a croaking sound and leapt behind the wheel. He floored the accelerator, smashing through the fence and into the huge golden sculpture of the Brahma bull. The bull snapped off its plinth, thundered to the ground, and rolled to its back, legs rocking skyward amidst clouds of steam. The driver's door swung open and deposited a passed-out Racine Kincannon on the grass.

Dani was near shock, so I made my way to Kincannon's snoring body, found a cellphone in his pocket, made the call, blood pouring from my palm. My good leg gave up and I crumpled to the ground, unable to move. Dani draped herself over me, crying.

And so we remained for several minutes, until the parade of blue-and-white flashers turned onto the Kincannon property and the curtain fell on the night from hell.

CHAPTER 51

Clair and Harry were at my place. The furor had subsided after three days, at least for me. The headlines continued unabated, though, from the *Mobile Register* to *The Wall Street Journal*, which page-one'd the headline, *Bizarre Crime Rocks KEI's Founding Family: A Tale of Hidden Children and Deadly Actions.*

"It's time for the five o'clock news," Clair said, picking up the remote. "Maylene's supposed to make a statement."

The television popped on, a scene outside the federal courthouse in Montgomery. The word *LIVE* floated in the upper corner of the screen.

"Look in the crowd . . ." Clair jabbed her finger at the tube. "Was that Dominick Dunne?"

"What's Dominick done?" I asked, thumping in on crutches, my foot in a soft cast and fabric boot, a six-week sentence.

"A writer. He does a crime show on cable. Kind of a 'Crime Styles of the Rich and Sleazy'."

I watched the camera pan the crowd, zero in on Maylene. She was flanked by two high-wattage lawyers and a woman Dani had once pointed out as a major PR type. Maylene shouldered past the lawyers to a bank of microphones on the courthouse steps.

"Maylene's going to talk," Clair said. "Here it comes."

"Here comes what?" Harry said.

"Whitewash and obfuscation and stonewall. She'll try to dump everything on Crandell, since he's not around to give his side of the story. She'll wrap the boys in her wings until the lawyers can get under the hood and tear the wires from the legal engine; years of obfuscation set to come. She'll spend millions to pervert the system."

The camera zoomed in on Mama, face pale and hair white, her eyes tiny black dots. We fell quiet and listened to the reporters' questions, were knocked back by Maylene Kincannon's answers.

". . . I never expected to be so deceived . . . garden of vipers and scoundrels . . . years of lies and scheming from my own children . . ."

"What the hell?" Clair said.

". . . culpable members of my family have been removed from all positions with KEI, no longer welcome in my home . . ."

"Jesus," Clair said. "She's tossing them to the wolves."

". . . support all efforts of our state's judicial system to mete out appropriate punishment for vicious crimes and deceits . . . testify myself if needed . . ."

A reporter asked a question about the children kept in the house. Maylene jutted a righteous chin.

"My only concern was for the finest care for the children and a life where every wish was fulfilled, every care given. In retrospect, I should have paid more attention to what was occurring elsewhere."

Maylene paused. Dabbed the pinpoint eyes with a tissue. She gestured off-camera for someone to join her and turned back to the microphones.

"My job now is to reestablish my relationship with the one son who has been so horribly maligned, one that I was manipulated to believe had terrible and incurable psychological problems, when in fact . . ."

Lucas Kincannon joined his mother, putting a loving arm around her oxlike shoulders. Kissed her powdery cheek. Several people applauded the spontaneous warmth of the moment. Lucas wore a dark suit, white shirt, and superbly knotted tie. He tucked his hands in his pockets and looked into the cameras with gentle shyness, referring questions to his mother or the lawyers.

Clair stared at the television in disbelief. "Lucas did abduct a woman, right? Mrs Atkins? With that purse bit?"

Harry said, "Rumor has it the old lady's revisiting her story. She may have misunderstood a few things the lad was requesting. I doubt Miz Atkins has any worries about the collapse of Social Security."

Maylene's voice lightened and she began chirping about "letting the sun shine on a bright new day in Kincannon stewardship".

"Sun shine or s-o-n shine?" Clair said.

"*. . . fostering change, while continuing a legacy of caring for the community . . .*" Mama intoned. "*. . . companies now under the expert supervision of professionals . . .*"

"Lucas is going to be the new Buck," I said. "Except that Lucas has the brains of a physicist and enough business acumen to grab the reins in weeks instead of years."

"Weeks?" Harry raised a dubious eyebrow. I flicked off the television.

"The whole show's not taking place in Montgomery. Take a ride with me, Harry."

Save for the upended bull, the Kincannon estate seemed unscathed by the bloody hurricane that had blown across its stately grounds three nights ago. The guardhouse was empty. Harry got out and pushed the gate aside. We drove to the house where I had been imprisoned. The door opened to a stately and somber face.

"Hello, Miss Gracie. We'll just be a minute."

She started to speak. I held up a silencing finger. "If you want peace, you'll let this happen."

She nodded and stepped aside. I led Harry across the floor to the elevator. My pry marks remained in the door, but it had been polished to a brassy sheen. We stepped inside. It lifted, the bell *bing*ing as we stopped.

I leaned against the side of the car as the door opened, drew Harry back with me.

"Grace, hon?" said the voice. "You bring that brandy?"

We stepped into the room. Buck Kincannon Senior was sitting in a chair by a window overlooking the woods. Sunlight streamed through the glass. He wore a dark velvet robe and slippers. His feet were propped on an ottoman. *The Wall Street Journal* was in his hands.

"I see the Asian market's on an upswin—"

He turned and saw Harry and me. He froze, his eyes open so wide they seemed little more than white.

"Auuh," he babbled, waving the paper. He let his mouth droop wide, tonguing drool down his chin. He swiped his hand across his mouth, stared at his saliva in wonder.

"Give it a break, Pops," I said.

We stepped back into the elevator. I pressed down. Miss Gracie was sitting on a couch. Holding her breath.

"One question," I said to her. "How did Taneesha get involved?"

Miss Gracie sighed from somewhere deep.

"I listen to WTSJ, play it soft over the sound system. Lucas liked listening, especially to Taneesha. He followed her from DJ to reporter. After it seemed clear Dr Rudolnick wasn't coming anymore, Lucas wrote an anonymous letter to Miz Franklin. The letter didn't say much, just that the doctor worked for the Kincannons, had done some strange things, maybe something a reporter might check into. That's all. I didn't know what was in Lucas's letter, but I did mail it for him."

"I figured it was something that simple. You helped Lucas escape, right?"

She looked away, but I stared at her face. She said, "One of the electric locks on his door went out. Pouring water in them does that."

I nodded, started to turn away. Her hand touched at my arm. "You won't tell people about . . ." Her eyes glanced toward the man upstairs.

"It would accomplish nothing, Miss Gracie."

She whispered, "Thank you."

Harry and I stepped outside. The grass of the Kincannon estate was so bright and green it seemed illuminated from beneath. A warm breeze sung through the trees.

"How'd you know, Cars?" Harry said. "About Daddy Kincannon?"

"Ory Aubusson put the bug in my head, bro. He said Buck Kincannon let himself go crazy because it was better than having to look at Maylene every day. It got me thinking."

Harry frowned. "Mama Kincannon has to know."

"I suspect they both played their roles. She got to exercise control, Daddy Kincannon got . . ." I tried to find words.

"Heaven?" Harry said.

"Or maybe just a form of freedom. There he sits in his own private world, everything he wants, waited on hand and foot."

"She loves him, doesn't she? The Grace woman?"

"I have a suspicion Daddy Kincannon and Miss Gracie go way back together. Twenty-three years at least."

I thumped across the lawn toward the car, Harry beside me. He said, "How much of a hand you think Daddy Kincannon had in this?"

I shook my head. "We'll never know. A finger, certainly. He knows Buck, Nelson, and Racine lived their lives poised at the brink of self-destruction. All it took was reaching critical mass, as the physicists say. Adding enough energy."

"Lucas," Harry said.

"Bang."

We reached the drive and turned to the house, a white refuge tucked deep in the trees.

I said, "I'll bet Buck Senior's spent four years teaching Lucas about the business. The boy's ready to take over."

"The company thrives," Harry mused. "While Daddy continues in his own private heaven. And Mama?"

"I think she'll stay out of Lucas's way."

We reached the car. I set the crutches aside and leaned against its sun-warm body, regarding the house for a final moment. Harry leaned beside me, arms crossed.

He said, "Do you think Lucas knew he was putting Taneesha Franklin in danger to accommodate his plans?"

"Lucas knew exactly what his family was capable of doing if threatened. Taneesha's questions were a threat. Lucas needed a threat to start the ball rolling."

Harry considered my words.

"But that would mean . . ."

I couldn't help but laugh. "Exactly. Lucas is every bit as amoral as his brothers, just ten times smarter." I clapped Harry's wide back. "Ain't it a grand day in hell, brother?"

EPILOGUE

I dropped Harry at his house, then stopped by Dani's home. Beginnings are always easier than endings. But endings are better when you can say you've learned something important. We both had that much, at least.

It was twilight when I crossed the bridge to Dauphin Island, the sky near dark, the western horizon painted with crimson. Pulling to my house, I saw Clair on my deck, standing at the railing and watching a flight of pelicans skim the foam at the surf line.

Three hours had passed and I was surprised she'd stayed. I parked, hobbled upstairs, moved straight through the house to the deck. She turned from the railing as I stepped outside, the night breeze rippling over her white sundress, her arms bare. She pushed a tousle of dark hair from her eyes as I crossed the deck.

"I'm surprised to see you here, Clair."

"You've been running, going to meetings, dodging the press. I haven't had a chance to see you alone, to tell you that . . . I was so afraid . . ."

She began blinking away tears and I pulled her close. Her head leaned against my chest and the rising moon drew a white line across the water. I suddenly knew the length and breadth of her existence as fully as I knew my own, felt her heart in my chest and my breath in her lungs, as if we had lost our boundaries. The world shivered and eased to a stop. Everything became still and peaceful and silent.

"Clair?" I said.

She leaned her head back, her eyes both frightened and expectant. Her lips were parted. I pulled her close and pressed my lips to hers. It started as a chaste kiss, blossomed into something more. Long seconds passed before she leaned away, her hands on my shoulders, her eyes damp, her head shaking.

"What?" I said.

"We can't be doing this, Carson. We just can't."

"Tell me why."

"First off, I'm forty-four, you're . . . you're –"

I put my finger over her lips and smiled. "I'm thirty-two, Clair. Forty-four and thirty-two. That adds up to, what? Seventy-six. That averages out to, uh . . ."

"Thirty-eight."

I said, "So what's your gripe against two thirty-eight-year-olds kissing?"

I waited for her answer.

Coming soon from HarperCollins, the fourth novel in JACK KERLEY's Carson Ryder series

LITTLE GIRLS LOST

CHAPTER 1

"The Gumbo King is stepping out, and
all the pretty women gonna jump and shout …

Her eight-year-old heart pounding, Jacy Charlane crouched behind a table of turnips and tomatoes in front of the small grocery and watched the Gumbo King approach. He was singing, his king-sized voice bouncing between storefronts and apartments on the four-lane avenue.

The Gumbo King, he's so fine, kissing all the
women and blowing their minds.

The Gumbo King was a white man, big, but not fat. He was wearing a yellow felt crown and a purple vest. His tee shirt and jeans were black. Jacy found it strange that if the Gumbo King wasn't singing, you never heard him coming, like cotton balls were glued beneath his shoes.

Whenever the Gumbo King turned his brown eyes on Jacy Charlane, they stole her voice and turned her knees to pudding. The Gumbo King was scary, and in the past she'd always run when she saw him coming.

But today was different: Someone in the city was stealing little girls. Gone, like they'd been snatched by goblins. One disappeared last week. Another got took just last night. People were whispering about it on the street.

The Gumbo King is struttin' down the street … all them gumbo lovers know Gumbo King's got the treats …

Jacy thought a king might be able to help find the girls. Especially one who owned his own place to eat and a humungous window sign with THE GUMBO KING written in red light beside a flashing gold crown.

The Gumbo King walked closer. Jacy swallowed hard and stepped from behind the table, blocking the king on the sidewalk. He stopped singing. Jacy felt the Gumbo King's shadow stop the sun.

"You're that Charlane girl, aren't you?" a voice boomed from up where birds flew. "Jacy, is it?"

Excuse me, Mister King, but two little girls are disappeared and please sir you would Highness your help…

Jacy felt the rehearsed words crash together in her mouth. She closed her eyes to hide. The Gumbo King rapped the top of Jacy's head with a knuckle.

"Knock, knock, girl. I know you're in there. I command you to speak to the Gumbo King."

Jacy pressed her palms against her eyes. She felt the sun return to her shoulders and when she opened her eyes the Gumbo King was walking away, singing again.

… So if you're aching and empty and
don't know what to do, call the Gumbo King
and he'll see you through."

Jacy felt like crying, ashamed she was too scared to talk to a king. She ran home and closed herself in her room, thinking to herself…

Who steals little girls? What do they do with them?

CHAPTER 2

Detective Carson Ryder traced his latex-gloved finger slowly over the mattress, as if reading in Braille. His eyes were closed, his head canted in concentration, intensifying the impression of a blind man searching for messages. After a few moments he sighed and pushed black hair from his forehead, opening his eyes to survey the small, dank-smelling room.

Like most in the neighborhood, the cramped apartment was furnished on poverty's budget: bare bulb in the ceiling, three-legged chair in a corner, torn paper curtains at the windows. The bed was a mattress on the floor, sheet pulled aside, amoebic shapes staining its surface.

A battered chest of drawers flanked the mattress, the red leg of a pair of tights drooping from a drawer like a wind sock on an airless day. Atop the chest sat a photograph in a listing frame, a black girl, eight or nine, whimsical twigs of hair poking from her head. She had laughing eyes and a smile one tooth shy of perfection.

"My baby, you've got to find my baby," a woman wailed from outside the bedroom, her voice rising toward hysteria.

"Where were you last night, Ms Shearing?" a policewoman questioned. "What time did you get in? When did you last see LaShelle?"

The woman replied with a sound like a keening gull. Ryder closed the door. Another minute and the woman would be screaming.

"Is it blood?" Ryder asked the bespectacled, rope-skinny black man crouched beside the mattress, his tie flung over his shoulder.

"Old blood," deputy chief of forensics Wayne Hembree said, lifting a mattress button and studying its underside with a penlight. "Hell, Carson, this mattress has probably been around since the Battle of Mobile Bay. Nosebleeds. Menses. God knows what."

Ryder let his eyes drift to the window, morning sun backlighting brick tenements across the street. A sultry day promised and being delivered, continuing a late-September heatwave as hot and fetid as lions' breath. Right on schedule the woman started screaming. Hembree winced and turned his moon-round face to Ryder.

"You see the kitchen window, the grating torn away?"

Ryder nodded.

"Think this is another one, Carson?" Hembree asked. "Abduction?"

Yes, Ryder thought. But didn't allow the word to reach his lips. He stepped into the hall outside the small apartment. It was quiet, the woman escorted away. He turned and shot a final glance at the mattress. Sunlight beamed through the window, lighting dust motes in the air. They drifted to the bedding like pinpoint flares.

"You leaving, Carson?" Hembree asked.

Ryder froze. "Is that a loaded question, Bree?"

The tech's eyes narrowed behind thick eyeglass lenses. "It's been a crazy couple of months. But it'll all settle out for the best. Forget the politics and do your job."

"Squill's back and in charge of the department," Ryder said, walking out the door. "And what the hell is my job any more?"

The Hundredth Man

Jack Kerley

A body is found in the sweating heat of an Alabama night; headless, words inked on the skin. Detective Carson Ryder is good at this sort of thing – crazies and freaks. To his eyes it is no crime of passion, and when another mutilated victim turns up his suspicions are confirmed. This is not the work of a 'normal' murderer, but that of a serial killer, a psychopath.

Famous for solving a series of crimes the year before, Carson Ryder has experience with psychopaths. But he had help with that case – strange help, from a past Ryder is trying to forget.

Now he needs it again.

When the truth finally begins to dawn, it shines on an evil so twisted, so dangerous, it could destroy everything that he cares about...

"Superb debut novel. A headless torso, the heat-soaked Alabama nights, a detective with a secret. Fantastic"

Sunday Express

ISBN 13: 978-0-00-718059-2

Jack Kerley Audiobooks

The Death Collectors

read by Kerry Shale

Thirty years after his death, Marsden Hexcamp's "Art of the Final Moment" remains as sought after as ever. But this is no ordinary collection. Hexcamp's portfolio was completed with the aid of a devoted band of acolytes – and half a dozen victims, each of whom was slowly tortured to death so that their final agonies could be distilled into art.

When tiny scraps of Hexcamp's "art" begin appearing at murder scenes alongside gruesomely displayed corpses, Detective Carson Ryder and his partner Harry Nautilus must go back three decades in search of answers.

Meanwhile an auction has been announced and the death collectors are gathering. These wealthy connoisseurs of serial-killer memorabilia will pay millions to acquire Hexcamp's art – unless Carson and Harry can beat them in their quest for the anti-grail.

Now available on Audio CD or Double Cassette

Kerry Shale's voice work has already earned him the title of "the best-known American voice on Radio Four", according to the *Evening Standard*. An experienced narrator, he is also the winner of 3 Sony awards for radio acting and writing.

Cassette: 0-00-721172-4
CD: 0-00-721173-2

The Straw Men

Michael Marshall

Fourteen-year-old Sarah Becker has been abducted, snatched from a busy shopping precinct in downtown LA. Judging from the state of the girls whose bodies have already been found, her long hair will be hacked off and she will be tortured. She has about a week to live.

Fromer LA homicide detective John Zandt has an inside track on the perpetrator – his own daughter was one of the victims two years ago. But the key to Sarah's whereabouts lies with Ward Hopkins, a man with a past so secret not even he knows about it. His parents have just died in a car accident, but they leave Ward a bizarre message that leads him to question everything he once believed to be true.

As he begins to investigate his own past, Ward finds himself drawn into the shadowy, sinister world of the Straw Men – and into the desperate race to find Sarah, before her time runs out.

'Brilliantly written and scary as hell. A masterpiece'

STEPHEN KING

'Instantly moves him into the Thomas Harris division'

Guardian

ISBN 0-00-649998-8